COLTON GENTRY'S

Third Act

COLTON GENTRY'S *Third Act*

A NOVEL

JEFF ZENTNER

New York Boston

Grand Central Publishing
Hachette Book Group
1290 Avenue of the Americas, New York, NY 10104
grandcentralpublishing.com
twitter.com/grandcentralpub

First Edition: April 2024

Grand Central Publishing is a division of Hachette Book Group, Inc. The Grand Central Publishing name and logo is a trademark of Hachette Book Group, Inc.

Print book interior design by Jeff Stiefel.

Library of Congress Cataloging-in-Publication Data

Names: Zentner, Jeff, author.
Title: Colton Gentry's third act : a novel / Jeff Zentner.
Description: First edition. | New York : Grand Central Publishing, 2024.
Identifiers: LCCN 2023025628 | ISBN 9781538756652 (hardcover) | ISBN 9781538756676 (ebook)
Subjects: LCGFT: Romance fiction. | Novels.
Classification: LCC PS3626.E447 C65 2024 | DDC 813/.6--dc23/eng/20230606
LC record available at https://lccn.loc.gov/2023025628

ISBNs: 9781538756652 (hardcover), 9781538756676 (ebook)

Printed in the United States of America

LSC-C

Printing 1, 2024

For Sara

Every love story is for you

PART I

CHAPTER 1

May 2015
Charlotte, North Carolina

Colton Gentry is hurting, which lately means that he's drunk and very much so.

Not a gentle buzz but rather the kind of inebriation that involves spontaneous crying when you tell a friend how much they mean to you. The skin over your scarlet heart thin as a baby robin's.

This wouldn't be a problem but for his being onstage in front of a capacity crowd of almost twenty thousand at PNC Music Pavilion in Charlotte, opening for Brant Lucas on his Dirt Road Dance Party tour. Even this precarious combination wouldn't necessarily be a concern—Colton had certainly performed good shows while four sheets to the wind before—except that in his sightline is a ruddy-faced man, dark crescent moons of sweat under his armpits in the sultry, breezeless Southern spring heat, trying to get his attention. The man is flipping him off with one hand and holding defiantly aloft in the other a "Colt .45" T-shirt with an antique revolver silkscreened on it. It strikes Colton as mordantly funny that the guy paid twenty-five bucks for one of his T-shirts, only to taunt him with it.

Before Colton had played a note of his set, the normally impatient tolerance that greets a stadium act's opener had yielded to something more weighted and hostile. It was nothing specific Colton could have pointed to (until heckle-tax-paying man)—but the electricity in the air. A twinge in the part of his gut that's attuned to danger.

"Fifteen minutes, Colton."

Brant Lucas's stage manager's terse voice coming through Colton's in-ear monitors startles him from his momentary stupor. He's only played a couple of songs and wasn't expecting the fifteen-minute warning so soon. No detail escapes the stage manager, and she's surely noticed Colton's bleary, unfocused gaze, slurred speech, and unsteady footing. And maybe she senses too that this crowd has it in for him. He decides it might be best if he doesn't study the concertgoers too closely for the remainder of his set. He and his band play another song to tepid, cursory applause.

His short-lived resolution fails him as soon as he notices that another man has joined the T-shirt brandisher. He's holding high a crudely lettered sign that says "From my cold dead hands!" One of his warm, living hands has its middle finger extended, to match his new compatriot's.

Magmatic fury surges perilously from beneath Colton's solar plexus. His face reddens. Sober, maybe he'd be thinking *Hey, man, let's sit down together and crack a cold one, and I'll tell you about my buddy Duane and what he meant to me and how shattered I am that he's gone, and we can put our loves on the scale and see whose outweighs whose*. But sober is back home, curled up on the couch, wearing a bathrobe and watching *The Bachelor*, and he is here. He draws a deep breath to try to calm himself. He's going too long between songs, and he knows it.

He looks over to see his rhythm guitarist approach. For the thousandth time in the last few weeks, he wonders what might have been if he could have afforded to hire Duane for this tour. *It was nothing compared to the cost of not hiring him. You were too proud to even ask for the friend discount.*

"Hey, Colt? You good?" Ever the professional performer, Colton's guitarist grins broadly while asking the question, so to all observers it appears that they're sharing a quick private joke.

Colton swelters under the lights and in the humid air. His building rage has reached the base of his neck. He forces himself to return his guitarist's smile and nods. The one thing he still has in his life that's good, that brings him unambiguous joy, is that feeling when the crowd cheers for him. Maybe between the drink and the smattering of perfunctory applause that has broken through this crowd's antipathy, he can find some sort of refuge, he thinks.

He gives his acoustic guitar a couple of quick strums and steps back to the mic. A pack of five frat boys with shaggy hair, pastel polo shirts, khaki shorts, and flip-flops or boat shoes have joined T-shirt guy and cold-dead-hands man. They cup their mouths and, in unison, shout "Libturd," cutting through the buzz of the crowd. Then, all five theatrically turn their backs on him in unison, guffawing at their own bayonet-sharp wit.

The scalding anger is now at the back of Colton's throat, like burping up stomach acid after eating too much Nashville hot chicken, which is exactly how he spent one of the last times he saw Duane alive.

A few more minutes. A couple more songs. Pretend you're back in high school, on the football field, it's fourth and goal, you're down by five, there are ten seconds left in the game, and you're holding that ball with your fingers between the seams, ready to throw. You've always been clutch.

His band starts in behind him. He inhales to sing. At the precise moment he's about to, someone sounds a deafening blast on an airhorn. Colton's mind immediately flashes to Duane, and the piercing AR-15 shots that were the last thing he heard.

Grief undermines your structural integrity. It crazes your foundation. Alcohol does the same, from another direction. Sometimes they meet in the middle, and when they do, once-solid things crumble. When the crumbling begins, it quickly becomes catastrophic. Somewhere, deep inside himself, where the ember of good judgment still smolders, Colton Gentry knows he's about to make a terrible mistake. But he just doesn't care.

"Hey, no, hang on," Colton says into the microphone, waving his band off. They're keenly attuned to his direction and come to a tentative, clattering halt. For a second or two there's a coiled, anticipatory silence in the assembled crowd and among the musicians onstage.

Colton turns his gaze to the small clump of hecklers. He points at them and speaks into the mic, his voice booming and reverberant. "Lemme tell y'all something. Y'all listening? Screw your guns. Okay? No, actually fuck your guns and fuck you. Lemme tell you—"

That's when Colton's mic cuts off. Before he could say *about my buddy Duane and how much I loved him*. Even as far gone as he is, he's surprised Brant Lucas's hypervigilant stage manager has allowed him this much rope.

Now her voice crackles in his in-ear monitors like a downed power line. "You're done. Offstage. Now."

A gray-green miasma of groans and boos wafts off the audience like the stench from a road-killed skunk.

Out of the corner of his eye, Colton sees his rhythm guitarist approaching again. His genial, aren't-we-having-fun ersatz smile is gone. In its place is pallid mortification. He's visibly searching for the right words. "Hey, bro . . . this is—I dunno, man."

Colton won't meet his gaze. He's got a show to finish, stage manager be damned. He claps. "Let's go. 'Honeysuckle Summer' to close, and then we're off."

His band shoots each other uncomfortable glances. *We're not actually going to try to play another song, are we?* their eyes say. The boos have become a sustained drone, like an airliner spooling up for takeoff.

Brant Lucas's stage manager saves them. She strides across the stage to Colton, grabs his forearm with a bear-trap grip, and puts her lips directly to his ear. "What'd I say? Off. Now. Done."

Colton regards her for a moment through his fogged eyes and lowers his gaze in defeat. A hurled Mountain Dew bottle flies past him, nearly hitting his shoulder. Someone shouts, "Honey, suckle my balls!" A chant of "We want Brant" replaces some of the jeering. Colton and his band slink offstage to rancorous applause and catcalls. He tries to walk without too much weaving, to preserve some semblance of dignity. He fails.

Backstage, as they file toward the green room, Colton, already aware of the gravity of what he's done to his own career but also to his band's financial prospects, tries to touch his bassist's shoulder, a gesture of contrition. His bassist flicks his hand off. None of Colton's bandmates will make eye contact. They haven't been together through thick and thin. They aren't buddies. This is a pickup band of skilled touring musicians who needed a paycheck and so they chose this gig over others, learned and rehearsed a bunch of Colton Gentry songs, and now he's certainly just gotten them fired.

Colton wishes, after being perp-walked offstage, that he'd taken a last look at the crowd, hostile though they were, assembled before him in the dark, their cell phones glowing here and there like fireflies. He always loved that in better days—the pinpricks of light from people texting those they love and recording memories. A small, luminous city of humanity spread before him. *You may never see it again.*

Another stone of heartbreak to pile on his chest.

CHAPTER 2

Colton sits alone in the green room, face in his hands, head spinning. As his tide of adrenaline ebbs, the urge to retch constricts his innards. His sweat-logged T-shirt adheres clammily against his skin in the air-conditioning. His band rebuffed every attempt to apologize. *Dude, you can't possibly think an apology in the state you're in means jack*, his drummer had said.

He senses someone standing before him.

"Hey. *Hey.*"

Colton looks up into Brant Lucas's face.

"Stupid, insane, or both? Which?" Brant asks.

Colton starts to speak.

"Or both and drunk," Brant interjects.

"All these choices you're giving me." Colton had been ready to apologize, even though Brant had generally been a prick to him on this tour and otherwise. But now?

"So a smart-ass too." Brant's harried makeup artist catches up with him and lifts the bill of his John Deere cap—which has never been within ten country miles of any tractor, John Deere or otherwise—to touch up his foundation. She obviously thought she'd have more time for this.

"Definitely drunk. That one for sure."

"After I helped you. You stupid, ungrateful clown sonofabitch."

"Now that one *you* chose."

"Only reason you were here was as a favor to Maisy."

"One minute," Brant's stage manager calls.

"She ain't gonna bone you, man," Colton says. "According to *Us Weekly*, she prefers hockey players." He pantomimes hitting a puck.

Brant shakes his head. "You're pathetic."

"Seems to be the consensus."

"Thirty seconds," the stage manager calls.

With a final glare at Colton, Brant turns on the heel of one of his $1,500 black ostrich Luccheses, and trots off in the direction of the stage, dodging one of his roadies.

Colton hears the crowd erupt as Brant takes the stage.

Brant's voice is muffled coming through the walls. "Y'all, first I wanna apologize for y'all's having to listen to that. America's the greatest country on Earth, and it's because of our God-given freedoms. Now who's ready to party?" The crowd loudly expresses their party preparedness. Brant starts in on his most recent radio hit, "High Lifes and High Trucks."

His head already swimming, Colton wants nothing more than to close the circle by drinking himself into a blackout—it's the forgetting that he craves more than anything. But now Brant's tour manager steps in front of him.

"Colton? We need to chat."

"Lemme check my calendar."

The tour manager walks over to the green room door, closes it, and returns. "This isn't a fun conversation, and I wish we didn't need to hold it in your present…condition, but Brant has directed that you be separated from the tour."

"Separated?"

"Fired."

"Then why not just say fired. Damn, son."

"Soften the blow."

"Ought to say what you mean."

"Because that's worked wonders for you."

"Touché, big hoss."

"Gather your things. We'll have a car take you back to the hotel. You'll fly home in the morning. Any questions?"

"You know if there's an open mic nearby? I was hoping to play those last few songs tonight."

The tour manager eyes him with incredulous disgust. "You're sure taking this well. If I'd just said the worst thing you can say to a country music audience, I'd be in no mood to joke."

Colton holds up his thumb and forefinger, almost touching, and squints through the gap with one eye. "I'm a lil' bit tipsy. Case you didn't notice."

"Oh, I did." The tour manager leans in close, like he's about to share some juicy bit of scuttlebutt. "You baffle me. Here you are, thirty-seven—"

"Thirty-eight. Just turned."

"Even better. You get your first big record deal when you're in your twenties. It flops. Now you're married to Maisy Martin, one of the biggest acts on Earth, you're just shy of forty, you have this 'Honeysuckle Summer' single catch fire out of nowhere, and now you're getting a second chance, the break a lot of musicians *never* get. And you? You win the lottery and then wipe your ass with the ticket. Help me understand."

Colton pauses for a long time before speaking. "Remember that mass shooting at Countryfest in Tampa a few weeks back?"

"Of course. Seventeen people died. Horrible."

"One of those seventeen was Duane Arnett."

"I know. Brant auditioned him for lead guitar a few years back."

"Duane was my best buddy. We roomed together in East Nashville when I moved to town. He and I'd sit in those flimsy white plastic chairs in the backyard on summer nights. You know the ones? Where it collapses if you lean back?"

"Yeah."

"We'd listen to Waylon and Merle, drink Coronas. Cicadas all around. Us sweating our asses off. Talk about girls, life, music, whatever. He was the first person I told when I met Maisy. He was best man at our wedding on Cumberland Island. I loved him. Like a brother." *I must be really starving to talk about this if opening up to even this asshole feels so good.*

If the tour manager feels chastised, he scarcely shows it. "Guess that explains your interview with Fox News a couple weeks back. Should've left things at 'We have a gun problem in America that we need to fix.' That wasn't ideal, obviously, seeing as it brought out the hecklers at shows—"

"Maybe if Fox hadn't edited out the part where I talked about Duane so I'd look more like a villain, I wouldn't have hecklers."

"Yeah, Colton, maybe. Or maybe they wouldn't have given a shit. Anyway, you're a professional musician. You should be used to dealing with noisy drunks. You can survive that. Not this."

"Well, thanks, man, for your sympathies. And the great advice."

"Look, I'm truly sorry about Duane. That can't be easy. But sorry won't cut it here. We still have a job to do."

"Yeah, I know. Anyway. You asked me to help you understand." Colton meets the tour manager's eyes. "I was missing someone a whole lot tonight and every night. Feeling a little lonely in this world. Simple as that. Nothing else to understand."

CHAPTER 3

He awakes to pounding on his hotel room door; a phone full of texts and voicemails from his agent, manager, label, and wife (although it feels strange to use any sort of possessive with her); and a head largely devoid of memories from the night before, but for the biggies. Where the inside of his skull lacks for recollection, though, it more than makes up for with blinding, searing pain.

"You packed?" the tour manager asks when Colton answers, as though the answer isn't plain from looking past him into the dark recesses of the room, where clothing is strewn about like dead branches after a storm, mixed with the flotsam of empty minibar bottles. As if Colton's standing before him in his boxer-briefs, still reeking of drink, leaves him doubting.

"Just gotta throw a few things in a suitcase," Colton mutters, scratching his sternum.

"Well, the van is downstairs right now. You're on a flight back to Dallas in an hour and a half. So I suggest putting your ass in high gear."

Colton nods, and so gently as to seem tender, closes the door in the man's face.

The airport bar is the only place where you can drink without judgment at nine thirty a.m., and so Colton sits and has a bit of the hair of the dog that ended his career while he waits for the next flight to Dallas, having missed his scheduled flight. He wears a faded black denim jacket that it's too hot for and sunglasses, both to block out the light and to lend some marginal disguise. Not that he need worry too much. He inhabits that odd twilight that precedes true fame where many people who have heard and love his song could never pick him out of a crowd. Still, he gets a few dirty looks.

He texts Maisy. Heading home. She texts back a terse K, see you there. He wishes she would have said *call me*, even though he wouldn't have, even though she's already implicitly (or perhaps explicitly—he wouldn't know because he hasn't listened) extended that invitation with the three voicemails she left.

There's a bank of televisions in the bar, and one is tuned to CNN. Continuing his recent pattern of acting against better judgment, Colton allows himself to watch. He immediately regrets it.

In other news this morning, country musician Colton Gentry is once more embroiled in controversy for anti-gun comments he made onstage last night in Charlotte, North Carolina, while opening for Brant Lucas, just weeks after stirring outrage by stating his support for gun control after the mass shooting at a country music festival in Tampa, Florida. A concertgoer captured the moment... Gentry could not be reached for comment. His management company, Big Sky Artists, released a statement saying, "Colton Gentry's profane and inappropriate comments do not reflect the views of Big Sky Artists, which supports the right of peaceful, law-abiding Americans to keep and bear arms."

Colton stares into his screwdriver. Duane had been his first celebratory call when he signed with Big Sky. Full circle.

A businessman sitting a few feet away stirs his Bloody Mary with a celery stalk, nods at the screen, and says, vaguely in Colton's direction but without looking over, "Bet that went over like a fart in church."

It's obvious the man has no idea with whom he speaks, and Colton can't help but smile at the moment's absurdity. "When I was twelve, my buddy Ryan ripped ass in church. Real wet one. Mid-sermon. I'd say a solid forty percent of the congregation enjoyed it thoroughly, and the sixty percent who pretended not to still let him in the door that next Sunday."

The businessman grunts and chuckles, eyes still glued to the TV. "That poor son of a bitch would have been better off going in on everyone's mothers. Bet there were at least a couple of people in that crowd who don't love their mothers."

Colton pulls a twenty out of his wallet and slaps it down on the bar. Then he hurries to catch his flight.

CHAPTER 4

September 1996
Nashville, Tennessee

It was already late afternoon when Colton pulled up to the tiny, ramshackle East Nashville bungalow. Across the street, a faded Oldsmobile Cutlass rested on blocks in the oil-stained driveway and a Rottweiler strained at the length of grimy clothesline binding it to a diseased oak. The house to the immediate right of the bungalow had ankle-length grass and a ragged square of blue tarp duct taped over a missing window. On the porch of the house to the left, a sunburned and barefoot pregnant girl who looked (generously) seventeen energetically told someone over a cordless phone that she was done with their shit.

Still, Colton's freshly wounded and lonely heart thrummed ecstatically at sighting his first home away from his parents.

As he stepped down from the cab of his pickup and pulled his guitar from behind his seat, he heard the tinny jangle of someone chicken-pickin' fast and clean through scales on an unamplified Telecaster. He ambled up the cracked and uneven concrete front walk and saw the source of the flurry of notes—a young man roughly Colton's age sat on the porch. He had shaggy shoulder-length blond hair and muttonchops, and he wore a 1970s-vintage fringed buckskin jacket, suede cowboy boots, a hemp choker, and a broad-brimmed black Stevie Ray Vaughan hat with a concho hatband. His head was lowered in concentration, as if praying.

He looked up as Colton approached and gave one of the sunniest grins Colton had ever seen. He rose and carefully leaned the Tele against his wicker kitchen chair. "You Colton?"

"Yup. You Duane?"

"Duane, or friends call me Dee-wayne. Everything you've heard's a lie." He stepped down from the porch and extended a handshake to Colton.

Colton took it. "Really? 'Cause I heard you could play your ass off on guitar."

Duane smiled even more broadly and looked away bashfully. "Hell."

"Felt bad interrupting you."

"Feel bad instead for looking like a damn movie star and not warning me. I mean shoot, son." He spoke with a syrupy drawl, exuding a warmth that put Colton at ease.

"Come on now." Colton shifted bashfully on his feet, his shoulders relaxing down a half inch.

"Come on your damn self. Now I won't be able to bring any ladies I'm hoping to woo back to the house."

Colton glanced earthward, licked his lips, and grinned ruefully. "Yeah, well, I've sworn off the ladyfolk for now, so no problem there."

"Uh-oh. Seen that look before. If nothing else, makes for good songs, huh? Speaking of, let's have a gander at that there guit-fiddle." Duane nodded at Colton's guitar case.

Intuiting he was in the presence of a true connoisseur, Colton set it down, opened it, and pulled out his guitar.

Duane took it carefully, looked it up and down, and whistled through his teeth. "Vintage Gibson," he murmured. "Look at that tobacco sunburst finish."

"1978 J-45. Was my dad's."

"Mind if I take a lick or two on it?"

"Go for it." Colton realized as he said it that he'd never let anyone play his guitar before. But he already knew it was in the best of hands.

Duane strummed it. Made some quick adjustments to the tuning.

Then he deftly began fingerpicking one of the most gorgeous and intricate melodies Colton had ever heard.

"What is that?"

Duane smiled faintly. "Just making it up." He played for a few more moments before handing the guitar back to Colton. "That is one sweet axe, roomie. Once we get you moved in, lemme make some adjustments to the neck, get your intonation dialed in purty."

"Sounds like a plan."

"Let's haul your stuff inside 'fore someone takes a notion to swipe it."

They strolled to Colton's truck together.

"Anyhow, Dee-Wayne, I'm the least of your concerns with the ladies. I'd be much more worried about them getting jealous of that hair."

Duane chortled and clapped Colton on the shoulder, tossing his mane theatrically. "I do got that *sal*on shine, don't I, brother?"

They spent the remnants of the daylight moving Colton in before supping on a bachelors' meal of scrambled eggs and a couple bricks of ramen seasoned liberally with Cholula. Later, they went out in the scraggy backyard with its mange of grass to build a bonfire of wood scraps, windfall sticks, and pine cones in the rust-laced sawn-off oil drum that served as a firepit. The temperature plummeted the moment the sun dipped below the horizon, and the warmth felt delicious on their skin.

Colton poked at the fire with a stick, sending up a shower of sparks. "You're from *England*, Arkansas? Like the country?"

"You know it, guvnuh." Duane did his approximation of an English accent—no Sir Laurence Olivier, he.

"How much like *England* England is it?"

"Well, ain't been yet to compare. But I'll venture to say: not much."

"I'm from Venice, Kentucky. It's spelled like Venice in Italy even though it's pronounced *vuh-neese*."

"Any time there's a city in the South named after a European city, you got a better chance of getting the pronunciation right if you pronounce it *any* other way than the European city."

"Pretty much."

"Running dry there?"

"Might could use a fill-up."

Duane pulled another Corona longneck from the cooler by his feet and handed it to Colton, who cracked it open. Then Duane slumped back in his chair, hands behind his head, and gazed off at the illuminated towers and neon of the Nashville skyline, just visible above the treetops. "Been here a year. Sight never gets old. Best part about this house."

"You mean it ain't what you said about how the basement floods every time it rains?" Colton started to lean back in his white plastic chair but quickly caught himself as the legs buckled.

Duane chuckled good-naturedly, and then his face returned to an uncharacteristically (or so it seemed to Colton) somber and contemplative cast. "All them lights. Every light a star. City of dreams, brother," he murmured in an awestruck tone. "Been imagining myself here since my papaw taught me how to play an E chord when I was nine. How 'bout you?" Duane plucked a joint from his jacket pocket and sparked it up in one practiced motion, taking a long drag before offering it to Colton.

Colton waved him off. "My dream's a little newer. But I been hustling to catch up. Hell, I've written probably fifteen songs in the last month."

Duane exhaled a cloud of smoke and coughed. "Play me one."

Colton hesitated for a few moments. Finally: "Guess I better start getting used to it, huh? One sec." Colton went back into the house and retrieved his guitar. Duane hit pause on the Larry Jon Wilson CD in the Emerson boombox sitting on an upside-down plastic bucket. He stuck his pinkies in his mouth and gave a piercing whistle. "We now welcome to the Opry stage…Mr. Colton Gentry!" He clapped and cupped his hand to his mouth and mimicked the *haaaaaaa* of crowd noise.

Colton ducked his head and grinned. He mock-bowed. "Uh, okay.

Thanks for coming out tonight, folks. I'm gonna play y'all one of my newer songs. It's called 'Honeysuckle Summer.' I wrote it about someone after I got my heart broke. Here goes." Of all the songs he could have played, he didn't know why he picked that one. But he did. As soon as he began playing and singing, his heartache, loneliness, and anxiety over his new life vanished momentarily into the darkness like the sparks from the fire. A sense of pure purpose—one that Colton hadn't realized he'd been missing—filled the void.

Duane looked on in rapt, stoned wonder, and when Colton finished, he leapt to his feet and erupted in raucous hoots, applause, and whistles. "I said got-*damn* son! Now that's a *song*. Lord *almighty*. You're putting that on your first album. Done deal."

"Aw, I don't know, man. Still a little raw for me. Can't believe I even had the balls to play it for you."

Colton put away his guitar and sat again, and they drank and listened to the crickets and Townes Van Zandt and Vince Gill. Every so often Duane would look over at Colton and offer some variation of *That song, man. Damn.*

Colton had gotten a warm, pleasant buzz on when he turned to Duane and asked, nodding at the skyline, "What you think, man? We got a shot?"

Duane looked at Colton for a couple of seconds and then looked back at the city with a knowing, serene smile. "We'll make it," he said quietly. "They say Nashville's a ten-year town. But we'll pay our dues and work our asses off and make it. Two of those lights are for us. I'm gonna get me a tricked-out, restored seventies Bronco. Buy up a little piece of Arkansas by the lake and spend time there fishing or duck hunting when I'm not on tour or doing session work. I'm gonna do it all with—" He set down his beer, raised his hands and waggled his fingers. "How about you?"

"I'd like to buy my folks a nicer place than what we had when I was growing up. It was fine, but I want to say thanks to them for raising me." He paused. "And while I'm doing it, I hope my girl from high school sees me making good."

Duane cracked up. "That's the main one right there, ol' boy. That girl's gonna see you do real good. Guaran-damn-teed." Duane said it with such confidence, Colton couldn't help but trust him.

Under the stars, in the shadow of the lustrous city of dreams, they drank and talked and listened to music deep into the night. A capacious sense of good fortune had descended upon Colton, and he knew two things for certain in that moment:

First, that he and his new buddy Duane would indeed make it.

Second, that he would love Duane always.

CHAPTER 5

May 2015
Dallas, Texas

It's never felt like home to him, this eleven-thousand-square-foot, $10 million, Spanish Colonial–style mansion with its red tile roof, indoor and outdoor swimming pools, home theater, yoga studio / spa, and tennis court in Dallas's Southlake neighborhood. Maisy's money bought it, so it was mostly her call on the design and decor.

When Colton steps inside, it's cool compared to the stifling heat outside, but not the pore-closing chill one might expect from looking at the house, which appears in every way a fortress against the world. Maisy has a comfortable temperature range of between 78 degrees and 82 degrees. Her money; her thermostat.

The air is luxurious with the perfume of red berries, clove, and pepper. He stands in the entryway, still wearing his sunglasses. A couple of mini bottles on the plane kept his headache at bay. His guitar sits at his feet in its road case, along with his suitcases, where he set them down.

He hears the hurried slap of bare feet on the zebra wood flooring of their living room, then on the gray slate floor as Maisy turns the corner into the entryway. She wears the athletic leggings, Lycra tank top, and Prada ball cap with her honey-blond ponytail pulled through it that's her uniform when she's not on a red carpet or touring. Technically, she's touring now, but Dallas is a quick Gulfstream flight from Phoenix, where Maisy's headlining her own tour tomorrow night.

They regard each other from a short remove. Her expression is an indecipherable amalgam of disgust, sympathy, and pity. He thinks he must look to her much like he feels—as though he slept in a shipping container with a troop of baboons.

"You could've returned one of my calls."

Colton removes his sunglasses, revealing red-rimmed eyes. "Something smells good."

"New Jo Malone candle. I like it, but I need to *love* a $500 candle."

"If you don't love the way that wildly expensive candle smells, you really won't love how I smell."

The competing currents of Maisy's expression flow together into a reluctant half-smile. She finally approaches him, and they embrace. Not as a husband and wife or even as lovers, but as what they are at that moment—two people with some history, who have loved each other, one of whom desperately needs a hug. The kind involving quick, reassuring back pats, not melting into each other with increasingly deep sighs—the sort of hug that Colton requires.

They separate and look at each other again. *She's so stunning*, Colton thinks. It's impossible to imagine her existing as anything but a megastar of some sort. It's always mystified him why she picked him over everyone else. If only for a while.

"You smell like you had a lot of fun last night," she says.

"I didn't."

Another half-smile. Sadder this time. "You eaten?"

"I'm still full from all the shit I ate last night."

"I sent Kendra out to pick up some salads. I'll check in." Maisy pulls her phone from her thigh pocket and composes a quick text. Colton's never grown accustomed to the difference their age gap makes in dexterity with electronics.

"I'm in more of a big disgusting greasy bucket of chicken mood, but it's fine."

"John Greco called *my* cell looking for you. Didn't you call him back?"

"I told him I'm not discussing *Breaking Bad* with him until he's finished the series."

"He's the head of our label."

"Is he?"

"I don't think you're grasping how serious this situation is, and if you deflect with another joke, I'm gonna lose it. Everything you've worked for for twenty years is at stake."

"Yeah."

"*Yeah.* That's your answer?" Her voice is rising.

"Tell me what you want me to say, Maise."

"That you have a plan to fix this."

"I have a plan to fix this."

Maisy folds her arms and regards him with deep skepticism. "Really?"

"No."

"What happened out there? Like, I'm not trying to rub it in. But."

Colton shakes his head and runs his fingers through his hair. It's been steadily accumulating silver over the past year. "I had too much to drink. But mostly I was just used up inside. Us. Duane. Everything."

"We've talked about the alcohol many times."

"And I've told you each time that I'm fine."

"You're *clearly* not fine."

"I'll be fine."

"I told you that if you couldn't go on because of Duane, you should just come home."

"I know."

"I told you I wouldn't be pissed."

They stand for a few moments in silence. They certainly haven't run out of things to say. And yet they have.

"You gonna apologize?" Maisy says finally.

"I'm sorry. I—"

"Not to me. I've tried to get you to get rid of *your* guns."

"You stuck your neck out to get me on that tour."

"Brant owed me. He didn't pay me enough to be on that idiotic 'Short Shorts and Long Nights' song. I was talking about a public statement."

Colton considers it for a second. "Thing is, I meant what I said. Even drunk. I ain't about apologizing for what I believe." He pauses. "Besides, would it do any good?"

"Probably not," Maisy says softly.

"Then I think I'll skip the public groveling."

She meets his eyes. "I always admired that about you. You don't crawl on your belly. You have integrity. But sometimes you need to grovel in this business."

"I might be in the wrong business."

"You say that now, but I bet you'll change your mind in a few weeks. Anyway." She sighs and reads a text. "I have a lot to do while I'm here, and I'm flying back to Phoenix at five."

"I thought your show was tomorrow. Can't you stay tonight?"

She doesn't answer.

Throughout their brief conversation, he's begun to feel invincible—not in the way of someone who can't lose, but of someone with nothing left to lose. "Maise?"

She looks at him.

"Was getting me on that tour a parting gift?" he asks quietly.

She opens her mouth and closes it again. She shuts her eyes and raises both hands to chest-level. "I don't wanna talk about this right now. Not the time."

Colton gives her a melancholy smile. "You know how you make me pull off your Band-Aids? How do I do it?"

"Quick."

"Quick. Draw it out less."

Maisy looks down. Then off to the side. Then upward. Finally to him. "My parting gift to you is the very expensive, private, and effective rehab program in Sedona I'm putting you in and paying for. Kendra's been on the phone all morning making the arrangements."

Colton nods. His heart aches like it's being beaten into a container too small for it. But there's some strange relief in this. You can't truly deal with the worst until the worst happens. "That Eklund dude? Erik? The hockey guy? From the *Us Weekly* story?"

"Emil." Maisy breaks eye contact again.

"Is it him?" Colton asks quietly. "I won't be mad."

She says nothing.

"So yes?"

"Colton. Seriously—Kendra's going to be back with the salads any minute."

"Yes?" Colton's voice is calm in defeat but brittle with hurt.

She inhales deeply through her nose. "Yes."

"That why you're rushing back to Phoenix tonight?"

"And for other stuff." Her voice quavers.

Tears gather in Colton's eyes. He blinks them away quickly. His throat aches to match his heart. "When that story dropped, you told me—" He feels ridiculous saying it. Like he can negotiate her back into a no.

"I know." Maisy's eyes well too. She draws a long shuddering breath. "We haven't been good for a while."

"Guess not." Colton pauses. "How long?"

"That we haven't been good?"

"No. With Eklund. How long?"

"A while." Maisy rests her elbow on her wrist and buries her eyes in one hand. "I never wanted to hurt you."

"So, what, did you decide I had too many teeth or IQ points, or—"

"Colton."

"What?"

"Please."

"Please what?"

"Can we be adults about this?"

"Making jokes instead of getting in my truck and driving out to whip his ass *is* me being an adult."

"Fair enough."

"You've put a Buick-sized dent in my ability to enjoy Predators games now."

"I really didn't want to do this now, with everything you're going through. Duane. Last night."

"If we're done anyway, I'm not gonna stick around and be a drag on your career for nothing."

"My career is my last concern right now," Maisy says, but that's never been wholly true of her priorities. Third-to-last (maybe second-to-last in a pinch) is the best she could ever do. Still, she says it with conviction.

The pain finally courses in, like the moment after a car accident, when the initial shock of impact has worn off and the body's pain receptors are ready to be heard. "Couldn't you have waited until we were officially done? Spare me the humiliation?"

"Well, as you may know, sometimes people don't think things through carefully before they act, thus humiliating people they care about."

"Walked into that one, didn't I."

A few beats of silence pass. Their house's sound insulation mutes outside noise, so when it's quiet, you can hear your own heartbeat.

"Were we real?" Colton asks finally.

"I sure as hell didn't marry you to advance my career."

They laugh a little.

"It was real for me," Colton says.

"Oh, I know. We've abundantly established that you don't let career considerations guide your behavior." More half-hearted laughter.

Colton's eyes fog with nostalgia. "You remember that time we went to Husk and dropped like $500 on dinner and drinks to celebrate *Live and Love* going platinum?"

"I was so wasted."

"You're like 'It's open mic night at the Bluebird. Let's go.' So, we ran back home, picked up a couple of guitars, and headed there. Everyone was freaking out. We skipped the line."

"I'm so glad I don't remember this night. I must have been terrible."

"You were amazing. You go up there and you play 'Under the Stadium Lights,' and you're so loose and free and happy. So beautiful. I wanted to ask you to marry me all over again. I got up there and played 'Honeysuckle Summer' publicly for the first time, dedicating it to you."

"Even though it's about your high school girlfriend."

"What? No—"

"Colton. I've always known. And I've never minded. It's the best song you've ever written. That's why I pressured you to put it on the album. Probably also why you always acted like it hurt to play. But not that time, sounds like. Now I wish I remembered."

They don't say anything for a few moments.

"I wish I could live that night over and over again," Colton murmurs.

"I wish that too." Maisy steps forward and kisses him on the cheek. She smells like creamy, smoky sandalwood, green herbs, and suede. He doesn't know if she means she wishes she could also live in that night forever or if she wishes that for him. It doesn't matter anymore. The security system beeps and they hear the rustle of plastic bags, the jingle of keys, and footsteps.

"They didn't have ahi tuna," Kendra calls from the kitchen. "So I got you grilled salmon instead. I texted, but you didn't answer."

"Salmon's great," Maisy calls back. She turns to Colton. "Let's eat." She starts toward the kitchen.

Colton steps forward, taking her wrist and stopping her. He raises her hand to his lips and kisses it. He rubs his cheek on the back of her hand.

Her eyes brim again as she gently pulls away. "Come on. You'll feel better after you eat."

"Go ahead. I'll be there in a sec."

It's the best conversation they've had in months. Maybe in the last couple years. Which isn't saying much.

After she's turned the corner, he breaks. The weight of his life and loneliness and failures is unbearable. Tears cascade down his cheeks. He slumps onto the hard slate and sits, holding his head in his hands, trembling with quiet sobs. He puts his sunglasses back on and has a stark realization: he's broken a pact he made to himself almost twenty years ago—one meant to prevent him from hurting the people he loves and himself—and reneging on it has cost him dearly. The God of Broken Promises has brought his sword down on what he had with the second woman he ever truly loved and never deserved.

Colton finally pulls himself back to his feet but remains rooted to his position in the entryway, the opulent perfume of a $500 candle swirling around him, and he has the sensation that he's standing in the lobby of some palatial hotel—one that would have him only as long as he could pay the exorbitant fee, but that was no home of his.

FOR IMMEDIATE RELEASE

Big Sky Artists has determined, after careful consideration, that it will terminate its working relationship with Colton Gentry in light of Mr. Gentry's comments impugning gun owners and gun ownership. These comments do not reflect the views of Big Sky Artists or its roster of artists.

FOR IMMEDIATE RELEASE

Loud Sound Records unequivocally condemns the recent derogatory, misguided, and insulting comments made by Colton Gentry regarding gun ownership. Because of these comments, Loud Sound Records will be dissolving its contract with Mr. Gentry and will not be doing further business with him.

FOR IMMEDIATE RELEASE

"The Cow Patty and the Doofus in the Morning Show on the Big 98.3—The Barn" holds as sacred those personal rights conferred by the hand of the Almighty upon all Americans under the United States Constitution, including and especially the Second Amendment. Cow Patty and the Doofus cherish the right to keep and bear arms and believe in the inspired vision of the Constitution's drafters—that a free and armed society is a safe and peaceful society. Therefore, they will be immediately removing all Colton Gentry songs from airplay now and in the future to express their vehement disagreement with Mr. Gentry's calumny against those who would exercise their sacrosanct constitutional right of gun ownership.

FOR IMMEDIATE RELEASE

The GOP of Cheatham County will be holding a Colton Gentry album-smashing party at the Cheatham County Fairgrounds on June 6. Admission is $5, $2 with a Colton Gentry album to throw on the pile. There will be a bounce house for the kids, live music from the Harpeth River Bluegrass Boys, and food vendors. Special thanks to Stapp Brothers Construction for supplying a bulldozer.

JOINT STATEMENT OF MAISY MARTIN AND COLTON GENTRY

It is with sorrowful hearts that we have decided to amicably end our marriage. This was one of the most difficult decisions we have ever had to make. We will always cherish the years of love, companionship, and song we shared as we move forward in friendship. We request respect for our privacy as we navigate this trying time.

CHAPTER 6

June–September 2015
The Southwestern and Southeastern United States of America

THE FLOODWATERS RECEDE, REVEALING A NEW, RESHAPED LANDSCAPE THAT little resembles the old.

Colton labors hard to get sober. He works the program.

The news cycle moves on while he's cloistered away in the monastic rehab program. He has no internet. No cell phone. Little contact of any sort with the outside world. Lots of time to walk in the desert and let the scorching sun burn him clean. Time to perform a searching self-inventory and work on his recovery. Time to consider the new life he's going to lead when he gets out.

Music is out. As has been pointed out to him, he had received the rare grace of a second lease on creative life in his waning thirties. He's not getting a third. Even if there might be a space for him somewhere someday, he's too wrung out to seek it.

No one has come recruiting him to be their cause célèbre. That only happens when you make a courageous, sober, cogent, passionate public case for something, consequences be damned. It doesn't happen when you have an onstage meltdown and go on a profanity-riddled, drunken harangue in response to hecklers, no matter how morally sound your position may be. Going into rehab immediately after only cements your unreliability as any sort of figurehead. What if getting clean tempers your passion? Throws cold water on your fire?

His divorce from Maisy is swift and sure. He's grateful for his isolation from the media—both him from its eyes and it from his eyes. The death of a marriage is painful enough without having to see your partner painting the town with her new beau splashed across magazine covers in grocery store checkout lines. Maybe you can insulate yourself from some of the blows in a suit of armor made of money, but Colton wouldn't know anything about that.

He's also awoken to the reality that the garden of friendships he's cultivated over the past twenty years was seeded with mostly professional colleagues—who are no longer his professional colleagues.

And yet, through it all, he hasn't apologized. He will not. He wouldn't have even if he thought it would make a difference and restore him to his old stature. He's not even entirely sure he wants to be restored. Tasting fame didn't make his life appreciably better. It only resulted in a lateral shift of higher-stakes problems. And besides, kowtowing would have felt like a betrayal to Duane's memory.

After leaving the divorce with almost nothing, he's faring poorly financially. Maisy made him get rid of all of his furniture when they moved in together (*I'm petrified to even imagine what that futon has seen*, she'd said). They had a prenup, and "ironclad" didn't begin to describe it. If Colton and a motley heist cohort had donned black ski masks and endeavored to rob Maisy's bank, the prenup would have been waiting for them at the entrance, its muscles oiled and gleaming, a bandanna tied around its head, wielding a machine gun. Not that Colton especially cares for the thought of living on the dole from his ex-wife and his replacement anyway.

He doesn't even have a record deal. In fact, he has a negative record deal. Under his contract's morality clause, which forbade public statements that "provoked controversy" and "invited widespread public condemnation," he owed his label back the advance it paid him.

Still, he's making his amends, following his program. And this is costing him too. He tracks down the members of his band and pays them their lost tour wages out of his own pocket.

His resume is thin. No college. From the time he was eighteen, he never held any job that was incompatible with being an up-and-coming country musician. Never stayed at any one job for more than a couple years. For the last five years, being married to Maisy allowed him to focus solely on music.

He still owns the black 2004 Ford F-150 XLT he bought with the advance from his first record deal. He's kept it while Maisy's gone through Bentleys and Mercedes G-Classes (she has Lululemon leggings that have outlasted her cars). He's sitting in it now, going seventy-eight on I-55, north of Memphis. Open plains have funneled into dense green forest and arrow-straight longleaf pines lining the interstate.

He made a brief detour to England, Arkansas, to visit Duane's parents. This brings him a little comfort. Not much. He hopes it brought some solace to Duane's parents. He felt like a liar telling Duane's parents that their son died doing what he loved. Duane didn't love getting shot while pausing during a song to make sense of the series of sharp reports he heard.

He stood at Duane's gravesite and said, out loud, *I sure wish this wasn't the way you got your little piece of Arkansas, Dee-Wayne. I love you, brother. Until the day I die. I'll never forget you.* If Duane is listening to him anywhere, it's here, in the hometown he always wanted to return to.

It wasn't long after that stopover that Colton had his first post-rehab close call. He passed a gun shop billboard emblazoned with a huge AR-15 and "Get your Man Card here." Seeing this instrument of his friend's death sent him spiraling with such swift brutality that he had to pull off to the side of the road to call his sponsor. He found a meeting in a Baptist church basement in Palestine, Arkansas. That night he stayed in the seediest motel he could find that didn't charge by the hour, both to stretch his dwindling cash and because he wanted to be around people who had other things to worry about than anything he'd ever said or done.

Lonely though Colton is on this cross-country trip, listening to the radio also doesn't offer much comfort—he can't rest on any country station or most pop stations for more than a few minutes without hearing a Maisy Martin song. So he listens to a Larry McMurtry audiobook. Bags, suitcases, and other sundries fill his truck bed. He hopes it doesn't rain—he's tempting fate in this Southern season of looming thunderheads and surprise ten-minute afternoon frog stranglers—but he knows by now that God will help himself if he wants anything else from Colton, and there's little he can do about it.

Laid across the seat behind him is his Gibson acoustic in its road case. Sometimes he'll hit a bump and hear it creak, getting the momentary impression that he's on tour again, hurrying to make the next venue in time to soundcheck and relax with a beer before he goes on. It feels like those few moments when you wake up from a long nap during a period of travail, one of those slumbers so deep you can't remember who you are or where you are when you awake, and for just a few seconds, you get to exist, conscious, but free of pain and worry, before it all deluges back.

CHAPTER 7

September 1995
Venice, Kentucky

"Colt." His dad shook him. "Look alive, bubba."

Colton rolled over onto his back and groaned, shielding his eyes with the crook of his elbow from the sunlight piercing his blinds. "What?"

"Told you we had a job today."

"The game went late last night."

"That's why I let you sleep 'til nine. Up and at 'em."

"Dad."

"Tell you what. You want to be with me today, make a dollar, you'll meet me in the truck. Ten minutes." He slapped Colton's bare shoulder and left.

Colton sighed and sat upright, rubbing his eyes until stars formed on the backs of his eyelids.

"Sweet roll and a glass of orange juice on the counter for you," his dad called.

Wrenching himself from bed, Colton threw on a pair of jeans, his battered work boots, and a ripped white T-shirt. He pulled a U of Kentucky baseball hat over his bedhead, brushed his teeth, put on deodorant, and splashed water on his face. He chugged his orange juice and took his donut out to the truck, where his dad had the AC cranked against the stifling heat of the Western Kentucky September morning. Bugs rattled in the weeds, a harbinger of a scorching day.

They drove for a while in silence.

"Hell of a pass to end out the third quarter last night," Colton's dad said. "Still thinking about it."

Colton beamed, flush with pride. "I had to dump the ball. Was about to get hit from two sides."

"Keep throwing like that, it's the Cowboys after MTSU."

"Naw, I don't wanna live in Dallas. Plus, you'll have an easier time seeing me play if I end up with St. Louis."

"Not if you buy your mama and me a little house in Dallas."

Colton smiled. "So what's this job?"

"Finishing up a deck on Eddie Lawler's house that I've been working on this week. I think he might have a girl who goes to your school."

"Luann Lawler, probably."

"She run with you and your buddies?"

"Naw. She's a little—I don't know. Different. Artsy. Something."

Colton's dad looked at him. "I hope y'all ain't ugly to her. Way you said that."

"Naw. She just kinda does her own thing. She moved in last year."

"Guess Eddie took over as big boss at the med center. They ain't hurting for money."

The Lawlers lived in the Cumberland Highlands neighborhood, the only part of Venice where houses had three-car garages. When the pair pulled up, Mr. Lawler greeted them. He was a slender, courtly, gray-haired man, older than Colton's dad. He led them around the back, where an order of lumber awaited them. They scoped things out, made measurements, and unloaded their tools. Colton's dad set out the boombox and got his CD wallet filled with Merle Haggard, Waylon Jennings, Willie Nelson, Johnny Cash, Loretta Lynn, and Dolly Parton albums. With some tunes going, they set to work.

Colton was sore from the hits he took and fifty-yard throws he made the previous night, but in the late summer sun, his aches dripped away from him like wax melting down a candle and his muscles glowed under his skin. He and his dad got into their rhythm. Measuring (twice). Sawing (once). Hammering nails. Calling something new into being with their sweat and companionship. Colton relished the dusty, tangy smell of sawn lumber and the metallic scent on his fingers left by handling countless nails. Tradition dictated that around the half-hour mark into a job, he and his dad started singing along with the boombox. Both had strong, clear, beautiful voices and could keep a tune. This was one of Colton's favorite parts about working with his dad. Sometimes he'd pretend he was onstage and would sing into his hammer like a microphone.

Around eleven, Colton peeled off his perspiration-sodden T-shirt and draped it over a branch.

Minutes later, Luann emerged from the house in a canary-yellow sundress, her dark, wavy hair—the color of Cherry Coke when the sun hit right—in a messy ponytail, bearing a tray with two glasses and a pitcher filled with amber sweet tea and clinking ice cubes. "My dad said y'all might be thirsty."

"He thought right," Colton's dad said, wiping sweat from his brow with the back of his forearm. "Colt?"

"Yessir," Colton said. He waved awkwardly at Luann. "Hey. Luann, right?"

"Yeah."

"I'm—"

"Colton. I know. Who you are." She looked away, blushing, as she said it.

"Didn't want to assume."

"You play football, and we're in high school in Kentucky."

Colton smiled.

They took glasses and drank and drank again until they'd killed the pitcher.

"You want more?" Luann asked. "I can tell my mom to make some for lunch."

"Cool, yeah," Colton said.

"You look pretty sweaty," Luann said.

"I mean, it's hot."

"Yeah. Anyway."

Colton watched her go back inside. It was strange to see her in such an intimate context as her own home, especially when they were having their first ever conversation. She was an enigmatic figure, as a newcomer to their school. She'd moved in from Lexington junior year. She hung out with Mara Bloom—known throughout Venice High for her artistic acumen, her Nine Inch Nails and Marilyn Manson T-shirts, and her ornately hand-decorated Chuck Taylors—and Tyler Garrett. The star of Venice High's theater program, Tyler was roundly rumored to be gay, gossip he spent little energy trying to dispel, the courage of which Colton respected.

Colton and his dad returned to work. The deck was taking shape, and Colton felt gratified—he was as proud of their two-man crew as he was of his football team. He found himself, strangely, hoping for Luann's return. He wanted to show off their work to an audience. At twelve thirty, Luann came back out with a book tucked under one arm, a tray of pimento cheese sandwiches and Lay's potato chips precariously balanced in one hand and, in the other, another full pitcher of ice-cold sweet tea. She placed the tray and pitcher on a portion of the finished deck and called, "Here's your lunch," interrupting Colton's and his dad's singing. She took a sandwich off the top of the pile and walked over to a shady spot in the backyard where there were a couple of yard chairs. She kicked off her Birkenstocks and sat cross-legged in a wicker chair, book open in one hand and eating a sandwich with the other.

Colton and his dad sat side by side, eating. Colton was on his second sandwich when he felt himself drawn toward where Luann sat—it felt impolite to be in such close proximity to a classmate without saying anything. "I probably ought to go say hi."

His dad gave Colton the knowing smile he used to give him when he saw through one of Colton's ruses for staying up past his bedtime *(If I don't finish the movie, I'll just stay awake thinking about it anyway).* "Be rude not to, wouldn't it."

Colton rose quickly and walked away so his dad wouldn't see his face blooming scarlet.

"Hey," Colton said.

"Hey," Luann said, not looking up from her book.

"The sandwiches are good. You make them?"

She scoffed and looked up finally. "Like I cook."

"Technically they're not cooked."

"You know what I meant."

"I don't know you all that well."

"Thank my stepmom. She made them."

"I will."

"So, good deck, I guess. I'm not a deck expert."

Colton smiled. "I can take partial credit for that. You excited to have a place to read?"

"I obviously have a place to read already." Luann met his gaze.

He noticed her eyes, which were hazel and inscrutable but radiated a resolve and intelligence seldom seen among their peers.

"Another place, then. What you reading?"

Luann held up the book. "*Interview with the Vampire*."

"So, what, like a guy asking what's your favorite kind of blood to drink, what's your favorite coffin brand, what sunscreen do you use?" Colton thought he almost saw her smile, but she caught herself.

"It's very weird talking about books with a shirtless dude." Luann recrossed her legs. She had chipped blood-red polish on her fingers and toes.

"I can leave," Colton said, feeling self-conscious and coarse. He was unaccustomed to girls trying to dissuade him from shirtless dialogue, and he was now wondering if he was a bad shirtless conversationalist and they'd all been too polite to tell him.

"I was just saying."

Colton appreciated the reassurance. Her jousting was a novelty to him, and he was intrigued, interested to see if he could sneak past her guard. He didn't often get the chance. "When you go to the pool with a guy, do y'all just not talk?" He didn't think she went to pools very often with guys.

"Not about books."

"Is it a good book?"

"Sure."

"Would I like it?"

"Didn't you just barely say we didn't know each other?"

"Is it the kind that's easy to like? I don't need to know you to know that you'll like some stuff."

"Such as?"

Colton thought for a second. "Reese's peanut butter cups."

"I—"

"If you're about to say, 'I don't like Reese's peanut butter cups' just to argue, I'll know you're lying."

Luann smiled at last. "I was gonna agree."

The breakthrough. "Finally. Lord above."

Blessedly, this drew a laugh from Luann.

"Colt?" his dad called. "Hate to interrupt y'all, but Luann's folks ain't paying us to chat."

Colton turned to Luann. "Well. Guess I better get back." He was starting to enjoy himself. He liked something about Luann. What it was, he couldn't quite say. He started to walk back.

"Is building a deck hard?" Luann asked.

Colton turned. "I mean, not if you know what you're doing."

"I wanna learn." She slipped on her Birkenstocks and set her book on her chair as she stood.

Colton eyed her face for some indication of jest, finding none. "What do you mean?"

"Show me how to build a deck."

"Are you...allowed?"

"It's my house." She started walking toward where they were working.

Colton turned to his dad. "Hey, Dad. Luann—"

"I heard. Luann, is it okay by your folks?"

"Dad? Dad?" Luann called until her dad came outside. "I want to help them and learn what they're doing."

Luann's dad looked to Colton's dad. "Will she get in your way?"

Colton's dad shrugged. "Nope. Long as you're okay."

Luann's dad sighed. "I know damn well I'm wasting my time if I try to say no. Lulu, no power tools. That's where I draw the line."

Her face brightened with a triumphal expression. Colton shared in it, pleased at the prospect of further interaction.

"Go change into something better for working, for heaven's sake," her dad said.

She ran inside.

Colton and his dad went back to work. She returned moments later wearing denim cutoffs, a white ribbed tank top, and burgundy Doc Martens.

Colton smiled at her approach. "Now you look like a construction worker."

They got to work. Colton showed her the best way to hold a hammer and where they were driving nails. He relished getting close to her. She smelled like fresh, aqueous, green fruits. Pear. Melon. Cucumber. Colton got a whiff every time she flipped her hair, which was often, and it made his head spin a little each time. After a while working in the close heat, she smelled like new sweat too, and that was also nice.

At first glance, she didn't appear the manual laborer. She had fine wrists and delicate, pretty fingers. But she was a quick study, wasn't squeamish about wielding the hammer, and had good aim, so within minutes, she was hammering in nails like a pro. She joked while they worked, narrating their labors in a New York construction worker voice.

Eventually, Colton and his dad went back to singing, although with Luann present, he held back out of self-consciousness.

"You're a good singer," Luann said between songs.

Colton's face reddened even beyond the flush in his cheeks from exertion and waved her off. "Naw, we just fool around."

"You have a country singer name."

"Folks have said that. You like country?"

An expression of disgust. "No."

"You've been suffering in silence this whole time?"

She shrugged. "It feels like deck-building music. Just don't make me listen to it when I'm not building a deck. Which is most of the time."

"Who do you listen to?"

"Tori Amos. Björk. PJ Harvey. Liz Phair. The Cranberries."

Colton looked at her blankly.

"I can acquaint you," Luann said.

Unable to overcome his self-consciousness about singing now that he knew Luann was paying attention, Colton chatted with her while they worked. They took a break to drink some sweet tea and sat on a finished portion of the deck, swinging their legs back and forth. The sides of their thighs touched lightly. Colton didn't know whether he'd sat close to Luann or she'd sat near him. Maybe it was both.

"You're a better deck builder than I expected," Colton said. "Not because you're a girl," he hastily added.

"Because I'm a deck-building virgin?"

Colton blushed and looked away. "Yeah."

"You're a nicer person than I expected."

Colton was taken aback. "You thought I was mean?"

"I dunno. You're like this big football player guy."

"Lots of guys on the team are nice."

Luann gave him an oh-please look.

"What?"

"To who?"

"Have football players been mean to you?"

"To Tyler."

"Well. Yeah. I guess that's probably true."

"You guess?"

"But I'm not okay with it. Just so you know."

"Good."

They sat quietly for a while, the only sound the steady buzzing of insects in the vegetation. Colton stole sidelong glances at Luann. He liked her face, he knew, even as he was still trying to decide whether he found her attractive. How had he not noticed her before? The answer was, of course, social status. He had it. She didn't, which had made her invisible to him, as wrong as that now seemed.

She caught him looking at her. "What?"

He quickly looked away. "Nothing. So you hang a lot with Tyler and Mara."

"Yep."

"Are you, like, an artsy person too?"

"An artsy person?" She imitated his voice.

"Why you gotta give me a hard time?"

"Aw. Is your life hard, Mr. Quarterback King of the School?" She gently kicked the side of his foot, and his leg swayed sideways.

He nudged her foot back with his. "I'm just trying to talk to you. Dang."

"We artsy people are temperamental."

"Apparently. Should I go put my shirt back on? Would that make this conversation easier?"

"No," Luann said, and it might have been Colton's imagination or wishful thinking, but she said it quickly and emphatically. She smoothed her hair and (again, maybe wishful thinking) blushed. "Yeah. I guess I'm an artsy person. Not like them, though."

"Like what?"

"Like... architecture is my thing."

Colton studied her face for some tell that she was giving him further grief, but nothing. "Designing buildings?"

"That would be architecture."

"You wanna be an architect?"

"Am I blowing your mind here?"

"That why you wanted to learn how to build a deck?"

"Bingo."

"Wow," Colton said. "You really are different."

"Not usually a compliment." She tapped the side of his foot again with hers.

He returned the tap. "I meant it as one."

"Better have. What about you? After you graduate?" She picked a fleck off his shoulder.

It felt like a butterfly alighting on him. "Playing college ball."

"You good enough?" She plucked another something off his biceps.

"Already got a scholarship to Middle Tennessee State. I threw three touchdowns last night. We're supposed to win state."

"Only one state? What about the other forty-nine?"

Colton grinned and shook his head.

"Just saying," she said. "One out of fifty isn't a great percentage."

The bottom hem of Luann's tank top rode up, exposing a strip of the pale skin on the side of her midriff. Colton pressed his chilled, condensation-soaked glass to the spot.

She yipped and doubled over sideways as if stung. "I'll get you back for that."

They giggled together.

Colton's dad glanced over with an amused expression.

Colton caught it. "Okay," he said, sighing. "Back to work." He rose and extended a hand to Luann to help her up even though she probably didn't need assistance.

And even though she probably didn't need to, she took his hand, then hopped down from the deck. Her fingers were soft against his.

They continued working in the subtropical afternoon until the livid yellow of the sunlight sweetened to gold and the shadows lengthened on the lawn. They finished and stepped back from their work to admire it.

Sweat plastered a lock of hair to Luann's face. Her cheeks glowed pink and she beamed.

"She was a big help," Colton's dad said to Luann's parents, who had come outside to see. "Wouldn't have finished so soon without her."

"Lulu's a sass mouth but a good worker," her dad said.

"What now?" Luann asked Colton.

"Clean up, load the tools back in the truck." He retrieved his T-shirt from the branch and donned it. It felt like a warm embrace on his skin. "This was fun. I'm glad we got to hang out some."

"Me too. Maybe I'll see you in the halls sometime or driving to Megan Strickland's house."

Megan was a cheerleader who lived a few streets away from Luann. She and Colton had gone out a few times. He was surprised Luann had noticed.

Colton set the circular saw in the truck bed and accepted a tool belt from Luann. "Or...we could hang out sometime on purpose," Colton said hesitantly. He hadn't thought this through. There were Byzantine social politics at play. But sometimes he spoke first and worried about the consequences later.

Luann squinted against the brightness and shaded her eyes with her hand. "You think?"

"Why not?"

"Because."

"Because why?"

"Because...I don't know."

Colton was entirely unaccustomed to this level of resistance. "I thought we had fun today. I had fun."

"Me too."

"Tell you what," Colton said. He rummaged in the cab of the truck and came up with a pencil stub and a faded blank invoice. He scribbled on it as he walked Luann back to her front porch. "Here's my number. You wanna hang out sometime, call me."

Luann looked at the paper in his hand skeptically. "Hang out and do what?"

"I don't know. Talk, listen to music, build a deck, whatever."

"Toss the old pigskin?"

"I mean...if you want?"

"Country karaoke night?"

"You making fun of me?"

"Teeny bit."

"Call me?"

"Maybe."

"Maybe?" Colton gave her his most winning smile, the one with the lowest failure rate.

"Maybe." She took the invoice and extended her hand for a handshake, once again affecting her New York accent. "Pleasure workin' with ya."

He shook his head and took her hand, holding it for a few ticks longer than necessary. "See you Monday."

"Yep."

He started down to the front walk, where his dad was getting in the truck.

"Hey, Colton?" Luann called after him. "Real quick?"

He turned around to see Luann holding the hose. He had no time to react before she doused him with a spurt of water, drenching anew his sun-dried T-shirt, plastering it to the muscles of his chest and abdomen.

"Told you I'd get you back."

CHAPTER 8

September 2015
Venice, Kentucky

THE EMPTINESS INSIDE HIM CLAIMS MORE TERRITORY AS HE EXITS OFF THE interstate onto the network of state highways and routes that will take him home. Kudzu engulfs trees and twines up telephone poles like Christmas lights. The houses along the way are a mix of sprawling estates with large, new-build homes with flashy boats sitting in their driveways, and mold-scabbed and sagging trailers bedecked with Confederate flags, menageries of rusted cars sprouting up, dandelion-like, on the lawn. Gas stations advertise live bait, Hunt Brothers Pizza, and sometimes barbecue. The occasional whitewashed church and cornfield break up the dense wall of foliage that lines each side of the road.

He drives into the outskirts of town, his heartbeat quickening with anxiety as he wonders how he'll fit his life back into the smallness of Venice after all he's done and seen away. *Everything right where I left it.*

But that isn't quite true, is it? The last time he was here, albeit briefly, was a couple of years back when he was on the rise. Beautiful, famous, rich wife. They had had their issues, sure, in their few years of matrimony, but things were mostly pretty good. New record deal and album in the works with the influence and support of said wife. He felt inspired and vibrant creatively. He was keeping so busy that even when he was at their Nashville condo, just two and a half hours away, there was rarely room in his schedule to visit Venice. When he wanted to see his mom, he usually flew her out to Antigua or Cancún or whatever exotic locale where he and Maisy were vacationing.

Venice might seem the same, but none of that was where he left it.

He passes the turn to Cumberland Highlands and a compulsion grips him to flip around and drive past Luann Lawler's home, to view the deck he and his dad and Luann built on a sundrenched Saturday afternoon almost exactly twenty years ago. He wants to remember a minor but unambiguous triumph—one time when he built something and it stood against time and storms.

But he can't. It's too devastating to consider driving by the house and seeing the deck gone—torn up and replaced with something newer and better—and witnessing one more work of his come to naught.

And the visual reminder of what happened with Luann would surely be the proverbial last straw, so he drives on.

His childhood home is on Venice's east side—the blue-collar part. Literally the wrong side of the railroad tracks that bisect the town. He drives through downtown, which sits on the banks of the Cumberland River, to see what may have changed. The Cotton Blossom, a gift store, appears to be long gone. Improbably, Meyer Menswear is still there, with Harris Tweed jackets on faceless mannequins in the window. Even when Colton was a kid, he never saw anyone in there. He realizes Meyer Menswear has outlived his musical career and chuckles in spite of himself.

Venice has seedlings of bohemia sprouting. There's a yoga studio/day spa called Lotus Flower next to the tragic muddy canal that flows through downtown, from which the town derived its name—as if in mockery of its Italian namesake. The downtown theater appears to have become an art mall. Occupying the 1920s-era neoclassical-style bank building is an upscale-looking restaurant called Field to Flame. By its name and appearance, Colton clocks it as a hip Southern farm-to-table restaurant of some stripe. He makes a mental note to take his mom there for lunch or dinner one of these days soon—before his scant funds are completely tapped. Or before the restaurant goes under from lack of patronage, a victim of the Venetians who prefer the Olive Garden.

He turns into the driveway of the 1950s-era brick ranch where he grew up. *If you'd held on for a year or two more, you might have made buy-your-mom-a-big-beautiful-house money.* He only made buy-your-mom-a-house-like-the-one-she-already-lives-in money. And even then, only briefly. He pulls his cap low and hopes no one is watching his official surrender—when he walks up to his old front door, guitar case in hand, and enters. Icarus finally plummeting into the tempestuous sea.

"Mom," he calls from the entryway. "I'm ho—here." He almost says "home" but catches himself. He's not yet ready to admit, even to himself, the extent of his defeat.

Colton's mom hurries in. Before he can even greet her, she squeezes him so hard he can barely breathe. They haven't seen each other since everything happened.

"I love you no matter what," she murmurs into his ear. "I know you miss Duane, sweetie. I do too. He was a good man and a good friend. I'll never forget how much fun I had dancing with him at Charity's wedding."

They hug for several moments, swaying gently. It's the first time in a long while that Colton has felt truly loved by anyone, but the second time in mere months that he's found himself sobbing in the entryway of a place that he used to call home.

Not a great ratio.

CHAPTER 9

"You hungry?" Colton's mom asks. "You didn't text to say when you were getting in, and I didn't want to fix dinner until I knew."

"Tired from the drive mostly." Colton rubs his face. "Maybe later." They sit at the kitchen table. The one at which Colton grew up eating Cheerios. He scratches at a divot on the tabletop and tries to remember if he noticed it as a kid. He looks at the floor. "Back where it all began," he murmurs.

"Colton," his mom says softly, resting her hand on his. "You're a young man with your whole life ahead. This'll blow over, and you can start again."

"You know how every time you turn on the country station, the Dixie Chicks are playing?"

"No."

"Precisely." But using logic to checkmate your mom out of still believing in you feels like no great triumph.

"I'm so proud of you. Nothing will ever change that. I know your dad would've been too."

"I can't decide if I wish he were still around to see all this going on. He'd have seen some high highs and low lows."

"It would've only been high highs to him."

Colton nods and looks away, tapping the table while he fights for composure. He doesn't need his mom thinking all he does is cry anymore as now he mourns his dad again alongside Duane. He clears his throat a couple of times. "I saw this fancy-looking restaurant downtown. Fire and Flame. Something like that."

"Field to Flame."

He snaps. "That's it. I wanna take you before it goes under."

"Would you believe there's a two-week wait to get in? People come from Paducah, Clarksville, Bowling Green, even Nashville and Louisville."

"Really?"

"Supposedly it's great."

"Been yet?"

"Never braved the wait, but Lynn's been a couple times and she said it's one of the best places she's ever eaten at."

"Huh. More's changed here than I thought. What else is new around town?"

"Since you were here last? Not much. There's a new Harbor Freight by the Hog Heaven. Oh! Guess who I saw the other day at the Foodland?"

"Who?"

"Derrick Giles."

"No kidding? You talk to him?"

"No. Y'all kept in touch since high school?"

"Not like we should've. Some, for the first few years after I moved to Nashville and he was playing football at Mississippi College. But then we sorta fizzled."

"Might do you some good to track him down and reconnect."

"Or it might just remind me of everyone I've let down in my life." Colton runs his fingers through his hair and yawns. The fatigue from the drive and of bearing the weight pressing down on him has caught up. "I might take a nap. Then we can talk dinner. Maybe watch some *Law and Order*."

"I've started *Grey's Anatomy*."

"I met Katherine Heigl once."

"Was she nice?"

"Seemed fine to me."

Colton's mom stands. "I've got your room ready."

Together, they get Colton's things loaded in. He reclines on his old bed, closes his eyes, and stares at the redness behind his sun-illuminated eyelids. Tired though he is, he can't sleep. Without warning, the craving for a drink wallops him with dizzying force.

Just something to blunt the edge. One drink.

You don't do single drinks. You're an alcoholic.

It's easy. One and done.

One won't dull the pain. You'll have as many as it takes to do that. And you have nowhere left to fall but off the edge of the earth.

You have nothing left. No job. No wife. No friends. No home of your own. Drink is all you have left that brings you any pleasure.

Getting sober was salvaging the last bit of dignity you had left.

You're back lying on the same bed where you used to have wet dreams. Don't worry about losing any more dignity.

He opens his eyes, sits up, pulls out his phone with trembling hands, and calls his sponsor, who happens to be a Grammy-winning R&B artist. One of the perks of his fancy rehab.

"Leon? It's Colton."

"What it do, my man? You good?"

"Not good, bro. I'm back home. In my old bedroom. Spinning out. Thinking about drinking."

"You haven't yet."

"No."

"Can you get to a meeting?"

"I looked into meeting schedules before I got to town. Made notes somewhere."

"Pull them up. While I'm on the line with you."

Colton puts Leon on speaker and searches around on his phone.

"Okay...looks like one just started at this church a few minutes from here."

"Can you get there?"

"Yeah."

"I'll stay on the line with you. You got this, bro."

"It's great to hear someone say that, Leon. You have no idea."

"I got a lot of idea."

"Okay. Heading out."

The meeting is small, in the United Methodist Church basement. No one recognizes him—or at least no one lets on that they do—and that's a plus. He's especially grateful there's no one in the group with whom he went to high school. Based on his experience, there are more than a few classmates who could have ended up here too.

When it's over, his shaking hands have steadied; he no longer has the sensation of hanging on a cliff face. Instead, he'll cling to his sobriety for another day, and that's a green shoot of triumph growing up amid the arid plains of defeat.

He steps out into the humid but cooling dusk. The air smells like the hallway between seasons. The sky is the lapis lazuli of a new evening in early autumn, and there's a bright, clean waxing gibbous moon rising. In the distance he can hear a train horn.

You will never have nothing. You will always still have this. At least this. No one can ever take it from you, because it was never yours to lose.

CHAPTER 10

THE NEXT MORNING, WITH DEW SPECKLING THE GRASS, COLTON ARRIVES AT the cemetery with a handful of flowers from his mom's garden. The thought of entering a Venice grocery store or flower shop filled him with nearly paralyzing panic.

He crouches by his father's lichen-fuzzed workingman's headstone. He's been absent from here for even longer than he's been gone from Venice, his last few short visits leaving little time to commune with those who have passed.

He feels a potent desire to speak out loud, the way people spill out to a therapist or confess a crime. "Second time at a gravesite this week. First time was Duane. Remember that time we all got ribs together? You liked him...Everyone did. He got killed. That's how I ended up back here. I'm sorry I haven't stopped by in so long."

Colton scans the grounds. He's alone. It's ridiculous, to be speaking aloud the way he is, but he feels catharsis, his shoulders less taut than they've been in months. It's a slight respite from gray despair, and it's healthier than the other temporary cure he knows.

He gathers himself. "I did okay for a while, Dad. I made the kind of music we used to listen to together. A lot of people heard it. Maybe some—" He breaks down and weeps. He's tired of crying. But there's much to cry about. *Grief is so much worse when you're mourning many things, including the deaths of essential pieces of yourself.* He takes a deep breath, wipes his eyes, and continues. "Maybe some fathers and sons listened to my music together. But I had my day in the sun, and it's over. It's all gone. The wind took it. I'm nothing more now than I was when you were around. My life hasn't amounted to much. So I hope you saw me somehow when I was doing good. I hope—"

Colton wants to say *I hope I made you proud, Dad*. But there's no amount of waiting that will allow him composure enough to speak the words, and he knows it.

He leaves.

CHAPTER 11

September 1995
Venice, Kentucky

THE FOOTBALL CAROMED OFF THE UPPER RIM OF THE HANGING TIRE IN Derrick's backyard.

"You even trying?" Colton asked.

"I'm still thrashed from last night," Derrick said. "Where were you?"

"Too tired. Worked all day with my dad. Actually, you know where? Luann Lawler's house. You know her?"

"We had English last year. Smart as hell. Always arguing with the teacher."

"She and I hung out some while we were working."

"And?" Derrick took the ball from Colton.

"She was cool. You ever talked with her?"

Derrick hurled the ball, missing the tire entirely. He trotted to retrieve it. "Why you asking?"

"I dunno."

They flopped down into nylon-web lawn chairs. Derrick pointed at Colton with the football. "You're into her."

"Naw."

"What about Jess?" Derrick flipped the ball into the air.

Colton reached over and intercepted it. "We're not officially going out."

"So you're available for Luann."

"I wouldn't mind maybe, possibly hanging with her again." Colton flipped the ball in the air.

Derrick swiped the ball. "Finally the truth. Sheeit."

"She's not my usual type."

Derrick tried to spin the football on his finger like a basketball. "Probably be good for you. You should date girls who are smarter than you."

"Easy for you to say."

Derrick brayed fake guffaws and slapped his knee. "Just for that, I'm not inviting you for dinner."

"Quit playing."

"Nana's cooking up chicken and dumplings and greens and mac and cheese." Derrick theatrically rubbed his stomach in huge circular motions and dabbed at the corners of his mouth with an invisible napkin.

"Come on, Big D," Colton beseeched. "D Rock, baby, come on now."

"Peach cobbler for dessert. With vanilla ice cream. *French* vanilla. I don't know what the French are doing to their vanilla, but it's working." Derrick closed his eyes in bliss and sniffed, wafting air toward his nose with his hand. "I can smell its sweet aroma."

"Dude. I'm sorry. You're a genius unlike anything Venice High has ever seen. Don't make me beg."

"Look how all dignity went out the window the minute I mentioned peach cobbler. Shameful."

Colton returned home several hours later, so full he could scarcely breathe. The smell of burnt microwave popcorn singed his nose when he entered. His beagle, Cooter, bounded in, skidding on the floor, to greet him with animated yips. Colton's dad, mom, and sister, Charity, were watching *The Fugitive* in the living room. It was one of seven VHS tapes they owned. His dad loved to do the "every henhouse" speech in unison with Tommy Lee Jones, never quite getting the order right.

"Hey, Colt," Charity called. "There's a message for you on the machine."

"Okay."

"It's a giiiiiiiirl," Charity sang out, reveling in performing the trope of a sitcom annoying younger sister.

Colton didn't respond, generally finding that the best approach, and went to the answering machine, where the blinking red light set his pulse quickening. He hit the button.

"Hey, Colton. This is Luann. Calling to say hi like you said. Call me back." She gave her number.

It was exactly the message he hoped for.

CHAPTER 12

September–October 2015
Venice, Kentucky

COLTON HAD BEEN BACK FOR FIVE DAYS WHEN HE STARTED GETTING cabin fever—or, more accurately, boyhood-home-to-which-he's-returned-a-broken-man fever. His mom remarked offhandedly that they needed garbage bags and, eager to venture out, he volunteered.

He'd awoken in one of those upbeat moods you sometimes experience during trying times, when that slippery perspective is within reach for a few hours, when the clouds part for a second and you're reminded of the blue sky behind them. He was relatively young and in decent health, especially now that he was sober. He had at least a few people in his life who loved him unconditionally. He lived in a free country that sometimes went as long as two weeks between mass shootings and had clean water to drink and abundant food. He had tasted greater success than most people ever would, doing something that he loved. He had gotten to hear a song he wrote played on FM radio. What percentage of humans ever experience that? And even the most carefully managed artistic careers didn't last forever. Popularity waned even for artists who didn't speed the process along with soused rants.

The early days of autumn had put him in mind of the cycles of the world, how things die and regrow. *Was what he had in his life before his great fall any more beautiful than an autumn leaf right before it falls? Might not spring come for him, too?*

He arrives at the Foodland still riding relatively high. Even so, he has a moment of hesitation in the parking lot. He sits in his truck, breathing down the jitters. *C'mon, man. Don't lose your nerve now. What are the chances you even get recognized by someone who didn't know you from high school?* Unwilling to yield to the more timorous angels of his nature, he enters.

He picks up the garbage bags and a bouquet of flowers for his mom. He manages to walk by the cold beer aisle without too much temptation. He's careful to select a checkout line with no tabloids, lest he see Maisy and the Hockey Player on the cover.

While he waits, a voice behind him says, "'Scuse me."

He turns to see a woman in an oversized Realtree hoodie, jean shorts, and flip-flops. Now facing her, he's hit with the smells of cigarette smoke and vanilla cupcake frosting.

"I ain't trying to be a stalker or nothing, but are you Colton Gentry?"

Colton clears his throat and rubs his beard self-consciously, bracing himself. "Yep."

"Thought so. Kinda hard to tell."

He'd grown out his beard and his hair, which was a few months past his normal haircut schedule. "What'd you say your name was?" he asks.

"Kaelee Joy. There was that one song of yours that was on the radio. Summer something."

Colton could hear the spelling of Kaelee's name when she said it. " 'Honeysuckle Summer'?"

"Maybe."

"It's probably that. That's my only song with summer in the title. Definitely the only one on the radio."

"Could be. Been a while since I've heard it."

Funny how that works. He begins losing his grip on the festive balloon he's been holding all morning, the one making him feel lighter. "Yep. Lotta turnover on country radio."

"Ain't you married to Maisy Martin?"

Colton loses his grip on the balloon and it floats into power lines. "I—Yeah, used to be."

"Not anymore?"

"No." He hopes Kaelee Joy will take his terseness as a hint and move on.

"What happened?"

"We, uh—you know, I'd as soon not discuss it." Up ahead of him an old man is paying for his groceries with a check. Naturally.

"I like her."

"She's very popular."

"Can't hardly turn on the radio without hearing her."

"Mmm-hmm."

"Wanna sign my grocery list?"

"Sure."

She hands him the list and produces a ballpoint pen advertising a tanning salon.

As Colton is about to add his name to the list underneath *Eggo waffles* and *tampons*, a man who looks like a shaved, sunburned hog's ass walks up. He smells like mildewed cotton. He sports a Punisher logo baseball cap with wraparound Oakleys perched on the brim and Realtree Crocs and has a large bulge of chaw in his cheek. In one hand he clutches an Aquafina bottle with some tea-colored liquid sloshing in it. He eyes Colton warily.

"Hey, Kody, this is Colton Gentry, the singer," Kaelee says.

"Oh yeah?" he responds gruffly.

"He's signing my grocery list."

"Nice to meet—" Colton starts, hand extended.

"Nuh-uh. Screw that." Kody snatches the list roughly out of Colton's other hand. He glares at Colton.

"Kody! Lord." Kaelee covers her face with her hand and then raises it in a he's-always-grabbing-grocery-lists-out-strangers'-hands-but-what-can-you-do-but-love-him-anyway-for-the-rare-and-beautiful-flower-of-a-man-that-he-is gesture.

"Naw. You wanna get up onstage, shit talk me? I ain't about to have your autograph in my house."

People begin to stare. Someone holds up a phone, filming. Colton reddens. "Hey, brother, I—"

Kody sticks his finger in Colton's face. "Ain't your brother, bubba. Tell you something else, okay? Maybe you used to be from here, but you ain't no more. Go back to LA or wherever you live now." He crumples up the list and throws it on the ground.

"Kody, I still need that list," Kaelee mewls. "There's stuff on it I gotta get from Walmart's."

Colton's brain froths with anger and humiliation. He considers calmly and rationally explaining to Kody why he had said what he said. But something tells him Kody doesn't do calm and rational. He thinks of just popping Kody in the mouth, but that idea has several important drawbacks: (1) getting his ass whipped—Kody didn't look like his skull was protecting anything terribly important, and you never want to get in a fight with someone who has little to lose; (2) getting his ass sued—Colton had had his fill of lawyers over the last year and hadn't made out well; (3) getting his ass sent to prison, which actually might be the only rung on the ladder lower than he currently occupied and would probably end up costing his mom a pretty penny; and (4) further public humiliation, which came as a free bonus to possibilities (1) through (3).

He chooses the one path that might do the least harm. Without another word, without making eye contact with any of the murmuring rubberneckers ringing the scene, Colton carefully sets his loaded basket on the floor, out of the way, and casually walks out, as though he'd always intended to stand in line for a while, get in a verbal altercation with a fellow shopper, and leave without buying anything.

After this experience and for the rest of his first two weeks back, he only leaves home to attend AA meetings each day, slinking in and out like paparazzi await him outside. But that was only ever a true problem when he was on Maisy's arm.

He sleeps later than he ought. He feels himself bogged down in the mire of a sustained depression. Nothing feels right. Nothing offers pleasure. Every experience, every sensory input feels like it's being run through a filter that shades it a sickly yellow. He limps through an omnipresent murk of shapeless anxiety. But without health insurance anymore or much of a bank balance, it goes untreated.

With a tried-and-true, relatively inexpensive way to (temporarily) feel a little better (or at least forget how awful he feels) just a bottle and a glass away, every day is a struggle to stay sober. It doesn't help that the circle of people who care whether he's sober or not has constricted to a number he can count on one hand.

It does help to open up during his meetings, though, which he utilizes as makeshift talk therapy. He also tries to use a different sort of liquid to drown his sorrows—sweat—by busying himself during his limited waking hours working on projects around the house and yard. He might not have the money to buy his mom a McMansion, but he's eager to help her however he can.

His isolation remains almost complete. His label ran his official social media accounts. They haven't offered to turn them over to him and aren't likely to. It seems pointless to ask anyway, as his follower count took a hit after his onstage meltdown. He had his own private accounts, but they too have gone largely neglected and now doesn't seem like a fun time to fire them back up. He hasn't kept in touch with many people from high school or his early music days. His life got too busy over the past few years.

Worse yet, he hasn't once touched his guitar since he returned home.

Nights he spends watching *Grey's Anatomy*, *Law and Order*, or *NCIS* with his mom. During one such watch session, as he's about to suggest they take down one more episode before packing it in for the day, she turns to him.

"Honey."

He looks at her but says nothing. He knows from her tone what's coming, and he's been dreading it. And he doesn't even know exactly what *it* is.

"I want you to take as much time as you need."

"Okay." Colton sinks farther into the sofa.

"I'm worried about you."

"I'm fine, it's just—I'll figure things out. I promise I'm not going to be in your hair forever."

"That's not what concerns me. It's that I can tell you're hurting, and you're my baby."

"Like I said, I'll pull out of it."

"One thing that worries me especially is the being so alone."

"Let's watch some more *Grey's*. How can I be lonely when I'm with my favorite scrubs-wearing crew of implausibly sexy doctors who hate each other but still sleep with one another?"

"Colt."

"I'm not alone. I have you."

"You do. But you need other friends—some that aren't fictional."

"Lord, Mama. It's like I'm seven and you're telling me to go ask the other kids on the playground to play."

"Well, it is a little. Sometimes a mother knows."

"I don't wanna do this. I'm thirty-eight years old and a goddamned failure in every way. My life's collapsed around me. I don't need friends. I need a time machine."

He and his mom look at each other for a second.

"Sorry for using the Lord's name in vain," he says quietly.

"You don't get a time machine. You get to rebuild."

"Yeah."

"What about Derrick?" his mom says.

"Dr. Derek Shepherd, aka McDreamy? Sure, let's watch some more of him." Colton picks up the remote.

His mom puts her hand over his and pushes the remote down. "Derrick Giles, smarty pants."

"I told you we lost touch."

"And I told you I think he's back living here."

"So?"

"So reconnect."

"People love when you show up back in their life like 'Hey, everything went to crap and I'm alone now, so I guess you'll do.'"

"If Derrick showed back up in your life, hurting, needing a friend, after he'd had a rough go of things, would you turn him away?"

Colton sighs, defeated. "By the way, I made us a reservation at Field to Flame. Little mother-son date," Colton says finally, eager to change the subject, as he picks up the remote again. This time his mom doesn't stop him.

CHAPTER 13

September 1995
Venice, Kentucky

THEY MIGHT HAVE RESEMBLED GREAT WARRIORS OF YORE, ENTERING SOME paradisiacal afterlife, these young titans of Venice High's football team, as they streamed into the parking lot, lightning arcing between purple thunderheads towering above them.

Derrick and Colton walked together at the rear of the cohort.

"...So what did you say?" Colton asked.

"I was like, 'Nana. Come on now. You will *not* like *The X-Files*. It is not a show for nanas.'"

"Which made her want to watch it more."

"Man. She straight posts up on the couch. No lie—very next scene dude gets his head sliced off."

Colton cackled. "I can only imagine her reaction."

Derrick clutched his heart, closed his eyes, looked heavenward, and pretended to swoon. "*Oh Lord Jesus, oh Jesus. Lord, no. Get out, Satan.*" His imitation of his nana was spot on.

They both laughed.

"Guess she learned," Colton said.

"She learned? Homie, *I* learned. Now my ass is forbidden from watching *X-Files* at home."

"You can watch at my house. I'll hook you up."

"Colton?" A familiar voice from the side surprised him.

Luann leaned against the fender of a red Jeep Wrangler. She wore short cutoffs, her Birkenstocks, a black choker, and a black crop top exposing a tiny line of midriff under an oversized, unbuttoned flannel shirt that looked like she might have swiped it from her dad's closet.

Derrick threw Colton a sly smile and slapped him on the pec. "Holler at you later, bro." He strode away.

Colton walked over to Luann. "Hey."

"Missed your call back. Figured I'd just come find you."

"Cool. Nice Jeep."

"It's dumb. My dad didn't even ask what I wanted. He just got what he thought a girl would like."

"Nine times out of ten he's right. What would you have gotten if he asked you?"

"Orange Karmann Ghia. But I didn't come to talk cars."

"I was gonna ask."

A peal of thunder boomed, as if on cue.

"That," Luann said. "Let's go watch it."

"The storm?"

"That's right."

"For real?"

"It's my favorite."

"Why?"

Luann's bravado totters. "Because...I don't know. It's awesome. Are you in or not?"

"Now?"

"You know a way to rewind a storm?"

Colton rested his hand on the hood of Luann's Jeep and leaned on it. He looked to see if any of his teammates were watching this scene unfold. They weren't. He was glad. It would be complicated to explain. "I got homework."

"Like you worry about that."

Colton, busted, grinned. "Can I drive your Jeep?"

"Nope. Get in."

"We gotta hit a pay phone on the way, because my folks'll wonder why I didn't come home right after practice."

"Cool. Let's go."

Luann drove fast and confidently, running through the gears like a road-seasoned trucker, a scrunchie wrapped around the gearshift. She worked the pedals barefoot and on long straightaways rested her left foot with its chipped red polish in the open driver's side window. The passenger window was open as well, and muggy, sultry air that smelled like scythed kudzu and the electricity of a coming storm poured in, whipping through their hair. Meanwhile, she had the AC cranked.

"Doesn't having AC on while your windows are open defeat the purpose?" Colton asked.

"Not if you're pretending it's already autumn like I am." Lightning scored the sky, creating a millisecond of daylight. "That was a good one," Luann murmured. "This is *the* storm."

"*The* storm?"

"That ends summer. It's gonna feel like fall for the first time tomorrow. Happens every year. It'll get hot again, but this is the night summer gets knocked on its ass."

"This is definitely not how I thought we'd be hanging out for the first time."

"It's not the first time. We built a deck."

"You know what I mean."

"What did you expect?"

"I dunno. A movie or something."

"How well do you get to know someone during a movie?"

Colton stuck his hand out the window to catch the air. "Not very well."

"You can talk while you watch a storm."

"Where we going?"

"My secret storm-watching place. How was practice?"

"Same as always. You coming to the game on Friday?"

"There's a game?"

"It's homecoming. You didn't know?"

She shrugged and turned hard onto a gravel road, fishtailing, dust rising. "Okay, now roll up your window."

"You didn't know about homecoming."

"Maybe now you mention it."

"I guess you're not going to the dance?"

"Why? You wanna go?"

"I already asked someone."

"Who?"

"Jess McElroy."

Luann nodded, her eyes determinedly fixed on the winding gravel road illuminated by her headlights and the increasingly frequent flashes of lightning. "She's pretty."

"We're just friends."

"Y'all gonna have sex after?"

Colton thought for a moment that he'd misheard. "Whoa."

"Just asking."

"You and I barely know each other."

"So?"

"So I wasn't expecting it."

"Not ladylike enough?"

"No. I don't care about that."

"So, you never answered my question."

Colton hesitated. "No. I don't know. No."

"But you want to."

"This some sort of test?"

"Just curious."

"Can we change the subject?" The truth was that the answer to her question was no, because the center of gravity of what he found alluring was abruptly shifting, but it seemed like a betrayal of Jess to say it out loud to this new interloper. Luann's blasé forthrightness in both of their encounters thus far signaled to him that he was dealing with an entirely different breed—one unbound by the conventions of social status where you were only allowed to speak with a certain deference to those who outranked you. And that meant that Luann had chosen her social station. Just as he respected her friend Tyler's refusal to genuflect to peer expectations, he admired her willingness to occupy the strata that made her most comfortable, even though she had the money and looks that would make climbing the ladder easy.

"We're almost there anyway," she said.

The unbroken tunnel of forest they hurtled through opened wide into a large, treeless plot on a high bluff overlooking the Cumberland River. Lightning reflected in the slow-moving water below. Luann skidded to a stop. She reached behind Colton and grabbed a gingham blanket. Colton caught a whiff of her sweet, verdant scent, and it made his head swim pleasantly.

She hopped out, blanket in hand. "You can't watch a storm from behind glass."

Colton followed her to the edge of the bluff, where Luann was spreading out the blanket on a grassy patch. "Where are we? Someone gonna shoot us?"

"Hopefully not, considering my family owns this land."

"For real?"

"My dad says he's gonna build a house here someday."

"You could drop a fishing line off the deck into the river."

"Cool."

"Not a fisherwoman?"

"No."

"Ever been?"

"Not really."

"I'm gonna take you."

"Oh yeah?" Luann said, dropping to a cross-legged seated position on the blanket. She patted the spot beside her. "Sit. I'm not gonna jump you and make you cheat on Jess McElroy."

Colton was glad it was too dark for her to see him blush. "She's not my girlfriend," he muttered and sat beside her, wrapping his arms around his knees.

"Then why are you gonna have sex with her after homecoming?"

"I thought we were changing the subject."

"More like changing your diaper." She pushed him, and he almost toppled over. They chuckled as Colton righted himself and inched slightly closer.

They watched the storm silently for a while. The thunderheads advanced like an invading army. The view was unbroken—rare in heavily wooded Western Kentucky—and spectacular. Luann was visibly energized by the tempest's approach. She hummed with electricity herself.

"You ever just sat and watched a storm before?" Luann asked reverently, as though in church.

"Not on purpose."

"There's nothing like it. The power. It doesn't even notice you. Makes you part of it."

"Do you do this alone?"

"All the time." Lightning illuminated her in profile. Wind whipped her hair across her face. The air smelled like river water and distant rain. "You have anything like this? Something that…consumes you, but you love it because of that?"

Colton thought. "Yeah. Football." He was a little embarrassed by how pedestrian it sounded compared to hers, but it was true.

"Tell me about it."

"You don't care about football."

"I still want to know why it consumes you."

Colton paused to consider. "When I throw a touchdown pass and the crowd goes wild; hundreds of people, it's like it's...washing over me. All that emotion. And joy. We went on a family trip to Gulf Shores a couple years ago, and I waded out in the Gulf and the waves crashed against me and I had to keep from losing my balance and getting swept away. It was awesome, being part of something that powerful and huge. That's what it feels like to me to hear people cheering when I've done something good."

"You get it," she said quietly.

The wind rose steadily, cool and feral, and the crashes of thunder increased in frequency and volume. It was like watching a freight train approach.

Luann pointed across the river, where the lights were hazy and soft around the edges as if viewed through Vaseline-smudged glass. "The rain. It'll be here in a sec."

Colton rose. Luann didn't follow.

"Wanna get inside the Jeep?" Colton asked.

"You can," Luann murmured, eyes trained on the horizon, ready for communion.

"Ain't scared of getting wet." Colton sat, this time close enough to Luann that the sides of their bare arms touched. She had goose bumps.

"You saying I need to get you back more effectively for the thing you did with the cold glass when we were building the deck?"

"Oh no, I'm terrified of hose water specifically. You got me real good."

"What you're scared of is my creativity."

"After what I've seen of your idea of a good time? Lil' bit."

They squinted against the grit kicked up by the intensifying gale. The veil of translucent silver rain crossed the river.

The first drops hit Colton's and Luann's faces, large and bracingly cool, presaging the cold front that advanced at their back. The downpour thickened.

Then the deluge swept over them. It felt like standing under a showerhead, monsoon-like. Their clothes were soaked through completely in seconds. Luann sprang to her feet and shriek-giggled in excitement, opening her arms like she was inviting the storm to dance. She tilted her head back and closed her eyes, drinking from the sky. Thin black runs of mascara mapped her cheeks with a network of highways.

Colton followed her lead. Her ecstatic lack of inhibition was contagious, and he gave himself to her rapture. The vigor of the storm filled his heart.

When they were done frolicking in the rain, they got back into Luann's Jeep, sopping. For a while they only laughed and then they were quiet, trading bashful glances, as the storm waned.

"I feel like in summer when you get out of a pool and you let yourself air dry," Colton said, breaking the silence. "I love that."

"Me too." Luann started her Jeep and the AC came on full blast. She quickly turned it down. "Can't have the star QB catching cold before the big game."

She started to put the Jeep in gear, the windshield wipers clacking.

Colton put his hand on her arm. "Hey."

She looked at him. Her hair was plastered to her face in chaotic waves.

"This was fun," he said.

Luann smiled enigmatically. "Life's too short to do boring, ordinary stuff."

"Yeah," Colton said, mostly to himself. And he was, in that moment, caught in the thrall of a longing—so forceful and pure that it rivaled the storm's intensity—to spend far more time with Luann, doing non-boring, extraordinary stuff.

CHAPTER 14

Colt .45! Colt .45! Colt .45! The jubilant chant, which Derrick initiated, reverberated in the Venice High Wildcats' locker room. Derrick was right to be celebratory. He and Colton had combined for no fewer than three touchdowns, on their way to a 36-7 rout of Cadiz High School, their traditional rival. The team bore Colton up on their shoulders.

He let their accolades wash over him like the cheers of the crowd when he connected with a good pass.

Funny thing, though: each time he'd thrown a touchdown and was basking in his kudos, he would scan the crowd looking for Luann. He had no warrant to hope that a girl who loved architecture and watching storms had somehow shown up this once to watch a football game, but that's not how hope works. Even though he didn't spot her, she could have been there somewhere, hidden among the faceless masses. Still, the overwhelming likelihood of her absence threaded with leaden filaments of melancholy a moment that should have been one of unalloyed triumph.

Luann was correct about the storm being the turning point. The night of the homecoming dance was as crisp and dry as it ever got in September in Western Kentucky and there was the faintest whiff of dry leaves and woodsmoke on the air from someone eager to bring autumn into being through fireplace and force of will.

The boys—all football teammates—barely perspired in their boxy navy blazers. The girls' upswept hairdos eluded the cruel ravages of humidity, their corsages bright and fragrant on their freshly tanned wrists. They supped at the Gondolier, Venice's finest pizza and pasta restaurant. (*Endless breadsticks, just like Olive Garden!* None for the girls, though. Their local pageant queen mothers had taught them that a lady was not to be seen engaging in an unseemly act like eating.)

They arrived fashionably late to the dance, surreptitiously passing back and forth a flask that had been covertly filled from one of their dads' Wild Turkey bottles. Their eyes acclimated to the dim light of the Venice High gymnasium as they entered to the closing strains of "Fantastic Voyage" by Coolio. The crowd parted to allow them passage. Several students high-fived Colton and Derrick, who walked side by side, their dates on their arms.

Jess looked the part of the trophy date—blond, eyes the shade of an apple Jolly Rancher, high cheekbones. She at least pretended to love all of Colton's and Derrick's jokes. The other girls in the group liked her (or feared her; it was always hard to tell), including Derrick's date, Alyssa Sullivan, one of Jess's cheerleading teammates. Jess never said anything that put Colton on his heels or made him blush (nor did she ever challenge him). She was who Colton was supposed to be at homecoming with.

The group stood at the edge of the dance floor. The boys elbowed each other and cut up, and the girls gossiped and snickered. Colton was staring briefly off into space, lost in the Tim McGraw song that was playing and feeling the heat of whiskey in his head, when a rush of murmurs swept through the girls. Colton looked in the direction of their stares.

Tyler Garrett, Mara Bloom, and Luann had entered. The three of them looked altogether more confident than they had any right to, by the girls' clear estimation, from their up-and-down assessments of Mara's vintage black lace dress, worn with her Chuck Taylors, and Luann's form-fitting, short, midnight-blue dress with spaghetti straps. The girls convened an emergency council and whispered urgently among themselves: *...too short...is she thinking?...not her color...with those shoes?* One of the boys said, "Where's Tyler's gown?" and they guffawed heterosexually while Colton squirmed.

Then Luann saw him glance at her, and she gave him a slyly knowing look that somehow instantly conveyed: *I know your secret. You would give anything to be with me, finding out what I'd also rather be doing than this.*

And she was right.

Colton slapped the nearest of the boys on the shoulder and said "Gotta piss" to establish his cover. Meanwhile, in his mind, as he exited the gym into the hallway, he sent up an entreaty to the God of Small but Vital Coincidences—the one who makes you read the word *bevy* on the page of the book you're reading exactly as someone says it out loud, the one who makes you pick up the phone to call someone, and there's no dial tone, because you just answered a call from the person you were about to call before the phone could even ring.

Colton did go to the bathroom, so as not to be a liar. After, he washed his hands slowly and thoroughly, to stall and increase his chances of the encounter he hoped for. He left the restroom and heard the muted strains of "Achy Breaky Heart" emanating from the gym.

And there she stood, waiting.

"Hey," Colton said, pulse and breath quickening. "This is a surprise."

"That's exactly what you said when we hung out the other night."

"Guess you're full of surprises."

"So it seems."

They stood close, and Colton leaned in to speak, as though it was too loud to be heard otherwise, but it wasn't really.

"How'd the game go?" Luann asked.

Colton deflated. "We won."

"I know. I saw, dork."

Colton reinflated, larger than before. "You were there?"

"No, it was on ESPN."

"I can't believe you came."

"You had plenty of people cheering for you."

"Quality, not quantity."

"And I'm quality?"

"You are. You look really pretty, by the way."

Luann started to say something but looked away. There were chaperones in the hall, and passersby shot discreet glances at the unexpected interaction between Colton and Luann.

Billy Ray belted his final bars and the opening notes of Whitney Houston's "I Will Always Love You" wafted out of the gym.

Luann opened her arms to Colton, like she did to the storm earlier that week. "Wanna dance?"

Colton laughed, unsure of whether she was joking. "Um. Here?"

"Why not?" Her face was soft yet stone serious.

"Uh."

Luann, clearly done with Colton's dithering, stepped in closer to him and placed his hands on her hips before putting her arms around his neck. She didn't lock her hands around his neck like the clasp of a necklace, as Colton was used to. She held the back of his neck in her palms. This simple and unexpected intimacy sent blood rushing to every reach of him. The considerable charge of static electricity they'd generated in their previous interactions arced at that point of contact.

Colton drew her close and then closer. She came up to his chin, and he was drinking in the floral shampoo scent of the crown of her head. Colton felt her body through the satiny fabric of her dress, quaking slightly under his hands, which would have been trembling too if he hadn't learned to steady them with his unconscious mind, to grip things surely while adrenaline flooded his system.

Colton also had a well-developed sense of spatial awareness, to be on guard for would-be sackers penetrating his team's defenses from behind him before he could pass. He saw, in his peripheral view, that the species of gawker that stopped to stare at him and Luann merely talking was exponentially more interested in the spectacle of the two of them slow dancing in the hallway. But dancing with her felt too good and anyway, his field of vision was narrowing by the second to Luann and nothing but.

Luann shifted her hands on the nape of his neck, and then let one hand slide slowly down to his chest. She had this unerring instinct for little movements and mannerisms that drove him wild with desire. Or maybe it's that everything she did was setting him aflame.

"This must be why you're good at throwing a football really far," Luann murmured.

"What?"

She tapped on his chest. "This… situation."

Colton drew her nearer still. He let his hand slip a fraction of an inch lower on her waist, to the beginning of the curve there. Not so much as to be ungentlemanly. Now their bodies were almost completely pressed together. He felt her warmth. He leaned down to her, inhaling her cool, sweet scent, his lips brushing the rim of her ear. "I think we should hang out more."

"Way more." The tip of her nose grazed his chest, as if she were smelling him.

"I'm glad you came to the dance."

"Me too."

"I wish I had asked you."

"Oh well." She sounded wistful.

"Do… you wish I asked you?"

A flutter of activity caught Colton's attention out of the corner of his eye. It was Jess, with two of her friends.

Jess halted when she saw Colton and Luann clinging to each other. Colton quickly stepped back from Luann and turned to face Jess. But he didn't speak.

Jess did. "Um. Colton. I was looking for you. They're doing the homecoming king and queen announcement after this next song. And—" She eyed Luann icily. "You disappeared."

"Hey, Jess," Luann said. She reddened and sounded like she was about to apologize but didn't.

"Sorry... what was your name?"

"Luann."

Jess gave her a wide, phony smile. "It's so cool how you didn't let not having a date keep you from coming." Her voice dripped with venomous sweetness.

Luann smiled back but said nothing. She turned to Colton. "I better get back to my friends." She turned before Colton could say anything (not that he would have) and walked away briskly.

Jess watched her, as though to make sure she wasn't leaving a trail of breadcrumbs for Colton to follow.

His ears burned. This was the most personality Jess had ever shown, and Colton didn't enjoy her meanness.

"Jess." He considered explaining that Luann had initiated the dance, but the thought of even pretending like he hadn't gone along willingly revolted him. And Jess wouldn't have bought it anyway.

Jess and her two ladies-in-waiting breezed past Colton toward the women's restroom. "See you back inside," she said over her shoulder, without turning around, in a tone suggesting the "see" part would be in the most strictly literal sense, with no social interaction whatsoever.

Colton reentered the gym and joined the boys.

"You been dropping a dookie or what?" Derrick said. "You were gone forever."

"Ran into Luann."

Derrick's eyes widened and he raised his eyebrows like they were air quotes. "You ran into Luann."

"Didn't plan it."

"Maybe not. But still. You didn't *not* plan it."

Colton grinned guiltily. "We danced."

"Danced."

"And while we were dancing, Jess came out."

Derrick cracked up. He doubled over and rested his hand on Colton's shoulder. "Whooooo, man. You got busted, G."

"She did not seem happy."

"Aw, naw, for real? Homie, if you had just asked Luann to dance in here, in front of everyone, it would've been fine."

"You think?"

"Maybe. Better than getting snagged red-handed though. You gonna be lucky if you come out of this with one woman."

"Guess we'll see, man."

Derrick put his arm around Colton's shoulder. He smelled like Cool Water, his brother Darius's signature fragrance. "She worth it, .45?"

Colton put his arm around Derrick's shoulder. "I think so, D Rock."

Jess came in a few minutes later, her two friends flanking her. She gave Colton a tight-lipped, dead-eyed smile. She said maybe fifteen more words to him the rest of the night, even after he was crowned homecoming king and she homecoming queen.

Fair enough. She knows where I'd rather be.

Colton called as early on Sunday as was reasonable.

"I won't apologize for asking you to dance, just so you know," Luann said.

"You shouldn't."

"I won't."

"Good. Don't."

There was a relaxed silence where they listened to each other breathe.

"What're you up to today?" Colton asked. He'd been planning on going over to Derrick's to throw the football and maybe fish for an invite to Nana's Sunday dinner table, but that could wait. "Wanna hang out?"

"Yeah. Hey."

"What's up?"

"You asked me when we were dancing if I wished you'd asked me to the dance."

"I remember."

"I didn't get to answer."

"No, you didn't."

"The answer's yes."

CHAPTER 15

October 2015
Venice, Kentucky

COLTON HAS NEVER BEEN A PARTICULARLY ADEPT CYBERSTALKER, SO IT TOOK him a while to chase down Derrick. When he finally did, he murmured out loud, "Damn, D Rock. You done good for yourself." He'd gone and gotten himself a law degree and was deputy public defender in their county.

Colton dialed Derrick's office. The receptionist said he was in court and would be done around five.

Colton now sits on a bench on the town square, outside the courthouse, in the warm October afternoon. He got there at 4:07 p.m. because he has nothing but time. He fidgets and bounces his legs as he rehearses how to greet his old friend.

After a while, the courthouse doors open and a man and woman, both wearing suits and carrying large red folders, exit. They chat merrily, like they just won something, as the man dons a pair of sunglasses. Colton has seen what the man looks like after he's won something. They'd celebrated more than a few victories together.

As Derrick nears, Colton stands.

Derrick doesn't look in his direction, still midconversation. "...Man, when she sustained that? I thought aliens had abducted and replaced her. I don't even usually bother with—" Then he sees Colton and freezes.

All of Colton's canned scripts depart his mind, leaving him to smile sheepishly and wave.

Derrick turns to the woman he's walking with. "Hey, Yvonne, go ahead without me." He lowers his sunglasses, peers at Colton over the top, and chuckles. "I'll be damned. Do mine eyes deceive me?"

Colton keeps smiling. He puts out his arms as if to say *in the flesh*.

"Colt .45? *The* Colton Gentry? Pride of the Venice High Wildcats?"

"*The* Derrick Giles. D Rock. Big D. What's up, bud?"

They close the distance between them and embrace, pounding each other hard on the back, chuckling.

Derrick sizes him up. "Bro, I didn't hardly recognize you with that beard. Grizzly Adams–lookin' ass."

Colton rubs it sheepishly. "Trying on a new look." And it's functioning exactly as intended if one of his old best friends struggles to recognize him.

"What you doing back here?"

"You know. Life changes."

"Yeah," Derrick says softly, more serious now. "Wanna grab a beer? Catch up?"

Colton shuffles his feet and scratches his beard. "Can't get a beer. That's one of the life changes. Buy you a cup of coffee?"

Derrick claps him on the back. "Let's do it, baby."

They walk the short distance to a nearby Christian chain coffeehouse called Good News, order, and sit.

"So," Derrick says. "Colt .45."

"Dude, look at you. Fancy-ass lawyer."

Derrick grins. "I dunno 'bout that. I'm a public defender who represents broke people. I make a fraction of what my friends from Tulane make at their DC and Atlanta firms."

"Gotta feel good though, man."

"Bro. I can't lie. It does, for real. Lotta times anyway. Like, you just caught me coming out of a hearing where I got the state's key witness excluded. That means they got no case, and they'll have to dismiss."

"Your new version of running the ball into the end zone."

"That, and I coach Pop Warner, so I get to live vicariously."

"You ever defended anyone we went to high school with?"

"*Psssssh.* Homie. Remember Todd and Terry Cobb?"

"The twins?"

"Yeah, who smelled like a skunk carcass stuffed with bleu cheese. They'd smuggle ferrets into class and get busted for having nunchucks and ninja stars and drawing those weird *S*'s on their lockers. I might as well give those two a punch card so every tenth time they get arrested they get a free soft serve. Dumbasses."

I don't know if Todd and Terry Cobb are doing a whole lot worse than me, ol' buddy. If they have their own places (prison doesn't count) and wives or girlfriends to go home to, they've got me beat.

They're quiet for a moment or two while they sip their coffee.

Colton clears his throat. "Hey, man. Um." He looks at his hands, takes a deep breath, and then meets Derrick's eyes. "I wanna say I'm real sorry. About us falling out of touch. Not checking in with you more. I feel like a bad friend. I been thinking a lot about what it means to be a good friend after I lost one recently. I wish I had been that good friend to you."

Derrick smiles sadly and nods. He looks like he wants to make a joke but reconsiders. "Well. Man. I ain't gonna lie to you. It hurt when we lost touch. Felt like you were ready to move onto becoming a star and forget about all the little people."

Colton shakes his head. "Not at all, bro. It was kinda the opposite. I'd moved to this big city where all these talented people are pursuing the same dream as me, and I wasn't special or a star anymore. I was a nobody working from the ground up. Plus, I was dealing with a broken heart. Meanwhile, y'all were crushing it playing college ball, getting your educations. I was happy for y'all, but jealous. It hurt to be reminded how I was getting left behind. So I guess I subconsciously tried to avoid those reminders. Then, by the time I was in a place in my career where I was feeling secure, it felt too late to pop back up in your life."

"Nana used to ask when you were gonna come home and have dinner with us, and I'd say 'I dunno, Nana. He's too busy up in Nashville getting famous.'"

Colton's heart slips like the gear on a failing transmission. "How's your nana? Is she still with us?"

Derrick's face clouds. "She passed a few years ago. Ninety-three. She had a good life."

"I'm so sorry, D. She was a good woman."

"Thanks, man. How's your family?"

"My dad passed a few years after I moved to Nashville. Colon cancer."

"Aw, for real? Damn. That's rough. I'm sorry."

"Yeah." Colton affects a huge fake smile. "Anyway, fun catching up! See you later!" He makes like he's going to stand and leave.

For a second, time collapses, and they laugh with abandon like they're seventeen again, with no gulf of years between them.

Derrick turns serious again. "I invited you to my wedding."

"I know, man. I'm sorry." Colton hangs his head and twists the corner of his napkin into a point. "I meant to tell you I couldn't make it. I was supposed to tape this thing for CMT and naturally that didn't even happen, and by then it was too late to get there and I meant to send you something and it slipped my mind and by the time I remembered—"

"In high school, I sometimes imagined us being best men at each other's weddings."

Twisting the knife. "You heard I was married?"

"To Maisy Martin. Gabi showed me the pictures in *People* magazine. Looked like you had some blond hippie-looking dude as your best man." Derrick sounds wounded.

"That's Duane...or was Duane." Colton momentarily falters. "He's the friend I recently lost. He got killed in that mass shooting at that country festival in Tampa."

Duane covers his mouth with his hand. "Damn, Colt. Bro, I'm so sorry."

"Thanks, bud. Anyway, that's the roundabout reason I'm back home."

"Heard about it on the news."

Colton stares at the table, his face smoldering.

"I was proud of you, homie. What you said. In my job, I have to take a lot of positions people don't like. And I still wouldn't want to be a country singer speaking out against guns. Brave stuff, bro."

Colton meets Derrick's gaze. "I was broken, not brave."

"What I saw was my buddy from back in the day speaking truth to a whole lot of people who didn't wanna hear it. Whatever might've motivated you."

Colton tries to think of a time he's felt better about himself in the last year and can't. He feels like crying. He clears his throat. Before he can speak, though, Derrick continues.

"Anyway, man, this has been cool, catching up. I best get home."

They stand. "You wanna get together again sometime?" Colton asks tentatively.

Derrick looks at him for a while. "Man, I dunno. Let's let bygones be bygones. It's all good."

It takes a moment for Colton to understand exactly what Derrick is saying. And it's more or less exactly the reason he was so reluctant to track down Derrick in the first place. "Right, yeah. No problem. But can I get your address anyway? I owe you a wedding gift."

Derrick smiles sadly. "Nah, man. Forget it."

"D Rock?" Colton says quietly but firmly. "Just gimme your damn address."

He smiles, shakes his head, and writes his address on the back of his business card. He hands it to Colton.

The sun descends as they leave the coffee shop, the sky purpling overhead. The downtown streets, quiet and vacant, are bedecked in autumn finery—hay bales topped with orange and white pumpkins alongside brown cornstalks surround a lamppost on the corner. A cool breeze wafts past them, carrying hickory smoke from some nearby restaurant, and sweet hay and the aged-paper scent of dry corn leaves from the fall display.

Derrick closes his eyes. "Smell of football season. Déjà vu."

"Great seeing you, D Rock."

Derrick turns to Colton and slaps his upper arm and grips it. "I know things been better for you, bro. But listen. I've seen a lot of people at their lowest, you feel me? And there's a path back. It's long and hard. But it's there."

"You know the joke I would've made back in the day when you said 'long and hard.'"

"Ain't too late."

"Naw, man, I'll pass and just sit with your inspiring sentiments. By the way, my next marriage, if there is one? I'm asking you to be my best man."

"No way are you ever getting two women to agree to marry you." Derrick slaps Colton's arm one more time and gives it a squeeze. He walks off with his suit jacket slung over his shoulder, hanging from his index finger.

A rogue wave of melancholy batters Colton as he watches Derrick walk away. *Now that I've wrecked my future, I have time to focus on wrecking my past.*

He knows a sure antidote to this feeling—to all feeling, really. It would be so easy. He could walk a couple of streets over to that Field to Flame place he's taking his mom on Friday. They'd probably have an open spot at the bar this early on a weeknight. He could scope it out, preview the menu while he nurses a bourbon neat. They look like they'd have a nice selection. He could order an expensive one—a Pappy Van Winkle or a King of Kentucky—as a way of limiting himself to one. Or two. *No, just the one—how hard could that be?* To take the edge off; to turn his sadness dial a couple of notches back to neutral. He's lost so much; must he deprive himself of this fleeting pleasure too?

His heart rate rises and he salivates at the thought. He starts walking in that direction.

Then he remembers that October is beautiful, and there will be more of them but only if he's around to see them.

Choose beauty and sorrow over numbness and oblivion. Choose it again and again. Choose it as long as you have any choice.

He stops, turns on his heel, and heads quickly to his pickup before he can crumble.

CHAPTER 16

October 1995
Venice, Kentucky

Colton waited at Luann's Jeep after school while students streamed into the parking lot and drove off. The day was cool, and the sky was the faded blue of October. A few dry leaves skittered on the asphalt. This time of year always imbued him with a quiet exuberance. It had something—but not everything—to do with the onset of football season.

When he saw Luann approaching, his pulse spiked and he suddenly didn't know what to do with his body, which hummed with want of her.

He leaned up against her Jeep. Then he just stood by it. He scuffed his feet on the ground. When she saw him, she smiled, and he worried that he was about to dampen her good mood.

"Hey," she called as she neared.

"What's up," he called back.

"No, you still can't drive my Jeep." She arrived, unlocked the door, and put her backpack inside. She grabbed her scrunchie off the gearshift and tied up her hair. One long piece hung down beside her face.

"How was your day?" Colton asked, trying not to let on how anxious he was.

"Good."

Colton wanted to continue into flirtatious banter, but being late to football practice was a hanging offense. "Hey, uh." He looked at the ground. "Anyone say anything to you about the dance?"

"No. Why?"

"Apparently Jess told people she walked up on you unzipping my pants."

Luann's face registered surprise and then bemusement. "Huh. That didn't happen at all. I'd have remembered."

"You not mad?"

"Should I be?"

"Sucks to be lied about."

"Only when you care about the people lying about you."

Colton studied her for some hint of counterfeit bravado, finding none. He'd never met someone so blithely undeferential to high school social hierarchy. "What if Jess tries to make things tough for you?"

"I have how many months left of seeing these people before I graduate and get out of here?"

"Fair." The idea of Luann's leaving landed on Colton in a way he wasn't prepared for.

"I have Tyler and Mara. That's enough."

Without thinking, Colton asked, "You hanging out with them Saturday night?"

Luann leaned against her Jeep. "Why?" She had a flirtatious lilt in her voice that sent a delighted shiver through Colton.

He leaned against the Jeep, mirroring her. "Because I think you should hang out with me."

"You asking me out?"

"If you wanna call it that."

"Okay."

"Yes?"

"Yes." Then she added, "My friends think I'm weird for hanging out with you."

"Luckily I don't much care what they think either." *A lie.*

"Good. You like haunted houses?"

"Sure."

"There's a decent one about an hour away. Wanna come by my house at six thirty?" Luann asked.

"Yeah." Colton looked at his watch. "Damn. I gotta be at practice in three minutes or it's my ass. Call you later?" He started quickly away.

"Hey, QB," Luann called.

He turned but continued walking briskly backward.

"I don't regret that dance."

He smiled. "Me neither."

As he sprinted to practice, a singular image remained fixed in his mind like a jewel in its setting: the hazel of Luann's eyes, catching the afternoon light—the browns, greens, and golds luminescing, the color of sun passing through leaves.

They drove fast in the fading light, with a moon rising cloud-white over the cornfields and tall trees blurring past them. They had the windows down and leaf-smoke-scented air cascaded over them. Colton was glad he wore his faded denim jacket with the faux sheepskin collar.

They went through the Bucky's drive-through before leaving. They ate cheeseburgers and shared a greasy brown paper bag of fries and battered pickle spears, which rested on the bench seat between them in Colton's pickup. He clutched a large Cherry Coke in a foam cup between his legs. Luann, in a baggy sweater, jeans, and Doc Martens, held her Dr Pepper and sat cross-legged in her seat.

"Your dad was nicer than I expected," Colton said. "I mean, he was cool when I came to work on the deck, but I wasn't taking out his daughter."

Luann rolled her eyes. "He's starstruck by the local football star. Such a dork."

"Hey, I'll take that over him hating me."

"What's your middle name?" Luann asked.

"Random question."

"Just want to get to know you."

"What's yours?"

She leaned back in her seat and propped her feet on the dashboard. "Charlotte."

"Luann Charlotte Lawler. That's a pretty name."

"Your turn."

"Dean."

"*Colton Dean Gentry.* You were already at a nine out of ten on the country singer name scale, and that middle name takes you up to ten out of ten."

"Speaking of music, what are we listening to?" Colton nodded at the stereo, where a tape with a hand-lettered label played.

"'Linger' by the Cranberries."

"This lady has a weird voice."

"I like weird stuff."

"I'm into it." *Also, it reminds me of you. And lately I love anything that does that.*

"This tape is a mix I made for you."

"So it's the Cranberries and—"

"Tori Amos, Björk, Indigo Girls, Liz Phair, PJ Harvey, Mazzy Star. My favorites."

They ride for a while and listen to the music.

"You said you like weird. I'm pretty normal," Colton said.

They held each other's gaze in the firefly phosphorescence of the dashboard lights for as long as was prudent. Colton turned his eyes back to the road, and Luann followed suit.

"You do seem fairly normal at first," Luann said, more serious than she'd been all night. "But then you start to notice there's something about you that's special. It doesn't have anything to do with how far you can throw a football or how you look with your shirt off or any of the other reasons people think you're special."

Colton waited for her to continue. She didn't. "Leaving me on a cliffhanger?"

Luann plucked a fry from the bag and dangled it a few inches from Colton's lips. He bit at it, and she pulled it out of reach. He tried again and she yanked it away once more. She attempted a third time, but he wouldn't take the bait. She gently brushed the fry along his lips, then held it on his upper lip like a mustache. When he still held firm, she started rubbing the fry on his lips like she was applying lipstick. He finally went for it, accidentally nipping the edge of her finger.

"Ow!"

He rested his hand on hers. "Sorry. Did I get you for real?"

"Barely. I was kidding."

Colton didn't move his hand. He liked the way Luann's hand felt under his.

"This is gonna sound stupid," Luann said.

"What?"

"What we were talking about. Why you're special. There's something bright and powerful in you. Best way I can describe it. I can sense it. You remind me of a storm that way. That's why you're not normal."

Colton felt like his body fluoresced on a cellular level on hearing this. And she said it with so much conviction that he believed her.

And still he didn't move his hand.

They pulled into her driveway, and Luann unbuckled her seat belt. "Wanna walk me to my front door?"

"Absolutely."

They stepped into the shimmering forty-nine-degree air. The black sky above them was awash in stars, clean of the haze of humidity. The crickets in the bushes chirped in drowsy chorus. Colton and Luann reached the porch, and their breath misted in the small circle of white light.

"So," Luann said, suddenly jittery and bashful.

"So," Colton said, reflecting her nervousness and excited apprehension.

They neared each other.

"So," Luann said again. This time she held Colton's eyes.

Now they stood almost as close as the time they danced.

And then as close.

Then closer.

Colton put his hand on the side of Luann's face, with his thumb rubbing the spot behind her ear, and kissed her, deep and slow—it felt like wading into a summer-warm river against the chill around them. He tasted the chemical fruitiness of her cherry lip gloss. She kissed him back with a hunger and longing that surprised him, making a sighing purr that sent a rush of molten heat spreading below his belly. She pressed her hips to his. He buried both hands in her hair like he'd always wanted and imagined her heart beating in a flurry to match his own.

Luann slipped her icy hands underneath his shirt and ran them along the smooth, warm bare skin and taut muscles beneath. "Warm me up."

"You getting me back *again* for the cold glass?"

"Maybe."

"I don't mind this time. You past curfew?"

She sighed and looked at her watch. "Yeah. Okay. One for the road." She got on her tiptoes and kissed him so fervently their teeth clicked together like pool balls. He pressed her back against the wall beside her front door, lifting her up slightly.

Finally, they broke the kiss. This time, Luann said only "Call me," and with a smile that sent one last effervescent surge of longing fizzing through him, slipped inside.

Colton drove home with both windows down, letting the chilly air buffet him, drinking it in. He sniffed at his collar for some lingering hint of her, the way the artificial cherry of her lips persisted on his. A deep, delicious ache swelled low in his pelvis, causing him to involuntarily whoop and punch the steering wheel in an ecstatic momentary rapture. He turned up the volume on Luann's tape. The song "Linger" by the Cranberries blasted through the speakers and spilled into the autumn night. When it ended, he rewound to roughly the beginning and listened again.

Damned if she ain't got you wrapped around her finger, like the song says.

CHAPTER 17

October 2015
Venice, Kentucky

COLTON FEELS A RUSH OF PRIDE IN HIS OLD (FORMER?) FRIEND AS HE ARRIVES at Derrick's home in Cumberland Highlands. It isn't far from Luann's old house, matter of fact. On the seat next to him is a giftwrapped blender with a card attached.

Colton draws a deep breath, gets out, and walks to the front door. He rings the doorbell, and a boy who looks like a young Derrick with glasses answers, a brown and white pit bull at his heels, barking animatedly.

"Mom! Door!" the boy hollers. "Petunia! Shush," he says to the pit bull.

Derrick has kids. And didn't even tell me. "What's up, lil' man?" Colton says. "You a fist bumper?" He puts out his free fist and the boy bumps it. "I'm Colton. I knew your daddy in high school. What's your name?"

"Xavier."

"How old are you?"

"Eight."

"Dang. Eight? Your daddy gonna give you the keys to his car soon?"

Xavier laughs. He looks like Derrick when he smiles. "I'm too young."

A woman wearing black skinny jeans and a soft white cotton shirt enters the foyer. Colton has been in rooms with some of the most beautiful people in the world, and she would not have looked out of place in any of them, with her sharp cheekbones and effortlessly chic style. Maisy trained Colton well enough to recognize the unassuming clothing as expensive. She smells like cocoa butter and luxurious French soap—jasmine, tuberose, ylang-ylang, and neroli.

"Can I help you?" She looks and sounds wary.

"Ma'am. My name is Colton Gentry. I'm a friend of Derrick's from high school. Nice to meet you."

"I'm Gabrielle, Derrick's wife." Recognition slowly dawns on her face. "I thought you looked familiar. Was he expecting you?"

"No, I just wanted to drop this by." He holds up the gift.

"Xavier, will you invite Mr. Gentry in?"

"Wanna come in?" Xavier says to Colton.

Colton grins. "Who am I to decline such a kind invitation?" He steps inside. Petunia approaches him cautiously. He lets her sniff his hand and pets her.

"Derrick's out back grilling," Gabrielle says. "This way."

Colton looks around as he follows Gabrielle through the living room to the kitchen. "You have a beautiful home."

Gabrielle waves him off. "Between my work schedule and Derrick's and chasing the kids, it's a mess."

In fact, it's immaculate and decorated so thoughtfully as to make Colton wonder if maybe Gabrielle had an interior design show he somehow didn't know about, despite the many nights he'd spent indulging Maisy's HGTV addiction.

"What do you do, Gabrielle?"

"I'm an anesthesiologist at the Venice location of Western Kentucky Med Center."

"Wow. My high school buddy married a dang anesthesiologist. I'm impressed." *I don't know if I'm still entitled to call him my buddy.* Gabrielle's demeanor, while cordial, is not giving him confidence.

"Will you remind him how lucky he is?"

"Every chance I get. I knew someone at Western Kentucky Med Center. I think he was in management. Eddie Lawler?"

Gabrielle's face illuminates. "Eddie! What a sweetheart. He retired a few years back, but he was there when I started."

"Good guy."

"Very. I'm glad he's getting more time to golf and visit his grandbabies."

Grandbabies. The word hits Colton like a slap. *Grandbabies. Multiple.* He envisions Luann holding one baby while she chases a toddler. *Grandbabies.* You have grandbabies with someone. Who? Jealousy writhes in his belly. *Visit his grandbabies.* He wonders where Luann ended up. If she were close by, Eddie wouldn't need to be retired to visit frequently.

Colton is glad Gabrielle's back is to him so she can't see his face as he worries, terrier-like, over this unexpected morsel of information she's tossed him. He's self-conscious enough tonight.

They exit into a sprawling, shady backyard. The trees wear gold and red motley. Derrick stands on the patio in front of the grill, which looks like something that could be driven to victory on a racetrack. He looks up through the white smoke and surprise registers. "Colt .45?" He opens his arms as if to say *Not bad, what I've got going here, huh?* while still holding the tongs. Gabrielle delivers Colton to Derrick and then heads in the direction of the far corner of the yard, where a little girl plays on a swing set.

Colton and Derrick slap hands.

Derrick nods at the wrapped gift. "Bro, what are you doing?"

Colton sets the gift on the patio table. "Open it."

Derrick shuts the lid on the grill. He pulls the card off the top, sets it down, and tears off the paper.

"It's a blender," Colton says.

"I can see that."

"Very belated wedding gift."

"You didn't need to do this."

"I did, man. I hate that I wasn't there. Open the card."

Derrick picks up the envelope and opens it. He pulls out a wrinkled cocktail napkin with a signature. He squints at it.

"That's Dr. Dre," Colton says. "I got it at the VMAs a few years ago. I had to get through his entourage. They all looked at me like I was dogshit until I mentioned I was married to Maisy Martin. Pretty humiliating. But I got that for you. I'd always meant to send it to you, but I'd keep putting it off because I didn't know your address and I was embarrassed to contact you after all that time."

"He was my favorite rapper back in the day."

"I know."

Derrick looks at him for a while. Then chuckles. "Come here, bro." He pulls Colton in for a half hug. His embrace lasts longer than it would if it were mere nicety. It feels reconciliatory to Colton. He hopes against hope that his gambit worked.

"Anyway, I'll leave you to your family," Colton says, not wanting to press his luck. "Your *beautiful* family, by the way."

"Stay for dinner."

"Nah, man, I don't wanna be in your hair. I'll—"

".45? You're staying."

Colton smiles. "All right." He pulls up a chair. He nods in Gabrielle's direction. "As I was saying? Bro..."

"I know. Don't ask how I convinced her. I don't know myself. She's Charleston royalty."

"The ladies always loved you. They're gonna love your son too." Colton gestures at Xavier, who throws a tennis ball for Petunia. "What a beautiful kid."

"He gets it from Gabi. Here's another one who gets it from Gabi."

Colton turns as Gabrielle walks up with the little girl. She indeed has her mother's elegant, symmetrical bone structure.

"Can you introduce yourself?" Gabrielle says, throwing a sideways, quizzical glance at the blender.

The girl looks bashful and hugs her mom's leg, burying her face in her side.

"Hey, baby girl," Derrick says. "This is Daddy's friend from back in the day. Tell him your name."

The girl peeks out. "Imani," she says shyly.

"Imani," Colton repeats. "What a pretty name. Fist bump?" He crouches, painfully, and extends his fist. Imani bumps it. Colton makes an explosion sound—*kapssssssssh*—and rolls onto his back from his crouch. Imani giggles. Colton rotates back to a sitting position.

Xavier returns with the tennis ball, panting from his game of fetch with Petunia. "Are you famous?" he asks Colton. "Our mom said you were."

"Xavier," Gabrielle says. "You don't have to answer that," she says to Colton.

Colton laughs. "It's fine. Ah. Hmm. I was a little famous, then I said some things that people didn't like, and now I'm not famous anymore."

"Daddy showed us that video of you talking. He said we're not allowed to use the cusswords you said," Imani says.

"Unless?" Derrick says.

"Unless we're saying something really important like you did and we need people to pay attention," Imani says.

"Hey, you were listening for once!" Derrick turns to Colton. "I wanted my kids to see that sometimes you have to say unpopular things to a lot of people."

Colton scuffs his feet. "Well, that video didn't show my finest hour, but I'm still honored."

Imani has already moved on. "Daddy, push me on the swing," she says.

"Mani, I'll push you," Gabrielle says. "Let Daddy and his friend catch up."

"No. Daddy push me."

Derrick and Gabrielle meet eyes. "It's useless arguing. She gets that from you," Derrick says. "Colt, you wanna watch those steaks and burgers? I just turned them."

"Sure thing."

"C'mon, baby girl," Derrick says. He and Imani head for the swings, Xavier following.

Gabrielle waits for them to clear earshot, then leans into Colton, and in a low tone says, "I don't know if D will ever mention it, because he's funny about stuff like this, but we saw you in concert in St. Louis, I wanna say it was 2007 because we were pregnant with Xavier."

Colton looks at her in shock, trying to read her for some sign of joking. "You serious?"

"For real! You were opening for... oh... He had to marry Nicole Kidman because he's prettier than every other woman."

"Keith Urban. Nice guy. Did y'all have a good time?"

"We did! We're more Drake and Rihanna folks; country's not generally our thing—"

"Hey, fair enough, not mine either anymore."

Gabrielle laughs. "But no, we had a great time. We got treated like celebrities. All these sweet white ladies who'd dragged their boyfriends and husbands to the show coming up to us like 'We're so glad y'all are here.'" Gabrielle did a spot-on impression of a Southern white woman.

"If I'd known you were there? I'd've gotten you in for free, VIP treatment."

"D didn't know how to get in touch with you. But honestly, even if he did, he'd have *wanted* to pay full price. We had a fancy dinner with nice wine before the show, and he was so proud. He was like, 'I got a job where I can pay for my lady to enjoy a night out like this.' Colton, he was making $38,000 a year with the public defender."

"Way we grew up, that would've felt like a lot of money." Colton checks on the meat.

"The whole drive home, we listened to your album. He just kept going, 'You believe this? Me and this guy were homies in school. He's doing so good.'"

Several tributaries of sadness converge into a greater whole and pass over Colton. "Sure felt like I was then."

"He was heartbroken you weren't at our wedding."

Colton hangs his head and stands with his back to Gabrielle, busying himself with the grill. "Yeah," he says quietly. "I should've been."

They watch as Derrick roars and plucks Imani off the swing, mid-arc, tossing her in the air and catching her. She screams, breathless with giggles.

"If I seemed at all hostile toward you at first, that was why," Gabrielle says. "I always tell D, 'Better be careful what you tell me about people wronging you. Because I'll hold the grudge *for* you long after you've forgiven them.'"

"D deserves someone like you. You think he's forgiven me?"

"He's proud. He had to try to push you away first to protect himself. He won't try again after failing."

"What does Derrick know about failing? I could teach him."

"For what it's worth," Gabrielle says, still looking at Derrick and Imani, "I see too many patients with gunshot wounds as they're about to go into surgery. Some barely older than Xavier. You were right to say what you did."

Colton winces inwardly at the thought of Duane lying on a hospital gurney, bleeding wounds pocking his body. "Appreciate that. Although I was pretty drunk when I said it, so no courage points." Talking about Duane and being drunk, he feels the urge to drink. The smell of the grill and the warmth of an early fall night don't help.

"The alcohol didn't give you courage; it just removed inhibition and diplomacy. Speaking of drinks, can I get you anything? La Croix, Mexican Coke, Perrier?"

Colton turns the steaks and burgers. "I wouldn't say no to one of those Mexican Cokes. It's all about that real sugar."

Derrick comes running back holding both Xavier and Imani under his arms.

"You been watching that meat? That's Wagyu beef."

"Like a hawk. I can't believe we both know what Wagyu beef is," Colton says. "When did we get so damn—sorry, dang—fancy?"

Derrick lowers his kids to the ground.

"You cussed," Imani crows triumphantly. "You say lots of cusswords."

"Beg pardon," Colton says, blushing.

"Ain't no thing," Derrick says. "Only grown-ups get to say cusswords, Mani."

"Look at you, all good with kids," Colton says.

"You got any kids?"

A sharp twinge bores into Colton's chest, right above his stomach. "Naw. We talked about it some. But it was never really on the table." There's a long, awkward silence. "I love kids, though. I would've loved being a dad."

"You talking like your life is over, bro. You're a young man," Derrick says. "Under that beard, you still look like a country music star. And believe me, based on my clients, you want to be a father bad enough, someone will indulge you no matter how old you are."

Gabrielle makes a horrified noise and backhands Derrick in the chest. "Ugh. Derrick."

"I'd like to avoid having kids by impregnating an eighteen-year-old on a conjugal visit, good buddy, but I appreciate you looking out for me," Colton says.

"I'm just sayin'," Derrick says.

"Well, stop sayin' and help me with plates and silverware," Gabrielle says.

Colton helps Derrick and Gabrielle set their patio table and put out the spread. They hold hands and say grace.

"The potato salad is Nana's recipe," Derrick says.

Colton nods and spoons some onto his plate, then puts his plate on the table where the potato salad bowl was and sets the bowl in front of him. Derrick's family laughs.

"I see you knew Derrick's nana," Gabrielle says.

Colton grins, swapping back the bowl for his plate. "I was telling Gabrielle earlier, I love y'all's house."

"Tell you what, never thought I'd live in the Highlands," Derrick says, finishing a mouthful of steak. "Didn't Luann live around here?"

That same twinge as a few minutes ago. Same place in his chest. "Um. Yeah, few streets over."

"Now, who's Luann?" Gabrielle asks Colton.

"High school girlfriend. Eddie Lawler's daughter, actually. That's how I knew him."

"You had a girlfriend," Xavier says accusingly.

"Just you wait, lil' man," Colton says, poking him in the stomach.

"You ever talk to Luann?" Derrick asks.

"Man, I lost touch with her after everything went down," Colton says with what he hopes is enough finality that they don't press further. They don't.

They sit around the table, talking and eating. The day surrenders its heat as the sun dips below the horizon, and Derrick lights the kerosene patio heater.

Xavier and Imani ask if they can model their Halloween costumes for Colton. Gabrielle says they may, but after that it's bedtime. They rush upstairs and return minutes later, breathless. Xavier is dressed as a Minecraft character; Imani as a cat.

"Man! Y'all are ready to clean up on the candy," Colton says.

"You have plans for Halloween night?" Derrick asks. "You wanna come trick-or-treating?"

Imani grabs Colton's arm with both hands and hangs on to it. "Come with us."

Colton laughs and lifts her slowly off the ground. "Sign me up."

Gabrielle claps once, sharply. "Okay then. That means you two don't need to try to squeeze any more time out of Mr. Colton and you can get ready for bed. Let's go. Teeth brushed. Baths." She escorts the children into the house.

Derrick and Colton relax back into patio chairs and listen to the crickets.

"This was the most fun I've had in . . . five years?" Colton says.

"Any time you wanna come on over, bro. Throw the football with the kids."

"This life you've made, man. What I wouldn't give."

"You did your thing, bro. You made music. You played for thousands of people. That's gotta mean something."

Colton smiles sadly and stares off into the dark reaches of the yard. "Gotta mean something." He says it as a statement, but it rings in his mind as a question.

Colton sits in his truck in Derrick's driveway for a few moments, summoning the will to leave, his knuckles turning white as he grips the steering wheel. He yearns for the life he's just temporarily occupied—more than he desires a drink, which he very much wants.

He'd forgotten what abundance feels like, and the rush of it returning to him for one night is the dolor of running hot water over frostbitten fingers.

CHAPTER 18

October 1995
Venice, Kentucky

In the way that only teenagers can, they relinquished all footing and slid into each other, making out ravenously before Colton had to run off to his practices and talking by phone late into the nights.

Now, Colton shivered with the quiet electricity of entering the sanctum of Luann's bedroom for the first time, under the chaste auspices of a study date.

"Door open, Lulu," Luann's dad called up.

"I *know*! Duh." She rolled her eyes to Colton in apology.

He looked around the room. It was spacious. Posters of musicians plastered the walls—Nirvana, Tori Amos, the Indigo Girls; boys—River Phoenix and Keanu Reeves; art—Klimt's *The Kiss* and Van Gogh's *Starry Night*; and buildings—black-and-white photos of the Chrysler Building, the Flatiron Building, and the Empire State Building under construction. She had a bookshelf flush with books. *Interview with the Vampire*, which he remembered from their afternoon deck building, and its evident sequels. Some Stephen King books. Books by authors whose names he didn't recognize. Sylvia Plath. Toni Morrison. J. D. Salinger. Anaïs Nin. Donna Tartt.

"You got a lot of books," Colton said.

"Who's your favorite author?"

Colton felt coarse and dumb. The true answer was "the Encyclopedia Brown guy," but that wouldn't do. "Man. Hard to choose just one."

"We gotta work on that."

Colton looked at her bed and envisioned her solitary, pedestrian rituals. Rubbing lotion on her legs. Curling the phone cord around her wrist while she talked. Sitting cross-legged and putting her hair in a ponytail. Painting her nails. Sleeping. He wondered what she wore to bed.

There was a dresser with various lotions and potions and perfumes arrayed on top. Colton wanted to open each and unmask Luann's signature scent—the one that made his blood warm.

Next to the dresser was a large table made of heavy, aged wood, worn by elbows and forearms to a shining honey-dark patina in patches, with a slanting surface and a gooseneck lamp clamped to one corner. It played host to piles of drawing pads and stacks of what appeared to be college applications.

Colton went to the table. "What's this?"

Luann joined him. "A drafting table. It belonged to my mom's dad. He was an architect."

"Runs in your blood." Colton touched the stack of college applications. Cooper Union. Cornell. Rhode Island School of Design. Besides the last, Colton had no idea where these schools were. "These where you want to go to architecture school?"

"No, I just enjoy writing things letter by letter in individual boxes."

"Ask a stupid question, huh?"

"You excited for MTSU? You're not going too far away."

"Playing college ball is all I've ever dreamed of. Everything I've worked for. It's my purpose." Colton was embarrassed at how emotional he felt himself becoming talking about this. He quickly redirected. "You're going far, looks like. I'm guessing Cooper Union isn't in Kentucky."

"New York City."

"You been there?"

"My dad took me and my stepmom a couple years ago when he had a conference there. I've wanted to live there ever since."

At this, an unfamiliar wistfulness descended upon Colton. "Never been."

"Bet you'd like it. You seem like someone who's open to new experiences." Luann sat with one foot under her thigh on the rotating stool in front of her drafting table and, using the table for leverage, spun around.

"Do I? Like what?"

Luann reached out and took his hand, raised it above her head, and twirled on the chair under his hand. "Me."

"You are definitely a new experience."

She wound up, twirled too fast, and tottered. Colton sprang to steady her. In her flailing for purchase, she knocked some of her sketchbooks onto the floor.

"Easy there. Don't want your dad knowing we're doing seated dance moves up here." He knelt to pick up the sketchbooks. One had fallen open to a pencil drawing of a skyscraper with clean, sweeping, modern lines. Colton held it up. "You do this?"

"Yeah."

Colton whistled. "Dang. Can I see more?"

"I don't know." Luann suddenly exuded apprehension.

"You watch me play football, which is my big thing. I want to sit in the bleachers for your big thing."

She hesitated for a long while before relenting. "Uh. Okay." She tucked a lock of hair behind her ear and stood so near Colton's elbow he could feel her body's warmth.

Colton leafed through the book. More pencil drawings of structures. Houses. Shops. Animals. Trees. All rendered with a sure, precise hand. There were elements that were photoreal combined with more dreamlike imagery, but with a cohesive vision.

"Wow," Colton murmured. "You ever show these to anyone?"

"Just Mara and Tyler."

He kept leafing through, murmuring *wow* and *damn* at intervals. Then he got to a folded paper stuck between two pages.

Luann made a small cry of dismay and darted for the paper. But she was at an awkward angle and missed. Colton's athlete reflexes kicked in and he held the book out of Luann's reach. "Hang on."

She jumped for it. Colton again dodged and held the book from her, laughing.

"Colton. Come on."

"You know you're just making me want to see it more, right?"

"Gimme it."

"Is it a porno picture? Huh? You drawing butt-nekkid people?" He held her at bay with one hand and raised the book out of reach with the other.

"Colton." She sounded upset and verging on frantic.

"Okay, sorry," Colton said gently, handing her the book. "I was just teasing. I won't look if you don't want."

She took the book and held it to her chest.

"I apologize. I love your art is all. If you ever want to let me see, I'd be honored."

She reddened, sighed, then removed the loose piece of paper and handed it to him, looking away.

He raised both hands, palms out. "I don't want to look if you'd rather I didn't."

"Just—"

Colton slowly unfolded the paper, watching Luann's face for some withdrawal of consent. Seeing none, he viewed it. It was a drawing of a young man. "Aha, you thought I'd be jealous if I saw..." His words trailed off as he studied the picture more closely. "This looks like me."

Luann said nothing, but the vermilion of her face deepened.

"Guess you have a type, huh?" Colton continued. "But this dude's hair is how mine was last year before I let it grow out."

"Yep."

"Wait." Colton held up the drawing. "Is this—"

"Yeah," she said quietly.

"Why is my hair how I had it junior year?"

"Gee, I dunno."

"You did this last year?"

"Hey. Ding ding."

"But we didn't even—we hadn't."

"We didn't even. We hadn't."

Colton held her eyes. "That long?"

"That long."

She played it so, so cool that day we met. He studied the portrait again. It looked exactly like him, but better somehow. Like she had drawn him emanating some invisible luster, obscured from even—and perhaps especially—himself. She had captured that bright and powerful something she saw in him.

He handed back the paper.

She tucked it back in the book, and exhaled a deep, jittery breath. "Whew. Wow. Okay."

"Thank you for letting me see. You're incredible." He pulled her to him and kissed her. She trembled palpably.

"Now you have to tell me about something you don't show anyone," Luann said.

"All right." He thought for a while. "Here's one. Few years back, my dad gave me a guitar and taught me how to play a little. So sometimes I get it out and play and sing. Makes me feel good. Relaxed or something. I don't know."

"You ever play for anyone?"

"Not really. Other than my dad."

"You have to play and sing for me sometime."

"Whoa. That wasn't the deal. I only had to tell you."

"New deal is you have to play and sing for me."

Colton hesitated.

"Or no more sugar for you," she continued.

Colton sighed loudly in capitulation and looked ceilingward, but a smile crept onto his face. "Fine."

They eventually ended up studying after all, sitting side by side on the floor, their backs against Luann's bed. Luann worked through calculus problems. Colton was supposed to be reading *The Scarlet Letter*, but the words beaded up on his eyes and rolled off like raindrops on a freshly waxed car. Consuming him instead was a vision of Luann, seated on her stool at her drafting table in a pool of white light from the gooseneck lamp, her right foot tucked under her left thigh, a keenly sharp pencil in hand, a rebellious lock of wavy dark hair hanging down below her chin, sketching him from memory, summoning from the ether a more perfect version of him he didn't know existed. Before a word had ever passed between them.

He couldn't have explained why, but nothing had ever moved him more.

CHAPTER 19

THE EDDYVILLE DEFENSIVE END WHO SACKED COLTON WEIGHED 350 POUNDS if he weighed an ounce, and he might as well have been a diesel locomotive for all the delicacy with which he executed the tackle. Colton lay on the gridiron grass, desperately trying to withstand vomiting from the explosive, neuron-searing agony in his left knee. One clear thought pierced the TV-on-the-wrong-channel static in his brain: *You'll be lucky if you ever walk normally again, much less finish the season, much less ever play football again.*

As he was borne from the field on a stretcher, the crowd's applause replaced the tense silence that had hung in the air after the play. If he had his wits about him, he might have savored it, knowing as he did even then that it might be his last chance.

On the other hand, though, he might have realized that Luann was standing in the bleachers at that moment, hands not applauding but covering her mouth, her breath short in horror and fear, watching him carried away.

And that thought would have somehow anguished him worse even than his demolished knee.

Some prodding, palpitation, and an MRI later, a grim doctor delivered the diagnosis: a severely torn ACL. Colton would need surgery and he would be on crutches for the next six weeks. But that news alone didn't account for the doctor's somberness. Rather it was this: in his learned medical opinion, even with surgery and a best-case recovery, Colton would never again play football at even close to the level that he once did. For all intents and purposes, his football career was over. It was only a matter of time before MTSU withdrew their scholarship.

"I know how hard this must be to hear," the doctor said.

Hard to hear? Colton felt like he was listening to a judge pronounce a death sentence.

CHAPTER 20

The doorbell rang with trick-or-treaters. The Highlands didn't get a lot—too many sprawling yards and long driveways were a drag on candy-harvesting efficiency.

Luann paused *Candyman* and rushed to the door with a bowl of full-size Three Musketeers. She had personally seen to it that any intrepid trick-or-treaters who made the trek would find a kingly reward.

Colton shifted uncomfortably on the sofa, his damaged leg extended and resting on an ottoman. He was due for another dose of ibuprofen. He was having about as much fun that night as he could be having, circumstances considered. Luann's parents were away at a Halloween party, so the young couple had the house to themselves. Luann's parents had correctly calculated that Colton wouldn't be in the mood to get into much trouble with Luann in their absence.

Colton had been invited to the Halloween rager at a former teammate's parents' cabin, but that was another thing for which he wasn't in the mood. He had little interest in hearing his former teammates drunkenly discuss their plans for collegiate bacchanalia while he awaited MTSU's inevitable scholarship withdrawal.

But more than anything else, Colton wanted to be with Luann and Luann only. She satisfied every social hunger he had and then some he didn't know he had. Nothing felt small or cloistered or lonely when it was just the two of them. Luann was making the greater sacrifice tonight. He knew she was missing out on good times by choosing him over Mara and Tyler, not for the first time.

He heard her conversing brightly with the kids at the door, gasping appropriately in feigned terror. Then she called, "Hey, Colt, you gotta see this." She was giggling.

Colton rose slowly from the sofa and collected his crutches, which were resting beside him. He made his way laboriously to the entryway. Luann stepped back from the door, where a boy of maybe six or seven stood in a note-perfect miniature replica of a Venice Wildcats uniform.

Colton grinned. "What's up, little dude? You a Wildcat?"

The boy nodded shyly.

"That's not the best part," Luann said. She crouched by the boy. "Tell him who you are."

"Colton Gentry," he said softly.

Colton's smile widened and his spirit lifted above the gloom for the first time in weeks. "Hey, what a coincidence. That's who I am too."

The boy's face brightened. "Really?"

"He's only ever seen you with your football helmet on," the boy's delighted-sounding mother explained. "My husband takes him to your games."

Used to take him to my games, you mean.

"You want him to sign your football?" Luann asked.

The boy nodded. Luann sprinted back into the house.

"How's your knee?" the boy's mother asked.

"It's...healing, I guess."

"You gonna be able to play any more this season?"

"No."

"Well, there's always college."

Sure, that can never be suddenly yanked away. Colton nodded but didn't respond. Luann brought over a black marker.

The boy handed Colton his Nerf football, which he signed before returning. "What's your name, champ?" Colton asked.

"Caleb."

"Caleb, give me five."

Caleb, beaming, gave him five.

Luann dropped several Three Musketeers bars in Caleb's pillowcase.

"Y'all made his night. Thank you so much," Caleb's mother said.

Colton and Luann bid them farewell and made their way back to the couch.

"How cool was that?" Luann said, snuggling up to Colton and laying her head on his shoulder. "You were so cute with him."

"I love kids," Colton said, more forlornly than he intended. He didn't want to bring the night down by letting on that he was now spiraling.

"What's wrong?"

"Nothing. Let's get back to the movie." Colton reached for the remote.

Luann moved to block him. "I wish you'd talk to me."

Another prolonged silence. Then, "That was the last autograph I'll ever sign."

"I doubt it."

"When am I ever going to hear applause again? Who's going to ever want my autograph again? Who'll even know my name? Football's out. That was, like, my thing."

"Football isn't all people clap for. Football players aren't the only people who get asked for autographs."

"It's the only thing I do well enough for people to clap for and ask me for my autograph. *Used* to do well enough, I mean."

"Now."

Colton paused. "What do you mean?"

Luann tucked her feet under Colton's thigh for warmth. "Like, football's your thing now. But there are other things."

"Like?"

She pondered. "Musicians get applause and autograph requests."

"I'm not a musician."

"Beg to differ. I've heard you sing."

"What, goofing around during work?"

"And literally every time we're listening to music together, you're singing along. I don't think you even realize it."

"That's all just screwing around."

"Some things you can't fake. Even goofing off, you have a great voice. You obviously love music. You told me you and your dad used to play the guitar together and sing. And..." Luann trailed off.

"What?"

She spoke gently. "Well...you have more time now."

"Thanks," Colton said glumly. "For that reminder."

"Hey." Luann reached out and turned his face toward hers. "If you put that time toward music, you'd get good fast. Practice. You know how. You weren't born knowing how to throw a football."

Luann seemed to believe in him so completely. It was spreading to him, the way the first tongues of flame start to creep up and lap at the higher logs of a bonfire. It was the first time in days he had felt anything resembling hope. What she was saying maybe wasn't so far-fetched. Before Colton started playing football, he spent a lot more time with his guitar. He and his dad would play together and sing. And what did he have to lose? The worst that could happen is that he'd come up short and he'd be in no worse a place than he already was.

"Okay," Colton said. "I'll try it."

"Swear?"

"Swear."

"Because you owe me. Remember how you promised you'd play and sing for me?"

"I know. Now let's unpause the movie. Or I'll say 'Candyman' five times and summon him."

"Colton."

"Candyman."

"Don't."

"Candyman."

"You butthole. Don't. This is exactly how teenagers get killed in movies."

"Candymmmph—"

Luann saved them from the curse of the Candyman by swiftly climbing onto Colton's lap and shutting him up with a kiss, one that would kick off an unbroken string of kisses that ended only when Luann's parents came in the front door and Luann leapt off him like she'd awoken from a NyQuil slumber to find herself dry-humping an anthill.

Luann drove him home and helped him to the front door. There, they put a fitting epilogue to the make-out session they'd ended prematurely at her house. Then, with an impish smile, Luann handed Colton a blank piece of notepaper and a ballpoint pen.

"What's this?" Colton asked.

"There's something else you do well enough to get applause and autograph requests for," Luann said. "Except I'd definitely prefer you don't spread it around as much as your other talents."

They laughed. Colton used his front door as a writing surface and signed the paper, *To my biggest fan from your biggest fan. Kisses, Colton Dean Gentry.*

He slipped inside and checked in with his parents, who had gone to bed. After making his way to his room, he lowered himself carefully to the floor and pulled his dust-bunny-adorned guitar case from under his bed. He blew the dust off it and opened it. He always loved the spicy, sweet, tangy smell of wood and glue that greeted him every time he opened the case.

He pulled out his guitar and cradled it on his lap like it was a sleeping toddler, suddenly consumed by an overwhelming urge to tune it up and play. He knew that doing so would wake his family, though, so he resisted. *Tomorrow,* he thought. *First thing.*

He knew exactly the song he'd start figuring out.

CHAPTER 21

October 2015
Venice, Kentucky

COLTON AWAKES THE MORNING AFTER THE COOKOUT AT DERRICK'S HOUSE with the news of Eddie Lawler's grandkids, the laughter of Derrick's children, and the words of the Serenity Prayer all reverberating in his mind. *God, grant me the serenity to accept the things I cannot change, courage to change the things I can, and wisdom to know the difference.*

Colton doesn't consider himself long on wisdom, but he has enough to know what he can change, and by God, he has the courage to change at least one thing.

He almost trips over the guitar case protruding from under his bed as he's leaving his room and pushes it farther under. Outside, it's a serene, cool, overcast Sunday morning. The only sound in the neighborhood is the cawing of crows and the dry brown leaves, the texture and color of aged hymnal pages, skittering on the driveway. A trail of leaves swirls out of the bed of his truck as he drives first to Pawsitive Vibes, a tragic, locally owned pet supply store next to a vape shop in a strip mall on the outskirts of Venice. There, he buys a collar, a leash, poop bags, a sack of kibble (the expensive stuff), some treats, a set of doggie dishes, a bed, and a raccoon dog toy.

He proceeds to Man's Best Friend, a shabby cinderblock dog shelter on the other side of town. He enters, and the musk of unwashed dogs wallops his nostrils. Shrill, frantic barks reverberate through the building, echoing off the bare concrete floor and drab white walls. Colton didn't do much research into which of Venice's animal shelters was the sorriest, but if this weren't it, it must be damned near, and that's exactly what he seeks.

A man with long, greasy hair and an unkempt goatee who could be anywhere in age from a rough twenty-five to forty-five sits behind a counter at the front, scrolling absentmindedly on his phone. He looks up. "Mornin'. What can I do you for?" he says as Colton approaches. His glasses look like he lets the dogs lick them clean. Judging by his odor, he's doing the shelter dogs in his ward a kindness, not making them envious of how often he gets to bathe.

Colton rests his elbows on the counter. "I want your sorriest, most broke-down-ass dog."

The man chuckles, barely hesitating. "I think Petey fits the bill."

"Talk about him."

"Petey, aka Petey Poops, is as much of a mutt as they come. We're not even sure he's one hundred percent dog. He could have some possum or raccoon mixed in there. He's old—no idea how old. He's blind in one eye and can't hear very well. His right hind leg is messed up—we think he was used as a bait dog for dogfighters—so he doesn't move real quick, not that he has much energy anyway. Not a big barker either. But he's a sweetheart. Oh, and we call him Petey Poops because he has diarrhea a lot." The man makes sure he has Colton's eyes. "A *lot*."

"Sold. Lead the way to Petey."

They walk down a long corridor lined with chain-link enclosures. Dogs of sundry sizes and breeds hurl themselves at Colton with frenzied, deafening barks.

"They all think you're here for them," the man shouts over the din.

Colton winces and nods.

Petey's kennel is near the end. They arrive to find him lying on a dingy mat, his head resting on his paws. He looks up solemnly but doesn't bark or otherwise move to acknowledge them. He's small and lean and looks to be around twenty-five pounds. He has black, coarse, wiry fur, streaked with silver and the odd patch of white. He has a graying beard and mustache. One eye is black, the other is milky as though with a cataract. All in all, he does, as promised, look like the offspring of a schnauzer's congress with a possum atop a pile of shredded newspaper.

"Hey, Petey Poops, look alive!" the man says. He turns to Colton. "He doesn't get his hopes up anymore."

"Can I pet him?"

"Sure thing." The man opens the kennel.

Petey finally rises, painfully. His hind leg is mangled and crooked. He limps arthritically toward Colton. Colton crouches, his own infirm knee groaning. He looks Petey in the eyes and scratches the coarse, greasy fur behind his ears.

"Not to put my thumb on the scale but Petey has about three weeks left before he's put down. Either you take him, or he crosses the ol' Rainbow Bridge—either way it's a comparative win for Petey. He hasn't had a good life."

"What's your name, man?"

"Larry."

"Larry, let no one accuse you of being overly sentimental."

Colton continues petting and scratching Petey. It's obvious, from the way Petey is soaking it up, that he hasn't had loving contact in a long time.

"We have a little play area out back if you wanna 'run' "—Larry makes air quotes—"Petey around and see if you're a good match."

"Naw, I'm good," Colton says. "Petey's coming with me."

CHAPTER 22

Colton assists Petey up into the passenger seat of his truck. Petey makes a faint, high-pitched whine and curls up. Colton gets in and is about to start the truck but stops and turns to Petey.

"Hey, Petey. Name's Colton. I'm your new dad. Maybe you've had a few, but I'm gonna be the best of them, and you'll know it because you'll never wind up in a dump like this again, people calling you Petey Poops. Lord almighty. That's another thing: no more getting called Petey Poops. Not by me. I've crapped the bed some in my time too. Metaphorically speaking."

Petey sniffs and licks his lips.

"I got you this." Colton offers Petey the raccoon dog toy. Petey noses at it but lowers his head.

"Maybe in time. Here, let's try something else." Colton hands a treat to Petey. This time Petey goes for it, but gently, tentatively. "That good? Here, have more." Colton gives him another. He starts the truck and goes to put it in gear but stops himself. It feels freeing to talk to Petey. Like opening up at Duane's and his dad's gravesites. Silence is fertile soil for grief to grow like creeping vines and cover you up.

"Bet you're wondering why you, Petey. Well. Because I had a good life and it started going down the crapper and I screwed it up the rest of the way. And now I don't have much of anything or anyone. No house. No career. No wife. No kids. Dead dad. Murdered best friend. Not many living friends. And I wanted someone to love and someone who'd love me back and right now people mostly aren't fitting the bill. And also, um—" Colton's voice cracks as he dams back tears in his throat with that swallowed-too-big-an-ice-cube ache. "I wanted to feel like my life mattered. So, Petey. That's why I picked you. I'm gonna take care of you, buddy. And that'll be one good thing I don't screw up." Tears stream down his cheeks, running into his beard. He quickly wipes them away with the backs of his wrists. "I had this plan that if I had a son, I'd name him Duane. But that doesn't look like it's gonna happen, so I thought that's what I'd name you. But I'm looking at you now, and you're a Petey. So you stay Petey."

Petey eyes him morosely.

"You're welcome." Colton clears his throat. "By the way, you don't like Swedish hockey players, do you?"

Petey looks away.

"I knew I could trust you. We got a lot in common. You got a jacked-up leg. I got a jacked-up leg. You got some gray in your beard. I got some gray in mine. No one wants you around. No one wants me around. On the diarrhea thing, though, you're on your own. At least until I stop into Bucky's for some fried pickles."

Colton puts the truck in gear and drives Petey back across town to Pawsitive Vibes. He has Petey washed and groomed, nails clipped, and teeth brushed. When they're finished, Petey still isn't beautiful, but his appearance is much improved and he smells immeasurably better. They put a little elastic bowtie on him to wear with his new collar.

Colton arrives home, aids Petey to the ground, and leads him inside. "Mom," he calls.

His mom stops puttering in the kitchen and comes to greet him. "Colt?"

"Meet your new granddog, Petey."

Colton's mom wipes her wet hands on her sweatshirt and bends down to pet Petey. "Hi, boy, you look older than me." She stands back up. "This is a surprise."

Colton rubs his beard. He meets his mom's gaze. "I needed him. I'm sorry," he says quietly.

His mom says nothing but nods with a tight smile and puts her cool hand to his cheek. Tears well in her eyes.

Colton and his mom watch TV for much of the rest of the day, Petey dozing at their feet. Larry didn't misrepresent his lack of vigor. But no one minds.

As the day unspools, Colton says to Petey, "You've spent enough time indoors, looking at white walls, I bet," and takes him out in the backyard. He spreads a fleece blanket over the layer of brittle, fallen leaves on the lawn. Raking would wait until tomorrow. He has nothing but time.

They lie close together in the cool and stillness of the afternoon, sometimes dozing, sometimes listening to the wind breathing through the balding branches of the trees ringing the yard. The smell of machine-drying laundry wafts all around. A flock of geese overflies them, honking in time with their wingbeats. Leaves spiral down, one by one, coming to rest on them, as though the world is slowly showering them with confetti in celebration of their new union. With no one around to judge them broken and flawed, they're perfect under the bright gray harvest sky, shining like polished silver.

"I love you, Petey," Colton murmurs into the crown of Petey's head. "The rest of your life is gonna be good. I promise."[1] Colton rests in the quiet of his new companionship, and for the moment, his existence seems marginally less desolate. This feeling will pass. It will pass. But for the first time in a long time, he feels fortunate.

---

1 Petey will not die in this book.

The hazy optimism that briefly enveloped Colton disperses when he discovers a lump on Petey's belly.

"Dogs can have hernias?" Colton asks, kneeling by Petey on the floor of the examination room. "He wasn't, like, lifting weights or helping a friend move."

"Petey's getting up there in years. I could give you a list of his issues, but the inguinal hernia repair is probably at the top," Dr. Greg says.

"Man, I came to you because I couldn't imagine someone named Dr. Greg delivering bad news."

Dr. Greg looks at Petey and back at Colton, eyebrows raised. It's all he needs to say.

Colton holds his breath. "What's the damage?"

"You're looking at about $2,500 for the surgery. I could get you in next week. I just had a cancellation. Got pet insurance?"

"Doc, I ain't even got people insurance."

"Well, I'd recommend looking into it. Petey's going to be expensive."

This might have been a bad time to fall in love with someone costly. Colton sighs long and looks deep into Petey's gentle, apologetic eyes and melts. He scratches Petey behind the ears. "We'll figure it out, buddy," he murmurs, kissing Petey on the top of his head. "Whatever Daddy's gotta do to pay the bills, he'll do. We'll get you fixed up."

CHAPTER 23

December 1995
Venice, Kentucky

Luann's dad answered the door, wearing a Santa hat and a cable-knit sweater. The warm cinnamon, clove, and citrus potpourri of mulled cider emanated from inside the house. "Colton, come in!" he said cheerily, standing aside. "Merry Christmas!"

"Merry Christmas, Eddie." Colton entered.

"Can I get something for you?"

Colton shifted the large wrapped box tucked under one arm and adjusted his grip on the handle of his guitar case. "No, sir, got it okay."

Luann's dad's face turned serious. "Listen, Luann told me about MTSU. I'm so sorry."

"It wasn't a surprise. I wasn't much use to their football program anymore."

"Still."

"Luann's been great. Helping me through it."

On cue, Luann appeared at the top of the stairs. She smiled at Colton. "Come up."

"Supper should be on in about a half hour," Luann's dad said.

Colton went upstairs. Luann greeted him at the entrance to her room with a long kiss. She stood barefoot on the toes of his boots.

"Hang on," Colton murmured. He set down his gift and his guitar case carefully and lifted Luann. "Okay, where were we?" She wrapped her legs around his waist and they kissed some more as he carried her into her room.

"I'm intrigued about what you've brought," Luann said.

Colton grinned. He picked up the box and handed it to Luann. "Open it."

She did. A loamy, arboreal smell floated out. She reached in and pulled out a juniper bonsai tree in a square, black-glazed ceramic pot. She gasped. "Is this real? It's teeny!"

"Yep. It's called a bonsai tree. Like Mr. Miyagi had in *Karate Kid.*"

"This is beautiful." Hushed awe threaded through Luann's voice. "How did you know to get this for me? Not even I knew I wanted this."

Colton's cheeks rosied with pride. "I was with my parents at the mall in Clarksville and there was a store called One World Village. And it had a lot of stuff that was sort of arty and cool. I thought you'd like this. Anyway, there's a little card in there they gave me that tells how to take care of it."

Luann fished in the box, pulled out the card, and studied it. She set it on her drafting table. "I like how much thought you put into it. Now I'm giving you your present."

"I have more for you."

"Hang on. Let me give you yours first." She went to her bed and retrieved a long, narrow box. She handed it to him and stood back in anticipation.

Colton opened the gift. The rich smell of leather greeted him on opening the box. It contained a long, padded strap of ornately tooled whiskey-brown leather, with "Colt .45" embossed into it. Colton's breath caught in his chest. "Wow," he whispered. "This is rad."

"It's a guitar strap," Luann explained. "'Colt .45' is what they call you, right? I asked Derrick."

"My junior high coach gave me that nickname."

"Someone spoil my surprise? That why you brought your guitar?"

"No. That's the other part of your present." Colton opened the case and pulled it out. "And your gift couldn't be better timing." He fitted the ends of his new guitar strap over his acoustic's plastic buttons and slung it on.

Luann clapped and clasped her hands together in front of her chest. "You gonna play for me?"

"And sing. Like I promised."

Luann jumped onto her bed with a bounce and sat cross-legged.

Colton fished his pick out of his pocket. He drew a deep breath. "Whew. Jitters." He took another nervous breath and exhaled in a rush. "This is a song you might recognize." He went in his mind to the place he would go when he needed to deliver. The place where he couldn't lose; where he was a champion.

He had practiced this song perhaps hundreds of times, rewinding the mix tape Luann had given him again and again. Like he was throwing a football through a hanging tire. He didn't try to imitate it exactly—he made it his own. He watched Luann's face. Her eyes incandesced and she gasped and covered her mouth with her hands as recognition slowly dawned, then broke over the horizon as he began singing.

It was "Linger" by the Cranberries. As he played and sang, he experienced the sensation of levitating above the two of them, watching from outside himself. It was transcendent. Not even throwing a perfect touchdown pass felt like this.

The final notes had no sooner faded than Luann leapt from her bed and stood in front of him, her body humming like a high-voltage power line. She allowed Colton to remove his guitar and set it back in the case before she pounced. She took him to the ground. It was the most Colton had ever enjoyed being tackled. She kissed him again and again.

Colton stole his lips back long enough to say "I kept my promise."

They rolled onto their sides, where they lay, breathless and facing each other. "Think I got a future in music?" he asked.

"And then some."

"Should I move to Nashville after graduation and try to make it as a country musician?" He was joking.

Luann was not. She reached over and stroked his cheek. She said, quietly and soberly, "You are an absolute star, Colton Dean Gentry. I'd buy your albums. I'd go to every show. I'd follow you around the country in a VW bus."

Colton ran his index finger along Luann's top lip. "Should I do it really?"

Luann met his eyes dead on. "You miss people applauding for you?"

"Like you wouldn't believe."

"Then you should. Because there's a lot of people applauding in your future if you do."

"The thought of trying to be great at something else scares me. Football took so much. I don't know if I could handle coming up short again."

"You don't seem like the type to fear the pursuit of greatness. Go after this. You might fail, but what if you don't?"

He could see she was graveyard serious. It was then Colton decided that that's exactly what he would do. And a great weight took wing and lifted off his spirit. Now, a path out of the wilderness—one he didn't need two working knees to travel.

He was still reeling and dizzy with the exhilaration of this new lightness when Luann stood, went to her drafting table, picked up a wrapped object, and sat back down, offering him the rest of his gift. Colton unwrapped a framed pencil drawing of the two of them together, watching a storm, at their secret place on the bluff overlooking the Cumberland River, executed with even more than her usual skill. "I consider that our first date," Luann said. "Wish I'd had the courage to make it official by kissing you that night, like I wanted to."

"Me too." And Colton realized that his nascent plan only made it more certain that they would be going their separate ways in mere months, even though he knew it was already an inevitability from her end. And this dispiriting notion dragged him earthward.

"Lulu, Colton," Luann's stepmom called up the stairs. "Supper's on."

They kissed again, long and slow. Luann got to her feet and helped Colton up. He winced as his knee twinged.

When they came downstairs for supper, a massive spread took up the long oak dining table. Luann's parents, grandparents, aunt, uncle, and cousins were seated already. Colton went around introducing himself. As he got to Luann's uncle, he asked Colton, not a hint of joking, "Hey, who were y'all listening to upstairs when we got here? He's fantastic."

CHAPTER 24

January 1996
Venice, Kentucky

Deep January, and dusk glittered with the glassy tang of coming snow. Low clouds tinged gray and rose-gold swept fast across the twilit sky at the front's advance. It was forecast to flurry several inches—a blizzard by Western Kentucky standards. There was not a chance Luann—and by extension Colton—would miss it.

Colton put his Boy Scout training to work and soon he and Luann sat before a crackling blaze at their storm-watching spot at the bluff. Still, she shivered, and Colton hugged her to him to stem the chattering of her teeth. Her nose and cheeks glowed pink in the amber firelight.

Colton roasted marshmallows until they were a rich, blistered bronze. They made s'mores and licked the lingering stickiness from their lips and fingers. Luann lapped a smear of chocolate from the corner of Colton's mouth. They watched the light frolic among the ruby embers as the fire burned low.

Luann slipped her icy hands under Colton's shirt, the way she did the night they first kissed. "What are you thinking about? You seem pensive."

I'm thinking about what I'm going to do without you when you go to college and leave me behind. How I'll live without this. But Colton said, "Technically I'm now wondering what *pensive* means."

"*Thoughtful*. What're you thinking about?"

Colton was still trying to find the words when a snowflake fell. And another. Then more. Innumerable.

Luann jumped to her feet, and Colton followed her as quickly as his knee would permit.

"Come on," she murmured. She took Colton's hand and led him to the edge of the bluff. The air smelled of spent fire and snow and cold soil. Below them, a long, silent barge with blinking red lights navigated languidly downriver. Across the water, the lament of a distant train horn and railroad crossing bells.

Snow fell thick now, absorbing sound. They turned their faces skyward and stuck out their tongues, so the snowflakes landed and melted sharp and metallic on them. Flakes stuck in their eyelashes and whispered and skittered down their shoulders and arms.

The flurry lasted a while and then lightened. Soon, only a few flakes were falling, drifting slowly downward, sometimes hanging suspended and bobbing in the air, then continuing earthward. The clouds thinned to a lucent, auroral veil over the moon, bathing the falling snow in white light.

It was beautiful to the point of holiness, and Colton and Luann stood in hushed reverence.

Colton spoke the only words worthy of that moment. "Luann?"

"Yeah?"

"I love you."

Her hand tightened in his and he sensed a tremor passing through her. "You mean that?" she asked quietly.

"With all my heart."

Several moments passed before Luann responded. "You know how I don't talk much about my mom and stepdad?"

"Yeah."

"I was six when my parents divorced. My mom remarried when I was eight. A couple years later, she and my stepdad had a kid, and from then on, they've both been distant and weird to me. Like they wanted to focus on their new family and forget me. So I'm distrustful about love."

"You've never mentioned that."

"Not a fun topic."

Colton looked her deep in the eyes. "I love you, Luann. Believe that."

"I love you too, Colton."

His heart leapt like a murmuration of starlings taking wing. Every reach of him filled with light.

He wondered how anyone survived this feeling he'd just named; this delirious sweetness. Maybe no one did. Maybe that was the point.

CHAPTER 25

November 2015
Venice, Kentucky

As he holds the door open for his mom and gets his first look inside, Colton registers that Field to Flame is easily the most crowded public place he's been in since flying back to Dallas. A sheen of sweat rises on his palms and his pulse speeds. He immediately senses a few pairs of eyes discreetly alight on him with recognition before politely moving on. Colton is the sort who looks and carries himself like someone famous, even if people aren't exactly sure who he is.

The restaurant's interior, built into the old bank building, is an impeccable balance of hip and rustic. The whitewashed exposed brick walls are hung with black and white photography of farm life, framed vintage botanical prints, and aged, rust-scabbed agricultural implements. The floor is crafted of wide, pitted-and-scarred reclaimed hardwood planks, rubbed to a dark, deep amber sheen. Industrial pendant light fixtures with warm yellow Edison bulbs hang from the antique-tin-sheathed ceiling above. The tables are heavy and wooden, farm-style, with clean, simple, sturdy lines, as are the chairs. The kitchen is partially exposed, and flames lick from the mouth of a visible brick oven.

The bank's preserved vault sits open in the back of the dining area, and it appears to be in use as a storeroom for foodstuffs. Immediately to the right, upon entering, the bank's teller windows have been converted into a well-stocked bar. Colton averts his gaze almost immediately, like he's just made eye contact with someone he hoped wouldn't be at a party.

The restaurant smells like a heady mélange of roasting vegetables and meat and garlic sautéing in browning butter. It's warm inside against the chilly gloom of the drizzly, leaf-strewn November evening outside, and the dining room buzzes with animated conversation. It's packed. At a few of the tables are obvious adventuresome locals, but there are also tables full of clear out-of-towners—older, wealthy-looking bohemian and academic types. A fair number of more heavily and artfully tattooed and pierced twenty- and thirtysomething couples than one generally sees in Venice. These patrons wouldn't look out of place as Field to Flame servers, who weave efficiently in and out of the tables, dressed in indigo chambray shirts with rolled-up sleeves and brown duck canvas aprons with rivets. On one wall, there's a hanging with a quote:

> *If beyond the pearly gates, I am permitted to select my place at the table, it will be among Kentuckians, and the food, I hope, will be Kentucky style.*
>
> —Thomas D. Clark

"Folks look happy," Colton's mother says. "Good sign."

"I don't guess I'd be pleased if I'd waited this long to get in and the food stunk."

"Hard to believe there's a place like this here."

"And doing so well."

The hostess greets them brightly and leads them to their table. It's a prime location, right beside one of the tall windows that line the front of the restaurant. They can see the downtown lights reflecting off the wet black pavement outside.

"Oh, that's fun! Look!" Colton's mom slides a triangular object toward Colton.

"Is that a peg game? Like at Cracker Barrel?"

"Yep."

"Tell you what, whoever's running this place sure knows what will put Venetians at ease."

Colton's mom starts playing. "I have never once won this game."

Their server—a stunning young woman with black hair, fringe bangs, a septum piercing, and sharp, angular black line tattoos on her forearms and ring-adorned fingers—arrives. "Hello, folks. I'm Bianca, I'll be taking care of you tonight. Here are some menus. Have you been our guests before?"

"First time," Colton says.

"So, we're a farm-to-table restaurant. That means our offerings change daily based on items' availability and the growing season. Tonight, we're celebrating winter squash and greens with our pumpkin seed pesto and heirloom peanut pumpkin gnocchi with sage brown butter sauce, roasted butternut-kabocha squash bisque, and Red Russian kale salad with heirloom Arkansas Black apples and Belle Champ goat cheese from Hopkinsville, Kentucky. Most items on the menu should be available, although a little while ago we sold out of the baby back ribs with apple cider–pecan barbecue sauce. Have you had a chance to look over our drink offerings?" Bianca asks. "Can I get you something while you peruse the menu?"

Colton had resigned himself to having a nice Diet Coke with his meal, but the drink menu offers an array of inventive non-alcoholic options. His mother orders a Buffalo Rock ginger ale with pickled peach juice and lime. Colton orders a mulled apple cider shrub with soda over ice.

He pulls the peg game to him. "I think the trick to this is you have to start from the outside and work your way in."

For a few moments, the pair plays in amiable and easy silence.

"This reminds me of that restaurant that you and Maisy took me to in Nashville for Thanksgiving the year after you two got married," Colton's mom says.

Bianca returns with their drinks, served in mason jars, of course. They order the pimento cheese, pickled serrano peppers, and benne wafers plate and the twelve-month Broadbent country ham, cheddar biscuits, and assorted pickles plate as appetizers.

"Maise and I used to go to that restaurant a couple times a week," Colton says after giving their server a chance to retreat.

"And who can blame you. That was one of the best meals I've ever had."

"You get spoiled quick, living that way."

Bianca arrives with their appetizers and they order their entrées. For Colton's mom, it's the paddlefish with citrus butter sauce, paddlefish roe, Carolina Gold risotto, and charred asparagus. Colton opts for the Heritage Farm pork blade steak with Broadbent bacon and sorghum baked beans and Kentucky hot slaw. They add the hearth cornbread with cucumbers and raw onions for their table.

Colton's mom takes a bite of a benne wafer smeared with pimento cheese. "Mmmmm. Out-of-this-world good."

Colton nods with a mouthful of cheddar biscuit and country ham.

"Our waitress is pretty," Colton's mom observes after Bianca brings the cornbread with cucumbers and onions.

"I think you're supposed to call them servers now."

"Our *server* is pretty." Colton's mom bites the end off a pickled green bean and holds the rest daintily between her finger and thumb like a joint.

"If you're getting at what I think you're getting at, answer's no."

"What?"

Colton raises an eyebrow. "Mama."

"She's pretty. That's all. Kind of artsy-looking. You always liked artsy. She looks like that girl Raleigh you dated for a while in Nashville, the model with all the tattoos. Just an observation."

"Oh, you're just *casually* observing. And no, I didn't always like artsy. That was a taste I developed."

Colton's mom smiles slyly.

"Listen, first of all, she must get hit on nonstop—"

"Well, probably, but you're a higher quality of man."

"Every creepy dude's mama thinks that. Anyway, Bianca's doing her job. She don't need me angling for her number."

"Well."

"Also? She's at *least* ten years younger than me."

Colton's mom bites a slice of cornbread dressed with raw onion and cucumber, covering her mouth while she speaks. "Maisy was younger than you."

"And *that* worked out famously."

"Was the problem the age difference?"

"The problem was a lot of problems."

"You thought about getting back into dating?"

Colton sighs and jumps a peg on the peg game. "Little bit." Truly a *little* bit—he didn't view his dating prospects in Venice in a sunny cast and accordingly limited the amount of contemplation he devoted to it.

"You seem lonely sometimes."

"That's what Petey's for."

"What do you think the odds are Petey's gonna leave us a surprise on the kitchen floor for when we get home?"

"That or the couch. Hundred percent."

"I'm rooting for kitchen floor," Colton's mom says. "Linoleum."

"Way to jinx us. It's gonna be couch."

Before long, Bianca arrives with their entrées. "Everything tasting good?"

"Incredible," Colton says.

"Can I get you anything?"

"No, you're doing a fantastic job. Thank you."

Colton's mom takes in the plate in front of her. "I feel like I should snap a picture. It's so pretty."

"Do it. People take pictures of their food." Colton looks at his plate and then around the restaurant while his mom holds her phone over her plate. "I feel like I'm back in Nashville or Dallas. I truly cannot believe I'm in Venice right now."

"Is that a good feeling?"

"Good and bad." Colton takes a bite of his pork blade steak and mutters an involuntary *damn* under his breath.

"You miss it? That life?"

"Some parts."

"Like?"

"The food. We ate good. And I miss playing music."

"You think you'll ever get back into it?"

"Lord, Mama, you're playing all the hits tonight. Getting back into dating. Back into music."

"We're at dinner. Aren't we supposed to talk?"

"Let's do some politics and religion."

"We can chat about the weather if you want."

"I'm not saying that."

"I'm not trying to be a bad date. It can feel good to talk."

"Nah, you're right. It helps to open up." Colton takes a bite of his baked beans and thinks for a moment. "Honestly? I'm done in music."

"No." His mom says it as an incredulous gasp.

"Yeah."

"You don't want to?"

"Not even that. I mean it's over for me from an industry perspective."

"How can that be? You were making a lot of people a lot of money."

"I wasn't making enough people enough money. And waiting in line behind me were about a thousand hungry, cutthroat twenty-four-year-old country bros with six-pack abs who are anxiously elbowing past each other for the privilege of stepping over my corpse and making a lot more people a lot more money than I ever did or will. And they'll say all the right things. Or at least keep their fool mouths shut. You get second acts sometimes in the entertainment industry. You don't get third acts. I was on my second when everything went to crap."

"Can you switch to some other kind of music?"

"Like rap?"

"You gotta try this. It's like butter in your mouth." Colton's mom offers him a forkful of her paddlefish and risotto. "No. Like rock. You were never the most twangy of country singers. You sound kinda like Gregg Allman. Rock musicians are always speaking out about guns. They won't punish you for that there."

"That plan's bass-ackwards. You hit thirty-eight as a rock musician, that's when you start looking to country music as your second chapter. That's what Darius Rucker from Hootie and the Blowfish did. That's what Jewel did. That's what Richard Marx did. It does not *ever* go the other direction—from country to rock. You can leap from country over to pop music like Taylor Swift did or like Maisy's doing right now. But you better be a smoking hot, driven young woman with a giant, passionate fan base who'll follow you over."

"Other types of country music then. Bluegrass."

"Not a bluegrass guy. They're hardcore."

"I sometimes hear country music on the Murray State radio station that they don't play on normal country radio."

"That's called Americana or alt-country, and they pride themselves on authenticity. They can be plenty snooty about it and they look down on mainstream country. So if I tried to switch over to Americana, I'd hit a wall. Not real deal enough."

"You grew up in a town of twelve thousand in Kentucky."

"Try telling that to some trust-fund kid from Portland with a handlebar mustache, an anchor tattoo on his wrist, suspenders, and a banjo."

Colton's mom sets down her fork. "You're a real downer."

"Realistic is all," Colton replies gently—he is, ultimately, grateful for her unfailing belief in him. There aren't many people like that in his life anymore.

"So what's the plan?"

Real good question. Colton shakes his head but says nothing.

"Sorry, Colt. Didn't mean to kill the mood."

"I know."

"You've been down before, baby. Remember when you hurt your knee? You had to forge a new path then. You can do it again."

"Older you get, the harder it is to reinvent."

They go a time eating without speaking. Then Colton feels a gentle tap on his shoulder mid-bite. It's Bianca.

"Sir, excuse me. Chef wanted to meet you, if that's all right."

"Mm. Mmm-hmmm," Colton quickly chews his bite, swallows, and wipes his mouth with his napkin. "No problem."

From behind him, he hears an approaching woman say, in an amused and oddly familiar voice, "Well, Bianca, your celebrity-spotting skills are improving. This is indeed a country star. But it's not Dierks Bentley. It's Colton Gentry. And I would know."

Colton turns and finds himself staring at a ghost.

CHAPTER 26

May–August 1996
Venice, Kentucky

A SUMMER-HUMID NIGHT IN MAY. A THIN CRESCENT MOON IN THE WEST, incandescent and sharp against the blue-black sky. The world pulsed with new growth, perfumed with ivy and clover.

They lay on a blanket at their spot on the bluff. They gazed up at the stars arrayed above in creamy swirls and made out ferociously, tasting salt on each other's skin. Something was different about that night. Their blood ran hotter, more animal and charged, closer to the surface of their skin, to their swollen lips. Like it held some liquid intelligence that knew they would soon part.

Luann, face flushed, whispered, breathless, into Colton's neck, "Make me feel like we're watching a storm." She wasn't talking about the heat lightning in the distance that broke the black of the sky, and they both knew it.

Afterward, they held each other. Luann rolled over to Colton and lay with her hair fragrant and splayed across his bare chest, listening to his heart. She traced toward the hollow of his throat and stroked it with her index finger. "If I could live on your body in a little cabin, this is where I'd build it," she murmured. "Where would you live on me?"

"Nowhere," he said into her hair. "Because if I lived on you I couldn't be with you." He felt her smile.

She pulled Colton's white T-shirt to her and hugged it and pressed it to her nose. "Can I keep this?"

"I'd give you literally anything you wanted right now. But why?"

"I want to take it to Cooper Union and sleep with it. Because it smells like you." Luann caressed his cheek. "You look sad."

"Thinking about us a thousand miles apart."

Luann traced her fingers along his eyebrow. She loved exploring the architecture of his face. "We're not a thousand miles apart now. We're really close actually."

"Never close enough." Colton stroked her lips with his thumb. "What are we gonna do?"

"Talk every day on the phone. See each other at Christmas and jump on each other."

He'd never loved or been loved so fiercely. He didn't know where to put it all or what to do without it. It was like tasting warm bread after days of fasting, knowing you would be locked back in an empty room for weeks more.

She inhaled muggy air rich with the sensuous fragrance of white flowers. "This is my favorite season. Not quite summer. Not really still spring. I call it Honeysuckle Summer."

"Honeysuckle Summer," Colton repeated quietly. "I like that."

Summer passed like a reverie.

Afternoons of lazing beside Luann's neighborhood pool on white plastic chairs, the hazy air redolent of chlorine, coconut sunscreen on sun-bronzed skin, and cut grass.

Firefly-bedazzled, star-swept nights; lightning against purple thunderheads; chirring of crickets. Driving backroads aimlessly, wind the temperature of a fever on their faces; lying on a blanket at the bluff, tangled like a necklace in a pocket.

They gripped one another like they were clinging to the same riverbank root to keep from being swept downstream and parted forever.

Too few days.

Linger.

CHAPTER 27

November 2015
Venice, Kentucky

It's Luann.

Dressed in white. It's her eyes—the same voltaic, radiant intellect. It's her cheekbones—sharper now, if anything, without the softness of childhood. It's her dark, wavy hair, pulled back. It's her.

Colton pushes back his chair with enough force that he nearly knocks it over and stands, almost involuntarily. The way you would if someone you assumed to be long dead walked into the room. His heart beats such a frenzied staccato he can feel it echoing in the hollow chambers of his lungs, which struggle to hold oxygen. "Lord almighty," he murmurs. "Luann?"

"Hey, Colton. Been a minute, huh? Look at that beard."

Colton's brain is a scramble. He doesn't know what to do. He can't shake her hand. That's never what they've done. As if it's muscle memory, he hugs her. She hugs him back. He feels a slight trembling under his hands, even though outwardly she seems to be playing things much cooler than he is. Underneath the smells of busy kitchen and cooking food, he detects hints of vanilla, cardamom, and dryer sheets. It's her.

Her body feels the same pressed against his. *She's still alive. She exists. She's twenty years older. She's here. He's touching her. It's her.*

They break the hug and stand back and assess each other. Colton falters for words. His mom rescues him.

"Luann!" She stands and hugs Luann.

"Hello, Mrs. Gentry."

"Janet. Please. I always told you that."

"Janet. It's wonderful to see you again. You look well."

Colton's mom stands back from Luann and grips her upper arms. "So do you. The last time I saw you, you were eighteen. You're all grown up now."

Luann smiles. It's her smile. "All grown up."

Even with this respite, Colton still struggles to form a coherent thought. "How. I— How on earth? You run this place?"

"Run it. Own it. Executive chef."

"This is *your* restaurant?"

"Yep."

"Good Lord. You've done an amazing job. Am I eating food you made?" He notices for the first time that she's wearing a high-collared chef's jacket with double rows of buttons.

"What are we eating tonight?" She scans their table. "The pork steak, looks like. The paddlefish. Nice choices. Good chance I made these."

Colton laughs and shakes his head. "I have . . . so many questions."

Luann laughs too. "Don't you remember all those times as a teenager when I talked about how much I love cooking?"

"I actually recall you specifically saying you don't cook, the first day we met."

"When we built the deck."

"Exactly."

"I changed my mind."

"Apparently. Your place is incredible, Luann."

"You enjoying your meals?"

"It's one of the best I've ever had. I'm truly impressed."

"Amen," Colton's mom says.

"That's what we like to hear."

"We made this reservation like a month ago," Colton says. "Y'all are absolutely killing it."

"Good. Listen, this has been so fun. As you can see, we're slammed tonight, so I better get back to the kitchen—"

"Hey. I won't keep you. But obviously you're back living here."

"Not far away, actually."

"I'm back too, for the time being. Would you like to…I don't know…catch up?"

She hesitates for a moment, and it's enough time for Colton's heart to drop to roughly thigh-level. But: "Sure." She produces a business card and hands it to him. It's printed on a luxurious, textured stock. In a clean, urbane font, it says: "Luann Lawler-Madsen, Executive Chef and Owner, Field to Flame." Below is her phone number and email.

Madsen. The father of Eddie Lawler's grandchildren?

Luann looks to Colton and his mom. "I know for sure Colton is a s'mores fan. How about you, Janet?"

"I love everything bad for me."

"Did y'all save room for dessert?"

Colton and his mom fall over themselves to answer yes.

Luann turns to Bianca. "Bianca, I'm going to do the s'mores crème brûlée with the smoked vanilla-bean marshmallow custard and Vosges chocolate for them."

"Luann, that is too kind of you," Colton says.

"Hey, for an old friend? That should be coming out in a little bit. Listen, I gotta run back to the kitchen. Great seeing you! You have my card." She hustles off toward the kitchen as Colton looks on.

Old friend. You have my card. These phrases fester in him. *Old friend. Old buddy. Old pal. You have my card. Let's touch base. Pencil each other in. Circle up.* This was not how he and Luann talked to each other when they talked to each other.

Colton and his mom sit.

"Wow," Colton says softly. "Luann Lawler. Well, I guess it's—" He looks at the card again. "Lawler-Madsen now."

"The last twenty years have treated her well. I always thought she was beautiful."

"Yeah," Colton murmurs. He stares in the direction of the kitchen, shell-shocked.

"She was pretty different from the other girls you'd gone out with before. Brainier. More ambitious. More spirited. Always had interesting things to say."

"All that and more."

"There were times Maisy reminded me a little of her."

"Me too." *Except Maisy never loved me like she did.*

Colton takes the final bite of his pork steak—the one Luann might have prepared with her own hands. It's the most succulent bite of all, fatty and rich, velvety on his tongue. "Luann was good at everything she loved. You know that drawing I had framed on my bedroom wall?"

"She did that?"

"Sure did."

"Then I'm not surprised at how good we're eating tonight."

Not long after their empty plates have been cleared, Bianca returns with large oval ramekins of the s'mores crème brûlée. Colton and his mom tap the caramelized sugar crust with their spoons until they break through to the smoky, marshmallow-infused custard and the layer of warm, molten chocolate and scratch-made graham cracker beneath. They take bites and their eyes roll back. It tastes like a winter night spent watching snow fall with Luann, feeling young and perfect. Now a stubborn pang has descended slowly over his heart.

She made this with her hands. For me. Knowing it was for me.

"If we weren't in public, I'd lick it clean. I've a mind to anyway." His mom scrapes at her ramekin, hunting for residual crème brûlée molecules. "You got quiet."

"Mmm-hmm."

"Seeing Luann get to you?"

"I wasn't ready. Like mentally."

Bianca returns to check on them. They sing the praises of their meal and request the bill. Absent from it is their dessert. It's still well over a hundred dollars. Colton pulls out his American Express and tucks it into the small leather portfolio the bill comes in, which, like everything else in the restaurant, is tasteful and beautiful. Luann overlooked no detail.

Bianca returns a few moments later, carrying the bill portfolio, a flustered and embarrassed expression on her face. She leans close to Colton, and in a hushed, apologetic tone says, "Sir, I'm so sorry about this. The card you gave me actually came back declined? Is there another one you want to try?"

"What? You sure?" Colton asks, even though he has no reason to doubt it.

"Yes, sir. I ran it a few times. Have you been traveling? Sometimes when people travel their card company puts a hold on the card."

Does voyaging from my bedroom to the yard to rake leaves and then wayfaring with Petey slowly around the block and then journeying back home to watch TV with my mama count? Because if so, yes, I've been jet-setting a fair bit. But he's happy to run with her face-saving offering. "That could be. I'll check with them."

Colton's mom opens her purse. "Honey, how about I—"

"Mama, no. Put it—"

"I'd love to treat you."

"Not up for debate." Colton tries to say it lightly, jokingly. He pulls out his wallet, extracts his Visa, and exchanges it for the useless Amex. "Try this one." He silently petitions the Almighty for a better result with this one, of which he is by no means certain.

"Yes, sir," Bianca says apologetically. "I'll be right back."

"Uh, Bianca," Colton calls softly after her. She returns. "Could you maybe—I don't know if you're required or whatever—but if you could maybe not mention this to the boss lady, I'd—" Colton makes a zipping motion over his lips.

Bianca titters nervously. "Oh no, no, of course not." She makes the same zipping motion and then a tossing motion. "Throwing away the key."

"Thank you." Colton almost added *You've earned yourself an extra big tip*, but he was not at all sure that was a promise he could make.

Bianca leaves and a stiff, awkward silence descends between Colton and his mom.

"Well," Colton's mom says finally.

"I'm trying to think what might've caused that. I had Petey's surgery bill, which was a lot, but—"

"You haven't worked in a while."

"I know, but. I gotta check in with Maisy's and my money guy on that."

"You think there's been some mistake?"

Sure don't. "Hope so."

On some level, Colton's known that the specter of financial ruin loomed, waiting for its opportunity. Now he can hear its moans and rattling chains outside his door. *Good job, NRA and Wayne LaPierre. You sure got me back for my sacrilege against your golden calf. Getting my credit card declined at the restaurant owned by my high school flame is more frontier justice than even y'all could've hoped for.*

Bianca returns. Colton holds his breath.

"That one work?" he asks tentatively.

"It did," Bianca says, beaming with obvious relief.

"It should. I stole it just this morning."

Nervous smile from Bianca.

"Kidding," Colton says.

"I figured. Y'all have a wonderful evening. And come see us again soon."

Colton starts to write a tip on the check, but reconsiders. He's unsure by how much the charge cleared. He opens his wallet and pulls out his remaining cash. Fifty-two dollars. He leaves it all. It's far beyond even a generous tip, but he hopes that if Bianca mentions anything about the payment fiasco to Luann, it's his magnanimity. And that sure wouldn't happen if the tip portion of his charge bounced.

As Colton and his mom are leaving, she asks, "You want to try to say goodbye to Luann before we leave?"

"No," he says so abruptly as to cut off all argument. Humiliation, combined with the fear and dread of his encroaching poverty and the shock of seeing Luann after twenty years, has left him gasping with want of a drink. And an abundantly stocked bar is staring him right in the face. After the meal he's had, he can only imagine how good and inventive the drinks are here. How deliciously they would sprawl on his tongue before blooming warm in his belly and numbing him. *Blessing in disguise that you can't afford any of them.* He's calling Leon the minute he gets home.

They hurry to Colton's truck in the cold mist, clutching their jackets around them. They get in and Colton starts the engine. They take a moment to collect themselves.

"Thanks again for that wonderful dinner, sweetie," Colton's mom says, rubbing her hands together in front of the heater vent. "It's one of the best I've ever had."

"Good." *Because it might be the last time for a while before I'm able to pick up the tab anywhere.*

Colton's mom says, "You know, I don't think that you ever told me what exactly happened with you and Luann back when."

CHAPTER 28

August 1996
Venice, Kentucky

Colton Gentry was hurting, which had sent him seeking the remedy he had been turning to with increasing frequency that summer, as Luann's departure drew near and with it, a tide of fear and sadness he didn't know how to contain unassisted. It wasn't something he thought he could talk about without crying, so no discussing it with his guy friends, even Derrick.

He sat in his truck, outside a teammate's lake house, listening to the distant whoops and hollers, and finished the last of the six-pack he'd brought. The end-of-summer send-off for members of the Venice High School football team was a proud tradition—a certified rager centered around the sort of bonfire that makes fire marshals sweat and personal injury lawyers salivate. Colton may not have ended the year as an official member of the Venice Wildcats, but he was an honorary teammate in perpetuity. Luann was taking the evening to finalize preparations for her move to New York, and the night after that would be their last together before parting. She'd leave the next morning.

The thought of that final night and watching Luann fade into the distance racked Colton with dread. Running into Tyler and Mara earlier at the gas station where he was buying the beer (the owner, a diehard Venice High football fan, could be counted on to "forget" checking IDs) had not helped.

Colton walked out of the store and saw Mara fueling her ramshackle

Toyota Corolla wagon, with more stickers visible than actual paint. Tyler was approaching the store.

"Tyler, Mara!" Colton waved.

"Hey," Mara called back warily. She'd never warmed to him, despite Colton's best efforts to win her over (which had included a solo trip to a local used CD emporium and a painfully awkward series of questions to profoundly skeptical employees, like "Who are some cool bands that someone who likes Marilyn Manson and Nine Inch Nails would listen to?"). Still, he wouldn't give up trying, not until the bitter end. Which this appeared to be.

"What's up, Colton," Tyler said as they passed. He sounded friendlier.

Colton walked up to where Mara was gassing up. She was wearing a Dinosaur Jr. T-shirt.

"Dinosaur Jr., huh?" Colton said. "I'm more into Dinosaur Sr. myself."

Mara forced a tight smile. "Good one."

"What are you and Tyler up to tonight?"

Mara shrugged. "Chillin'."

Colton almost told her his plans, but he had a sense Mara wouldn't think getting sloshed in front of a bonfire with a bunch of other jocks was terribly cool. "Same. Just chillin' too."

Mara nodded at the six-pack. "Drinking alone, huh?"

Colton smiled awkwardly. "Getting together with some friends. Obviously, I'd rather be with Luann. Probably you too, huh?"

"Yeah. We haven't gotten to see much of her this year, so..."

Slipped that in right between the ribs.

Colton winced and scratched the back of his head. "Yeah. I guess not, huh. Well, now neither of us get to see her much."

The gas pump clunked off and Mara replaced the nozzle. She faced Colton, her eyes hard and rimmed generously with black eyeliner. "And now you're gonna be a country star."

It sounded so stupid when someone said it with the slightest bit of cynicism. Colton's face grew hot. "I mean... I'll try."

"Meanwhile, Luann's pining for you in New York while you're getting down with the Nashville honeys in Daisy Dukes, right?" She sounded too pointed to be teasing.

"No chance."

"Are you aware Luann is talking about taking a year off from school to come hang out with you in Nashville?" Mara's tone made clear she didn't think Colton should be excited.

And indeed, Colton did not feel excited at this news. His stomach clenched. "I didn't know that."

"Well, she is. Which would be a bad idea, and you should tell her that if she suggests it."

"You've never thought I was good enough for her, huh?" Colton had thought this many times but had always lacked the gumption and opportunity to ask. Now he had the chance, and instead of courage, he didn't have much to lose, which can serve the same purpose sometimes.

"No offense." Mara leaned against her car and folded her arms. "You seem like a nice guy and all that. But for her? Nope."

Colton hadn't realized what a precarious state his heart was in until this interaction. It just got knocked off the slim ledge it was clinging to, into the void. "You think that hadn't occurred to me?"

"I don't know what you think about."

Tyler walked up and handed Mara some change and a peach Snapple.

"Anyway," Colton said quietly. "I better run. Good luck with everything, both of you."

He walked back to his truck feeling thoroughly battered. It's one thing to suspect for the entirety of a relationship that you're unworthy of someone. It's quite another to have outside confirmation.

Still, he put on a brave front at the party and tried to have a good time. It quickly became clear that cheap beer—and lots of it—would be his only shot at numbing the pain. The boy whose family owned the lake house raised a toast to Colton, their fallen leader, which the other boys weepily joined, lofting their red Solo cups in tribute.

Soon, though, the talk turned to girls. And then Luann. One by one his teammates, except for Derrick, came out in favor of Colton's making a clean break.

"She's fancy, dude. You're country. That can work in high school, but not after," one pronounced sagely.

"If you love someone, set them free, dogg. That's for real," another offered.

"It hurts, bro, but it's like when I dislocated my shoulder. Quick pain when you pop it back into place, but then it don't hurt no more," still another proclaimed.

Between his interaction with Mara and now his teammates, was he being pushed toward an off-ramp on the highway of long-distance-relationship heartbreak? Wisdom dwelled in the unlikeliest of places—even in the mouths of fools, which his teammates were. They were giving voice to things he would have thought himself had he ever allowed them purchase.

Was this the path? To put down his and Luann's relationship like a horse with a broken tibia? The thought was sour in his mouth like turned milk, but he was no stranger to doing exquisitely painful things with the hope of some future reward. That's all football ever was—every ladder sprint, every weight session that left his muscles screaming. That's what it was to leave football behind for music. He knew how to say goodbye to what he loved and press forward. *Maybe that's my life—I get to love things for a while and then say goodbye. I never stopped loving football. But the only way I was able to move on from it was to say goodbye.*

The voices swirled around Colton in his haze. Meanwhile, his mind churned. He stumbled away from the group into the cooler darkness beyond the fire. He needed quiet to weigh this new possibility, unthinkable until now. He sat on a stump with his head in his hands.

I could suggest it to her. Maybe she's been thinking about it too and she'll be relieved. Luann's smart and reasonable. We don't want to hurt each other.

I need to talk to her now. I need to do this while I have the courage. It's better this way. I'm not good enough for her.

Colton rose and tottered drunkenly toward the lake house. The raucous conversation and soused hollers faded behind him. Entering, he was hit by the stench of moldy carpet, dirty socks, and beer. He immediately tripped over the coffee table and tumbled onto the sticky, vaguely moist floor. He pulled himself to his feet and continued his quest. There it was. On an end table. A *Sports Illustrated* sneaker phone.

Colton almost lost his nerve. *You don't have to do this.* But he recognized this quailing as the coward in him talking. Everything worthwhile he had ever done had come from ignoring that craven voice.

He picked up the phone and dialed. Luann answered on the fourth ring, her voice mossed with sleep. "Hello?"

"Hey. It's me."

"What time is it?" she asked blearily, but still heartbreakingly happy to hear from him.

"Uh. Not sure. Were you asleep?" Colton was glad Luann had her own phone line. Whatever time it was, her stepmom and dad surely would have been less excited to hear his voice.

"Yeah. What's up?"

"I just—I don't know." Colton's heart had begun a fast roll. He felt his mettle draining.

"You okay? You sound different."

"I wanted to—I guess I needed to talk? About—I don't know. Us."

"Okay." Luann sounded more awake and now alarmed. "You still at the party?"

"Yeah, I'm at the lake house."

"You wanna talk tomorrow? I'm so out of it. I was packing all night."

"No. I gotta—" Colton cursed his muddled brain. He wondered if he should sleep on this. But slumber would dull his resolution to do what was necessary. "I was thinking about us being so far apart."

"Me too," Luann said, sighing. "I'm gonna miss you so much."

"That's actually what I wanted to talk about. I— Do you think maybe we should . . . I don't know. Like take a break or something?"

A gravid pause on the other end.

"Luann?"

"What are you talking about?" Her voice was bowstring taut.

"Just. I don't know. A break." He cursed the meekness in his voice.

"What does that mean?"

"You know. A break."

Another prolonged silence. "Like . . . break up?" Luann's voice sounded like chewing ice felt.

Colton rubbed his eyes and forehead. He sat on the floor with his back against the sofa arm. "Maybe."

"What is this?" Luann was fully awake.

"I just thought—"

"Are you *dumping* me? Over the phone, out of the blue at 12:47 a.m.?"

"Luann, I—" *Bail out. Eject. Abort.* But it was too late.

"It's a yes or no question." Her voice had the ragged edge of verging on tears.

"Maybe we should. Take a break. You're gonna be—"

"Are you *drunk* right now?"

"No. I mean I've had some to drink, but—"

"Oh, that's fantastic. You get wasted and wake me up in the middle of the night to dump me? The *day before I'm leaving*?" She was crying.

"Luann, shhh, don't cry, just—never mind, okay? Forget I—"

"Forget what? That my boyfriend who I loved woke me up to break it off less than two days before I go off to school? Yeah right, Colton. You bet. I'll go right ahead and forget that. Everything is cool."

"I'm not saying we should break up. I thought—"

She laughed bitterly. "You *thought*. Get some cheap beer in you and the truth all comes spilling out. How long you felt trapped? Huh?"

"Never."

"Sure." She wept on the other end.

"Luann," Colton pleaded. "Don't. It's okay, I'll—"

She collected herself, but her voice still quavered. "You know what? If this is the sort of chickenshit stuff you'll pull when you're drunk, you're gonna do it when you're sober after you finally get up the sack. So I'm done."

Colton was struck silent while he tried to process what he was hearing. "What? Wait. I don't get—"

"I'm *breaking up with you*. I don't want this anymore. I don't want you anymore. You must've lied when you said you loved me."

"I didn't. Never, ever. I—"

"I never should have trusted you. Do not ever call me or talk to me again."

The line fell mute. Then a dial tone like a flatlining EKG.

Colton stared numbly at the sneaker phone for a few moments like he was staring into a bottomless chasm. *Did I have to ruin the best thing I've ever had with such a cartoonish phone?* He hurled it away with a jingle, put his head in his hands, and moaned shapeless words of anguish. He pounded his fists on the floor. Far from the quick pain and then relief of popping a dislocated shoulder back in place, this felt like hitching his arm to a team of oxen and slowly yanking it the rest of the way off.

He slid onto his back on the gummy, yeasty carpet and sobbed, the rain-on-concrete smell of crying in his nose, tears running down his face and collecting in his earholes like warm river water as he looked up at the ceiling.

He wept until his head ached and the room spun slowly around him; until sleep took him where he lay.

He slept as if anesthetized; like his reptilian brain was protecting him from consciousness. He awoke only when the sun-blazed coral of the backs of his eyelids screamed him awake and he opened his eyes to see one of his teammates unsteadily stepping over him to get to the bathroom.

He rose to a sitting position and looked around his room, a piercing, shooting pain behind his eyeballs. His mouth was cottony, and he could only swallow with great difficulty. Boys were draped over couches, easy chairs, and in various attitudes across the floor, mostly in positions that would make a chiropractor dream of a new boat.

For a few blessed seconds, Colton remembered nothing of the night before and merely felt a terrible drumming at the base of his skull. But soon memories—specifically The Call—began emerging from the gloom like lantern-bearing harbingers. And metaphysical agony overtook the physical.

He evacuated the house as quickly as he could in his hungover state. It was 11:14 a.m. by the time he had located his keys, gotten his teammate to move the Pontiac Grand Am that blocked in his truck, and left.

As he drove, windows open to keep his own sour stench of booze and armpit sweat away from his nostrils, he recited a covenant with himself as a litany:

I am never drinking again.

I am never drinking again.

I am never drinking again.

CHAPTER 29

A SHOWER AND FOUR IBUPROFENS LATER, COLTON SAT ON HIS BED, HEADACHE ebbing, trying to summon the moxie to call Luann and attempt to put things right. In the cold, sober light of day, he knew beyond all doubt that it was her he wanted, near or far, in any form. He had made the misstep of his life.

He tried calling her five times. Futile.

On some level he had thought that when Luann said to never call or talk to her again, she maybe meant *Give me a few hours, then I'll be fine*. This was proving deeply wrong.

Finally, deciding he had nothing to lose, he drove to her house. Before everything had descended to hell, they'd had plans for tonight, and he hoped her night was still open. He arrived at her house and sat for a few moments out front, sweating. He gathered himself and walked up to her front door on trembling legs, his bad knee singing.

He rang the doorbell and wiped his palms on his jeans. He heard footsteps. His pulse rose, thudding in his ears.

Luann's dad answered. "Colton. Hello." His face was inscrutable.

"Hey, Mr. Lawler. Is Luann home?" Colton had no idea how much Mr. Lawler might know.

Mr. Lawler's expression came into sharper focus: pity. He did know *something*, if not all the details. "She's, ah." He rubbed his forehead. "Not available right now. I'll tell her you came by." His tone bespoke clear marching orders, which he was executing reluctantly but scrupulously.

Colton opened his mouth to plead to see her. But he had a notion of how far that would get him. He looked at the ground. He almost said *Please tell her I'm sorry*. But he couldn't. Instead, he croaked, "Okay, please tell her I came by."

Mr. Lawler looked at Colton. "I think she just needs time," he said delicately.

Colton met his kind eyes. He wanted to break open. *I love her. Tell her I'll do anything for her forgiveness. Tell her I can't live without her.* He nodded, turned, and walked away. He stole one look back, in case she had appeared behind her dad and was watching him leave.

He saw a closed door.

That night, despite his promise to himself that morning, he snuck some mouthfuls of bourbon from his dad's liquor cabinet. He still slept fitfully, spending at least a solid hour awake between 2:47 a.m. and 4:00 a.m., contemplating some grand cinematic gesture. Throwing pebbles at her window until she opened it and then serenading her. Working up a hasty cover of "I Will Always Love You." Casting his dignity onto the fire to attempt to thaw her heart.

Ultimately, he lay paralyzed in bed, staring at his cottage-cheese ceiling, cursing his gutlessness while the bleakness inside him rose like a river overflowing its banks after a gray week of torrential rain.

The next day, from an unfinished cul-de-sac up the hill from Luann's house, he sat in his truck and watched as she and her dad loaded her possessions in the family's Suburban. Before loading one bin, she pulled out a white piece of cloth and cast it on the lawn.

The car backed out of the driveway, its red brake lights stinging Colton's eyes. And then they were gone.

Colton's heart collapsed into a sinkhole of anguish and regret. A sob percolated up and then another, and then he shook and clutched his head in his hands. Finally, he composed himself and drove down the hill to Luann's. He walked over to the piece of white cloth that Luann hurled on the lawn.

It was the T-shirt he'd given her. He plucked it off the grass and pressed it to his face reflexively. There was the smell of his perspiration and deodorant. But now it mostly smelled like her. Sweet pears and melon. Fresh, cool cucumber. The olfactory signature of their love. She'd started sleeping with it clutched to her even before leaving. His head swam and his eyes filled with new tears.

He folded it as if folding a flag for the widow of a fallen soldier. He got back in his truck and drove home.

CHAPTER 30

November 2015
Venice, Kentucky

"So," Colton says. "That's what happened with Luann and me."

His mom says nothing for a while and then says, "Well, honey."

"Say it. I messed things up royally."

"I was just thinking how nice of her it was to make us that fancy dessert."

"Because of how I screwed things up."

"*You* said that."

"Some things go without saying."

Colton puts the truck in gear, and they drive home in silence.

Petey laboriously greets them at the door. Almost as though he'd sensed Colton's inner turmoil from miles away, he'd generously opted to deposit a big runny stool on the easily cleaned kitchen linoleum rather than the couch.

A small grace—but one nonetheless—and Colton welcomes any.

Later that night, while they're watching the local news together, and apropos of nothing, Colton's mom rests her hand on his forearm and says, "I'm glad you stopped drinking, sweetie."

"Seems best for everybody, huh?" Colton murmurs, eyes fixed on the screen, the relief a cold beer offered not far from his mind.

CHAPTER 31

Before turning in for the night, Colton pulls out his guitar case and rummages under his bed. He retrieves a dust-bunny-fuzzed football cleats box. He opens it for the first time in many years and withdraws a plain white T-shirt, yellowing with age like the pages of an airport paperback. He presses it to his face and inhales.

Faint as a whisper while watching a storm, she's still there. Somehow still there.

CHAPTER 32

He sleeps in fits and starts, dreaming about Luann. In one, they're married. In another, he's back watching her taillights disappear as she leaves for college, and he tries to scream after her, but his voice is a dry, impotent husk. He awakes with the dampness of dream tears on his pillow. The temptation to get in his truck in search of an all-night convenience store and a six-pack or two is strong. But he manages somehow, remembering how proud of him his mom had sounded the night before.

As soon as he hears his mom up and puttering around the house, he gets out his guitar for the first time in months. All morning and afternoon, he plays and sings, his fingers and voice shedding their scale as he builds up courage.

By nightfall, he's ready to give his sore fingers—their calluses having receded—a rest. And now they hold Luann's card. Running over its embossed letters, caressing its luxe linen finish. Many times he almost calls the number on it, and each time his courage abandons him.

Then he remembers: there was someone he left off his list on step 8 of twelve. One who he harmed while drinking—in fact, the first—and to whom he owes an enormous outstanding debt of amends.

He swallows hard and with a trembling thumb dials the number.

Luann answers on the third ring. "Hello?"

"It's Colton."

"Hey, Colton." Her voice is friendly but guarded.

"This a good time?"

"Sure."

"It was great seeing you last night. Mama and I couldn't stop talking about how good our food was."

"I'm so glad."

"I was surprised you were behind it. I mean pleasantly. But..." He can hear what sounds like kitchen noise in the background. *Better get to the point.* "Hey, I'd love to hear the story. I was wondering if you might wanna get together, catch up. If that wouldn't be too... weird."

There's a protracted pause on Luann's end that immediately rouses memories of the last time he and Luann spoke on the phone. A hesitation so long as to nearly give Colton space to lose his nerve. "Let's do it," she says.

"You sure?"

"Yeah, let's grab a drink."

"Could we... maybe do coffee instead? I'm not currently—um—I'm—"

"Yeah, no problem," Luann says quickly. "Coffee works better anyway. My schedule is nuts with the restaurant. I can generally squeeze in a little time in the afternoons between lunch and dinner. How's two thirty?"

"Two thirty's great."

"How's Tuesday?"

"Perfect. Where?"

"Not to toot my own horn here, but we serve the only coffee worth drinking in Venice."

"Works for me." Colton's head swirls. How do you end a conversation like this? When there's everything left to say, and you so badly want to confess your regret that it's twisting your heart and mind into a braid. "Hey, Luann..." He falters.

"Were you gonna say something?"

"It's really good to hear your voice again," Colton says softly.

CHAPTER 33

Monday morning, Colton calls his and Maisy's financial adviser. He confirms what Bianca already told him on Saturday night: Colton's broke. What little he has remaining is all spoken for. His finances are in their irretrievable death spiral.

He allowed himself to believe that this reckoning would never actually arrive. But here it is.

He thought his phone would ring eventually with fresh opportunities, new ways to earn a living. Surely when his life disintegrated, not *all* the pieces rolled under the refrigerator and out of reach, right?

Right?

He labors into the early afternoon, hunched over his laptop, googling "jobs Venice Kentucky," "how to write a resume and cover letter," and "jobs that don't require a college degree and allow you to keep your dignity."

The pickings are slim.

He heads to eBay to explore the market for the personal effects of B-list, flash-in-the-pan country musicians whose only moderately coruscating stars have faded, leaving them to eke out a living however they can.

PART II

CHAPTER 34

Colton stands in front of Field to Flame for the second time in less than a week, freshly showered, beard neatly trimmed. His heart's tempo quickens as he eyes himself in his reflection in one of the windows. His palms sweat despite the chill in the air. Acid bubbles sour in his throat, and he has an uncomfortable, queasy warmth low in his gut. He texts Luann that he's arrived. One of her employees comes to the door and lets him in.

It's eerily quiet after the bustle of dinner a few nights before. He can hear the faint clinking of pans and cooking implements from the kitchen mixed with the chatter of the staff. It smells like aged wood and steam off cookpots. His breath tightens as Luann hustles toward the entrance, wiping her hands on a towel.

"Sorry, tied up in the kitchen."

"No problem, thanks for making time." They give each other a quick, businesslike hug. *What is this?*

"Get your coffee order? Go nuts, we can do anything you could get at a coffee shop."

"Damn. Well then. Iced Americano? Black?"

Luann nods appreciatively. "All right."

Colton grins. "Guess I've gotten a little fancier since you last knew me."

"Marisa?" Luann calls toward the kitchen. "Iced Americano, black, and an iced caramel macchiato? Thanks!" To Colton: "Let's grab a seat by this window."

They sit, and a chevron of November afternoon sun falls across Luann's face. In this brightness, he can see the delicate lines that surround her eyes. She's more striking now than when she was eighteen.

They look at each other. Colton steals a glimpse at her hands. Same ones he once held. Same he taught to hold a hammer. Same that painted and drew for him. No ring. Interesting. *But maybe rings are a liability in a kitchen.*

He takes a deep breath. "Wow. This is..."

"Weird?"

"A little." He laughs. "Unexpected too."

"Can I address something right off?"

Colton's heart jackhammers. "Sure."

Luann smiles a little, with her lips pressed together tightly and toys with the table's centerpiece. "I was never the world's biggest country music fan. Still, I'm aware of your...situation and what I assume are the circumstances bringing you back here."

She says it with a tact that turns a knife in his heart. Not where he thought she was going. Colton coughs and shifts in his seat. "Ah. Yeah. That." He breaks eye contact and stares out the window.

"If this is uncomfortable territory—"

"It's definitely low on my list of favorite subjects, but—"

"We won't dwell. I just wanted you to know I respect what you said."

"Tell my record label. They dropped me like...I guess I can't think of something that gets dropped as quick as a country singer who speaks ill of guns."

"I think it took courage. I'm nervous every time I drop my girls off at school. I always hug and kiss them like I might not see them again."

Colton meets Luann's gaze for a second and then he looks at his hands. "I was, um. Pretty drunk at the time. I'm—" He almost says *I'm pretty brave when I'm drunk* but he catches himself. *That's not true, is it? Sometimes being drunk makes you awfully cowardly. And no one knows that better than the woman sitting directly in front of you.*

"Like I said, we can move on."

"Really it was because of my buddy Duane Arnett. He was my best friend in Nashville for years. We actually met right after you and I broke up. I was feeling pretty lonely, and he was there for me. Like he always would be. He was killed in that shooting at the country music festival in Florida. He and I—" Colton's voice breaks. Still, he feels a fist unclench in his chest. Even knowing Duane and Luann had never and now will never meet, there's something soul-salving in speaking of him to her. What he meant to him. A circle closing—now everyone he'd ever loved knew Duane's name, and this felt important for some reason.

"Oh, Colton. I am so sorry. When that happened, my heart was in my throat until I made sure you weren't there."

"You did that?" A potent rush of warmth courses through him, commingling with the grief momentarily.

"Of course," Luann says quietly. "Knowing that you were speaking out for a friend makes me appreciate what you said even more."

"It's great to hear you say that. I haven't felt like many people see it like you do. Suffice it to say, the haters have been louder."

"'Suffice it to say.' Man, it's weird hearing phrases like that come out of your mouth."

They laugh, Colton's sorrow ebbing slightly.

Colton says, "I'm a little more sophisticated now than when I was eighteen. And speaking of which…" He gestures around him. "I need the story."

As if on cue, Marisa arrives with their beverages.

Colton sips his iced Americano and his face wrinkles in ecstasy. "Mmmm. Damn." He raises it reverently. "You weren't lying about best coffee."

"We've looked into expanding into the space next door and turning it into a coffeeshop and takeout concept."

"Sign me up. I'll be there every day. So—"

"Yes. This. Okay. Well...I guess it started when I was at Cooper Union. I got a job waiting tables at this fine dining French farm-to-table restaurant called Ferme. That was my first taste of the restaurant business. It gave me a love of fine dining, but I didn't get in the kitchen at all. Fast forward to 2004, I got a job with the Madsen-Fisker Group, which is kinda the architectural equivalent of playing the Grand Ole Opry."

"Shot in the dark: that's where the 'Madsen' on your business card comes from."

Luann sips her macchiato. "Henning Madsen, rockstar architect. We got involved a little while after I started there."

"Look at you go." Colton plays it with a lightness he hopes masks his jealousy.

"Yeah," Luann says with a little mirthless chuckle. "So we pick up and move to Copenhagen in 2006."

"That's a long way from home."

"Yep. Anyway, got pregnant with my twins and—"

"Twins?!"

"Girls. Esme and Freja. They were born in May 2007."

"So they're eight?"

"Eight. Can't believe it."

"You got pics?"

She hands her phone to Colton.

On the screen are two beautiful girls with luminous hazel eyes—their mother's. One has wavy dark hair, just like Luann. One has strawberry-blond hair. Must be from her father.

"My goodness," Colton murmurs, a chimeric sensation of sorrow and joy passing through him. "If those aren't the two most precious angels. Which is Esme and which is Freja?"

"Dark hair is Esme; blondie is Freja. Easy to remember because Freja's the one who has a Viking princess name."

Colton stares at the photos with a twining of pride, envy, and regret. His tear ducts itch and his throat constricts. "You must be the proudest mama on Earth."

Luann beams. "Check back around bedtime or getting-ready-for-school time."

"Here we are. Twenty years later, you got these darling girls. Running your own restaurant. You're absolutely crushing it, Luann. I'm proud as hell of you."

She blushes. "Anyway, we're in Copenhagen. I speak zero Danish. It's oppressively dark and cold during the winter. I'm pregnant with twins and sick a lot. I have to stop working and go on bedrest. Henning is working sixteen-hour days, seven days a week. I'm lonely and desperately homesick. On one of the rare nights he's not working, Henning takes me to this Danish...barbecue place? Soul food? I honestly don't know what it was trying for."

"I feel like I'm watching two co-eds descend into a dark basement in a slasher film."

Luann snorts. "The barbecue sauce tasted like ketchup mixed with Diet Pepsi and sauerkraut juice with a dash of cinnamon."

Colton makes a dry-heave sound.

"I'm not finished," Luann says. "There were raisins and celery in the mac and cheese. They used spinach instead of collards."

Colton raises his hand. "I can only take so much of man's inhumanity to man."

"And the decor! They had, like, steer horns and cheap toy revolvers on the walls. It felt like they were mocking Americans—but unintentionally—while fetishizing the American South." Luann pauses for a second. "Oh, and it was called Lonesome Harry's."

Colton raises a finger, then slowly leans forward and bangs his forehead on the table, rattling their glasses. "I'm anxious to learn how the worst restaurant on Earth resulted in the best," he says after they've caught their breath from laughing.

"Well, that experience got me thinking about how if that restaurant had even remotely delivered, it would've been such a salve for my homesickness. The next day I emailed my dad for my grandma's biscuit recipe. I couldn't find the White Lily flour the recipe called for, so my first batches were like rocks. I got my dad to send me some White Lily, and my biscuits started turning out better."

"The biscuits we had the other night were the best I've ever had."

"Lots of practice. So it's helping my homesickness. Also, it's replacing the satisfaction I used to get from my work by engaging the same artistic muscles. I start branching out. My mom sends me more heirloom family recipes. I do the best I can with the ingredients available. I'm subbing prosciutto in for country ham, polenta for grits, stuff like that.

"The twins are born and they're a handful and I have terrible postpartum. I finally quit my job. We move back to New York City in 2008. Technically Brooklyn. Then it's on. I have access to a lot more and better ingredients. Our brownstone has a tiny yard, and I get a smoker. Raise chickens. I'm putting up my own preserves. Making these elaborate dinners every night."

"And you're all self-taught?"

"At that point. Lots of watching Food Network, reading books about cooking, trial and error. Then, in 2010, we hire a Norwegian au pair to help with the twins because I want to go back to work in the restaurant industry and go to CIA."

"Wait, you were a spy too?!" Colton says.

"Culinary Institute of America."

"At this point, I'd have believed spy." Colton sips his Americano.

"So I do a two-year online program while I'm working back at Ferme, apprenticing in the kitchen as a junior chef a few nights a week. It's hard, exhausting, dirty work, and I've never felt more alive. Meanwhile, I guess

Henning has also never felt more alive, because..." Her voice trails off and she looks at her hands.

"The au pair?"

"Bingo."

"Jeez. I wanted to be wrong. I'm sorry, Luann." Colton wants to say *I know the feeling, and with a Scandinavian too, no less* but stifles the urge. He can only be so raw today.

"We divorce in 2012. I'm sick of New York City, and I want to open a restaurant somewhere. So my parents pose a proposition. They'll put up the money for me to start a restaurant on one condition: I open it in Venice."

"Hardball."

"My dad's gentle façade hides steel. But at that point, I was missing my family and the South anyway. In fact, I was already considering Nashville, Louisville, or Atlanta. And opening a restaurant always comes with tremendous risk. I had no experience actually running a place, so that stacked the odds against me. I needed a support network. The girls adore their Mimi and PopPop, who watch them while I'm at work—they're over there right now. They like warm weather and having a yard to run in barefoot. It all feels right."

"So here you are."

"2013, I move back home. Get a great deal on this space. Opened in 2014. I work some of my media/PR connections from my preschool moms' group back in New York and get a couple of nice features in *Southern Living* and *Garden & Gun*, which kick things off, and—"

"Here you are."

"Here I am. I wanted it. Badly. So I went after it. I've always gone after the things I want."

Colton gives her a sly smile. "I do happen to know that about you."

Luann pinkens. "I guess you would, huh."

Colton sits back in his chair and regards her admiringly. "Luann. That is one impressive story."

"Didn't feel like it the nights I was up crying and wringing my hands, but... Anyway, enough about me. Tell me about the last twenty years."

The elephant in the room steps forward from the corner where he's been waiting patiently.

Colton clears his throat and studies the tabletop. He taps the peg game. "This was a genius idea by the way," he murmurs, stalling. "So. Before anything else, there's something I've needed to say for a long time."

Luann shifts in her seat. She smooths her hair and sips her macchiato. Her hand trembles almost imperceptibly.

Colton meets her eyes, his heart thudding. "I am so, so very sorry for how I treated you. I was a stupid, scared kid who knew how to take a hit on the football field, but nowhere else."

She doesn't say anything. She looks sad but smiles a little.

Colton continues. "I loved you so much, and I was terrified to lose you. And I ran like a coward. I regret it."

She's still silent. Colton can't tell if it's because she has nothing to say, doesn't want to say anything, or simply wants to allow him space to talk.

He continues. "I don't offer this as an excuse, but I was very drunk at the time—you know this. Alcohol's led me to some poor decisions and to hurt people I loved, and I'm sorry for hurting you."

Luann swallows hard. Her eyes brim with tears. She blinks them away, looking out the window. She turns back to Colton. "I envisioned this moment so many times over the years. You were my first love."

"And you were mine. But I didn't treat you like it."

"At various points in my life, I imagined every kind of response I could offer. Bitter ones. Angry ones. Conciliatory ones. Jumping back in your arms. Telling you to eat shit and die."

"All fair."

She pauses for a moment, takes a deep breath, and says, "How about this: thank you, Colton. It's good to hear and soothes an old wound."

Their eyes meet, smiles blooming across their faces.

"Wow," Colton says. "This is... I thought I'd never get a chance to say that." And yet, he's crestfallen. Like she's taking this too well. Which is evidence that she's truly moved on from him. *But what did you want?*

"Colton?" Luann says quietly. "How are you?"

"Today?"

"In general."

"I'm... you know. Fine."

"Fine?"

Colton licks his lips and drums his fingers on the table. He shakes his head and eyes the table. "Yeah."

"Because I know what you look like when you're feeling beaten down and hopeless. I can see it through that beard and the silver in it."

Colton sheepishly rubs his face. "I need to invest in some Just for Men."

"Silver suits you."

Colton nods and breathes in deep through his nose. He can't look at Luann for this part. "I lost my best friend in a senseless mass shooting. I lost my career when I vented about it, to the gun nuts' great delight. My wife then left me for a Swedish hockey player, to the tabloids' great delight. I'm back living at home with my mom, literally sleeping in my bed from high school—the same one you and I made out on. And I recently discovered that I'm broke, so if you know anyone eager to employ a failed country singer with a cubic shitload of baggage, let me know, because I have a life to rebuild." Colton immediately regrets unloading this on Luann, while it feels perversely satisfying, like lancing an abscess.

"So you *are* fine," Luann says. They smile ruefully at each other.

"In the plus column, I'm now completely sober."

Luann takes a breath, stirring her straw pensively. "There was never a moment when I wanted anything but the best for you. Not when I was at my lowest, feeling hurt and broken and abandoned. I've always been in your corner, even when I didn't think you were in mine."

Colton loses his grip and tears stream down his face. He wipes his eyes with his jacket sleeve. Turning from Luann and the restaurant, he stares out the window at the gray afternoon.

Luann pushes a paper napkin toward him, and he accepts it, wiping his eyes and nose.

"Very manly," he manages finally.

"No shame."

"Not just the crying. It's my whole trainwreck of a life. You seeing me like this—a big loser."

"I never had the pleasure of knowing Duane. But I'm sure he would be proud of all you've done and for the stand you took for him. I'm proud of you."

Colton composes himself for a few moments.

"Hey," Luann says gently. "Were you serious about looking for a job?"

"If I ever want to live anywhere but my mama's house again. Doubt I could even busk for change at this point. Not without people trying to fight me."

"Because I . . . might be able to help. One of my sous chefs, Marcus—he's my second-in-command—is moving, ironically enough, to New York City in December. So I need a new sous chef."

"Are you saying—" Colton tries to read her, but Luann's face is a mask of rumination.

"I'm saying. I could only pay twenty an hour—I wish it were more, but that's all I can afford currently. I don't make much more than that myself once all is said and done. But I have a group health plan for my employees we could get you on."

Colton leans back in his chair. "Wow, I mean, that's super generous of you. But I don't know the first thing about cooking."

"I beg to differ. You once roasted me the most perfect marshmallow I've ever had."

"I assume you'd need more done than roasted marshmallows."

"It's all an extension of the skill needed to roast a perfect marshmallow. I can teach you. You love good food, right?"

"I'm a patron of your restaurant."

"That's the most important criterion. You have familiarity with fine dining. I assume you and Maisy ate pretty well?"

"We tried."

"Listen. The Venice, Kentucky, labor pool isn't super deep in terms of fine dining familiarity, and I haven't had much luck recruiting elsewhere. Moving here is a bit of a tough sell for some. Then you need a work ethic. Zero concerns there. I've watched you build a deck. I've watched you throw a touchdown pass. I've watched you perform a song you taught yourself. I've had a front-row seat to your creative work ethic as you pivoted from football to music. I've never written a song, but I gotta think composing the elements of a song is similar to assembling the parts of a recipe."

"This is—wow. Is it cool if I think on it? I don't like to do anything halfway. I'd want to make sure I could commit one hundred percent."

"That's the kind of commitment I'm looking for. What do you think your timeline would be?"

"Day or two? That work?"

"Sure." She glances at the time on her phone.

"Have to run?"

"Gotta get back in the kitchen to gear up for dinner service."

"Yeah, sorry, I've kept you too long."

"Here's my final pitch: cooking for people is one of the most intimate and important things you can do. You can inspire emotion and memories and give comfort. Think of it like music for your mouth. You can express yourself and invent and be creative."

Colton nods. "This was amazing, Luann. Thanks for meeting me."

"I feel like I did all the talking. I want to hear what you've been up to too. Maybe we can do this again sometime?"

"I'd like that."

"Let me know about the job."

"Will do. Can I pay for—" Colton gestures at the empty cups on the table.

Luann waves him off. "My treat."

They stand and embrace. Colton leaves.

The air outside is cold and dry and claws at his face and hands on the short walk to his truck. He looks back at the restaurant, the House Luann Built. Her employees busy themselves setting tables behind the large windows. He watches for a few moments, wondering if he could be one of them and reveling in the new lightness of having finally laid down a burden he's carried for twenty years.

Let no one say there's no upside to your life imploding.

CHAPTER 35

"Hold up, man, gotta stretch," Colton says to Derrick. They pause their run, breath steaming against the cobalt dusk sky, and walk to a nearby bench. They sit, and Colton pulls his knee to his chest a few times, wincing. He massages the ligaments that surround it.

"We might be able to get one of Gabi's colleagues to look at that knee," Derrick says.

"Man, I lost my health insurance when I got fired from country music."

"Get you to the large animal vet, then."

"Take it from me and Petey: that wouldn't save me much. Tell you what, though. I might have a way to get some insurance."

"Got a lead on a job?"

"An offer."

"Son!" Derrick fist bumps Colton. "Do tell!"

"So, you know who owns Field to Flame, that new restaurant downtown?"

Derrick shrugs.

"This is the crazy part. Guess."

"Anthony Bourdain."

"Dude, come on."

"The way people been talking about that place? Plus that's the only chef I know by name."

"You'll never guess."

"Then stop making me."

"Luann."

Derrick stares at Colton and shakes his head. "Lawler?"

"Ding ding."

"You for real?"

"Buckle up." Colton tells Derrick the story of encountering Luann at the restaurant, meeting her for coffee, and the job offer.

"You gonna take the job?"

"I don't know."

"You afraid you can't take orders from your high school girlfriend?" Derrick asks.

"Dude, you did not know anything about our relationship if you think that's a concern."

"Bro, we all knew."

"You got the love of a good woman now. You know how it goes."

"Better than anyone. So what's the hesitation?"

"It'd be a commitment."

"And?"

"It's a lot to think about. I let her down once. I don't want to do that again."

"So don't."

"Think I should do it?"

"You asking my learned counsel?"

"I am, learned counselor. Advise me like I'm one of your clients." They stand and start walking.

"Take the plea deal."

"Yeah?"

"People get into trouble when they lack dignity. They want to feel big and powerful, so they do it the only way they know how, which is often illegal. Sell crystal. Hold up a convenience store. Whip someone's ass. We could solve crime if our country made folks less desperate for some shred of dignity. But that's another conversation."

"You think this job'll keep me out of trouble?"

"I think it'll give you dignity. So yes. Like Luann said, you'd be making art, bro. Food Network is wall-to-wall celebrity chefs. Entertainment. That's your business. This is a way back in, if only on a small scale. Put it this way: if you were one of my clients, and you had lost everything, and someone was offering you a chance to get back into doing something you love, but from a different angle, I'd say you lucky as hell."

They walk for a while in the dim light, saying nothing while Colton mulls. His knee throbs, which only further reminds him of the last time he came to a great crossroads in his life.

Colton flops onto his bed, hair damp from the shower. He puts his hands behind his head and stares up at his ceiling, pondering.

He hears Petey approach and hefts him up, where he cozies along Colton's side.

"Petey," Colton says, scratching Petey behind the ears. "I'm considering taking a job learning how to cook from my high school girlfriend. What you think?"

Petey raises one eyebrow, then the other.

"Luann is doing for me like I did for you, adopting you just before they could put you down."

Petey rests his chin on his paws.

"I'm starting to think I also might could use a smidge more social contact than I'm currently getting. What you think, Petey Peanut Butter Pie?"

Petey yawns.

"Your breath stinks, dude. Anyway. If you approve, I'll call Luann right now and accept before I lose my nerve. Speak now or forever hold your peace."

Petey draws a long, contented, snuffly breath.

Colton dials.

Luann answers, kitchen sounds in the background. "Colton?"

"This a bad time?"

"Normally, yes, but it's a lull."

"It's about the gig. I'm in. Let's...cook. Or whatever y'all say."

There's a silence on the other end that gathers weight until it starts dragging Colton's heart toward his knees.

"Listen, about that. I worry I didn't adequately convey how much I need this next hire to be a long-term one. We've had turnover in this position, and I need my next sous chef to stick around."

"You saying the offer's off the table?"

"The opposite. I'm saying the offer's on the table, but if you're going to do this, I need you to *do* it. Much as I would love to help you, I can't be the place where you wait for something to blow over."

He hesitates. *This is it.* "Loud and clear. I'm all in."

"Well. There's ready and there's *ready*. Let me make sure you know what you're getting into. If any seasoned restaurateur found out I was hiring someone with no cooking experience as sous, they'd think I'd lost my mind. It's just not done. This is me gambling you'll learn this as quickly and well as you've learned other things. So I'll need you to do your homework. You'll have to practice and study even outside work hours. And we're talking sixty-plus-hour weeks. Hot, dirty, stressful work. You're gonna get burned and cut yourself. Your back'll hurt from standing and bending. You'll have people send food back that you thought was perfect."

"There a downside?"

"Here's what you'll have going for you: Where I came up under chefs who didn't know me from Eve and loved yelling, I know you and want you to succeed and hate yelling. And I'm a damn good teacher. Too good. I've taken Waffle House line cooks and taught them fine dining well enough that they're leaving me for New York. So, with all that said..."

"You ready to take yes for an answer?"

"What if your label calls and says 'Hey, we screwed up. Come back.'"

"Ain't happening. I'm in. I see things through now. If anything, sometimes I even hang on too long."

"Well, we'll try not to do that either. Tomorrow morning, ten a.m. sharp. Wear comfortable clothes you can move in and get dirty. And don't go apartment hunting yet. You're gonna be spending your first few paychecks on the best knives you can buy, some books I'm going to recommend, and some good meals for your mom while you practice."

"Luann?" Colton hesitates. "I let you down once. I won't do it again."

"Okay," Luann says softly. "See you tomorrow. The front'll be locked. Come to the alley entrance." She hangs up.

See you tomorrow, Colton whispers up at the ceiling, wondering what he's just gotten himself into, hoping his life isn't about to become one huge bingo card of failure.

CHAPTER 36

A BRACING WIND DRIES THE STREETS AND SIDEWALKS OF THE RAIN THAT ROLLED through the night before, but Colton still sweats as if in summer heat as he approaches Field to Flame. He realizes how seldom he's downtown at this time of day. It's so sedate. He knocks on the alley door at 9:52 a.m.

"You okay?" Luann asks as she greets him at the door with an iced Americano.

"Why, do I look like shit?" Colton quickly slaps his hand over his mouth. "Didn't mean to cuss in your restaurant. Sorry."

"Profanity is a second language in a restaurant kitchen. And no, no one who didn't know you as well as I do would even notice."

"I'm nervous. Didn't sleep much. It feels like the first day of third grade."

"How did you manage to go onstage in front of arena crowds?"

With a little help from my buddy Jim Beam. "Totally different story. Should I be prepared for hazing, by the way?"

"We have a very strict policy against that. Being hazed when I started working in restaurants was a nightmarish experience, and I swore it would never happen on my watch if I could help it. Let me show you around the kitchen and get your paperwork done. Then I'll introduce you to the opening crew."

The restaurant is already aflutter with activity despite the empty dining room with chairs upside down on the tables, a cacophony filling the air—the hiss of running water, the snicking and clacking of knives chopping, the metallic clanging of pots and utensils, the whoosh of flame and steam. Stocks simmer on ranges, filling the kitchen with their hearty aroma.

"The opening crew gets in around nine," Luann says. "They get the stations set up; receive and inspect the food deliveries. We source ingredients from a few different farms in the area. Every day is a surprise because we serve what's local, fresh, and available. We have to think on our feet and improvise. You'll learn about all this."

Luann shows Colton around the well-lit, spotless, immaculately organized kitchen, gleaming like a surgical suite with chrome and stainless steel. The brick oven, smelling like cold ashes from the night before. The walk-in freezer. The locker room. The curing and ripening rooms. The walk-in boxes. Dry storage. She shows him the various stations. The meat station. The fish station. The entremetier station. The garde manger station. The coffee station. The plating area.

"I'm a bigger neat freak now than when I was eighteen," Luann explains. "The only way to run a kitchen is squeaky clean. Things need to be where you can find them when the heat's on. Now, let's get your paperwork done." They step into Luann's office, a disarray of Post-its and precariously stacked ledger books and documents.

"I know," Luann says as Colton sits across from her angular midcentury desk. "If I had to cook in here, I'd keep it tidier."

They fill out Colton's paperwork. Luann makes a copy of his driver's license and Social Security card. As they're about to exit her office, she goes to a rack in the corner, where several cloud-white chef's jackets hang. "Let's make you official. You still a large?"

She hands him one. It smells like freshly laundered cotton and the faint antiseptic tang of bleach. He dons and buttons it. It's soft and cool against his skin. He thought it would feel like wearing a prison jumpsuit, readying to serve his lifetime exile from music. Instead, it feels like being decked out in a football uniform, like joining a team. A sensation of pride. Opposite him, Luann puts on a jacket of her own and buttons. She rolls up her sleeves. Colton does likewise.

"Turn that in at the end of each shift," Luann says. "I only trust myself to wash them well enough."

Colton straightens his jacket with a snap and extends his arms by his sides. "How do I look?" He does a slow twirl.

Luann looks him over with a slight smile. "Like a chef," she murmurs and plucks a piece of lint from his shoulder.

She returns to the kitchen with Colton trailing behind and calls the staff together, identifying them by name and title: Dani, the opening sous chef; Taylor and Finn, the day line cooks; Reggie, the dishwasher; Katie and Will, the servers; and Ruth, the hostess. Colton celebrates inwardly that Bianca isn't working today. That's going to be awkward.

"Hey, y'all, real quick. I want to introduce a new member of the team: Colton Gentry. He and I go way back. Don't ask how far. He's coming on to replace Marcus. This is his first time working in a kitchen, so I'll be around more to train him. Show him a warm Field to Flame welcome, answer his questions. He learns fast."

Colton surveys his new coworkers. He sees vague recognition on a couple of their faces. Skeptical looks from others. Self-consciousness and embarrassment suddenly overwhelm him. He scratches his cheekbone, under his eye, and looks away bashfully.

"Speech!" Finn calls. He has an easy slacker smile, midtwenties shaggy hair, and tattoos (Colton has him beat, though).

Everyone laughs. Colton gives a lopsided grin. "It, uh, hasn't always gone well for me when I make speeches." Appreciative, sympathetic smiles from those who understand his allusion. "I'm honored to be working alongside y'all, and I hope to learn from you. Sorry in advance for my screwups and dumb questions."

"All right, y'all, let's talk lunch." Luann reviews the menu with the staff.

Bánh mì with duck sausage, bourbon-glazed pork belly, fresh-pickled carrots, cucumber, and daikon…

Duck fat fries…

Wagyu beef cheeseburger with Sweet Meadow Farm pimento cheese, fried green tomatoes, and Broadbent bacon jam…

Winter squash gratin…

Marinated cucumber, onion, and Arkansas Black apple salad…

Buttermilk biscuits with pawpaw preserves…

The line cooks and Dani ask questions. When Luann answers, they respond with a crisp, soldierly *Thank you, Chef.*

The meeting ends and the crew returns to work, prepping dishes and the dining area for lunch service. Colton follows Luann back into the kitchen. "Should I be calling you Chef? I always wondered if that was a real thing when I'd watch Food Network."

"I mean." Luann blushes. "Technically but—"

"Chef it is."

"I think we've got enough history to bend the rules."

"Naw, Chef. I don't want special treatment."

"Even though you're already getting it. Which, by the way, won't go unnoticed. I try not to hire assholes, but there still might be some bruised egos over you skipping the line to sous chef. So work hard, listen, be humble, be cool. Okay?"

"Yes, Chef."

"One sec." Luann goes to her office and returns with two canvas bundles. She unrolls them on a stainless-steel table. "Japanese knives. The best money can buy. You know how you wouldn't go onstage with anything but the best gear?"

"I didn't always go onstage with my best everything, but I get your point."

"Anyway, you can use my backup set. First, we sharpen. Using knives you haven't sharpened is like going into the recording booth with an untuned guitar."

"You don't have to liken everything to music," Colton says gently. "I'll get it."

"Sorry, I'm nervous."

"*You're* nervous?"

"Colton." Luann sets down the knife she'd started to hone with practiced, swift strokes.

"Yes, Chef?" Colton watches her hands. The skin on them looks thinner now, and the bones are more pronounced, but otherwise they're the same hands he knew. Still beautiful. He always loved them.

"We both know why I'd be anxious."

"It was your idea."

"And I don't regret my decision."

"Good, Chef."

"Yet."

"If you fire me, Chef, it'll be the second quickest I've ever gotten fired. Not by much, but still."

"You're enjoying calling me that."

"I am, Chef. I can tell from your face you like it too."

"When I was coming up through kitchens, I always looked forward to the day it was me being called Chef."

Colton starts to sharpen a knife ineptly.

"Here." Luann takes it from him and demonstrates again.

Colton tries again and then hands the knife to Luann to inspect.

"Getting there," she says, testing the edge. "Takes practice."

"You even gonna ask about the quickest I ever got fired?"

"Thought it might be a sensitive topic."

Colton picks up the next knife. "I'd been in Nashville a few years. Doing odd jobs here and there. One of my buddies comes to me, says he has a gig doing a bachelorette party. Wants to know if I want to do it with him. I've never played one, but money's decent, so I'm like, 'Sure.' I show up, guitar case in hand. I'm ready to cover 'Your Body Is a Wonderland,' all that. Then my buddy arrives, with a boombox, wearing this weird cheap cop uniform, all tight-fitting polyester. Looking like a damn Village Person."

Luann gasps, giggles, and covers her mouth. *"No."*

"He's like, 'Okay, cool, so you're doing country singer.' I'm like, 'Dude, of course I'm doing country singer. That's what I am. What are *you* doing?' Turns out he'd sorta taken for granted that he'd told me. He had not."

"I assume this is the point at which you got fired."

"Close. There was a little more dickering. I said, 'Dude, I'll play this thing. I will not take my pants off.' And he's like, 'I ain't standing there in a thong with a badge pinned on it and a police hat and aviators while you cover "Any Man of Mine" fully clothed. Strip or get out.'"

"*Strip or get out* is quite an ultimatum."

"Presents a real opportunity to decide what sort of man you are."

"And you chose get out."

"Thing is, I actually thought about it for a hot second. I was struggling to make rent and eat at that point." Colton almost smiles at the irony of saying "at that point," as though he's much better off now.

"Dignity wouldn't allow it?"

"If only. Had a hole in my boxers. Otherwise—"

Luann facepalms and laughs. "Bless your heart. Well. There'll be times working here you'll wish you'd gone the Chippendales route. Okay, all sharpened up? Now it's time to start in on our mise."

"Meez?"

"Sorry, kitchen lingo, short for mise en place. It's a French phrase used in cooking. It basically means prepping and organizing all the ingredients you'll need to execute your menu so you're not searching around frantically while you're in the middle of a rush. Every time you prep, there'll be some constants in your mise, some things that'll change based on the day's menu. Let's start with julienning carrots, cucumbers, and daikon so we can get them pickling for the bánh mì."

"Yes, Chef."

"You know what bánh mì is, right?"

"There was this little Vietnamese grocery in South Nashville where we used to get bánh mì."

"*We* meaning you and Maisy?"

"That's right," Colton says awkwardly.

Luann averts her eyes. "Hope mine measures up. Um. Okay. So. Let's teach you some knife skills." She demonstrates the julienne cut. "We're looking for uniformity of length and thickness. Every detail matters. People notice things that not even they realize they notice. You try now."

"Okay..."

Luann gently corrects his technique. "Those are a little on the long side."

Colton tries again. "Like this?"

Luann juliennes a carrot with lightning speed. "Like so."

"You're a machine."

"Hundreds of thousands of cuts. I once asked one of the chefs I trained under how I could get cuts that look like his and he said, 'Millions of cuts over twenty years.'"

Colton tries a few more cuts and feels a sharp sting in his fingertip. He sucks in his breath with a quick hiss and lifts his hand to inspect.

"You get yourself?"

He sees no blood welling at the spot. "Saved by what's left of the guitar callus."

"You losing them?"

"Yeah. I mean yes, Chef."

"No music at all?"

"Only occasionally."

"That makes me sad."

Colton sighs. "Yeah. Me too."

Luann holds up her hand and wiggles her fingers. "You'll get new calluses. Guess the only kinds of art worth doing make us tougher, huh?"

"Yep, Chef."

They keep cutting. Luann watches Colton like a mother teaching a toddler to walk. And like an unsteady child trying out new and untested legs, Colton has several more close calls. Luann shows him the white scars on her hands, the places where her craft signed its name on her skin.

Colton's mind keeps returning to a memory—a warm September day a little over twenty years prior, when he taught Luann how to properly hold a hammer and drive a nail.

Amid his bittersweet reminiscences, Luann teaches him the five tastes the tongue perceives—bitter, sweet, salty, sour, savory—and what they mean. She tells him about the messages that each send to the brain about what's being consumed. "Cooking is finding the balance between them," she says.

She teaches him how salt, acid, fat, and heat are used to transform ingredients to develop and bring the five tastes into their proper harmony. She's an excellent instructor—calm, quick to praise, able to explain things clearly, demanding and exacting without being oppressive or megalomaniacal. She reminds Colton of some of the music and recording professionals he'd worked with, the ones who wouldn't rest until every element of a song was perfect and who drew the best from their collaborators.

Luann hands Colton a sliver of raw, cantaloupe-hued butternut squash. "Taste this."

Colton eyes her quizzically. "You messing with me, Chef?"

"You're not in boot camp. You don't need to say 'Chef' after everything. And no, I'm serious. You need to know and understand your ingredients. Taste."

Colton tentatively puts the piece of squash in his mouth and starts chewing. "Mmmmmm." His eyes roll back. "Organic squash? More like *orgasmic* squash."

"All right, smart-ass. What are you tasting?"

"Some extremely uncooked squash."

"Do I need to start back in with the music metaphors?"

"No, Chef."

"Then tell me what you're tasting."

"It's, uh, crisp. Cool. The texture is kinda like a green apple or...no, more like a dry, fibrous cantaloupe."

"Okay, good."

"Wait. Can I get another piece?"

Luann hands him another slice, and he chews, brow wrinkled in thought. "Okay, no, it's more like a raw carrot in texture." Colton chews a second more. "Tastes kinda like raw carrot too."

"How so?"

"Sort of vegetable-ish sweetness? But smoother than a carrot somehow? Like it does taste sort of cantaloupe-y."

"What's it smell like?" Luann hands him the halved squash.

Colton sniffs it and hesitates. He draws it to his nose again and closes his eyes. "Halloween. Carving jack-o'-lanterns."

"Good. We want to know all facets of the food we prepare. Taste. Texture. Smell. The sense memories it evokes. Does it taste like it traveled a thousand miles in a Cisco semi or fifteen minutes in the back of a 1993 Ford F-150 from a farm owned by a guy named Hollis?"

"Fifteen minutes. Guy named Hollis. Randy Travis on the tape deck of his pickup."

Luann shaves off a thin piece and chews. "It tastes like here. Like home. Like something someone would work hard to grow so they could put their daughter through college. Like something someone's worried about and prayed for. Food has a narrative. We have to understand it so we can tell it."

"I'd have never thought to try uncooked butternut squash."

"Now what? How do you think you could use this ingredient?"

Colton ponders for a moment. "I guess you could use it in anything that would be good with raw carrots," he says tentatively.

"Such as?"

"Well. The bánh mì we're doing."

"You think?" Luann asks with a twinkle.

"Yeah. Julienne it up. Pop it in the pickle solution."

"And what would that add to the dish?"

"A little sweetness. Some tartness. Some crunch."

"Contrasting with?"

Colton considers the question, the flavors, seeking the vocabulary. "The soft fattiness and savoriness of the pork belly and the duck sausage."

"We'll make a chef of you yet. Speaking of pork belly, let's start glazing some." She reaches above them on a shelf and pulls down a bottle of Old Crow bourbon and hands it to Colton. "Okay, first things first, we're gonna need to—"

He doesn't hear what Luann says next. The bottle fits his hand like the lacquered walnut grip of a revolver. He freezes.

"Oh," Luann says. She gently removes the bottle from Colton's hand. "Sorry," she murmurs, looking away, flustered.

"No, it's—"

"I wasn't thinking about—I'll take care of the glaze."

"I want to learn my job."

"This officially isn't your job. I got it."

They keep working on the mise en place. Luann continues her tutelage, and Colton is grateful for it. It leaves no time to dwell. As they're on the cusp of lunch service and taking a quick breather, Colton says, "Tell me if this is a stupid idea." He'd been thinking it over, remembering fine meals he and Maisy had all over the country.

"Go 'head."

"What if you were to shave butternut squash really thin, like in strips, and then combine it with shaved coconut, which has kind of a similar texture and subtle sweetness."

"I'm listening."

"Then you do a salad out of it. Do maybe like a lime vinaigrette dressing."

"Peanut lime?"

"Yeah! Throw a little sriracha in there to give it some heat."

"We make our own chili sauce, but I like where you're going with this."

"You've got crunch with the coconut and squash, so maybe some soft sweetness with some raisins. Some of those golden raisins."

"Or some dried figs. Maybe some local honey in the vinaigrette to sweeten. How about a little salt and fat in there for flavor and so we don't get too healthy?"

"Bacon?"

Luann thinks on it for a second, mouthing bacon. "Mmm. No. That song's been played."

"Cheese? Goat cheese sprinkles?"

"How about turning up the funk and the salt with some gorgonzola crumbles? Sweet Meadow Farm supplies us a killer gorgonzola."

"There we go."

"I'd eat that salad. Tell you what: as soon as we can get our hands on some fresh coconut, it's going on the menu. And you're gonna make it."

"Yes, Chef." He beams.

Lunch, served from eleven thirty to two, is hectic. Dani mostly runs lunch service while Luann continues to ease Colton into the kitchen's rhythms. He burns his palm on a pan handle but otherwise acquits himself decently for a beginner. Everyone is patient with him.

The restaurant closes at two o'clock. Luann leaves to pick up her daughters from school, spend a couple of hours with them, and take them to their grandparents' before returning for dinner service. Dani assumes Colton's training in the interim. Together, they prep the mise en place for dinner service.

"Chef tell you about family meal?" Dani asks Colton as they start winding up their mise preparation.

"What's that?"

"Restaurant tradition and nice little perk of the job. Between lunch and dinner service, we make a meal just for staff. Everyone sits down as equals and eats together. Lotta times we use up leftovers. We go a lot simpler than our guest menus. We like to do quality, straightforward executions of familiar dishes with great ingredients. Rule is, everyone tries to bring in a family recipe or something they loved eating as a kid. Keeps us honest. Chef's big on us remembering our connection to food. She says in fine dining you can lose sight of that, and then food becomes an abstraction. More about you than the guest."

"Kinda like a guitarist who endlessly solos?"

"Exactly. Anyway, family meal is my favorite part of the job. There's something special about cooking for your coworkers who are there in the trenches with you, getting your back."

"So how'd you end up here?"

"I read the profile on Chef in *Garden & Gun* and connected with her philosophy of cooking. I was working at a restaurant in Louisville at the time. It had aspirations to be like here but wasn't willing to do what it takes. Too much corner-cutting. Cheap over fresh, bottled over scratch, that sort of thing."

"So you moved from Louisville to Venice just to work here? No family or any connection to the area?"

"Yep. Working for Chef was exactly what I'd hoped for."

"You're young. Don't you miss all the big city stuff? Friends?"

Dani shrugs. "I grew up in a small town. It was fine. Plus the goal was to work too hard to care. Learn as much as I could. I have a boyfriend back in Louisville. He's a chef too—we met at the restaurant where we both worked. Plan is to open our own restaurant together someday."

"It's nice when you and your significant other understand each other's work. I used to work in the same business as my ex-wife."

Dani chops okra to fry. "What business?" She doesn't sound like she's feigning ignorance out of some sense of politeness.

"Music."

"You're gonna sear that chicken on both sides for about three minutes. Eyeball it until it browns. Were y'all musicians?"

"This pan?"

"Next size up."

"We were both singer-songwriters."

"What's your ex's name?"

Colton stares into the heating pan as though awaiting a message from an oracle. "Maisy."

"Like Maisy Martin?"

"Like that."

"What's her last name?"

"Martin," Colton says quickly. "Okay, so before I pop in the chicken do I need to—"

Dani studies his face. "For real, though."

"For real. So do I—"

"Your ex's name is Maisy Martin exactly like the famous pop star Maisy Martin? Was she worried about getting sued or mix-ups?"

Colton clears his throat. "Not so much. So this chicken—"

"Season it with salt and black pepper…yeah, that's probably good. You can always add salt. Harder to take it away. And then…in the pan. Good. Now we're just gonna watch it. Turn down the flame a smidge. So did your ex use a stage name or—"

Colton sighs. No escape. "My ex is Maisy Martin."

Dani sets down her knife. "*The* Maisy Martin."

"Of popular music renown."

"You were married to Maisy Martin." Dani raises a skeptical eyebrow.

Even though mere moments ago, Colton wanted nothing more than for Dani to move on and continue thinking that he had been wedded to someone coincidentally named Maisy Martin, he's slightly offended by Dani's incredulity. He tightens his lips, nods, and nudges the chicken around the pan with tongs to prevent sticking.

"Like when she was starting out?"

"Like... until a few months ago."

Dani's eyes widen. "*Stop.* Are you *serious*? Dude, who *are* you? Like, I know you and Chef go way back, but..."

"Remember this summer when a country singer got himself in hot water when he ran off at the mouth onstage about gun control while playing an arena?" Colton can feel his face reddening.

"Sounds vaguely familiar, but I don't have time to follow the news."

"Well, assume that this last summer a country singer got himself into hot water when he ranted onstage about guns."

"Sounds like it would be poorly received."

"It was. That was me."

"Damn, dude." Dani chuckles to herself in disbelief. "I gotta google you."

"Naw, you don't."

"I'm teaching a country star how to make chicken and dumplings for family meal."

"*Star* would be very generous even during the best of times, and *former* would be a lot more accurate now."

"I can't guarantee chef-ing is gonna be as exciting as playing arenas full of screaming fans."

"Promise?"

Dani grins. "I still don't believe this. What's it like being married to Maisy Martin?"

"Had its ups and downs, and we'll leave it at that," Colton says. "Anyway, enough about me. You'd really wanna run a restaurant with your boyfriend? Y'all wouldn't be afraid of messing things up between you?"

"Naw. When you're running a restaurant, everything is on the line. No margin for error. You can't be in that business with anyone but someone you trust completely. And if you can't work alongside someone in the kitchen, you probably have no business being with them anyway." After a moment, she adds with a teasing lilt, "Chef must trust you a lot. Don't let her down."

Colton smiles apprehensively, nods, but doesn't respond.

Colton helps Dani prepare chicken and dumplings (Dani's grandmother's recipe), fried okra, turnip greens, and creamed corn (recipe from Reggie the dishwasher's mother). Dani allows Colton to assume a more hands-on role than at lunch, the stakes of family meal being somewhat lower, although, as Dani makes clear, it's no time for making bad food. Family meal is ready at around three thirty, and everyone sits down together to eat.

Colton ends up directly across from Bianca, his server from the other night. He experiences a brief flare of humiliation, but Bianca makes no big deal of it. He supposes that she went home the night she waited on him and googled him and imagines he sees on her face not contempt or pity but only the understanding that one does what one must to survive in the unsparing, unsentimental wilderness of free-market capitalism.

The food is delicious, which doesn't hurt. It's possibly the best chicken and dumplings Colton's ever had—his memory of Derrick's nana's notwithstanding. It's clear that Luann's talents extend to hiring. The staff's easy camaraderie reminds Colton both of his football days and playing with musicians who got each other. It feels good to be part of a team, part of the band again. And it feels good to feel good.

Luann returns at around four o'clock, and it's promptly back to business. They hold pre-service meeting. Three additional servers, including Bianca, have joined the two from lunch. Luann reviews the night's menu with the staff.

Pimento cheese with benne crackers...

Hearth cornbread...

Charcuterie board with local pickles, preserves, apples, cheese, and a country ham medley...

Sweet potato apple cider bisque with clove-cardamom cream...

Luann's family recipe biscuits with squash marmalade and persimmon jam...

Charred Grove Creek beef short ribs with black truffle purée, garlic smashed potatoes, and carrots braised and glazed in carrot juice...

Wilder Farm herb-roasted chicken with wild mushroom gravy, squash seed risotto, and mustard greens...

Kilt green salad with Broadbent's bacon vinaigrette and cornbread croutons...

Heirloom potato confit with Meyer lemon vinaigrette, and pickled green beans and asparagus...

Cinderella pumpkin bourbon chess pie...

Heirloom apple dumpling with cardamom ice cream...

Luann and Colton regroup to continue training and prepare the sampling plates to familiarize the waitstaff with the orders they're taking.

"Did Dani take good care of you?" Luann asks.

"Great care. It's pretty incredible that you're running the sort of place people like her seek out."

"Dani's a unicorn. Most up-and-coming chefs are not looking to grind out some time in Venice."

"I heard my name," Dani calls over from her station.

"I was bragging on what a good trainer you are," Colton calls back.

"He learns quick, like you said, Chef."

"How are Freja and Esme?" Colton asks.

Luann beams. "Aside from a minor hair-pulling incident on the way to Mimi and PopPop's that Freja tried to play off as an accident, they're good."

"Which parent do you think they take after more? You or—" Colton pretends not to remember Luann's ex's name. He makes a mental note to google him later.

"Henning? Depends. Freja gets mad like me. Kinda blows up, regrets it later, doesn't know how to apologize. Esme gets mad like Henning. Turns inward, shuts off, seethes quietly. They're both a lot more optimistic and affectionate than Henning. Who slivered this garlic, you or Dani?"

"That was me."

"I ask because if it was Dani, it's a little less perfect than she usually does. But if it was you, that's impressive."

"Thanks, Chef."

"Do you—" Luann hesitates as though reconsidering the question in real time. "Have any kids?"

A dull ache unfurls in his stomach. "Not—"

"Don't say 'Not that I know of.'"

"How'd you know what I was gonna say?"

"It may have been two decades, but I can still smell you about to drop a hacky joke. Like one of those dogs that can smell a seizure coming on in someone."

"No kids. But speaking of dogs, a rescue named Petey. Or Petey Pie. Or Petey Peanut Butter. Or Petey Peanut Butter Pie."

"Aw. A dog has to be a sweetie to warrant so many nicknames. When you leave tonight, grab him a nice fatty piece of pork belly as a treat."

"Your heart's in the right place, but you're not the one cleaning up the diarrhea."

"Fair enough."

"Your twins ever come by here?"

"Sure. Sometimes Mimi and PopPop bring them by for dessert. Their palates aren't quite refined enough to appreciate the dinner offerings. Even with dessert we only have about a forty percent hit rate."

"They're your kids; they'll come around. I'd love to meet them next time they're here."

"We can arrange that."

They work quickly to finish the tasting plates by five and bring them out to the waitstaff. Luann answers questions and explains the dishes, runs down the farms where the various components came from, and suggests wine pairings for the servers to recommend.

Then, like a wave breaking over them, dinner service begins. In the minutes leading up to the first customers walking in—a pair of patrician, professorial-looking gray couples on what looked to be a double date, followed by a Williamsburg-esque (Brooklyn, not Colonial) couple in their early thirties, abundantly pierced and tattooed—Colton feels the same anticipatory rush he used to feel first before games, then before shows. More customers trickle in as the dining room fills to happily chattering capacity.

Colton expected a chaotic, noisy environment in the kitchen during the dinner rush. But Luann runs a calm, orderly, efficient operation, even as the dinner rush crests around seven. Dani sticks around longer than usual to assist Marcus so Luann can keep training Colton. For a while, Luann entrusts Colton to work the garde manger by himself, assembling salads and cold appetizer plates. He screws up, sure, but most of his missteps are swiftly and easily remedied by his kitchen compatriots.

The night flies by. At 8:54, the last guests finish, pay, and leave, and the restaurant closes.

"I dunno if Chef told you, but you're good to sign out," Dani tells Colton at around nine thirty. "Great work today."

"Thanks for all your help. You know where Lu—Chef went?" he asks.

"Check by the alley door. She likes to hang there for a bit to catch her breath after we close."

Colton signs out, then exits through the alley door. Moonlight leaks into the alley from around the buildings. After the stifling heat and auditory and olfactory din of the kitchen, the autumn night is tranquil and tastes fresh and crisp—like chilled apple cider spiced with clove and orange zest. He breathes it in, and it's pore-closingly cool on his sweaty skin. Luann leans against the brick wall of the restaurant, staring up at the star-jeweled sky. She looks over at Colton.

"Hey, Chef," he says.

"Dani tell you you could sign out?"

"Yeah, and I did."

Luann props the sole of her right foot against the wall. "Then it's Luann. Don't call me Chef for free."

"What you doing out here?" Colton stands beside her and leans against the wall.

"Little personal ritual. When I first started waiting tables in New York, I'd go out back after a shift to smoke and think."

"You took up smoking?"

"Do I detect judgment?" She says it with a jesting air, like she doesn't much care if he is judging.

"I, of all people, have no place judging anyone for any sort of substance use. Or anything else."

Luann's manner turns serious. "Hey. About that. I'm really sorry about the bourbon thing earlier. That was thoughtless."

"Eh." Colton waves her off.

"No, I want you to know that I support your recovery. Anything you need."

Their eyes meet. "Well. Thanks," Colton says softly. "Maybe we could avoid scheduling me behind the bar."

Luann smiles. "Consider it done."

"So what led you to take up smoking? I remember both Mara and Tyler hanging out in the smoking section back in high school. But never you."

"I moved to New York City and felt lost and small and like a country bumpkin, so I had to armor myself with cool. If you ever tell my daughters I said this, I'll deny it, but smoking *does* make you look cool."

"Your secret dies with me."

"And...smoking made me feel good, and I was pretty heartbroken at that time." Luann doesn't add it pointedly—she's more matter-of-fact than anything—but it lands that way.

"Oh." Colton stares at the cracked asphalt, embarrassed.

"You develop any bad habits when you got to Nashville?"

"Besides country music?"

"Hyuck hyuck hyuck."

"I'll be here all week, folks! Try the veal! Ah, let me see: thinking up ways back into the graces of my girlfriend with whom I messed things up pretty royally is the first thing that springs to mind."

"And you think that was a bad thing?" Again, that tone of teasing with just enough acid to burn—no one can nail it like Luann.

"No. I was trying to recover from my joke earlier. Want me to go back to jokes?"

"I'm good."

"Plus, the high I was riding all day is wearing off and I'm not thinking straight." Colton unbuttons his chef jacket.

"Don't forget and leave with that, or you're responsible for washing it."

"I won't."

"Even I'll have my work cut out for me washing that one."

"Come on, I didn't do *so* bad."

"You'll end up wearing less of the food with practice, but you did great today."

"Did I?"

"You learn fast, just like I thought. It takes a special kind of man to be willing to take orders from his high school girlfriend."

"Luann, I would take orders *now* from *high school* you. You've never been anything but a genuine badass."

"There's been a lot of my life you didn't know me."

"Well. I wish it weren't so."

They're quiet for a while. The only sound is the muffled clanking of pots being washed in the restaurant behind them. A motorcycle accelerates a few streets over. A train in the distance. Luann shivers and rubs her arms.

Colton removes his chef jacket and drapes it gently around her shoulders. "Two birds with one stone. Now I won't forget to leave it with you."

"Won't you be cold?"

"I saved up heat from the kitchen."

"That how that works? You a cast iron skillet now?"

They listen for a few moments to the sounds of the night.

"It was cool seeing you do your thing today," Colton says. "You're one hell of a chef and teacher."

Luann looks happy. "I try to make the training experience more pleasant than my own, which, in fairness, is not hard."

"And you're a great manager. That crew in there loves you. I mean, you're knocking it out of the park."

She blushes, visible even in the low light. "Well."

"No, I'm serious," Colton says. "Look what you've built. I'm honored to be a part of it."

"It's too soon for a raise. You can stop kissing ass."

They laugh. "Am I keeping you from your kiddos?" Colton asks.

"They're asleep at their grandparents'. Whether I get home now or an hour from now makes no difference to them."

"Where do you live, by the way? It just occurred to me I don't know."

"Not far. Remember the Star Trek House on North Cedar?"

"You live in the Star Trek House?"

"Yep."

"I've always wondered what it looked like inside."

"A Richard Isenhour house right here in Venice."

"I could pretend I know what that means and let you think I'm cool, or I could continue the course of the day and admit I have no clue who that is. Richard…"

"Richard Isenhour. Midcentury architect from Lexington. One of my inspirations. And speaking of the course of the day, how you doing with all this?"

"I have a lot to learn. Obviously."

"You're entering a whole new artistic discipline. It's to be expected. Feeling good about learning?"

"It's funny, the last twelve hours or so have been some of the nicest I've spent in a long time. I got out of my own head. I spent time with cool people, learning how to make something for folks to enjoy. I feel pretty damn lucky."

"And that's with you feeling unsteady on your feet. Think what it'll be like when you're really comfortable."

"Can't wait."

"That mean I'll see you tomorrow?"

"Same time?"

"Same time."

"Count on it." Colton starts to say something else, but the alley door opens, cutting him off.

It's Grace, one of the servers. "Hey, sorry, am I interrupting?"

"All good," Colton says. "Just shooting the breeze with Chef."

Grace takes a deep breath and titters awkwardly. She holds a menu and a pen. "So. This is embarrassing, but. My aunt in Bowling Green is a huge country fan, and I mentioned we work together now and she kinda flipped out? Anyway, she asked if I'd get your autograph."

Colton grins. "Aw. Sure. What do you want me to sign? This menu?"

"Is that weird?"

"I've signed way weirder stuff."

Luann scoffs.

Colton turns to her. "Not what you're thinking. I'm nothing if not a gentleman."

Luann scoffs louder and more energetically.

"All right, now you're hurting my feelings." He turns back to Grace. "What's your aunt's name?"

"Faith."

Colton takes the pen and the menu. "I'm signing by the kilt green salad because I think I rocked those tonight. You agree, Chef?"

Luann nods. "You objectively rocked the kilt green salad prep tonight."

"Would you say I 'kilt' it?"

"I absolutely refuse to say that, on principle."

Colton props the menu on the wall, shakes the pen a couple times, and autographs with a flourish, as if he's signing a concert poster. "Here you go. Tell Aunt Faith thanks for listening and come visit us in a few months so I can show her my cooking skills too."

"I think... Aunt Faith might be interested in... other skills."

Colton blushes. "Ah. I don't know if, uh—"

Luann snorts. "You can tell Aunt Faith... well, never mind." Both Grace and Colton look to her with curiosity. She waves them off.

"Anyway," Grace says. "She's gonna freak. Thanks."

"Any time," Colton says. Grace returns inside.

"Colton Gentry," Luann says in a high-pitched, breathy, lovestruck voice, holding her hands over her heart and batting her eyelashes after Grace's been gone a few seconds.

"You only have yourself to blame. You know that, right?"

"I foisted music on you. I disavow all responsibility for Aunt Faith's libido."

This is an opportunity for Colton to ask her something he's long wondered—what she thought of his music. But he retreats. This has been a good day. *Why take the risk?*

As if a soothsayer, though, Luann asks, "You still know how to play 'Any Man of Mine'?"

"It'd be a bit rusty, but sure."

"You're playing it at the staff Christmas party."

"You allowed to boss me when I'm off the clock?"

"Okay, now you're back on the clock. You're playing it at the staff Christmas party."

"Yes, Chef."

CHAPTER 37

Colton drives past the Star Trek House—Luann's house now—on his way home. It's off his usual route, but he does it anyway. The house is dark, naturally, and he feels a pang knowing that Luann now occupies a house he'd seen and wondered about so many times growing up. He envisions her at the breakfast table with her two undoubtedly brilliant and precocious daughters eating some incredible delicacy she whipped up in minutes (maybe a Maisy room service favorite like brioche French toast with strawberries and powdered sugar. Maybe something like the crème brûléed oatmeal he'd had once at brunch in an unassuming café in Asheville, North Carolina). It seems blissful in his imagining. The pining deepens in him. He allows himself a single, evanescent moment of picturing a future for himself still worth looking forward to somehow.

He arrives home and his mother greets him at the door in her bathrobe. She smells like almonds and cherries and her face is shiny with moisturizer.

"You were gone longer than I expected," she says.

"Said it'd be a long day. Brought you some leftovers." Colton opens the refrigerator and puts a to-go container inside. He turns back to face his mom.

"Well, I know. That the way you want it?"

"Keeps me out of trouble. Not much time to be in my own head. I spent whole hours today feeling good, instead of just the few minutes after first waking up."

"You keep bringing home leftovers from that place, I better either learn some willpower or update my will. Was it awkward working under Luann?"

"Nah. She's a great teacher and boss. Everyone there loves her."

"That doesn't surprise me." She eyes him kindly. "Okay, honey, I'm turning in. I was nodding off through the news. Will you run the dishes?"

"Yep. Night, Mama." He kisses her on the cheek.

She turns back just before exiting the kitchen. "Guess now that you got a job you'll be looking for your own place?"

"You hustling me out?"

"Not hardly. Thought of you moving out makes me sad."

"We got a while yet. Lu told me I'd be spending my first few paychecks on fancy knives and cooking you practice meals."

"Those must be some *fancy* knives."

"Ain't much different from guitars. You need good ones."

"If you wanna pitch in with Thanksgiving this year, be my guest."

"Can't imagine a better way to practice."

After Colton's mom leaves, he hears Petey rouse himself from the warm spot near the heating vent in the living room where he likes to doze his days (and his nights) away. He hobbles into the kitchen, nails clicking on the linoleum, tags jingling. Colton kneels to pet him and kiss his muzzle.

"Brought you a treaty treat, Petey Pete," Colton murmurs into his musky neck. He stands and gets the Saran-wrapped nub of pork belly he brought home for Petey after all. He lets Petey nibble it from his fingers and basks in the warmth and adoration in Petey's large eyes.

Sometimes, on the grand cosmic scale, the certainty of joy must outweigh the mere possibility of catastrophe.

Just please aim for the linoleum, Petey.

Colton lies on his bed, letting the rigors of the day ebb from him. Naturally, he picks this moment to google his first love's ex-husband. *Oh cool, the first page is nothing but "This man is forever changing the way we view the spaces where we live and work," and "Meet the Danish architect who has created the greatest revolution in living spaces since humans left caves—and he's sexy too!" and "Can the mere sight of a building make you spontaneously climax? Architect Henning Madsen is on a mission to find out...and succeeding!" Oh, there he is giving a TED Talk.*

Colton does an image search. Madsen looks to be at least fifteen years older than Luann. "Dang pervert," Colton mutters. "Dirty old man. Ed Harris–lookin' sumbitch, huh, Petey?" He nudges Petey. Petey, snoring beside him, abstains from offering his view. Colton keeps scrolling. "Ed Harris–lookin' ass. But with more hair, I guess." A *lot* more hair. A sweeping mane of thick silver hair cascades off his head like a piece of architecture itself. He wears chic, square, black-framed glasses in several of the pictures. He's tall and jaguar-lean. In most photos, he's dressed in immaculately tailored clothes in elegant, severe dark tones. He looks as fun as having a pimple deep in one's ear canal.

Colton recoils with the intensity of the jealousy and resentment he feels for this man with the face of Ed Harris, the hair of Patrick Dempsey (after another seven years of dignified graying), and the workplace ethics of Bill Clinton. He's not sure exactly what inspires this ferocity in him. Maybe it's that Madsen is at the top of his profession while Colton is buried six feet below his and starting afresh. Perhaps because Madsen has two beautiful daughters while Colton has no children of his own and probably never will, and he's begun to acutely feel that loss of possibility.

Too worked up now to sleep, notwithstanding his fatigue, Colton navigates to YouTube and searches "cooking tips." He starts watching.

It dawns on Colton at approximately 3:37 a.m., when he rouses himself to pee and get a drink of water: Henning Madsen is, by all appearances, a complete rejection of who Colton is.

He spends another hour and a half spiraling before he can get back to sleep.

CHAPTER 38

November 2010
Stuttgart, Arkansas

Between them, they'd bagged eight ducks earlier in the day. But they'd spent the last couple of hours getting a buzz on, their shotguns propped against the crossbar of their blind as the gloaming darkened to the color of gunmetal and the wind picked up before an incoming cold front, carrying the decaying, earthy scent of marsh and reed.

"So the door opens and in walks…" Duane looked over at Colton.

"Well? You gonna keep me hanging?"

"Dolly."

"Parton?!"

"Naw man, Obama. Turns out he has a sister named Dolly Obama. Who knew? Yeah, Parton."

"Damn, son. Now I get why you wouldn't tell me until we were hanging out in person."

"I had to see your face," Duane said.

"Speaking of Dolly, you know I've been writing songs again?"

"No shit?"

"Tossing out a bunch but keeping some. If I get enough together for an album, you know what song I think I'm going to put on it?"

"The one we wrote together back when we lived in East Nasty? 'Cloggy Toilet Breakdown'?"

"I don't know that the world is quite ready for that masterpiece yet. Pearls before swine. Remember that song I played for you the night I moved in? 'Honeysuckle Summer'?"

"Dude, about damn time. I told you back then it should've gone on your first album."

"I think I've finally worked up the courage. Maisy's been bugging me to."

"I see how it is. Your new favorite blonde says jump."

"Hell, son, you'll always be my favorite blondie."

They laughed and sat in easy silence for a while, holding Colton's good news between them for warmth like a glowing ember.

"I wish we got to do this more," Colton said. "Our crazy schedules."

Duane reached over and clapped him on the shoulder. "Been too damn long, brother."

Colton offered his vintage sterling silver flask of Jim Beam to Duane. "Colder'n a well-digger's ass out here."

"I heard that." Duane accepted it, tipped it back, and sighed. He handed the flask back to Colton, who took a snort off it.

"What you doing for Thanksgiving?" Colton asked.

"I think Mandy and me are coming back here, hang with the kinfolk." He nodded at the bag of mallards and grinned. "Roast up some of these honkers, have us some Peking duck."

"You know how to make Peking duck?"

"I been getting into cooking lately. Trick is you go over the skin with a hair dryer. That's how you get it good and crispy."

"I'll be damned. I knew you were good with a hair dryer, but I never figured you for some fancy chef."

"It's fun, man. You should get into it. I know you love good food. How about you? What y'all doing for Turkey Day?"

"We're gonna go down to Dallas, spend it with Maisy's family."

"Man, things are really going good with y'all."

"Brother... can I tell you something?"

"Tell it."

"Maybe it's the liquid courage talking but I'm thinking of proposing."

Duane looked at Colton for a couple of seconds, his radiant smile breaking across his face. He whooped. "Right *on*. Right the hell *on*, brother!" He cackled and grabbed Colton in a hug and pounded his back.

Colton laughed. "We've broached the subject. I might pop the question around Christmas. Hell, maybe I'll do it at Thanksgiving when I can ask Maisy's dad for permission. If it happens, I'll need a best man. You available?"

"Abso*lute*ly, bud. I don't care if I gotta say no to Reba so I can be there."

Then, Colton said somberly, "I wish my dad could see all this. Being out here reminds me of him. We used to hunt together." The Jim Beam had loosened something in him, and he abruptly broke down weeping. "I miss him so much. Damn. Sorry." He wiped his eyes with the backs of his gloved hands.

Duane didn't hesitate. He yanked Colton in for another embrace. "Hey now. Hey, brother. Bring it in," Duane said quietly, ruffling his hair and kissing him on the top of the head. "All right now. Hey."

"But damn I'm a weepy-ass drunk. Been ten years he's gone."

"Grief ain't got a calendar, brother."

"I know that's right."

Duane chuckled to himself. "Remember that time your dad took us to that all-you-can-eat rib joint? I was full for a week. He was *delighted*. Kept going 'one more round' to the waitress."

"He slapped a twenty on the table and said here's your tip in advance." Colton laughed through his tears. "Said he knew he was getting his money's worth, taking a couple starving musicians... You know what I been thinking about a bunch lately?"

"What's that?"

"If Maisy and I get hitched, what it'd be like to have a couple kids together. I'd always just sorta assumed I'd be childless—you know how it is in our business. But last little while, it's been like a switch got flipped in my brain. If I was half the dad my pops was, I know I'd do him proud."

Duane looked at him and gripped his biceps. With the same steadfast confidence with which he pronounced, on a starry night in September 1996, that he and Colton would make it, he said, "Bud, you're gonna get every good thing in life your lil' heart desires. And I think you'll make a hell of a father. No, I *know* you will. Now let's pack it in. We got a bag full of honkers, your ass is out here crying, we've covered *all* the topics, and my nuts are about to freeze off."

CHAPTER 39

November 2015
Venice, Kentucky

COLTON MINCES GARLIC FOR HIS DINNER SERVICE MISE, HUMMING TO HIMSELF, lost in the meditative discipline of trying to achieve perfect cuts, when he hears Luann enter the restaurant, a couple of animated, high, chittering voices in tow. He sets down his knife with now-trembling hands and listens. *I'm about to meet Luann's daughters for the first time.* He's been bracing for this moment and still he feels unprepared. He draws a deep breath and exhales slowly, wipes his hands, and strolls out to the dining area on wobbly legs.

They sit at one of the tables, school backpacks on the ground beside them. They look older than in the pictures Colton's seen.

"...Maybe we can later, but for now you two need to do your math," Luann says.

"*Mom,*" they whine in unison.

"Really, guys? We have to go through this *every* time?"

Freja frowns, rests her cheek on her palm, and kicks her legs, bumping Esme's legs. "Can we have a treat?"

"*Ow*, Freja, *stop*," Esme says. "*Mom.*"

"Yes, but I want the bickering to stop. Okay?" Luann looks up to see Colton. She gives him an exasperated smile. "I'm so glad this is how you get to meet my girls for the first time," she mutters through clenched teeth. "Do we still have any of those honey-lavender crème brûlées?"

"Think we got a couple."

"I'm gonna run and grab those. Freja? Esme? This is Colton. He and I were friends in high school, and now he works here as a chef."

"I have heard *such* wonderful things about you two," Colton says, shaking first Esme's tiny hand, then Freja's. "Y'all mind if I sit?"

They shake their heads.

"Y'all doing some math or what?"

They nod.

"Shoot, I'm a math whiz. Ask me any math question."

The girls eye him skeptically.

"What's two plus two?" Freja asks finally.

Colton sucks a tooth, slaps the table, and leans back casually. "Five. Next question."

Freja and Esme look at each other and giggle. "It's *four*," Esme says.

"Pretty sure it's five. Next." Colton makes a *c'mon, gimme* gesture with his fingers.

"What's one million plus one million?" Esme asks.

"Ten billion." He raises his index finger to an invisible waiter. *"Um... check please."*

The girls again giggle raucously. "You are *not* good at math," Freja says. "You've gotten zero right."

"Oh yeah? What do *you* think one million plus one million is?"

"Two million," Freja says.

"Yeah, I don't think that's right."

"It is. Get out your phone and use the calculator."

"Nope. Show me on your fingers."

"I don't have that many fingers!"

"Fingers and toes, then."

"I don't have that many fingers and toes! No one does!"

Colton laughs. Seeing these feisty little girls feels like what it must have been to know Luann as a child. It sets his heart aglow.

Luann returns with the two crème brûlées and sets them in front of the girls.

"We were just having a little challenge where the girls ask me any math question and I answer correctly."

"He didn't get *any* right," Esme says.

"Oh, now *that's* shocking," Luann says. "Anyway, I gotta get back in the kitchen. And so does Mr. Colton," she says with an arched eyebrow.

"Yes, Chef. Be right along."

Luann leaves. The girls crack the caramelized lavender-infused crust on top of their crème brûlées, and each takes a bite. Their noses wrinkle as though they'd broken through the sugar to find a bowl full of toenail clippings and baby spiders.

"It tastes weird," Freja says.

"It's gross," Esme says. "Mom makes weird fancy food a lot."

"Your mama makes some of the best food I've ever had in my life, but I think maybe you gotta grow into it."

The girls push away their ramekins and look glum.

Colton feels an irresistible urge to reverse the downcast expressions on their faces. "Gimme a few minutes. We'll make this right." He hurries back to the kitchen.

"Could use a hand back here, Colt," Dani calls.

"I know, I know, be right there." He quickly rounds up a couple of bananas, vanilla-bean ice cream, whipped cream, some duck fat caramel, and a jar of maraschino cherries, cobbling together a couple of banana splits. His presentation leaves something to be desired by the time he haphazardly drizzles on some caramel and dusts each with a little sea salt, but he suspects the girls won't mind.

He bustles back out to the dining area and sets the bowls in front of them with a flourish. "Two banana splits."

"What's that?" Esme asks.

Colton looks at them, agog. "You've *never* had a banana split?"

They shrug and shake their heads.

"Well. You're in for a treat. Try it."

They hesitate.

"I'm better at making these than I am at math," Colton says. "That what you want to hear?"

They smile and dig in reluctantly. The first spoonful hits their lips and their eyes brighten.

"Yeah?" Colton asks.

They nod vigorously and fall upon their dishes like starving jackals, spoons clinking. A Pollockesque splatter of ice cream and caramel soon adorns their mouths. Colton watches their ecstatic faces, glowing inwardly.

"This is really yummy," Freja murmurs.

"Y'all are a great crowd." Colton stands and picks up the crème brûlée ramekins. "All right. I best get back to work before y'all's mama fusses at me. Enjoy." He leans in. "Nice meeting you, Freja and Esme."

Colton reenters the kitchen with the crème brûlée ramekins.

Luann looks up from her sauté pan. "What'd the girls think?"

"Hmmm. You know...kids are—"

"They didn't like?"

"It was maybe a little adult for them. I made them a couple of banana splits instead."

Luann turns to face him. "Colton."

"Yes, Chef."

"I'm trying to train my daughters' palates."

"I know, Chef."

"So if you go undermining me?"

"Sorry, Chef. Just it's hard to do math without a treat."

Luann points her spatula at the ramekins in Colton's hands. "We're not throwing those out. You're finishing them both." Her mouth turns up at the corners ever so slightly.

"I'll take my punishment like a man, Chef." Colton swallows a bite. He feigns gagging.

"Don't."

He starts wolfing the crème brûlée.

"Faster. Work's been piling up while you've been busy undoing my parenting."

"I'm sorry for undermining you." He gives her the smile that always used to get him out of trouble in high school.

Luann rolls her eyes. "No you're not." She gives the contents of her pan a quick stir and turns down the heat.

"How do you know?"

"Because I know that self-satisfied grin well. So did they like the banana splits?"

"Very much."

Luann's face softens. Not quite to the point of smiling, but close. Colton can tell she's avoiding eye contact lest he drag it out of her.

Colton finishes eating and takes the empty ramekins over to Reggie's sink. He returns to his station and resumes his prep. "You got some amazing little girls, Luann. Well done," he says after a while.

"They're a pain in my ass sometimes, but they're damn cute pains in my ass."

"They sure are."

As the hours pass and the tempo hastens for dinner service, Colton tries to immerse himself in his work and his memory of the jubilant expressions he wrote on Freja's and Esme's faces. He does this to forget the aching void that opened in him from watching Luann mother her daughters and briefly feeling like they were parenting together. A sensation somehow more in the bloodline of grief than anything else, and he would surely know.

CHAPTER 40

Colton unfurls his brand-new knife roll with a theatrical, magicianlike flourish. "Voilà. Korin knives, Chef, just like you said to get." He pulls one out and holds it, gleaming, to the light, like he's pulled Excalibur from the stone. "Pure Japanese steel. Split atoms with these." He slashes a couple of times in the air.

Luann and Dani *ooh* and *aah*.

"Fresh from the dishwasher," Colton adds.

Their expressions wilt immediately, and they look at him, aghast, as though each was silently waiting for the other to say what must be said.

Colton waits until the split second before one of them is about to speak. "Kidding!"

They breathe a collective sigh of relief.

"What kind of monster do you think I am?" Colton asks.

"One who would even joke about tossing Korin knives in a dishwasher," Luann says.

"I paid more for that set of knives than for my first pickup; you think I'm not gonna study up?"

"You? Who knows. Let's get them sharpened," Luann says.

"Done before I came. I arrived ready to work, Chef."

They set to work prepping their mise. "So how was your Thanksgiving?"

Colton asks. Luann closed the restaurant on Thanksgiving Day so her staff could spend the day with their families.

"Pretty low-key. My aunt and uncle and their kids came in from North Carolina. We had it at my parents' house. You get three guesses who cooked, and the first two don't count."

"Your parents still live in the Highlands?"

"Remember that property they owned on the bluff?"

"You asking me if I've forgotten about that place?" Colton says with a half-smile.

"I mean." Luann sounds flustered.

"Because the answer is no, Chef."

Luann blushes and turns her gaze toward her hands. "Anyway, they live there now. In a house I designed, actually."

Colton sets down his knife and faces her. "That's amazing."

"Still the design I'm proudest of."

"I always dreamt of buying my mom a nicer house. But, you know. Dreams don't always..." Colton trails off.

"Let's chop those shallots just a smidge finer. Well, your life isn't over yet."

"Yeah. We'll see."

"How about your Thanksgiving?" Luann asks. "Nice cuts on that celery, by the way."

"Practicing, like you said. Been watching YouTube videos. But Thanksgiving. Yeah, it was great. Charity and her husband and kids came in. We had it at my mom's house."

"You cook?"

"Of course. I did a broccoli-kale slaw and garlic smashed potatoes and fried the turkey. You inspired me to add a little goat cheese to the potatoes."

"Yeah? And?"

"It was delicious. Some fatty tang to wake them up, add some creaminess."

"Look at you, talking and thinking like a chef!"

"Then after dinner with my fam, I went over and had dessert with Derrick and Gabrielle. Took some pumpkin chess pie bars I made."

"Derrick..."

"Giles. From high school."

"I was gonna say."

"Yeah, he's living here now. Oh, and his wife, Gabi, is a doctor at the med center. She knows your dad."

"Small world."

"Can we not just skip over the fact that I made pumpkin chess pie bars?"

"*Forgive me.* Talk about them."

"Well, I thought the recipe looked a little plain vanilla, so—"

"Hang on. We don't use *vanilla* as a pejorative in my kitchen. Vanilla is a subtle, beautiful, and versatile spice and deserves respect."

"Sorry, Chef."

"Continue."

"Anyway—"

"Hey, did we get the cucumbers and mushrooms in the pickling solution?"

"Yes. Anyway, I thought the recipe looked a little *boring*, just sweetness and more sweetness, so I added some fresh ginger to give it some brightness and zing."

"Love it."

"Pinch of orange zest."

"Love."

"But that's not all. And a dash—just a dash—of black pepper. For a little heat."

"Colton! That sounds great! How'd they turn out?"

"Pretty amazing." Colton can't hide his smile.

They continue dicing, slicing, chopping, deglazing, sautéing, reducing, poaching for a while without saying anything other than Luann making subtle corrections to Colton's technique.

"Speaking of Derrick earlier, what about Tyler and Mara?" Colton asks. "They stick around here?"

"Remember in cartoons how a character would start to run, and their legs would turn and then they'd zip off so fast they left an outline hanging in midair? Pretty much that was both after graduation."

"Figured. Where they at now?"

"Mara's in Black Mountain, North Carolina, teaching art at Warren Wilson College. Tyler's in LA; he works as a producer on *The Ellen DeGeneres Show*."

"Was he there in 2014?"

"Yep."

"Maisy went on the show in 2014."

"Did you go with her?"

"Nah. Maisy flew solo for stuff like that." *Or at least I thought she was solo . . . maybe not.*

"We open soon," Luann says quietly. "We better step on it some."

Lunch service runs smoothly, thanks to the fine-tuned machinery of the kitchen crew. Colton, starting to feel the first inklings of competence behind the spatula, is beginning to relish the rush that working with his team under pressure offers. It gives the same dose of serotonin that taking the football field once did.

Later, as he's helping Luann prepare the tasting plates for the pre-dinner-service meeting (sliders of hickory-wood-fired Oak Creek brisket with house-made hot sauce and honey butter biscuits; Rolling Fork Farms Berkshire pork chop with apple hoisin and smoked beets; cedar-wrapped rainbow carrots with rosemary; candied butternut squash with mascarpone bouffant; roasted Green Door parsnip and Barefoot Farms sweet potato bisque), she says, mostly to herself, "How have I not asked you yet?"

"Asked me what?"

"Your best food memory."

"Gotta think for a second." Colton runs through his memory. Ironically, many of his finest food memories are now his worst ones, given that they involved things like midnight room service Wagyu ribeyes with lobster and lavish country music award banquets with Maisy. But he comes up with something—really his second-favorite food memory. Luann won't know.

"Remember my buddy Duane, who I mentioned when we had coffee that first time?"

"I do," Luann says quietly.

Colton tries to continue but he can't. Trying to talk with Luann about Duane is loss upon loss, sharpening and intensifying his bereavement, like sunlight through a magnifying glass. He stands motionless and tries to maintain his keel. Grief is an arsonist, stealing in under cover of dark to reduce you to ashes. You can expect it or not. But you can't prepare for it, and there's no defense. *Well, one maybe: self-immolate first.*

Lacking words, Colton turns back to his cutting board. He clears his throat a couple of times to try to banish the remaining waver from his voice before continuing. "You'd have loved Duane. He had this easy way about him. He was like... Owen Wilson mixed with a golden retriever. Hell of a guitar player. He was obsessed with Nashville hot chicken. He turned me on to Prince's and Bolton's when we first moved to town.

"So, anyway. Duane and I—this would have been in 2013, couple of years after Maisy and I got married—stars aligned and he and I are both in Nashville for a night. This is rare, because I'm always on the road with Maisy or splitting time between Dallas and Nashville, and he's constantly on tour. Anyway, we meet up; it's one of those gorgeous April nights. We get hot chicken on the bone and white bread and slaw and mac and cheese and take it up to this rooftop bar in downtown Nashville that overlooks Broadway.

"So, we're eating this hot chicken and our noses are running from the spice and we're washing it down with ice-cold beer, and we're talking and cutting up and watching the people mill around down on Broadway. We see this dude go down on one knee to propose and we jump up and we're hollering off the roof, *Say yes! Say yes!* Music's coming out of all the honkytonks. Everything was perfect—the food, the company, the night, everything. We just felt young and alive and like there was so much hope for both of us. We both had good things going in music and love. Life hadn't landed any punches on either of us, you know?"

Luann smiles wistfully. "You made it all the way to 2013?"

"Well, no knockout punches, I guess." Colton falls silent, remembering how he and Duane sat surveying the nightscape, the neon and music radiating from it like summer heat off asphalt.

Here we are, Duane had murmured. *From that sorry backyard in East Nashville to here, all these years later. You believe it?*

We made it, Colton had agreed quietly. *Just like you called it.*

To country music and lucky sons of bitches. Duane raised his bottle to Colton in toast.

Colton clinked his bottle with Duane's. *Country music and lucky sons of bitches.* He had gazed into the expanse of lights. He chose one for himself and one for Duane; lights that would burn steady and bright and wouldn't die.

Then, as if Colton's life is being written by the laziest writer in existence, the opening strains of the new Maisy Martin collab with Justin Bieber and Diplo begin playing on the battered radio over Reggie's dishwashing station, shocking him back to the present. Both Colton and Luann hear it. He hangs his head and laughs. It's all he can do.

"Is that—" Luann points toward Reggie's station.

"Yeah."

"You gotta be kidding."

"Speaking of knockout punches."

"You can ask Reg to change the station. I doubt he's a big Maisy Martin fan."

"He won't mind?"

"Reg minds very little. It's why he's so good at his job."

"Hey, Big Reg," Colton calls over.

"What up, Colt?" Reggie calls back.

"That's my ex on the radio. Can we change it?"

Reg shakes his hands off. "Still can't believe you was married to her. Long as we ain't got to listen to no country. I ain't trying to do that."

"Naw, man, me neither," Colton says. "Believe that."

Reggie fiddles with the dial and lands on a classic rock station. "I can get down with some AC/DC; how 'bout you?"

"Yessir, that'll work nicely."

"That a nightmare? Having your ex pop up randomly like that?" Luann asks.

"No, Chef, it's fun."

"I appreciate you respectfully addressing me as 'Chef' while sass-mouthing me."

"It's a nightmare for sure. I guess you find less occasion to be randomly confronted with your ex here."

"Yeah, not as much."

"So, Chef? You gonna tell me your favorite food memory? You must have a ready answer from interviews and such."

"I do. We used to have Sunday dinners at my grandma's house in Lexington before we moved to Venice."

"Was this the grandma I met at high school graduation?"

"Yep. My dad's mom."

"I remember her. Sweet lady."

"The sweetest. On the last Sunday before my family moved, my grandma cooked us this huge meal. Fried chicken, squash casserole, stewed turnip greens with fatback, corn pudding, creamy grape salad, country ham biscuits, big pitchers of sweet tea. Chess pie and banana pudding for dessert. Her greatest hits. Sent leftovers home with us. Everything tasted so good. She probably didn't do anything differently from normal—I think she always put her best foot forward for us—but it felt like this gloriously comforting final meal. I was bereft to be leaving Lexington, which already felt too small, for this tiny town in BFE Western Kentucky, four hours away. Felt like my life was ending. I'd been crying all that day. After dinner we went out on the porch and sat in rocking chairs and she said, *Everything's going to work out, Lulu. You'll make new friends, wait and see.*"

"That's a good one, Chef. I felt that."

"I don't go into quite as much emotional detail in interviews as I did just then."

"Have you gotten to cook for her?"

"No, she passed in 1996. Cancer."

"Whoa, ninety-six?"

Luann looks down and says quietly, "That was not . . . shall we say . . . the best of years for me."

Colton squirms, guilt wringing him. "I know she'd be proud. I wish you'd gotten to cook for her, though." *Among other wishes I have.*

Luann smiles, faint and sad. "Would've been nice." She clears her throat. "Okay, now we need to start the . . ."

Colton listens with half of his brain, and with the other, entertains a thought. He has no right—especially since he offered his own second-favorite food memory in its stead—but he wishes Luann's favorite food memory had been the same as his: a teenage jacket-weather night in October, driving too fast under the brilliant harvest moon, tawny and dried cornfields and flaxen hay bales lining the backroads, sharing a grease-Rorschached paper bag of Bucky's cheeseburgers and fried pickles between them, their hands sometimes touching accidentally (or not) as they went for a pickle spear, talking about nothing, laughing about everything, both falling in love for the first time, the world their very own gleaming orb of infinite possibility.

CHAPTER 41

They're slammed that night, as always on Friday, but there's a lull between waves.

"Colton, come here." Luann motions for him to follow her. They leave the kitchen and step into the dining area.

"What's up, Chef?"

"Take a sec. Look."

Colton surveys the room, filled with happy chatter, clinking cutlery, and beaming diners. "What am I looking for?"

"I remember you saying how one of the things you loved about playing football was the roar of the crowd. I assume it was what you loved about music. Behold the roar of your crowd."

Colton scans from table to table. At one, a table of ten with what appears to be three generations of a family, an elderly woman sits at the head of the table. She's wearing obviously her finest clothes. Her expression says that she feels celebrated. "Birthday," Colton murmurs with a slight nod. "Big one too, by the look of it."

"Mmm-hmm. My money's on ninety. I'm thinking first date over there." Luann nods toward a table where two men blush and converse with jittery, excited energy, stepping on each other's words, gesturing for the other to speak.

"I don't much miss that," Colton says. "Done with first dates."

"Taking a vow of celibacy?"

"Just a vow of no more first dates. From now on I only do third dates at the earliest."

"Wonder why more people haven't thought of that." Her smile fades. She nods.

"Not a first date there." A young man and a young, emaciated woman sit. They're dressed to the nines. She wears a motley silk scarf over a bald head. Her skin is tight across her cheekbones, and her eyes sit deep in their sockets. Her complexion is pallid and tinged at the edges with pistachio green. She and the man look deeply into each other's eyes while she pushes food, largely untouched, around her plate.

"Anniversary?" Colton says somberly.

"I'd guess." Luann pauses for a beat before she speaks again. "Look at everyone. Eating food you prepared. Letting it sustain them and strengthen them. Trading their money for memories. Celebrating their love and companionship. Your skill and craft bring honor to these moments. How's it feel to see this?"

Colton abruptly finds himself in the clutch of an emotion he can't name—maybe there's some untranslatable foreign word that captures it. An amalgam of joy, triumph, deep sadness, purpose. Pride. Dignity. Gratitude. Whatever it is, it silences him with a tautness in his throat. He finally clears it. "Feels real good, Chef," he manages while he can.

"One of the chefs I apprenticed with did this with me when he finally thought I'd believe what he was telling me." Luann starts back toward the kitchen. Colton goes to follow, but Luann stops him.

"I've never quite bought it when you said it was about the roar of the crowd for you. I think it was really about bringing people joy. Stay out here for a minute or two among those you've made happy. Soak it in. Make sure you do this occasionally." She looks back over her shoulder and adds, "During lulls."

Luann is right. The roar of the crowd only meant he was making people happy. Colton's been self-conscious about being seen in his chef's jacket—as though it were emblematic of his failure. But tonight, as he looks over the assemblage of exultant diners, he feels like he's wearing a uniform festooned with medals.

It's not the same as looking out over a darkened congregation of people lit only by the spectral pale glow of screens, swaying to his music, mouthing lyrics, but it feels good nonetheless.

While he surveys the crowd, a stone-faced man at a corner table subtly raises his phone toward Colton, undoubtedly snapping a picture or video. It's not the first time he's seen someone taking a furtive shot.

He's still a touch self-conscious about being seen in uniform and takes this as his cue to get back to work. He reenters the commotion of the kitchen to meet the next rush, pushing away any thought of how his former fans would receive such a photo.

Colton wipes sweat from his brow, takes a deep breath, and steps out into the alleyway. It's cold in a way that feels festive. "It was touch and go for a while there," he says to Luann.

"Get in the weeds?"

"I thought Taylor was gonna have my ass."

"He's harmless." Luann drums her fingers on her lips.

"I'm gonna buy you some candy cigarettes," Colton says.

"They still sell those?"

"They shouldn't, but if they do anywhere, it's in the great commonwealth of Kentucky."

"Maybe we should figure out how to incorporate candy cigarettes in a dessert. I remember them being pretty good."

"I bet you remember wrong."

"Not taking that bet."

A car passes on the street intersecting the alley, the strains of Mariah Carey's "All I Want for Christmas Is You" blaring and fading.

"So I ran across a picture of Henning Madsen the other day," Colton says nonchalantly.

Luann turns to face him and regards him with the most profoundly skeptical look he's maybe ever seen, and he's inspired his fair share over his life. "You *ran across* a picture of my ex-husband."

Still nonchalant, but faltering: "Yeah, I don't remember exactly what I was searching, but—"

"Were you searching 'most important Danish architects of the 2000s' perchance? That topic that so famously captivates you?"

"I think I might have been looking up who did the design for the new Tractor Supply store."

"The one on Rutherford Parkway?"

"Yep."

"The one that looks like, you know, a *big box*, hence the phrase *big box store*?"

"That where that phrase comes from? I thought it was because they have big boxes of stuff inside."

"So you google 'new Tractor Supply store Venice Kentucky,' and up comes a photo of Henning Madsen?"

"Weirdest thing."

"So odd as to be virtually implausible, in fact, thus pointing to the far greater likelihood that you googled my ex-husband specifically."

"Can't blame me for being curious."

"Look. If I'm being honest, I'd have googled your ex if she weren't already, you know, ubiquitous."

"Don't you love that I understand words like *ubiquitous* now?"

"Oh please. At no time have I ever felt like I needed to dumb down my speech for you."

"There *were* a lot of times when I only pretended to know the meaning of a word you said."

"You hid it well." Luann leans back against the wall of the restaurant, crossing her ankles. "So. I told you all about Henning. Tell me how you met and married one of America's biggest pop stars. I admit to some curiosity."

Colton points up to a patch of exposed starlit sky between low, pale orange clouds. "See that constellation there?"

Luann squints.

"Right up there, between the rooftops."

"There?" She points.

"Yep. That's called Archeron, the Greek word for *archer*. You can kinda see his bow there."

"Okay, that sounds not even remotely true."

Colton shrugs and grins and keeps staring at the evening sky.

"Wait," Luann says. "It's not true, is it?"

"I had you going."

"You done avoiding the question?"

"What was the question again?"

Luann scoffs and rolls her eyes.

"Okay, okay," Colton says. "Uh, Maisy. I guess this would've been 2009 or so. My career was in the toilet, and my management invited me to this awful party in some equally awful mansion in Belle Meade in Nashville. Guess they hoped I'd talk to the right person, and I was about five minutes from leaving when I did. I ran into Maisy at the food table. At that point, she was pure country still. She was a couple years off finishing second on *American Idol*. Star on the rise. Just moved to town and bought a condo on the twenty-second floor of the Viridian in downtown Nashville. I thought she was attractive and— What's that look?"

"I'm not giving a look."

"Hell you aren't. There was a look."

"No, just... how utterly intriguing. Finding Maisy Martin hot."

"Listen, I never tried to wear it as some badge of uniqueness." He wants to tell her that what really drew him to Maisy, far more than her looks (which was why he said "attractive," which has multiple meanings), was her magnetic verve, the sense that there was nothing in this universe she couldn't draw inexorably into her orbit, so why fight it, and this reminded him of the first girl he'd ever fallen in love with.

"You had more interesting taste in high school," Luann says, as though clairvoyant. Then she quickly adds, "*Sometimes* you did, anyway. So, you ran into Nashville's own Jess McElroy at the buffet table."

Colton chuckles. "Jess McElroy. Forgot about her."

Luann sighs and looks off into the dark, down the alley. "Not me."

"Anyway, I figured I had nothing to lose, and I went for it, chatted Maisy up. We talked about how sorry the food was at the party and how hungry we both were. She suggested we leave and go find some real food. I drove us down to Puckett's Grocery in Leiper's Fork. We got fried catfish and slaw and corncakes. Ate it on the patio. Maisy's in heaven. Nashville is the smallest town she's ever lived in, and she loves seeing the stuff she makes millions to sing about. Some folks were passing around a guitar and we each took a turn. I did 'I Still Love Someone' by Johnny Cash."

"And she did..."

"'Dreams' by Fleetwood Mac."

"I was hoping she had worse taste," Luann mutters. "That didn't make your best food memory?"

Colton scratches his cheek. "Naw. That one's taken a real dive in the ranking."

"Was it formerly your number one?"

Colton looks Luann dead in the eyes. "It was never number one." This is as close as he can bring himself. He imagines he sees the faintest light of understanding, and maybe even hope, dawn on Luann's face.

"So. Fried catfish leads to, what, married barefoot on the beach in Charleston?"

"Close. Cumberland Island in Georgia. Couple years later."

"Oh, right. But I nailed the barefoot on the beach part."

"Lucky guess?"

"Not really...I'd used you for a game of Two Truths and a Lie at a dinner party in Manhattan. One of my fellow partygoers read about your and Maisy's wedding in *Us Weekly* and showed me the article."

"Was I the lie or the truth?"

"My two truths and a lie were 'Ray Liotta once asked me for my number when I was waiting tables,' 'I've been bitten by a shark while scuba diving,' and 'I dated country star Colton Gentry in high school.'"

"Wait, were you—"

"Never been scuba diving. But Ray took quite a shine to me."

"Not surprising. Did your friends know who I was?"

"Not really. But your name felt real enough. Most people guessed Liotta was the lie. Anyway, good times seeing my first love marry a pop star on a beach while my own marriage was curdling." Luann sighs and her breath rises silver in the dim light.

"Well, we know how that turned out. You feel like telling me how you and Mr. Madsen got together?"

"You can probably figure it out."

Colton rubs his chin in mock contemplation. "Dance club. Lower Manhattan. Eighties night. Henning Madsen is there in tight red leather pants and a black mesh tank top. He's absolutely *working it* to Depeche Mode. It's mesmerizing."

Luann bark-laughs and covers her mouth with her hand. "Oh so close. Try 'grueling, grinding hours working on a design for an art museum in Barcelona.' He did once surprise me by flying us to Chicago to see Depeche Mode, though."

Colton shakes his head and mutters, "I knew it. So, what, he start hitting on you? Skeevy boss?"

"I thought he was so sexy. This suave, accomplished, handsome older man," Luann says with mock breathiness.

Colton shakes his head. "Dude looks like Ed Harris."

"And?"

"If you're into grandpas, I guess he'd be on the handsome end of the spectrum for grandpas."

"I thought he resembled Viggo Mortensen. That was the comparison he always got."

She's right. But honor demands that Colton resist. "*Aragorn?* You think that dude looks like *Aragorn*?" He tries to say it with a teasing lightness that obscures his jealousy. He cannot imagine he's fooling anyone, much less Luann.

Blessedly, she says, "We've officially reached my limit for talking about Henning for any single twenty-four-hour period. And I have a restaurant to finish closing."

"Is it supposed to snow tonight? It smells like snow."

"What I heard is starting around three or four in the morning."

"We need to put a dish on the menu that involves bread and milk for all the people who didn't stock up the night before."

"Maybe a savory bread pudding. Call it Kentucky Snow Day Bread Pudding. I'm assigning you to figure it out." She starts to head inside.

Colton calls after her. "Remember that time we went to the bluff and made s'mores and watched it snow?"

Luann turns back to him, her face at once soft and pained with nostalgia. She sighs. "Of course I do," she says before leaving him standing alone in the alley.

CHAPTER 42

December 2015
Venice, Kentucky

COLTON, COLTON, COLTON, HIS COWORKERS CHANT, LUANN LOUDEST OF ALL. They sit at tables amid Luann's cozy and festive holiday decorations (her architectural eye extends to the elements of room decor). Field to Flame's young tradition is that Luann closes the restaurant for the staff Christmas party and spends the day cooking for everyone. They eat too much—second, thirds, and fourths. Roast goose. Bacon-wrapped scallops. Apple-glazed beef short ribs. Cranberry-Brie bites. Cranberry sauce. Green bean casserole. Mashed potatoes. Yams candied in sorghum and topped with roasted marshmallows. Honey-balsamic-glazed brussels sprouts. Roasted beet goat cheese salad. Tiramisu. Cinnamon roll apple pie. Peppermint bark ice cream. They (with some exceptions, notably Colton and Luann) drink too much, and a raucous, convivial mood prevails.

Colton, Colton, Colton. The chant continues.

"Come on, we're having fun. Y'all don't want this," Colton says, in what he already knows will be a vain attempt at demurral.

Reggie chuckles. "You right, bro, but we can tell *you* don't want this, so we do."

"Shan-i-A, Shan-i-A, Shan-i-A," a well-served Finn chants.

"Remember back at the end of November when I ordered you to?" Luann says, Colton's coworkers egging her on. "You said, 'Yes, Chef.'"

Colton lifts his hands in a sorry-I-wish-I-could-help shrug. "I don't even have my guitar here."

Luann grins wickedly. "I had a feeling that might happen. Taylor?"

Taylor dashes into the back. He emerges with Colton's guitar case.

"I foresaw this sorry attempt to shirk your responsibility and arranged to obtain your guitar," Luann says. "Your mom happily threw you under the bus."

Colton can only smile and shake his head. He walks slowly over, opens his guitar case, and slings on his guitar. Everyone cheers and hoots. "Y'all know I got canned from this, right?"

"For running your damn fool mouth. You just shut up and sing, you'll be fine," Reggie says.

"Reg Limbaugh up in here." Colton sighs and gives his guitar a quick strum, tweaks first one tuning peg, then another, then strums again. It occurs to him that he's on the precipice of performing music for a crowd for the first time since July, and his heartbeat accelerates. He's barely picked up his guitar. "Y'all, I ain't gonna lie, I got stage fright."

Dani cups her hands to her mouth. "No more excuses!"

"All *right*. I used to play this for bachelorette parties, so y'all best get rowdy."

Luann produces a stack of papers and starts distributing them. "Lyrics so everyone can sing along."

"You really don't leave a thing to chance, do you?"

"Never have."

"You had confidence you'd break me down."

"Always have."

In the beat before Colton's pick first hits the strings, he totters between melancholy and anxiety. This is his first audience since the one that booed him offstage. *It's quite a downgrade in size, but not in quality.* He's worried that this will make him miss music, a feeling he's successfully suppressed out of necessity.

He also realizes that this is the first time he's performed sober for any audience in a very long time.

He draws a breath from his diaphragm and launches into "Any Man of Mine." He sheds his qualms almost immediately and finds the charisma that made him a minor star. He's a little rusty on guitar, but he soon finds his footing. It helps that his thoroughly soused coworkers make for one of the most boisterously enthusiastic crowds he's ever performed for. He's gathered in this last month or so that no one can party like restaurant people. They roar out the chorus with him. When he finishes, they clamor for more.

For the next hour and a half, attempting to quit after each song, Colton plays the most crowd-pleasing covers he knows. By the end, he's soaked in sweat, standing on one of the tables in his Red Wings (Luann must have been having fun indeed, because he doesn't get in trouble for it), his voice hoarse and fingers aching from singing and playing unamplified over a noisy throng. He ends with a joyous singalong of "Frosty the Snowman."

Playing music again feels like looking once more upon the face of someone he loved, after a long absence. A feeling with which he is now quite familiar.

"More!" Reg bellows.

"Encore!" Bianca echoes.

The others take up the chant. *Encore, encore, encore.*

Colton meets Luann's gaze and holds it.

"Play 'Honeysuckle Summer,'" she says with a lightness, while her eyes remain serious.

Colton's breath stumbles. She's never let on that she knows any of his songs. It doesn't seem like she's messing with him. And he's glad, because part of him has always wanted to play it for her.

Colton smiles a little and says, "Yes, Chef." He plays it. He sings of watching summer storms with a girl under the night sky of Kentucky and of driving too fast down moonlit dirt roads.

Most of his coworkers don't know this one, so they sit in rapt silence (or at least as much so as a room full of drunk people can manage). While he plays, he remembers how every time he played it in concert, he made one or two achingly futile scans of the crowd to see if somehow, improbably, Luann had showed up to see him perform for thousands. Every time, he finished the song with that curious mix of joy and sorrow that comes from making something beautiful for someone who you know will never experience it.

He'd given up hope of ever looking out in the crowd and seeing Luann. But this time, there she is.

When he finishes, his coworkers applaud rapturously, and the party winds down.

Luann claps. "Listen up! No one asked Santa for a DUI for Christmas. If you need a ride home—and you do—I rented a fifteen-passenger van. See me for a ride."

Luann starts clearing dishes from a table.

Colton goes to her. "Need help with anything?"

"Nah, I'm gonna run everyone home, then come back to clean up."

"Let me pitch in."

"I threw this party for y'all. Go home. Have fun. You work enough as is. Lord knows."

"Pot calling the kettle black there. You got two little girls waiting for you."

"They've been asleep for hours. Or at least they'd better be, or Mimi and PopPop are in trouble."

"Look. I'm maybe the most sober person in a five-mile radius. I didn't even touch the bourbon yams. Let me chauffeur everyone."

They stare each other down. Luann capitulates with a dramatic sigh. *"Fine."* She hands Colton the plastic-tagged key to the van. "Out front, the big white—"

"Do you think I'm unfamiliar with fifteen-passenger vans after being a starving touring musician? I've probably spent more time behind the wheel of one of those than you have in a kitchen."

"Don't bank on it."

"Yeah, maybe not." Colton cups his hands to his mouth. *"Y'all!* The

Avoid-a-DUI Express is leaving the station. All aboard!" Colton pumps his arm and makes a *woo-woo* train-whistle sound.

As the van crew files out, Reggie says to Colton, "Colt, you know I hate country. Talking about your hound dog dying and your girl cheating and whatnot. But that last song you played was fire. For real, though."

Colton regards Reggie solemnly, putting his hand on Reggie's meaty shoulder. "Big Reg, if I know anything about you besides that you hate country, it's that you would never, *ever* lie to spare my feelings."

Venice is compact, yet it takes Colton forty-five minutes to get everyone dropped off. He parks the van where he found it and goes inside, where Luann appears to have made little headway.

"Luann?" he calls. "I'm back."

"Everyone get home safe?" Luann asks, emerging from the kitchen and drying her hands on a towel.

"Safe and sound." Colton hands her the key. "You been working the whole time I was gone?"

"Doesn't it look like it? Don't answer that. Just got done squaring away the leftovers. We got family meal for the next couple days too." She surveys the dining room. "I guess I'll be here another few hours."

"*We'll* be here another few hours."

"You helped enough by driving everyone. Go home."

"Make me."

"I'm your boss. I order you to go home and relax and let me get this."

"Tough tinsel, Chef. I'm helping."

Luann smiles. "You're fired."

Colton smiles back. "Now you *truly* have no leverage to make me leave." He stacks plates and takes them to the dishwashing sink in the kitchen, depositing them in the water. He returns for more.

"You sounded amazing tonight," Luann says.

"You think?"

"You know better now than ever before that I don't mince words about when things are good or bad."

"My first time playing music for people in a while. Well, I guess it hasn't even been a whole year. But man, feels like a long time."

"Hope I didn't put you on the spot too much."

"Naw."

"You were a compelling performer from the first time I ever saw you play."

"'Linger' by the Cranberries."

"Yep." They smile.

"I still love that song," Colton says.

"Me too."

"I ever tell you I met Dolores O'Riordan?"

"Lead singer of the Cranberries?!"

"No, sorry, a Subway sandwich artist named Dolores O'Riordan. I can see how that would be confusing."

"Crack your jokes, smart-ass, but hopefully you now appreciate the artistry that goes into making a good sandwich."

"Oh, trust me. But no, it was at this MTV thing where Maisy was presenting. I actually..." Colton smiles to himself and shakes his head as he wipes crumbs off a table into his palm. "I told her about you. Said I'd covered her to impress my high school girlfriend."

"What'd she say?"

"She asked if you were impressed. I said I hoped."

"You know damn well I was."

"I told her your name."

Luann stares at Colton for a moment. "You mean I get to report back to teenage me that Dolores O'Riordan knows my name?"

"Tell her Colton made it happen."

"She's going to wish it was because Dolores moved into a building she designed."

"Then tell her that."

"I'm not lying to her and robbing you of credit!"

"I just want whatever'll make you happy," Colton says to Luann's back as she wipes down a table.

"The truth will always make me happier than a lie."

"Then truth it is."

They work for a while in busy silence, too often not in the same area as they bustle to and fro between the kitchen and the dining area, sweeping, straightening, tidying. They go back to the dishwashing station to tackle the hillock of dishes.

"I have a new appreciation for Reg," Colton says.

"One of the first lessons ingrained in me in food service was that a good dishwasher will make or break a kitchen. They're the anchor. He's our highest paid hourly employee."

Colton scrubs a large soup tureen. "Sounds fair to me." Suddenly, he's caught in the thrall of an irresistible urge—one he's been fighting for a while now. "So...speaking of music earlier. I've been wondering about something for a long time."

Luann scrutinizes a pan. "You gonna wash this one?"

"I literally just did."

"With what? Beef tallow?"

"Come on. It's not that bad."

She drops it back in the water. "Not if we were on a cattle drive."

"But damn you're a hardass."

"I'm so awful for *forcing* you to stay and work. Anyway, you were about to ask me something."

"Lost my nerve."

"Lost your nerve."

"Yep."

"You chicken?"

"No."

"Huh? You a big old chicken? *Buh-cock. Bock bock bock buh-cock.*"

"That is a *frighteningly* good chicken impression."

"I used to raise them, so…"

Colton pulls his hands from the water and shakes droplets off them. He leans on the edge of the sink. He can't make eye contact. He starts to talk and shakes his head. "Man, this is so— Okay. I'll just ask. Did you ever listen to my music?"

Luann finishes drying a pot that passed cleanliness muster. She turns to Colton. "What's the answer you're hoping for?"

"Please don't," Colton pleads. "You can torment me on anything else."

"I'm not teasing you," she says quietly. "Younger me needs to know. She's demanding this price, not me."

"I'm hoping for yes. There was nothing I wanted more than for you to see that I made good. Well, good-*ish*. Before I pissed it away. I wasn't so excited for you to see that part. I looked for you in the crowd when I played New York City at the Garden in 2006. Dumb, huh?"

"You did?"

Colton blushes. "Like I said. Dumb."

"If I'd known, I certainly would've considered it. I'm glad I didn't know. That would've been a painful decision, even by 2006." Luann doesn't say anything for a while as she scrubs at a persistent spot on a pan. Finally: "Yeah, I listened to your music. Not during those earliest years. It was all too raw, and I couldn't stand to bleed anymore. Hearing your voice would have yanked open the stitches. Believe it or not, it's easy to avoid inadvertent exposure to country music in New York City and Copenhagen."

Colton smiles sadly. "I believe it."

"Little harder in Kentucky. I was driving to my parents' one night to pick up the twins and I had the windows down and I was flipping through the radio. I hit a country station and I heard 'Honeysuckle Summer'—great phrase by the way. Who was the genius who thought of it?"

"Tell you what: going forward, you can have one hundred percent of the royalties. That's gonna be—" Colton looks upward as though in thought and counts on his fingers. "Zero dollars. But seriously, thank you."

"I wasn't going to write a song about it. One of us needed to. Anyway, I heard it. And...it got me pretty good. Pulled over and cried. I'd been fighting with Henning over the visitation schedule, and then I hear your voice for the first time in almost two decades and it was...a lot. I'd tried my best to hate you over the years. It would've made things easier. And it never took. Listening to that song, I realized it would never take. I imagined how happy you were, and I was so proud of you my heart wanted to explode."

Colton's eyes prickle with imminent tears. "Now you know how I feel every day I come to work." He gets it out quickly before the swelling lump in his throat cuts him off.

They meet each other's eyes and hold the moment between them for what feels like a long time. *God, you're beautiful.* Colton wonders how many times he's thought that. *How many stars in the sky? Add one more.*

"Weren't you worried about getting emotional when I played it tonight?" Colton asks finally.

Luann chuckles. "Dude, I'd just witnessed you covering 'Jolene' while standing on a table and wearing a Santa hat someone had chucked at you while yelling 'Santa panties.' I knew I was gonna be fine keeping it together. And by the way, hit that table real good with the bleach solution."

"Already done. And besides, there was a tablecloth on it."

"I saw that pan earlier. Do it again."

He does. They wrap up the cleaning. "I think we're about good here," Luann says.

"You know what I could go for?" Colton says. "A few minutes in the alley. You got a sec?"

"I was just thinking that."

They go out in the alley and lean their backs against the brick.

"So," Colton says. "I don't know the etiquette or whatever about giving your boss a present. I hope this is okay." He rummages in his pocket and hands a vintage sterling silver floral-etched cigarette case to Luann. It's warm from his body.

Luann gasps. "*Colton.* You did *not* need to do this. This is—"

"Open it."

She does. The smell of cinnamon and clove wafts from it, perfuming the space between them.

Colton beams. "Milled northern white birch toothpicks, steeped in my proprietary blend of cinnamon and clove essential oils and two others. Let's see if you can guess."

Luann pops one of the toothpicks in her mouth. She smacks her lips a couple times. "Cardamom?"

"Yep. One more."

She gnaws at the toothpick and wrinkles her brow. "Fennel?"

"Close. Star anise."

"Damn it. It was fifty-fifty."

"Still. Impressive."

"No, I'm the one who's impressed. This is, like, a perfect balance of flavor. In a *toothpick.*"

"Took me a few batches to get the proportions right."

"I'm dead serious—make me another batch to put up at the front, and I'll buy them from you."

"I ain't gonna charge you."

"I insist on paying you like I would any of our other suppliers."

"After all these cooking classes you've paid *me* for? Hell."

Luann starts back inside. "Hold on."

"Where you going?" Colton asks.

"Be right back."

After a few moments, Luann returns with a gift bag. She hands it to him. "For you."

Colton hefts the bag. "If you've just gone and filled this with some Broadbent country ham from the kitchen, I'll know."

"You wouldn't complain."

"Didn't say I would."

"Look inside."

Colton reaches into the bag and pulls out the contents. He unfurls it in the dim light and holds it at arm's length with both hands. It's a white Waylon Jennings baseball T-shirt with faded black three-quarter sleeves. Colton's voice is hushed in awe. "Is this—whoa, this looks—"

"Vintage for vintage. I think it's from the seventies, maybe early eighties, by the look of it."

"Where'd you find this?" Colton sputters. "This would be $500 at a fancy Nashville vintage clothing store."

"Right here in Venice at the Grace and Mercy Thrift, second Christmas home during college. Two bucks."

"You've held on to this for almost two decades?"

"Thought maybe I'd take it back to New York. Sell it, make a little folding money. Never did."

"Why not?"

Luann wipes her hand down her face. "Oh Lord. It's embarrassing."

"Good thing the only person around to hear is someone you just watched standing on a table, playing 'Jolene' and wearing Santa panties on his head."

"That's *such* a good point. Okay. I held on to it because…I guess I'd fantasized that I'd give it to you someday. Under what circumstances, I had no clue. Turns out, it was Christmas in 2015, having just watched you standing on a table, playing 'Jolene,' and wearing Santa panties on your head. Life's funny."

"Life's funny."

"So? Do you love it as much as I thought while I was forking over two bucks for it?"

Colton looks at her. "However much you thought I would love it? Double it. Then you're halfway there." He starts to unsnap his denim Wrangler shirt. "No peeking."

"*Pshhh.*" Luann averts her eyes. "*Now* you're okay with stripping?"

"Nothing you haven't seen before. Well, except the tats." He dons his new shirt. It fits perfectly.

They turn to each other. "Merry Christmas, Colton," Luann murmurs.

They hug for a long time, swaying as though dancing. She's a familiar warmth against him in the chilly December night. Colton rests his cheek on the side of her head, and her hair brushes against and tickles his lips, sending a volt through him. *How bodies remember each other, the years be damned.* He can smell the fragrant spiced oils on her breath, and he wonders what it would be like to kiss her now.

When they finally stand back from each other, Colton says, gesturing at his torso, "So when were you planning on giving this to me? You tried to run me off like three times tonight."

"It was when you wouldn't let yourself be run off that I decided to." She cradles the cigarette case in her palm and runs her fingers over the etchings. "This is really cool."

"Took me forever to scrub out the cigarette smell."

"There's something I've been meaning to tell you," Luann says, vulnerability bleeding around the edges of her voice.

He gives her space to speak.

"Running a restaurant is lonely and scary. Sometimes I feel like I've wandered out onto the middle of a tightrope and I've just looked down. All to say, I've enjoyed having you around."

"I believe in you without reservations. Get it? Reservations?"

"Colton, please don't ruin Christmas."

"For real, though, I'm dead serious about my confidence in you."

They stand there for a while longer, saying little and savoring the easy, contemplative quiet between them before they have to go their separate ways. The distant, plaintive lament of a passing train carries toward them—the lone sound in the still winter night.

CHAPTER 43

January 2016
Venice, Kentucky

The new year comes, and this feels to Colton like crossing some threshold. No longer is he in the Year of Ruin. This is the Year of New Becoming.

Over the ensuing days and weeks, Colton works every minute Luann will allow. Even on Sundays and Mondays, his days off, he's practicing his cuts and honing his cooking technique, making meals for his mom and Derrick and Gabrielle. He reads the chef memoirs Luann recommends. He spends hours on YouTube and watching Food Network. Sometimes he even goes on field trips with Luann to visit farms, Colton being more fluent in Western Kentucky Country Boy than Luann (they don't generally tell the farmers Colton's full name—they never recognize him, and why tempt fate?).

When he's working, he lacks the time or mental space to revisit his defeats, and this is a welcome respite. Gone are the nights tossing and turning, trying to sleep while he replays his failings on an endless, spiraling loop. Despite being around alcohol every day, he feels less compulsion to drink—though the urge is still present, and he attends meetings regularly. He's not going daily, like in the first few months after rehab, but a few times a week. He's keenly aware that sobriety requires constant work and vigilance. He's communing with his higher power—

cooking. Conjuring sustenance with his hands. Combining disparate elements to create something beautiful. He knows he'll never master it completely, such that he can learn nothing more. It will always be greater than himself.

He learns a particular economy of movement. He lights burners with one hand while reaching for a pinch of kosher salt with the other, wipes down his workstation while stirring the contents of a sauté pan. He becomes adept at the delicate dance of the kitchen, calling *behind* while dodging swiftly around his coworkers with honed knives and piping skillets and artfully plated dishes. He burns and nicks himself less frequently. He develops muscle memory—the precision and speed of his cuts improve exponentially.

Still, there are bumps in the road. Nights he gets in the weeds and can't get out. The underseasoned dishes, the overseasoned ones. The undercooked ones, the overcooked ones. The dishes that get sent back. His improvement isn't an unbroken upward trajectory, but a steady ascent nevertheless.

He feels himself standing taller, prouder.

He relishes the camaraderie of the kitchen staff, including and especially when they're slammed and must depend on each other the most. It reminds him of being on a football team, calling plays under stadium lights, or being onstage with a well-rehearsed band jamming through a song live for the first time. The work is different, but the pressures are the same—and so are the rewards. His tendency toward steady-handed leadership in both sport and music begins to emerge in this new context.

The keen memory that once allowed him to archive and recall football plays and hundreds of song lyrics has turned, with singular focus, to remembering recipes, cooking techniques, and the business aspects of running a restaurant. His mind crackles with the heady rush of creativity and learning of a new artistic discipline. The part of his soul that music once fed feasts now on... food.

The butternut squash salad he invented makes it to the menu. It's well received. So is the Kentucky Snow Day savory bread pudding, prepared with brioche and venison sausage, and seasoned with smoked rosemary and thyme. An antique dispenser at the host's station dispenses Colton's custom-blend toothpicks as a sort of final bow of excellence for the restaurant.

Occasionally, during a lull, he'll emerge from the kitchen to survey the diners enjoying meals he prepared. He looks over them, feeling the pride and satisfaction with which he used to overlook an arena crowd.

Luann brings her daughters to the restaurant sometimes, and whenever they come, they find Colton and, each grabbing one of his hands and hanging from it, beg him to make them banana splits. He lives for that.

Too, he relishes the ends of nights, when his culinary labors are through, and he can chat with Luann in the alley. That's when he most feels like he's not a failure and his life is moving forward somehow, in spite of everything. Those sweet few minutes.

There are never enough.

CHAPTER 44

February 2016
Venice, Kentucky

"COLT?" HIS MOM CALLS. "YOU SEE TODAY'S PAPER?"

Colton spits out toothpaste as he readies for work. He swishes water, spits again, and wipes his mouth. "Since when do I ever read the *Star*?"

His mom doesn't respond.

"Mama?"

"Yep."

"Why'd you ask?"

"No reason."

Colton pulls on his T-shirt and makes for the kitchen, where his mom sits with the paper and a cup of coffee. "You just randomly decided today of all days to ask me if I'd read the *Venice Star*, a thing you know I never do?" He looks down at the paper spread before her. He picks it up and reads:

FIELD TO FLAME BRINGS COASTAL ELITE FOOD CULTURE, VALUES TO VENICE

by Brett Walsh, Opinion Columnist

Ever since Field to Flame opened on Main Street a couple of years ago, Venetians have had their own little taste of

> New York City under the guise of farm-to-table Southern cooking. That's fine if you like that sort of thing. As for me and my woefully unsophisticated palate, I think Cracker Barrel makes a better biscuit and Chick-fil-A fries a better piece of chicken. But I digress.
>
> See, the true problem with Field to Flame is not that it offers food at New York City prices and pretense—it's that it's now serving up a heaping side dish of elitist New York City values too. Allow me to elaborate. An anonymous source recently provided me with a photograph of former country star and hometown-hero-turned-goat Colton Gentry working at...

"What the *fu*—fun...times is this?" Colton mutters as he reads, face reddening, blood pressure surging. *Are they going to put their foot through the vase every time I glue the shards back together? Do I need to wear an old-timey barrel with suspenders before they'll be satisfied?*

Colton's mom pets the back of his hair. "Sweetie, Brett Walsh loves to get on his high horse."

"This is going to hurt the restaurant." *Meaning Luann.*

"I didn't even want to tell you because nobody reads his column."

"Hope not," he says to himself.

A few minutes later, Leon offers Colton the same assurance over the phone. *Print media is dead, man. Last gasp of an attention seeker. This trifling nobody ain't worth your sobriety.*

Colton hopes his mom and Leon are right.

He works his shift, the Serenity Prayer looping through his head, dread enrobing him, but nobody mentions anything.

Maybe Mama and Leon are right.

SHAD HAGGERTY: Good evening and welcome to *The Patriot Report*. I'm your host, Shad Haggerty. Tonight, we'll be talking with Brock Steele about his new book, *No Easy Pay: The Navy SEAL Way of Closing Deals*. Then, we're discussing the hoax of global warming with Dr. Richard Hode. But first, we begin tonight's show with a recurring segment—the Loudmouth Liberal Loser Roundup. [sound effect of whip cracking] This is where we check in with some loony liberal who's displayed even less common sense than your *average* liberal and gotten themselves in hot water for it.

Tonight's Loudmouth Liberal Loser comes from a viewer who sent this in. Who remembers Colton Gentry? No one? He was the B-list country singer who said this: [roll video of Colton Gentry rant at concert]. Boy, it takes a genius to go off like that in front of a country music crowd. Guess he didn't learn much from the Dixie Chicks.

Mr. Gentry's local newspaper reports that after being dumped by his record label, country radio, and his sugar mama Maisy Martin [Borat "My Wife" sound drop], who ran off with an NHL player [Austin Powers "Yeah Baby" sound drop], he's gotten himself a job—get this [chuckling]—as a line cook at a restaurant called Field to Flame in his hometown of Venice, Kentucky [descending slide whistle sound effect]. Well, Mr. Gentry, I doubt this new job pays as much as your old one, but at least you won't have access to a microphone while you sling hashbrowns, so maybe you'll hang on to this one [descending trombone sound effect].

CHAPTER 45

Colton senses something amiss the moment he walks into the restaurant, the way soldiers can smell an ambush. The phone at the host's station is ringing when he enters. Luann answers and hangs up quickly. No sooner has she put the phone down than it rings again. Another terse exchange. She glances quickly at Colton and averts her eyes. She hangs up, reaches down, and disconnects the line.

"What's up?" Colton asks, nodding toward the phone, as she approaches, heading toward the kitchen.

Luann rolls her eyes and shakes her head. "People with entirely too much time on their hands and too little brain in their heads. Don't worry about it."

They work, prepping for lunch service. Luann is unusually quiet. Colton's insides writhe. "Everything okay?"

"Yep." A knock at the alley door. Luann goes to answer it. It's Ray with K&L Poultry, one of their suppliers.

Colton hears them talking in curt, clipped tones. He catches snippets.

Problem for us...

Sorry you feel...

nonnegotiable...

not a good reason...

since we opened...

If you reconsider...

Luann returns, looking vexed. "I'm printing some new menus. No chicken today."

"K&L flake on us?" Dani asks.

"We're done with K&L."

"Wow, just like that? They've been with us since we opened."

"Irreconcilable differences. I'll call Windy Gap, see if they can sub in. They raise a good chicken, just pricier. Probably too late for today, though." She goes in her office, and the hum of the printer soon follows.

The turmoil in Colton's gut intensifies. *Something is definitely wrong here.*

"Don't go running off on me," Dani says as Colton starts toward Luann's office. "We're already a woman down here."

"Be right back," Colton says over his shoulder. He enters Luann's office and shuts the door behind him. "Is this because of me?"

Luann looks up from her laptop, and her eyes are gentle but her expression is anguished. "You didn't do anything."

"Yeah, but is what's going on because of that Brett Walsh thing?"

"It's because of Shad Haggerty."

"That Fox News guy? What did he do?" Colton leans against the wall to steady himself on now-tremulous legs.

Luann rests her elbows on her desk, sighs, and rubs her temples. "You didn't hear?"

"You might say he and I aren't fans of each other."

"On his show last night, he said you were working here. Maybe the only truth that's ever passed his lips."

Colton's breath catches. An acrid nausea starts above his stomach. "For what purpose?" He runs his fingers through his hair.

"Well, assuming that's not a rhetorical question: to humiliate you. There's this idea that working in the service industry is somehow less worthy of dignity than other jobs."

"And to punish you for hiring me."

"Also."

"That what went down with K&L?"

"Ray's a prick."

"I know, but is that what happened?"

"He watches Haggerty religiously, I guess. All the times he's interacted with you, he didn't realize who you were. He gave me an ultimatum: you or him. I chose you."

Colton exhales a long breath and sinks into the chair opposite Luann's desk. He wants the thing that will reliably soothe him, albeit temporarily. It feels like every synapse in him is firing, begging for one thing, the gears in his heart and head shifting into overdrive. He knows where to find it. It's feet away. He could tuck the bottle in his chef's jacket or in a box that he'd carry back to one of the storage areas. He could take a few slugs from it—enough to dull himself and no more. Then he could restart his path, Luann and Leon and the rest of them none the wiser.

Please, Luann, put me to work before I can think about this anymore.

As though she heard him, Luann stands, walks to the printer, and removes the stack of newly K&L-free menus. "We're gonna sub smoked trout croquettes for the fried chicken." She rests her hand on his shoulder. "Come on. You'll be too busy trying not to screw these up to think about Haggerty."

He hopes she's right, but he's not holding his breath.

They plug the phone back in just before lunch service. It immediately starts ringing every few minutes. Colton overhears Ruth telling Luann that all but a fraction of the calls are abusive. Luann tells Ruth to unplug it again and says she'll put a note on the website that they're only taking online reservations for the time being.

Colton stews with guilty mortification. At this point, he's sure all his coworkers know what's happening and why. They're going out of their way to show him kindness—once, Reg walks past him and rests a huge palm on his shoulder for a second, in a brotherly gesture. Somehow, this only deepens his embarrassment.

Around the beginning of lunch service, faint chanting drifts in from the sidewalk, momentarily increasing in volume each time the door opens for a patron to enter, which appears to be occurring about half as often as normal.

"Assholes," Dani mutters to Colton while molding a croquette.

"Who's out there?" Colton asks.

"Seven or eight hobbyless people with some group called the Eagle League," Dani says.

As the day wears on and lunch service ends, the picketers go home. Colton assumes they've not seen the last of them, and he's right. They assemble in greater force shortly before dinner service. Eleven or twelve of them pace the front entrance with signs reading "Venice is a 2nd Amendment town" and "It's our right to bear arms—get over it," and "I'm a gun owner and proud!" Several of them tote AR-15s—matte black and menacing, like the instrument of Duane's murder—slung across their bodies. The sight makes Colton feel like his organs are made of frozen sand. Every nerve along his spine arcs, sending waves of sickly chills pulsing through him.

As he works, he can't stop the churning rage or the rampant litany of thoughts of how he brought this scourge on Luann. They drive him to distraction. He burns and cuts himself. He scorches food. All the footing, pride, and self-worth he's recovered over the past several months is dissolving like strychnine stirred into coffee.

During a lull (of which there are several—they have many canceled reservations, whether their patrons are taking a political stand or don't want to walk past a small militia to eat), Colton makes the mistake of looking up the restaurant on Yelp, to see the blight he's brought upon Luann's livelihood. Its rating now sits at one-and-a-half stars with 167 reviews, 98 of which have been left in the last twenty-four hours. Some of them at least pretend: *I ate here and got the worst food poisoning of my life!!!! This is the priciest, most pretentious restaurant ever! The waitress mocked my pawpaw, who's a veteran, for wearing his Navy hat in the restaurant!* Some abandon all pretense: *DON'T SUPPORT A RESTAURANT THAT DOESN'T SUPPORT YOUR 2ND AMENDMENT RIHGTS!!!!*

Colton wonders how much travail it would be to change his name legally. Maybe he could decamp to Seattle, or Portland, or San Francisco—someplace where he doesn't belong and where no one knows or cares who he is, and where people might even appreciate his vitriol against the sanctity of assault rifles. They would have vibrant restaurant scenes. He could get a kitchen job.

If only he alone bore the consequences of his actions. But now they were being visited upon Luann and her fledgling enterprise. Colton had faithfully done his homework, studying the restaurant industry. He knew enough now to spot how Luann walked a tightrope of benevolent risk in her restaurant operation. She paid her staff too well. She sent guests home too full and with to-go containers. She had little margin for error, and she made few, aside from the most glaring one: him.

But he was a blunder he had the power to fix for her, and he resolved to do just that after overhearing her, toward the end of the night, canceling an order with a supplier for a big upcoming job catering a wedding in Paducah.

Why the universe cursed this woman with me twice now, I don't know. But the curse ends now.

He finds her in the alley. His gut is queasy and ardent with acid.

She turns to him and opens the silver cigarette case he gave her, offering him one of the toothpicks he'd made. "Been a day. You look like you could use one of these." She's already chewing one.

Colton gives her a doleful smile and accepts it. He puts it in his mouth, the cinnamon oil burning.

"How's your hand?" she asks.

"The one I cut or the one I burned?"

"Thought it was the same hand."

"If only."

They're quiet while Colton summons his courage. He imagines all the good a drink would do him right now.

"Any more suppliers quit on us?" he asks, stalling, but also seeking further justification.

"Just K&L, and honestly, good riddance. Ray was always trying to look down my shirt. He made me feel like a stripper who was getting tipped with raw La Flèche chicken thighs." Luann gives him a wan smile. She looks more spent than normal at the end of a shift. Colton's eyes drop to the pavement.

"Luann. Chef. There's, um, something I wanted to discuss." He buries his hands in his pockets and studies his feet. His heart thrums. This conversation has an eerie familiarity.

Luann watches him, growing trepidation on her face.

He draws a deep breath. "I want you to know I'm so grateful—*deeply* grateful for everything you've done for me. But I think it's time I moved on."

Luann stands up straight from where she was leaning against the wall. She pulls her toothpick out of her mouth and flicks it down the dark alley. Colton can feel her eyes bore into him. "Why?" she asks quietly.

Colton can't meet her gaze. "You know why. They won't stop until you have no choice but to fire me. Trust that. They took their pound of flesh from me, and they won't be happy until they've got the other hundred and eighty-seven or so."

Luann stares into the darkness, laughs hollowly, and mutters, "I don't believe this."

"Luann, I'm so sorry. I don't know why this didn't occur to me—

I guess I thought they were content with how far they'd knocked me down. I thought—"

"You're dumping me again."

"No—I—"

"You're tossing me aside again for a trash reason. When will I *ever* learn with you?"

This draws blood. "Chef—"

"Don't *Chef* me. Don't hide behind protocol or turn me into an abstraction to make this easier on yourself. I'm *in* this for you. Like I've *always* been for you. *All* in. Always on your team. And I'm the one hard thing you *always* quit." Her eyes blaze and her words cut like a Korin knife fresh from the whetstone.

Colton stammers. "It's—it's not that. I—"

"I offered you this job on impulse. I saw you in need and hurting, and I'd be damned if I'd stand by while the world kicked you in the teeth. Then I tortured myself the whole time you were making up your mind. Wondering if I'd set myself up to get hurt again."

She's landed more than a few blows, and Colton has to fight to steady himself.

"Luann, I won't allow the stain of my failure getting all over what you've created here. I can't live with that. And that's what happens if I stay. You ask when you're going to learn with me? Good question. When *are* you going to learn with me? When do you figure out that I'm a hopeless screwup and one way or another every good thing in my life slips through my fingers and leaves me holding dust?"

She takes a step toward him, close enough now that he can't duck her glare. She stabs her finger at the wall behind them like she's skewering it to roast. "You think I built all this while having my head jammed so far up my ass it never occurred to me that this might happen someday? Huh? That the mob might come for you and me both?"

"No."

"It was the *first* thing that occurred to me. Guess the second."

Colton looks at her.

"Guess." She raises her eyebrows and sets her jaw.

"I don't know," he says quietly.

"That at some point, you'd try to bail on me again, saying it was best for both of us."

"I'm sorry I gave you so little cause to believe in me."

"Oh, spare me the self-pity. I *obviously* believed in you."

Colton unbuttons his chef's jacket. "There are men carrying assault rifles in front of your restaurant. The first time I quit on you, it was to protect me. This time, it's to protect you." He takes off the jacket and extends it to Luann.

She eyes it for a moment before taking it. "This time it's also to protect you," she says in a wounded hush. "I'll send your paycheck to your mom's." She turns her back on Colton and goes back inside.

Colton stands numb and still for a while. Without his chef's jacket or Luann, the alley is a cold, lonely, and dark place indeed. His resignation had gone differently than he'd thought. He knew she'd be mad, but he'd wanted to thank her for everything. In the turmoil of the moment, he forgot. Now he's too ashamed. In the back of his mind, he remembers how the pang of humiliation was one of the conditions that alcohol most effectively remedied.

He leaves without reentering the restaurant to bid his farewells to coworkers or retrieve his knife roll. It will be his costly atonement for what he brought on all of them.

CHAPTER 46

His hands quake on the steering wheel. His truck ticks and pops as the engine cools. The neon sign of the liquor store reflects red and liquid in a parking lot puddle from a quick spring cloudburst.

He's spiraling. There are no meetings this time of night. He tried Leon, but he's on tour and didn't pick up. His local sponsor didn't answer either.

Only a few minutes ago, he'd had something that stopped the hurting and made him feel worthy again. Luann, his work, his patient and generous coworkers—his team, his band. Gone. And how could he possibly rebuild again? Where could he go from here? Who would save him this time? He could have nothing of any consequence that his detractors wouldn't try to take away. There's naught standing between him and losing himself down the neck of a bottle. And right now that feels like the only viable option. Maybe his surrender will somehow bring the universe back into balance. Maybe if he ruins himself first, everyone else will lose interest.

He gets out of the truck and stands beside it. His heart beats a tattoo. He rests his hand on the door and leans over, staring at the rain-damp pavement, as though catching his breath.

If you do this, it will be the end of you. There is no "just once" for you when it comes to drink. All you will have left is the blackout of drunken oblivion.

Maybe that's not such a bad thing.

He turns and takes several steps toward the entrance. He can see through the glass door, a man in a Carhartt jacket is purchasing a bottle of tequila at the cash register.

It will be the end of you.

Then again, you can't disappoint anyone else when you're not around.

He takes another couple of steps. Suddenly, he thinks of Duane and how Duane would have wanted to live. How he tried to cling to life even as his blood abandoned him and his organs failed. How he fought to the bitter end.

Duane had no choice. You do.

He halts and sinks to a squat, groaning involuntarily through his teeth and pressing his palms to his temples, tears blurring his vision.

"Hey, brother, you okay?"

Colton looks up to see Tequila Man standing above him. "I'm—I don't know."

"You don't look like you're doing so hot." Tequila Man pulls out his wallet, opens it, and takes out a five. He holds it out to Colton. He nods toward the liquor store. "Don't spend this in there. Go get yourself a burger."

Colton stands. "Aw, man, thanks, but give it to someone in need. I'm all right. Just . . . having a moment. Lost my job and got in a fight with the lady tonight." *I may not have much left, but at least I'm not a liar.*

Tequila Man chuckles. "That'll drive a man to drink, sure enough." He claps Colton on the shoulder. "Have a good one, brother." He walks to his car.

Colton watches him leave the parking lot. He casts one final, protracted look back at the liquor store. The neon beckons in the dark. *Funny how they say "go toward the light" and "walk in the light" like those are always good things. Sometimes the light is a luminescent predator in the deep and you're a tasty fish.*

He clenches his fists and releases them. Clenches and releases. Runs his fingers through his hair. A sheen of sweat rises on his forehead and on his palms, and his scalp prickles. He breathes in and out until he grows dizzy. He can't think of much he has to stay sober for, but he decides to anyway, because he's alive. Not everyone has that much. *You can have a drink tomorrow. Not now. Stay sober tonight and you can have a drink in twenty-four hours. Promise. But not now. Not tonight.*

He walks back to his truck, gets in, and drives home.

"Busy night?" his mom calls from the living room couch as he enters. "You're a bit later than normal."

"Less busy than usual actually." Colton sits beside her. "What are you watching?"

"Oh, I don't know. I've been dozing off. I should turn in."

He has a moment of wild envy at the relative simplicity of his mom's life. No involuntary appearances on Fox shows. No one protesting any place she wants to be. No addictions save for scrapbooking. No exes in tabloids. No repeatedly letting down anyone whom she cares deeply about.

"I quit tonight," Colton says softly.

Colton's mom looks over at him. "I really need to get to bed. Sounded like you said you quit tonight."

"I sure did."

"Honey?"

"Shad Haggerty on Fox did a thing on me last night."

"Again?"

"Making fun of my new job. Calling out Field to Flame on national TV."

"That man is so ugly to people."

"Bunch of protestors showed up at the restaurant today."

"You have *got* to be kidding. Who has time?"

"Anyway, business was way down today. Our—Luann's main poultry supplier quit on her. She lost a wedding catering job."

"Did she ask you to resign?"

Colton shakes his head and slumps into the couch. "She tried to convince me to stay."

"But you couldn't be persuaded."

"Mama. I'm a millstone around her neck."

"Shouldn't that be for her to decide?"

"I think she cares about me more than she should."

"Sweetie, she's a big girl and she can make her own choices, and it sounds like she chose to stand by you."

"If this is about me moving out, I'll find something else. I'm thinking about going to Seattle or Portland or San Francisco and getting a kitchen job out there."

"It has never been about that, which I've made clear many times. You live here for the rest of my life as far as I'm concerned and then keep on living here after I'm gone."

"Then what is this about? Why do you care that I quit?"

"I care because that job gave you your self-esteem back. It was a night and day difference. It gave you purpose. You were happier than I'd seen you in a long time."

Colton looks at her, eyebrow raised.

"Mothers notice these things in their children. Am I wrong?"

"I don't know."

"You *do* know. You think Luann would have you back if you asked?"

"You mean if I pleaded?"

"You think that's what it would take?"

"At the very least. When we broke up, I even tried pleading, and it didn't work."

"Well, you obviously found your way back into her good graces eventually, or she wouldn't have hired you."

Colton checks an imaginary watch. "All right, I'll just check in with her in about, oh, twenty years or so and see if she'll give me my job back."

"Do you not have any regrets?"

"Oh, the one thing I have in endless supply is regrets."

"You know I love you no matter what."

"Then I guess I have two things in endless supply."

"I need to go to bed. We'll talk in the morning." Colton's mom pecks him on the cheek and rises from the couch.

"Mama, hang on one sec." Colton pulls his truck keys from his pocket and hands them to her. "I need you to hide these from me tomorrow. Don't give them back no matter what. Not if I beg or plead. Also, don't let me leave the house any other way."

"There something I should know?"

"Only that I made a promise to myself tonight that I can't keep under any circumstances."

Sleep proves predictably elusive. Colton dreams he's back in the kitchen, in the weeds. It's a good dream. He awakens partially and it's several seconds before he realizes it was a fiction, which wrenches him the rest of the way awake.

A mug of hot chamomile tea with milk and a couple of hours of googling kitchen jobs in Seattle, Portland, San Francisco, and Austin later, he's ready to try again. Out of nowhere, just as he closes his eyes, he remembers Luann's daughters and how he'll probably never get to see them again, never get to make them banana splits again and see the joy on their faces. Which leads to the realization that there'll be no more post-shift alley chats with Luann—his favorite part of the day. Back wide awake.

Colton tries searching kitchen jobs again, but the combination of the computer's glow and the depressing task isn't helping him grow sleepy, so he sits out on the back patio and gazes into the dark, predawn sky. A thought occurs to him, and it's the first time he's entertained it:

Maybe between the two of us, Duane was the lucky one.

CHAPTER 47

Colton and Derrick come to a stop, panting.

"I gotta walk the last little bit," Derrick says. "I'm beat. How you doing, bro? You're acting out of sorts today."

"Yeah, I'm good," Colton says. *If spending the last few days back on your pre-job schedule of moping around the house, half-heartedly browsing employment listings, and watching network crime procedurals with your mom is considered "good."*

"Hey, I wanted to take Gabi to Field to Flame for her birthday on Friday. We gonna have to walk through a picket line of amateur Rambos?"

"You know about that?"

"Talk of the town."

"Um. I don't know how long they'll be there."

"I forgot to make a reservation. You working tonight? Hook a brother up?"

"I... am not working tonight."

"Tomorrow?"

"Nope."

Derrick looks at Colton. "The next night? I need the reservation hookup."

Colton sighs and rubs his face. "Man, I quit."

Derrick raises both eyebrows. "You quit."

"Yeah."

"Bro, why? We talked last *week* and you were good as hell. You didn't—" Derrick makes a bottle tipping motion.

"I said I quit, not that I got fired. And no. I came close, but no."

"Well, I'm trying to figure out why you'd've done something crazy like that."

Colton relates the story of and reasoning for his resignation.

"So Luann did not even *hint* she wanted you gone," Derrick says.

"No, but—"

"You knew what was best for her."

"Come on."

"You knew better than she did what she needed."

"Well, no. I mean yeah, kinda. I didn't think she would do what she had to do."

"Which was fire you?"

"Like my record label, my management company, my agent, my wife, and all of country radio. Yes."

"It ever occur to you that Luann has bigger balls than all of them combined?"

"She'd probably insist you say ovaries."

"Name your body part. You know what you did to her?"

"What?"

"You cut her off at the knees from standing up to these assholes. How much you think she appreciates that?"

Colton sighs and shakes his head.

Derrick presses. He cups his hand to his ear. "Huh? I can't hear you. What I know of Luann? Not much."

"My mom basically said the same thing."

"Yeah, well your mom is a smart lady then. How *you* feeling about your decision?"

Colton hesitates before answering. "Not great."

Derrick squints and starts counting on his fingers. "Okay, so your mom thinks it was a bad idea, Luann thinks it was a bad idea, *I* think it was a bad idea, I know Gabi will think it was a bad idea when I tell her—and I will—*you* think it was a bad idea. There's one other person I know would have some thoughts."

"Who?"

"Duane. You spoke up for *him*. How you think he would feel, you throwing away a good thing to appease the people who got him murdered?"

Colton is silent for a long time as they walk. Every minute he spent not driving to the liquor store in the last few days, Duane had been on his mind. "Even if I wanted to go back, this is like when Luann and I broke up back in the day. I tried to grovel my way back in, but she would *not* have it. It's too late."

"People change, bro. They grow up. They soften. They learn to forgive." He looks pointedly at Colton. "I would know."

"So I go crawling back. I'm not sure if she'll have me. She had some strong words when I resigned."

"Don't go empty-handed. Remind her of your worth." Derrick pauses, considering. "What's the one thing she takes more seriously than anything else?"

"Food," Colton says without hesitation.

"So try a new recipe. Something that'll show all those protestors and Luann that you're serious about this new path. In fact, you could test it out on me and Gabi on Friday since you have more time on your hands. I'll buy the ingredients."

"Was this whole pep talk so that you could treat Gabi to a Field to Flame–quality meal after you blew it getting a reservation in time?"

"It wasn't *not* that. We'll want to eat at six thirty, and we'll only have the babysitter until ten, so the quicker you can clear out, the sooner Gabi and I can…" Derrick rests his hand on Colton's shoulder. "And, hey, listen, .45, one more thing. I know I talked a big game just now about not appeasing assholes, but even so, in a couple years when the public defender retires and I run for her seat, I'm gonna need you to not endorse me publicly, cool?"

Colton grins. "There anything else I can *not* do for you?"

"That's it for now."

Colton drapes his arm around Derrick's shoulder. "D Rock: I would consider it the greatest honor to not publicly endorse you for the office of public defender."

CHAPTER 48

STANDING IN THE DIM ALLEYWAY, COLTON TAKES DEEP BREATHS TO TRY AND calm his nerves. Anticipating how Luann will receive his entreaty for rehire, and how she'll judge the reconciliatory dish he prepared, has left him jumpy. He didn't end up testing the meal out on Derrick and Gabrielle. He wasn't confident enough in it to ruin Gabrielle's birthday dinner, opting instead for ribeyes and lobster, which were well received.

Colton fidgets and looks at his phone. He didn't see any protestors when he walked up to the restaurant, but he had come minutes before closing time, so it's possible they already left. Also, he assumed Luann had told them they were protesting in vain.

Luann is running late. *Oh right. She's a man down in the kitchen.* His jitters build.

Maybe she's not coming out in the alley anymore at the end of each night. Maybe she's afraid for her safety. Maybe it reminds her of me and so she doesn't do it anymore. Maybe—

The alley door clanks open and out steps Luann.

She sees Colton, gasps, and jumps. "Holy shit."

"Sorry, I didn't mean to—"

She leans against the wall, eyes closed, hand on her chest. "Asshole," she hisses. "We have a front door. You don't need to lurk in the alley like Ted Bundy."

"Did he lurk in alleyways? I thought his thing was luring into cars."

"Okay, then like... Kenny Ray McSecondAmendment. I don't fucking know. This is not remotely the point."

"I was embarrassed."

"Oh, *you* were embarrassed? Tell me, were you more or less humiliated than if you had to try to convince your employees and loved ones that you actually didn't fold to a bunch of gun cultists by firing one of your best workers; no, he up and quit on you to do you a *favor*."

"I don't know about my relative shame level. I just know it's really high. I came to say I'm sorry, Luann. And to see if maybe... you would consider having me back?"

Luann stares into him, her eyes stony. "You did *precisely* the thing I was most afraid you'd do when I hired you on—left me high and dry."

"I did," Colton says contritely.

"Only *now*, twenty years later, I have my daughters asking about you, wanting to know when you'll be back to make them banana splits again. And I'm stuck trying to think of how to explain this situation to them."

"I genuinely thought I was protecting you. But with some time to think, I see you're right and I was mostly trying to protect myself and my dignity. I was wrong."

"Here I thought I was older and wiser, and this is beat-for-beat what you did to me two decades ago."

Colton smiles a little. "Not quite. I've already gotten further with my apology than you ever let me get back then."

Luann folds her arms. "Thank a string of therapists."

"I hope I wasn't responsible for that."

"Don't flatter yourself. It was a team effort."

"I brought you something," Colton says, extending a small, waxed-paper-wrapped packet to Luann.

"What's this?"

"An offering."

She opens it.

"I hope it's still warm-ish," Colton says. "And that you have an appetite. Nashville hot chicken sandwich. My version."

"Okay. But only because I haven't eaten since breakfast. Missed family meal because I was doing *your* job." She takes a bite and chews.

"The bun is grocery store brioche. Best I could do. Obviously I'd prefer something fresher."

Luann covers her mouth with her hand. "This a red pepper aioli?"

"Nailed it."

She nods and her forehead wrinkles. "I'd lose it. It's fine but not earning its keep."

"I debated whether to put it on."

"Buttered bun, pickles, and done. The pickles are good. Nice crunch and tartness."

"Homemade. I used lemon juice instead of vinegar to change things up."

"The fry on this chicken is perfect. It's still crunchy after however long ago you fried it."

"I used cornstarch and rice flour in the dredge and double-fried it, Korean-style."

"Meat's tender."

"Boneless chicken thigh brined overnight in sweet tea."

"The heat is perfect. I love the smokiness."

"I used smoked honey."

"I'd turn down the salt by ten percent." She wolfs several more large bites while Colton watches. She finishes the sandwich and licks her fingers. She looks at Colton for a few moments as if weighing her options. "Workshop it some more. Then it's going on the menu. Sandwich for lunch; bone-in chicken for dinner."

Colton's heart pumps its fist. "Yes, Chef."

"I want you to hear me."

"I'm listening."

"Not again, understand? No more leaving me in the lurch. Twice is enough."

"Got it, Chef."

"Do it a third time, and it'll be this Earth you're leaving."

"Would you be cooking my final meal before I'm executed? Because—"

"You'll *be* the final meal. I really should not let you back, you know."

"I know. But I sure hope you will."

"At least you *pretend* to want to spare me pain. Not even pretend, actually. I think you sincerely want that, as misguided as your attempts to show it are. For a while there, I was into guys who didn't even pretend, and that wasn't fun."

"Wouldn't imagine. So, did I at least save you from dealing with protestors after I quit?"

"No."

"Persistent like hemorrhoids."

"Well, I didn't tell them you'd quit."

"Seriously?"

"And give them the pleasure? Yeah right. Also didn't tell your coworkers."

Colton does a double take. "What *did* you tell them?"

"That you were on vacation while things blew over."

"What would you have said if I hadn't come groveling back?"

"Guess I'd have crossed that bridge when I came to it. But I was pretty confident you'd come crawling on your belly."

"And that I'd persist in begging even as you tried to make me feel like it was futile."

"Exactly." Luann taps the tip of her nose with her index finger.

"You really got my number, lady."

"Cue you privately wondering how I'll keep the lights on with your sorry ass back in my kitchen."

"If I'm being honest."

"We're going to be too good to boycott."

"What's that going to look like?"

"We'll figure it out. We'll be people's guilty pleasure. They'll all say they won't patronize us on principle, but when push comes to shove, where are they going to go for their anniversaries and special occasions? The Gondolier? Bless their hearts."

"You sure about this? I checked—our Yelp rating is in the toilet."

"I'm aware. This is a fine dining restaurant in Venice, Kentucky. How much do you think we depend on Yelp to survive? People are going to hear about us from a friend and they're going to come. They're going to read about us in *Southern Living* or *Garden & Gun* and they'll come. They're going to hear about our take on Nashville hot chicken and they won't be able to stay away. And if those things don't happen? We're screwed even if we had a pristine Yelp score."

"What about the protestors?"

Luann scoffs. "Remember in high school when Jess McElroy and her crew scared me out of dating you?"

"I recall you gave Jess and company the proverbial middle finger."

"Oh yeah, I did, huh?" She opens her cigarette case with a flourish, pulls out a toothpick, and pops it in her mouth.

They're quiet for a while. Luann giggles to herself. She folds her arm across her chest, rests her elbow on her wrist, and buries her face in her hand.

"What?"

"It's just—it's so funny the wingnuts picked you of all people for this treatment. Like you're Michael Moore or something. Didn't you use to hunt with your dad, like all the time?"

"And with Duane. Hell, I'd go now if I had someone to go with. You interested?"

"Might be."

"Wait, really? I was joking."

"Sure, why not?"

"Well, for starters, in high school you *never* would have. You got mad at me for doing it."

"That was before I owned a restaurant specializing in local ingredients and sustainably sourced animal protein."

"True enough."

She looks at her phone. "It's late."

"You trying to get rid of me?"

"You're opening tomorrow morning."

"Figured. Night, Chef." He begins walking toward the street.

"Colton?" she calls after him.

He turns back to her.

"It's time to move out of your mom's house and find your own place. I want the stakes to be higher for you next time you try to quit on me. Maybe you'll think twice."

"You threatened to end my life if I did."

"Still."

"Will you help me set up my kitchen in my new place?"

"You'll need a lot of help, huh."

"Thanks for taking me back, Luann."

"Thanks for slinking back."

CHAPTER 49

True to what Luann said, no one treats Colton as though he's returning from anything but several days' break when he shows up for work. But Luann calls a meeting and Colton notices that every single Field to Flame employee is present.

Luann stands before them. "Hey, y'all, thanks to everyone who came in on your day off on short notice; promise I'll keep it quick and I'll make it up to you. But I wanted to take a moment to welcome Colton back to the Field to Flame family. I told y'all he was taking a temporary leave of absence, but the truth is he resigned. To protect what we've built here together. He has reconsidered.

"I apologize for not being completely candid with you. I guess it was partly wishful thinking on my part. I hoped Colton would come back before I had to fess up. Here's what I want y'all to know: we're a family here. We don't abandon family for financial advantage. That's not the way I want to live. I'd stand with any of you the way I'll stand for Colton, and I don't need any of you to spare me the trouble. I don't need my life to be easy that way."

"If Colt's sorry ass is worth it, y'all best believe yours is," Reg says, to chuckles.

Luann continues. "Business is down, obviously. Will it pick back up? Hopefully. In all candor, I can tell you I only have one plan at the moment: be so good that people will happily pass through armed protestors to eat here. You've all had that meal you'd risk your life for. We need to be serving that meal. Everyone having the best dining experience they've ever had. Every guest treated like a Michelin reviewer. You're all giving one hundred percent. We gotta give one hundred and ten. No compromises. Everything matters.

"Now is not the time to hold back that idea you've been sitting on. That menu item you'd like to see. That service area you think we should explore. Colton brought me some Nashville hot chicken yesterday that blew my mind."

"Blew your mind, Chef? You downplayed that," Colton says.

"It still needs work. Also, shush your sass mouth during my inspirational speech."

"Zipping my sass mouth now, Chef."

Marisa raises her hand. "The protestors aren't there in the morning. We could start doing takeout coffee and biscuits without totally opening front of house or doing a full sit-down breakfast. We're staffed in the morning anyway."

"Good News Coffee has had a monopoly downtown for too long," Ruth says. "And Marisa and I wouldn't mind picking up some extra hours."

"We could put out a chalkboard to promote it," Marisa says. "Call ourselves 'Caffeine to Brain.'"

"We could cut leftover biscuit dough into donut shape and toss them in the fryer," Dani says. "Call them 'bonuts.'"

"I love it," Luann says. "Y'all talk to me after. We'll figure it out. Everyone else, give me your ideas."

"We could make Colt wash dishes, and I'll stand out front and all the ladies will pour in," Reg says.

"Good idea, Reg, except you've obviously never seen Colton wash a dish. Remember, I said we've gotta be *good*."

Everyone laughs. An exuberant esprit de corps has prevailed.

Luann's tone turns sober. "None of you signed up for this. You want out, I understand. I'll give you an employment reference so glowing you'll need welder's goggles to read it."

"Y'all could easily get a job at the Gondolier cramming people full of defrosted garlic breadsticks like pâté geese," Dani says. Then, after an appropriate comic beat: "But then you'd be working at the Gondolier."

Luann smiles. "On that note, let's get to it."

"Hang on, hang on," Colton says. He goes to the front and stands beside Luann. He extends his hand, palm down—QB again. "Come on, everyone. Bring it in. Let's go."

"All right, let's do this." Luann puts her hand atop Colton's, Dani's on top of hers, then Reg, then the rest, crowded around.

"Count of three, *Field to Flame*," Colton says. "One . . . two . . . three . . ."

"Field to Flame!" they shout in jubilant unison.

"Bless your heart, you're so cheesy," Luann mutters to Colton as they break.

"We don't use *cheese* as a pejorative in this kitchen, Chef. Besides, you love it."

"I hate that I do."

Colton has been on teams that came from behind, defying long odds to win. He has a good feeling about this one.

CHAPTER 50

THE CLAMOR OF THE PROTESTORS LAYING SIEGE OUTSIDE—FIVE OR SIX OF them just in time for dinner—wafts into the kitchen. Colton tries to lose himself in his work and ignore them, but to no avail.

"Has it been like that?" Colton asks Luann, wincing and trying to steady his hands as he dices shallots.

She adjusts the heat on a burner under a pan she's deglazing. "Every night." She shakes her head in weary disgust.

"Y'all tried talking with them?"

"Have we attempted dialogue with the shouting people armed with assault rifles?"

"It's not an entirely stupid question."

"It is a teeny bit, considering you cited people armed with assault rifles and shouting as one of your reasons for quitting."

"Fair enough, but you never know."

"I'm hoping to wait them out."

Colton busies himself, a notion budding in his mind. He sets down his knife. "Chef, there any leftover biscuits from lunch?"

"A bunch."

"Mind if I borrow them?"

"For?"

"Community outreach."

Luann eyes him. "Come on."

"With the biscuits, I figure I at least got a shot."

"Let's not use the word *shot*."

"What's the worst that can happen? They're already parading in front of the restaurant hollering."

"*With guns.* I don't even like thinking about the worst. The times you've attempted dialogue on this issue haven't gone well."

"I was drunk then. Not now. You gotta give me a chance to fix this for you."

Luann puts her fist on her hip and regards him for a while. Finally she raises her palms in surrender, sighing. "Try it. But the slightest hint you're in trouble out there? I'm coming after you swinging a skillet."

Colton gets a tray of biscuits, a pitcher of sweet tea, and some plastic cups. He takes a moment to breathe through his butterflies. He wishes he could have one tiny drink to steady his nerves. A swallowful.

As he's about to push open the door, a whisper sounds in his mind, the small voice of his own better judgment that he was so often unable to heed or hear when he was drinking: *Approach them the way Duane would. Treat them like Duane would.*

He gathers every fiber of confidence he possesses into a sheaf and heads outside.

"Who's hungry, y'all?" Colton calls jovially over the chanting, like he's taking the stage again. He sets the pitcher of sweet tea and cups on the sidewalk and extends the tray of biscuits to the protestors, who quiet and look at him with a mix of wary befuddlement, contempt, and the faintest hint of embarrassment.

"Hey," one of the protestors—a bearded young man in sunglasses, a black Molon Labe T-shirt and black tactical pants, with a highly accessorized black AR-15 slung across his chest—says warily.

Colton's scalp prickles cold and his chest constricts at the sight of the rifle, so close to him. He wills himself to maintain composure. "I'm Colton." He extends his hand to the young man, who hesitates for several seconds before taking it.

"We know," the young man says tersely.

Colton gestures again with the tray. "Y'all gonna eat up here?"

"What'd you do to them?" A gray-haired woman scrutinizes the biscuits, as though scanning them for toothpicks with little skull-and-bones flags stuck in them.

"We take way too much pride in our biscuits to use them for evil. Tell you what—pick any three and I'll eat them right in front of you. How's that? Go ahead. Make my day."

A couple of the demonstrators smile in spite of themselves at the reference. A portly, gray-haired man with a Glock on his hip, who looks to be the woman's husband, grunts his assent and grabs a biscuit. "Hell, I could eat." He takes a bite and grunts again. "Ain't bad." Crumbs spill from his mouth.

"Yeah?" Colton says.

"Not as good as my mamaw's, but—" The man interrupts himself with another bite.

"We ain't trying to compete with mamaw biscuits," Colton says. "When that secret ingredient is loving you, specifically? Hell. Nothing tastes better."

A few reluctant half-smiles. More grabbing of biscuits.

"Wet your whistles?" Colton starts pouring cups of sweet tea, which the group also accepts. This time Colton doesn't have to offer to prove it's untainted.

After the group has had a moment to eat and drink, Colton says, "I didn't just come out here to show off our biscuits and tea. I wanted to introduce myself and give y'all the chance to say your piece. Cuss me out, whatever. So here I am. I'm listening." Colton is proud of how imperturbable he manages to keep his voice. *Like Duane would do.*

The demonstrators look awkwardly at each other. Finally, a large bearded man in a flannel shirt with a .357 revolver on his hip, wearing crepe-soled work boots with heels so worn he nearly walks on the sides of his feet, speaks. "Well, we didn't like what you said."

Colton nods but remains mum, giving the group space to air their grievances.

The gray-haired woman says, "We're not crazy people, and we don't deserve to be cussed out. We want to protect ourselves and exercise our God-given freedoms. That's all."

"It's not evil to want to be able to defend yourself from government tyranny," the young man with the AR-15 says.

"I hear you," Colton says. "I get it. Can I tell y'all where I'm coming from?"

The group nods and shrugs, *Sure, go ahead.*

"I haven't gotten much chance to tell this part publicly. My best buddy in the world was a guy named Duane Arnett. Unbelievable guitar player. He and I came up in Nashville together. He was my only friend on Earth for a while, at least how it felt. When my marriage started imploding, he was there for me. And then he, um." Colton's voice totters. He clears his throat a couple of times and swallows before continuing. He refuses to cry in front of this group. "He was killed a while back at that mass shooting at the country festival in Florida." A few murmurs of recognition pass through the group.

"I miss him. I feel his absence from this world every day. So that's where I'm coming from."

The group is silent for a few seconds. Finally, the hulking bearded man speaks. "My best buddy got killed a few years back during a holdup at the BP where he worked. All I could think about is if he had a gun on him, maybe it wouldn't've gone down like it did."

"Man, I'm real sorry," Colton says. "I know how that hurts. You must miss him."

The man nods quickly and looks away. "Yeah. I miss him bad. We was fishing buddies. Since we was kids."

"Duane and I used to fish together. We loved duck hunting too. What was your bud's name?"

"Terry."

"I bet Terry was a real good dude."

"Sure was."

Colton takes advantage of the ensuing silence to gather himself and choose his words. "Here's the deal, folks. I ain't a powerful man. The lawmakers don't listen to me. I'm no threat to your rights. I'm just a guy who has a different opinion on what sort of guns you should be able to walk up and buy. That's the beauty of America, isn't it? We can have different opinions. Did I cuss some when I expressed those opinions publicly? I sure did. If you really knew how much Duane meant to me, I believe you'd understand.

"Maybe y'all might like to see me fired, but I need this job. These ain't easy times we live in, and a man needs to work and make a living. I don't have any college. I can swing a hammer pretty good, but I got a bad knee that makes it tough to work construction. I got an old dog who's racking up the vet bills. My dad died, and my mama's gonna need help. I ain't getting rich here, y'all, believe you me. And when my ex-wife divorced me, it left me in a bad spot financially. The lady who owns this place, she and I go way back. High school sweethearts, in fact. She's a single mama raising two daughters on her own. She doesn't have it easy either. She took a real risk giving me this job because she knew there's a lot of people in this world who don't care for me. So that's my sob story. I ain't trying to throw myself a pity party. I'm just telling how it is. Y'all can do with that what you will."

Silence from the group. Averted eyes. As though maybe they have old dogs with failing bodies or aging parents or bad knees or exes or jobs that never let them get ahead.

"My older brother played football with you at Venice High," a skinny, acne-scarred young man who hasn't spoken yet says after a few moments.

"Who?"

"Ronnie Tate."

Colton brightens. "Hell, I remember Ronnie! He could run a football; dude went like a damn rocket."

"Yeah, he was good."

"How's he doing?"

"Got his own HVAC business in North Venice. Married, couple of kids. Doing well."

"Man, that's great. Will you tell Ronnie I said hi and I'm glad he's crushing it at life?"

"I'll see him Sunday. I'll tell him."

Colton looks at the group. "Folks, I gotta get back to work. Boss lady'll be on my ass if I don't. But I'm glad we got a chance to meet and talk some. Sometimes it's important to remind each other that we're all just folks doing the best we can. Y'all enjoy those biscuits and tea. Just leave the tray and pitcher and cups by the door when you go, okay?" Colton goes around, shaking hands with each demonstrator. He starts inside.

"It wasn't never anything personal," the large bearded man says after him.

Colton turns.

"People shit on us a lot. We were sticking up for ourselves, not trying to hurt you," the man continues.

Colton smiles a faint, sad smile. "Y'all have a good night. Hug the people you love."

He goes inside.

After a while, and without fanfare, they leave.

CHAPTER 51

April 2016
Venice, Kentucky

On the last Sunday in April, Colton and Petey move into their new home in East Venice—a 750-square-foot white cottage built in 1915. Railroad tracks run on a raised berm behind the chain-link fence in the backyard. It has patinaed heart-of-pine floors, and it smells like the mold that infests the shabby AC window units. There are two small bedrooms, a single bath, and a front porch with space for a pair of rocking chairs. Rent is $700 a month. The water pressure wouldn't strip paint off anything, but there's a half-decent gas range in the kitchen.

When the landlord showed Colton the house, Colton remembered how Maisy would talk about wanting to move into a tiny house like she'd see on HGTV. He'd suggest she try living in her 150-square-foot shoe closet (not to be confused with her primary, secondary, or tertiary clothes closets) for a few days to audition it. He doubted the reality would meet her expectations, like the truth of so much else.

Derrick helps him move in his spartan furnishings in the late morning and they finish by two, the April breeze drying their perspiration. They sit on Colton's front porch in a couple of rockers he got off Craigslist and split a Little Caesars pepperoni Hot-N-Ready, washing it down with ice-cold Ale-8s from glass bottles. Colton was prepared for Derrick to rib him about his humble new digs—he had comebacks at the ready. But

Derrick did no such thing. In the late afternoon, Derrick leaves, passing Luann and her twins as they come to replace him. Luann wears a short mustard sundress emblazoned with blue cornflowers. It reminds Colton of the dress she wore the day they built the deck. Her shoulders and collarbones are creamy and flecked with freckles under the spaghetti straps, and her wavy hair is gathered into a messy bun with two tendrils falling loose on either side of her face, framing it. She leaves her flip-flops inside the front door and pads around his house barefoot, dusty rose polish adorning her toes.

Colton seldom sees Luann outside of work, almost never attired in anything but her chaste chef's jacket. The sight of her in civilian clothes stirs delicious butterflies in him, like the feeling before he used to go onstage.

Luann brought a metal mixing bowl of rosemary-tarragon chicken salad and a framed pencil rendering she did of the Brooklyn Bridge, correctly surmising that Colton would be impoverished of wall décor. She assigns Freja and Esme to work in the yard, picking up twigs, rocks, and other detritus, and to sweep the floors, while she helps Colton put his kitchen in order. As she toils in the close heat of the confined area, a sheer dew of sweat rises on her brow, chest, and shoulders like condensation on a glass of lemonade. She smells like freshly shampooed hair and sunscreen on clean, warm skin.

Colton steals a glimpse at the exquisite line of her calf every time she stands on her tiptoes to put something away. While passing behind her, he puts his hand on the back of her arm for a couple beats longer than necessary and reflexively says *behind*, as is the practice in the restaurant kitchen.

Soon, Freja and Esme shirk their duties to hassle Petey. He doesn't seem to mind, and there's a bounce in his step as he hobbles around the yard with the twins giggling and giving chase and offering him his cherished slobber-glazed tennis ball. Luann opens the kitchen window to call them back to their tasks, but Colton intervenes. "Petey needs to play with kids more than I need help picking up my yard."

"They have to learn how to stay on task." Luann scrubs out a pan.

"They can learn tomorrow." Colton hangs one of his mamaw's cast iron skillets on his kitchen cart.

"Undermining my parenting yet again. I can already tell when you have kids you're gonna spoil them rotten."

"*If*," Colton says, and he hopes Luann doesn't press him about the melancholy permeating his voice. She doesn't.

Her hands are covered in soap suds. Colton joins her at the sink. He reaches over and tenderly lifts a lock of hair out of her eyes and tucks it behind her ear, pausing to live for a moment in the hollow between her ear and her jawline.

Taking his first break since lunch, Colton heads outside to give Freja and Esme dog treats to offer Petey, as though they need any aid getting in his good graces.

Unbidden, Esme tells Colton, "Mom said you quit working for her for a while."

Colton squirms. He scratches his cheekbone. "Ah. Yeah, I did. For a bit. But I came back."

"Mom cried when you quit," Freja says matter-of-factly.

"*Freja. Don't.* That's secret," Esme says.

"Mom didn't say it was."

"So?"

"Y'all," Colton says. "I won't tell your mom you said anything. And I also won't make her cry again."

"Sometimes people cry when they're happy," Freja says.

"Okay, then I'll try to only make your mom cry from happiness."

"Okay."

"You sure your mom wasn't crying out of happiness when I quit?"

"No, she seemed sad."

"Well, I'm sorry I made your mom sad," Colton says, indeed contrite but with a scintilla of inner jubilance to hear how Luann missed him.

Colton rejoins her in the kitchen. She casts him a glance and then another, more wary one. "What're you all Cheshire Cat grinny about?"

"Hmm?"

"*Hmm*? You're smiling like you have a secret."

"It's no secret I find chatting with your daughters delightful."

"I feel like ever since that first banana split incident, they view you as an accomplice in shenanigans."

"No shenanigans afoot."

"Mmm-hmm."

"Look. Want to know why I'm smiling?"

"Do I? And I'd call it a smirk."

"Because I'm happy. That's all."

"And the mischievous glint?"

"Because my being happy feels like I'm getting away with something."

Before Luann departs, she helps Colton select a location to mount her drawing. Then Colton steadies her with both hands on her waist while she hangs a set of windchimes on his porch. It could be his imagination, but she takes longer than necessary to do the job. He keeps his hands on her waist for all that time and for a few delectable seconds after she's stepped down from the chair she was standing on.

Freja and Esme weep when it's time to bid Petey adieu and go home. "We like how he smells like macaroni and cheese," they hiccup through tears.

In the calm solitude of the early evening, Colton lies on a picnic blanket in his new backyard and rubs Petey's belly. The humid, hazy air glitters gold from sunset through saffron-hued pine pollen. The aroma of cut grass, lighter fluid, and charcoal grill smoke hovers around them. It's turning Colton's mouth to the notion of using the last dregs of sunlight to grill up a couple of thick, rare sirloins for him and Petey.

It's not quiet, exactly. The creaking of insects floats atop the faint drone of a lawnmower up the street. Colton's windchimes jangle in the languid breeze. A train approaches and rattles past (Petey takes little notice—a good sign), with its horn sounding in the distance a few minutes downtrack.

Through it all, Colton replays in his memory the hours he spent with Luann, while she helped him nest; her daughters outside making a birdsong of giggling and ebullient shrieking. The seconds he spent holding her waist, his hands tasting her body's heat under the gossamer cotton of her dress.

In his heart there's a profound and forlorn stillness—such as attends losing what was never yours.

CHAPTER 52

"I DUNNO, .45," DERRICK SAYS.

"Come *on*," Colton says. "I've fed y'all how many times now? And when have I disappointed?"

"Not once," Gabrielle says, glowering at Derrick. "Baby, you trusted him to feed us for my *birthday*."

"Thank you, Gabi. I appreciate that," Colton says indignantly.

Derrick holds up his hands. "Just saying. I've never had Nashville hot chicken before. How'm I gonna know if it's good?"

"You *could* check in with your mouth and if it's telling you, *mmmmm this is tasty*, then maybe don't worry about how it compares to other Nashville hot chicken," Colton says.

"Excuse me, excuse me, I'm sorry." Derrick makes a time-out sign. "I thought the entire point was to do Luann's bidding to perfect your *Nashville hot chicken* with an eye toward it going on the menu. See, if you put a plate of fettuccine alfredo in front of me, my mouth would find that very delicious indeed. But it wouldn't taste like Nashville hot chicken. Am I wrong?"

Colton starts to respond.

Derrick cuts him off. "*Am I wrong?*"

Gabi rolls her eyes at Derrick. "Baby. Stop lawyering, shut up, and eat."

Colton peels back the foil covering the aluminum serving tray, revealing legs, wings, and breasts fried deep, glistening maroon with spice.

Derrick reaches for a piece. Colton halts him. "Hold up. There's a right way to do this."

He goes back to the kitchen and returns with a loaf of Texas toast and a mason jar of pickle slices and opens both. "First things first. You lay down a piece of bread. Then you put the chicken on top of that. The bread soaks up all the goodness."

"You mean the grease and spice," Derrick says, laying down a piece of bread and then a leg on top.

"Like I said. The goodness. Then—" Colton fishes several pickle chips out of the jar with a fork, shakes the juice off them, and garnishes the top of Derrick's chicken. "You eat the chicken with the pickles. The acidity and tartness of the pickles complements the spice and cuts through the fattiness and gives you some different texture."

"Any more hot chicken law I need to study before I, you know, eat my food?" Derrick says.

"Carry on, Counselor."

While Derrick and Gabi assemble their plates, Colton serves up the sides—a honey-mustard brussels sprout slaw and pimento mac and cheese.

They start eating.

A few bites in, Colton studies the faces of his fellow diners. "So?"

Gabrielle covers her mouth with her hand as she finishes a bite. Then she points at her plate and looks at Colton. "Ten out of ten. Five stars. Two thumbs up."

Colton flushes with pride (and the sandwich's heat). "Yeah?"

"Crunch is perfect. Spiciness, perfect. Makes your mouth sing, but doesn't overwhelm."

Colton looks to Derrick. "D Rock?"

Derrick gazes at his plate, his face solemn and pensive. He grunts a couple of times as though embroiled in internal debate. He nods slowly. Then he cracks. His face breaks into a wide grin.

Colton claps and hoots and points. "Boom, baby! *Boom.*"

Derrick shakes his head and goes for another bite. "Bro, I did not want to like this as much as I do, for your ego's sake. But damn, son."

"You think I'm ready to take it to Luann?" Colton asks.

"If I ordered this, I would leave supremely satisfied," Gabrielle says.

"Even if you passed up more haute cuisine options on the menu?" Colton asks.

"Even then."

"I still cannot believe that you of all people learned how to cook," Derrick says.

"That a yes on the chicken being ready for prime time?" Colton asks.

"That's a hell yes. Now shut up and let me eat," Derrick says.

"Save room because there's chocolate peanut butter mousse pie," Colton says.

Gabrielle's eyes roll back in gustatory bliss. "Derrick, does this qualify as attempted murder?"

They eat for a while. The pile of hot chicken in the serving tray shrinks.

"Speaking of Luann." Derrick has a mischievous glint in his eye. He leans back in his chair, sucking at a tooth, wiping his fingers on a heated, lemongrass-scented towelette Colton provided (he was testing every facet of the experience).

"Were we?" Colton says.

"You know damn well. What was she coming to do when I was leaving the other day?"

"Get my kitchen in shape. What're you getting at?"

"I'm just saying—sorry, baby." He looks at Gabrielle. "There was a cleavage situation."

"*A cleavage situation*," Colton repeats.

"A *distinct* cleavage situation."

Gabrielle gives Derrick a glare that would scour the seasoning from cast iron. "Mmmm, nope. No sir. I do not care for this phrase—*cleavage situation*—at all."

Colton leans back in his chair. "Can't say I noticed," he lies. "She's my boss." He thinks about her in her yellow dress, standing on her tiptoes to put away a glass.

"I'm just sayin': it's not everyone's boss who shows up to help them move in while sporting a cleavage situation," Derrick says.

"Utter the words 'cleavage situation' again, and I'm swiping my thumb across my plate and rubbing Nashville hot grease and pickle juice directly in your eye," Gabrielle says.

"I got it out of my system," Derrick says. Then he says to Colton, "But she wasn't always your boss. Y'all were hot and heavy back in the day. You telling me there's nothing between y'all?"

Colton reddens, his pulse throbbing in his temples. "Man, honestly, I ain't thought about it."

Derrick squints. "First you feed me Nashville hot chicken; now you feed me lies."

"Naw, bro. No dating until I'm a year sober is what they told me in the program. So it hasn't been on my mind."

"When is a year sober?"

"June 3."

"That's fast approaching."

Colton rises from the table, claps, and rubs his hands together. "Who's ready for pie?"

"Oh, all right," Derrick says.

"Luann and I have a complicated history. Me and pie, less so. Sounds like I have one taker. Gabi?" Colton asks.

She sighs and throws up her hands. "I am a weak, weak woman."

"Don't punish yourself for being human." Colton dishes up pie. "I call this Petey's Peanut Butter Pie. It's one of my nicknames for my boy."

"So why Nashville hot chicken of all things to be perfecting?" Gabrielle asks.

"Well, it's two things. The first is that my working at the restaurant has resulted in a downtick in business."

"Still?" Gabrielle's jaw drops.

"Yeah, enough to make us seek out ways to make up the difference."

Gabrielle raises her hand. "I can't. Ridiculous."

"Luann thinks Nashville hot chicken is about to blow up. And we'll be the only and best game in town."

"What's the second thing?"

"The, uh, second thing is—" Colton looks at Derrick and Gabi, and heartache unexpectedly engulfs him. He tries to speak, but emotion throttles him. *Someday, maybe, I'll stop living so close to the bone.* He looks away, clears his throat, and scratches his cheek. "Sorry," he rasps and thumps his chest a couple times. "Little acid from the spice. The second thing is that it reminds me of good times with friends."

CHAPTER 53

May 2016
Venice, Kentucky

Colton pulls up to Luann's house on Sunday night and parks behind her Volvo, his heart quickening. He's never been inside, and he's nervous to see what sort of home she's made for herself and her girls. Curiosity has long gnawed at him, so he's glad that inadvertently hanging on to his chef's jacket after Saturday's shift has given him an excuse.

He walks up to the door with Petey in tow. Colton values his life too much to show up to the twins' home without him. He rings the doorbell, hears two voices yell "Mom!" and then two pairs of small feet running. Freja and Esme open the door breathlessly. "Petey!" they shriek in unison and fall on him, hugging his neck from both sides, completely ignoring Colton.

Luann follows them. "Girls? Are we going to invite Mr. Colton in? Or at least acknowledge him?"

They ignore her too. They run out onto the front lawn with Petey and start throwing sticks for him to fetch. Luann shakes her head and rolls her eyes. "I swear I've raised my children with manners. Come in. To what do I owe this pleasure?"

Colton steps inside, handing her the chef's jacket. "Had to bring this by." Luann's house is cool and smells like an upscale spa—cedar, magnolia flowers, and grapefruit. "When you getting these girls a dog?"

"When I'm not working twelve hours a day." Luann wears black skinny jeans, ballet flats, a Parisian-looking white knit shirt with wide black stripes, and a slim black leather motorcycle jacket. She smells like fresh-laundered, sun-drying sheets; clean skin; figs; and the honeyed grape of linden blossom.

Colton eyes her up and down in the most gentlemanly way he can. *Lord have mercy, she's a vision.* "You look nice; what you all dressed up for?"

"Thanks. Well, nothing as of a few minutes ago. I had a thing but my babysitter just canceled on me and my parents are both sick with the flu, so..."

"I know someone who'd be more than happy to watch your kiddos so you can do your thing."

"All ears."

"Me."

Luann glances at Colton and laughs. Then she looks at him again. "Wait, you're serious."

"I'm free tonight. I even got Petey here with me. Let me be a hero."

"You don't want to do this."

"Sure I do. Your girls love me."

"Because you undermine me to win their favor."

"Still mad about the banana split thing?"

"Here I make them these gorgeous lavender-honey crème brûlées, and you swoop in with your banana splits—"

"Lavender tastes like shaving cream to a kid."

"Until you train their palates to have some sophistication."

"Hey, I drizzled some duck fat caramel with Himalayan pink salt on them."

"Ohhhhh, very challenging flavor profile there. Pure salt, fat, and sugar. Whoever'd have guessed you'd make a couple new friends with that. You know what?" Luann says. "Just to punish you, next week we're doing a panna cotta banana pudding with duck fat salted caramel and banana cake, and you're responsible for it. You like to make banana desserts so much, you can knock yourself out."

"Well it'll be a big hit, because apparently you can't go wrong with those flavor profiles."

"Anyway, no, you don't want to babysit tonight."

"I insist you allow me."

"It'd be weird."

"Would not."

"Um, yes, it would, because my thing is a date." Luann eyes him with raised, skeptical eyebrows. Gauntlet thrown.

Oh. Colton scrambles to hide his rush of mixed deflation and jealousy from showing on his face. *So much for Derrick's cleavage situation theory.* "Good. Now you can go because you got a babysitter," he says breezily.

Still with lifted eyebrows, Luann says, "You're okay with that?"

Colton laughs (maybe a bit too loudly). "Why wouldn't I be? Have fun!"

"I'll pay you."

"You can't afford me. I volunteer."

Luann scoffs. "Are you sure?"

"I'm sure. Now give me the damn tour already," he says with forced cheer.

She leads Colton through the entryway into the living room. He scans around in awe. Her style is still hers—echoes of her teenage bedroom abound—but updated and more sophisticated and adult. Everywhere his eye lands, there's something beautiful, elegant, interesting, or all three. Her impeccable decorating trends toward Scandinavian midcentury design, fitting for her midcentury modern house. "Your place looks like a West Elm, but nicer."

"Thanks?"

Colton gestures with his head. "That a Carl-Axel Acking chair?"

Luann turns to him, mouth agape. "How the *hell* did you know that?"

"Few years back Maisy was redecorating, and she hired Angelo Surmelis from HGTV to do it. Nice guy; we talked a lot. Learned a ton."

"Color me impressed." She continues showing him around the house. Aside from the kitchen's being somehow even more spectacular than he would have predicted, it's exactly the house he always imagined Luann would end up in, even if he didn't have the faculties at the time to envision the particulars.

After a few moments, Colton says with all the nonchalance he can muster, "So, who's this date?"

Luann shrugs. "You don't know him."

"I'd sure hope not. That would almost certainly bode poorly for you. Who is it?"

"He's an ophthalmologist."

"You don't wear glasses."

"We met on a dating app."

Colton snickers.

"Forgive me for not wanting to die alone."

"Will you ask him if when eye doctors are doing that *Which is better: one or two* thing if they ever just give you the same lens twice in a row to see if you're playing eye hooky?"

"I absolutely will not."

"You gonna give him a choice of outfits and ask him if he likes one or two better and then two or three better?"

"Really leaning into the one ophthalmologist joke you have, huh."

Luann opens the front door and calls to the twins, "Freja! Esme! Since Dawn can't come babysit, Mr. Colton is going to."

The girls squeal.

Colton grins. "See?"

Luann shakes her head. "They've had dinner. They can play until eight or so and then it's bedtime. They can get themselves ready for bed, brush teeth, all that. You have my number. And I left my parents' number on the fridge in case there's an emergency."

"Has it changed since high school?"

"Not in twenty years."

"Then I still remember it."

"This is so weird."

"Your high school boyfriend who still has your high school phone number memorized babysitting your twin girls on his night off from working for you at your restaurant while you go on a date? You think that's weird?"

"My *country star* high school boyfriend, yes."

"*Former* country star. What time you think you'll be back?"

"We're going to dinner in Bowling Green, so probably around ten?"

"Try not to judge the restaurant too harshly now that my Nashville hot chicken has passed your lips."

"I knew you'd make me regret my honesty. Straight to your head, like I thought."

"When's the dude gonna be here? What's his name?"

"J.D. And a few minutes."

"J.D.," Colton repeats back to himself quietly. *Hope it stands for "Just Disappointing."*

The doorbell rings after a few minutes. Luann answers. There stands J.D. in his be-khakied glory. Blue sport coat, loafers. He's good-looking in a milquetoast way, like the third most handsome man at your church.

"Okay, I'm leaving! Bye, kittens," Luann calls. Freja and Esme run to hug her goodbye. J.D. greets them formally and stiffly. He's clearly uncomfortable around kids.

Colton strides to the door.

"All right, we better get going," Luann says quickly as she sees Colton's approach. "We don't need to—"

Colton extends his hand past her, to J.D. "What's up, my man? Colton."

J.D. accepts the handshake. He has a soft, smooth doctor's hand. "J.D. Nice to meet you. Are you—"

"I'm just the babysitter, bud."

"Colton's a coworker," Luann says with a strained lilt.

"Well, now," Colton says with a rakish smile he knows from experience is one women like. "We go a *little* further back than that."

J.D.'s face betrays that he'd rather Luann's babysitter didn't have a smile women like. Or look like a famous country singer. Or go further back.

Luann shoots Colton a *What are you doing; knock it off* glare. "We went to high school together."

Colton answers her look with a *What? Lil' ol' me?* look. "All right, you two, y'all best be getting on. Have fun. Don't do anything I wouldn't do. Hey, real quick though, J.D.: when eye doctors do that thing where y'all are like 'Which is better, one or—'"

"Nope, Colton. We need to go," Luann says curtly. And she and J.D. leave.

Colton watches them walk to J.D.'s Lexus SUV, where J.D. opens the door for Luann. The sight makes Colton forlorn. *You didn't think she'd fall for you again, did you? You had your chance and blew it the first time.* He takes a moment to try to shake off his sadness and envy before he goes back inside.

Freja and Esme immediately accost him. "We want banana splits again!" Freja says.

"Banana splits, banana splits," Esme chants. The twins hang from Colton's arms.

He groans with mock exertion and lifts them off the ground, carrying them toward the kitchen. "Okay, okay! Let's see what ingredients Mama's got." Colton rifles through the kitchen. Her pantry is amazing. Her fridge is stocked with all sorts of delicacies. But conspicuously absent are any vanilla ice cream or bananas, necessary preconditions to the making of a good banana split.

"We're gonna have to go to the store real quick."

They head out to Colton's truck. "Can we ride in the back?" Freja pleads.

"I doubt your mama would like that much," Colton says. "Tell you what: I'll drive you up and down the street a couple times, and you can ride in the back. Then you have to get inside with me. Deal?"

"Deal!" the twins shout. Colton lifts each into the bed. They squeal and giggle as he drives ten miles per hour up and down their street a few times. Finally, he stops and makes them get in the cab. They sit three across the front bench seat.

"Can we choose the radio station?" Esme asks.

"We want 99.1," Freja says.

Colton briefly considers introducing them to Loretta Lynn instead but acquiesces apprehensively. Not thirty seconds later, Maisy's song with Justin Bieber and Diplo, "Losing Myself in You," still dominating the charts, comes on. Colton moves to change it, his hesitation validated. "Let's listen to—"

"*Nooooooo,*" the girls howl in unison.

"We love this song, and Mom never lets us listen to it," Freja says.

"She hates it," Esme says. "She thinks it has a bad message."

Colton smiles in spite of himself. "I'm not the hugest fan of this song either, but sounds like I'm outvoted, so..."

The twins cheer.

"Did you and our mom used to go on dates in high school?" Esme asks.

"We... were..."

"She said you did," Esme says.

"She's... uh... telling the truth. We used to go out."

"Did you kiss?" Freja presses gleefully.

"You know what I *did* do in high school?" Colton says quickly, his face crimson. "I played football. Your mama tell you that?"

"No," Esme says.

"Our dad says it's dumb that they call it soccer in America instead of football because you use your feet for soccer."

"Well your dad can..." Colton pauses to swallow his irritation before continuing, lest he tell two eight-year-olds their father can suck a big old salted cod or whatever Danish people do. "Have his own opinions about that, and that's okay. Either of you ever played football before?"

"Just soccer," Freja says.

"Who wants to learn how to throw a football?" Colton asks.

"*MEEEEEEEE,*" the twins shriek, making him wince.

Soon, they're driving back with bananas, Walmart's finest vanilla ice cream, caramel sauce, whipped cream, and a couple of Nerf footballs.

When they arrive, a rising, humid west wind buffets them. It smells like electricity and rain. Dark clouds mass on the horizon.

The three play in the backyard until it gets dark. Colton finds a bucket and sets it on a patio chair as a target and teaches the girls how to throw spirals, aiming for the bucket's mouth. Then they play a little two-on-one football—the twins versus Colton. The girls triumph. Petey watches from the sidelines, the world's most lackadaisical cheerleader.

By the time they're ready to go inside and gorge themselves on banana splits, the twins are breathless, their cheeks ruddy and sweat-glossed from exertion and merriment. The football tutorial was a famous success. Thunder growls in the distance.

At 7:48, Colton sends the twins to get ready for bed. At 8:03, he tucks them in.

"I'll be out in the living room, okay?" Colton says, turning out the light.

He retrieves a book from his truck. A light rain falls. Wind rushes in the trees with a sound like ocean breakers. Lightning scores the sky, illuminating towering thunderheads. Thunder rumbles, closer this time. Back inside, he reads until he grows dozy. Reclined on the couch, with Petey at his feet and his book on his chest, Colton drifts off.

A thunderclap jolts him awake, his heart pounding. He looks toward the twins' room and startles again.

Esme and Freja stand in the hallway, side by side in their matching pink nighties.

"Holy shi— Y'all haven't seen *The Shining*, huh."

"We're scared," Esme says. "Can we come out here with you until Mom gets home?"

"Go get your blankets." Colton turns out the lights in the living room.

The twins pull their comforters from their beds and return. Each nests on either side of Colton using their blankets, curling up against him. Following suit, Petey curls up nose-to-tail on the floor.

Even though the thunder outside continues to roll, gusting wind lashes rain torrents against the windows, and lightning periodically illuminates the room through the large windows as if daylight, the twins soon grow heavy with sleep and cease fidgeting.

Colton sits and feels the warmth of them nestled against him. He hears their breathing slow. He surveys the darkened living room that Luann immaculately appointed.

Inhabit this life while you can.

For these few brief moments, imagine all this is yours and you didn't squander all opportunity for it.

Pretend you were ever good enough for this.

He doesn't know what's worse—to have it for an hour or never.

He closes his eyes and listens to them breathe, his heart breaking with every breath.

CHAPTER 54

THE JINGLE OF PETEY'S TAGS AS HE STANDS AWAKENS COLTON. LUANN hovers over him and her sleeping daughters, watching with a tender expression.

"Hey," Colton says in a hoarse, drowsy whisper. "Sorry, I must've—"

Luann smiles and puts her finger to her lips. Lightning outside like a camera flash. She bends down to lift Freja.

Colton gets to his feet. "I got them," he whispers. He scoops up a sleeping twin in each arm. They bury their faces in his shoulders with a soft mewl. He bears them gently back to the bedroom they share, Luann at his heels with their bedding. He lays each in their bed, and Luann covers them with their comforters, tucks them in, kisses each on the cheek, and strokes their hair for a moment.

The pair make a quiet retreat, Luann shutting the door behind her noiselessly. They tiptoe to the living room and stand facing each other.

"How long were you standing there?" Colton asks, rubbing his eye.

"Few minutes."

"Swear I was being a vigilant sitter. Got a little sleepy."

Luann waves him off. "Guess the thunder scared the girls?"

"Wouldn't have expected that from your daughters."

"I was scared of storms too before I learned to love watching them.

Pays to confront fears." Luann nods at Colton's book, *Legends of the Fall*, on the coffee table. "That yours?"

"Yeah."

"Remember when we saw the movie?"

"I remember being on a couch with you while the movie played in front of us. I recall we didn't actually *watch* a lot of it."

"Thank Brad Pitt for that."

"I met him once. Should've."

She picks up the book and thumbs through it. "Looks like a pretty serious read."

"I was disappointed by the lack of pictures, but I've been sounding out the words."

"Didn't mean it like that. I never knew you as a huge reader is all."

"Picked it up on tours. Lots of reading time."

She sets the book back on the coffee table. "Be still, my teenage heart."

"What about your current heart?"

"Don't fish for compliments. It's unseemly."

"How was your date?" There's only one answer Colton wants.

"Meh."

That's the one. "Aw." Colton tries not to gloat.

"He was nice. Just... not very interesting."

"How was the restaurant?"

"It was nice. Just... not very interesting."

"So it's no Bucky's is what you're saying." *And he's no me.*

Luann shoots him a knowing grin.

"Well," Colton says softly. "Better luck next time?" He searches in his pocket for his keys. "I guess I'll—"

"Hey," Luann says, putting her hand on his. "You got somewhere to be?"

"Nah. Petey's here, so no need to check on him."

"Looks like we have a little storm left."

"You... wanna watch it?"

"Need you even ask? Hold on." She retrieves a towel. She opens the sliding glass door to the deck adjoining the living room and mops off the patio chairs.

Colton steps outside. The rain has mostly ceased. Water gurgles in the rain gutters, patters from the railings, and stands in puddles on the deck. The air, rinsed of pollen, has surrendered its heat to fuel the storm. It smells like petrichor and the sliced-cucumber scent of pure water on thirsty green plants and white blooms.

Luann sits and pats the chair next to her. "Sit your ass down."

"You're in high spirits for having endured such a boring date."

"Couple of glasses of Avalon Cabernet at dinner, and I'm a lightweight. Speaking of, where are my manners." She gets up and Colton notices a little wobble in her balance. She returns minutes later with two mason jars and hands one to Colton.

"This is?"

"Crushed ice, grapefruit juice, ginger beer, a shot of reduced fig balsamic vinegar, and a sprig of mint."

Colton takes a sip and nods, smacking his lips. "Damn." He raises his jar and clinks hers in toast. "To the two smartest, most well-behaved children on the planet."

"I'll drink to smartest. Most well-behaved is iffy."

"They were angels. Besides making me listen to 'Losing Myself in You.'"

Luann feigns gagging. "Hate that song."

"They said."

"It's not even that it's Maisy."

Colton eyes Luann with teasing skepticism. "It's a *little* bit that it's Maisy."

"It's a genuinely abysmal song. Like, what a message for young women: *subsume yourself in your boyfriend's personality.* How romantic."

"They said you felt that way. I guess we finally found something Scandinavian you don't like."

Luann eyes him quizzically.

"Every song on pop radio is written by one of, like, three Swedish dudes."

"I'm done with all things Scandinavian." Luann pauses for a second. "Okay, maybe not their furniture. But their songs and *definitely* their men."

Colton reaches over and clinks his mason jar against Luann's again. "Cheers to that."

"Did Maisy like watching storms?" Luann asks, casting her eyes downward.

"Total indifference. And we had good ones in Dallas."

"You ever try to get her to?"

"Never once. That was yours and mine alone. Always and forever."

Luann smiles and buries her face in her hand. "Ah, how I yearned to be interesting. I thought adopting that as *my thing* would make me intriguing and mysterious. Such a child of the nineties."

"Lemme tell you what. I've met David Bowie. I've met Dolly. I consider you the most interesting person I've ever encountered."

"You just said you met Brad Pitt. What about him?"

"You still win."

"Oh shut up."

"Hand to God."

"Such a liar."

"Will it lend credibility if I acknowledge this is my opinion and many people would disagree?"

"Marginally."

"Speaking of the nineties, your girls knew all about us dating. Well, not *all*, I hope."

"They're already to the age where I have to tap-dance to seem cool to them."

"And telling them we used to date is cool?"

"To them. And it has nothing to do with your celebrity."

"*Brief* celebrity. So did Henning like watching storms?"

"We never lived in a great place for that. But he usually found reasons why things I found beautiful were pedestrian and boring."

"What a cool guy."

"Yeah, good times. Anyway, when were you and the twins listening to the radio?"

"On the way to get banana split fixins."

Luann shakes her head. "I *knew* you'd continue your project of ruining them."

"Oh you haven't heard the half of it. I also bought them Nerf footballs and taught them to throw. Then we scrimmaged some."

"And?"

"Esme's got the arm. Freja's the bruiser. Get 'em both into Pop Warner ASAP."

"I may not be able to afford your babysitting rate, but I'm absolutely reimbursing you for those footballs."

"They were a gift," Colton says. "You've raised amazing daughters, Luann. I'm deeply impressed." *And don't get me started on the envy.*

"They were *so* excited to hang with you and Petey."

"Let's be honest: mostly Petey."

"No. It was you. They love you."

"You think?" A rush of pride passes through Colton.

"I *know*. When you've loved someone, it changes you, I believe. At the cellular, DNA level. They have my DNA, so they were born to love you."

A livewire silence dangles between them while Colton parses exactly what she's saying. A particularly spectacular bolt of lightning interrupts the moment as it bathes the retreating thunderheads in violet-blue iridescence. They both gasp involuntarily.

"One of my favorite things about performing was looking out over the crowd and seeing the little glowing cell phones in the dark. It reminded me of lightning against clouds at night," Colton says.

"When I lived in Copenhagen, we'd sometimes see the Northern Lights. They were spectacular, but I still missed this," Luann says.

"Never in a million years thought you'd end up back here again."

Luann sips her drink and nods slightly. "Me neither. But then I missed fireflies. And cornfields in October. And dirt roads. And stillness. And storms. Turns out I needed those things. But I'd be lying if I said I didn't feel like a failure sometimes. Like I retreated or something. And maybe I'm just telling myself I missed all those things to cover my shortcomings. I dunno. I'm a little buzzed from the wine, and I'm being too honest. In vino veritas."

"Yeah, I wouldn't know anything about knocking a few back and being too honest." Colton gives Luann a melancholy smile. "For what it's worth, I don't consider you a failure at all."

"Yeah, well, for what it's worth, I don't think you are either."

They smile at each other and then look away.

"So. You gonna go on another date with ol' J.D.?"

"You are *such* a dick," Luann mutters, shaking her head.

Colton stares at her, mouth agape. "What?"

"*What,*" Luann says in a mock-deep voice, approximating Colton's drawl. "*My name's Colton Gentry, and I go out of my way to intimidate Luann's date so he spends all night asking questions about me and then I act all innocent.*"

"First off, I don't talk like that."

"*Yes you*—I mean *yes I do.*"

"No. My voice doesn't sound like that. Secondly, I was being friendly!"

"Regular ol' one-man welcoming committee."

"Are you literally getting mad at me for being handsome and charming?"

"And then making my ovaries explode by picking up both my sleeping daughters and carrying them to their room and tucking them in."

"Again, not sure what you want from me."

"Colton. Were you jealous of J.D.?" She says it with a teasing lilt, but it's clearly a serious question.

"Lil' bit, yeah. Lil' teeny bit."

Luann sits quietly for a moment. Then she backhands Colton in the sternum.

"What was *that* for?"

"For dumping me twenty years ago. Asshole."

"You know I tried calling you two consecutive Christmases in a row after."

"I know. I almost called you back."

"I wanted to make things right."

"I don't think I would've been a receptive audience at the time."

"Ain't trying to split hairs here, but technically you're the one who dumped me."

"Just finishing what you started."

"I don't think I ever told you this, but I saw Mara earlier that night. And she basically told me she didn't think I was good enough for you. I'd always been insecure about that, and it had a big part in my actions."

Luann sighs. "Man, I wish she hadn't said that. She hated that I was always hanging out with you."

"Anyway, no sooner had the words come out of my mouth than I regretted them."

"It was the words coming out of your mouth at all. You fractured my faith in love, just as I was rebuilding it after feeling rejected by my mom and stepdad. I've never recovered completely."

Colton regards her for a long time. "You mean that?" he asks quietly.

Luann looks off and sips her grapefruit fizz. "Henning had his chance to restore it, and instead he shattered what you only cracked. This life is made to break your heart. What can I say."

Colton reaches over and with two fingers gently turns her face to his. "A lot of people would be surprised to hear this, but what I said onstage a year ago isn't my greatest regret. It's trying to spare myself the hurt of being apart from you by cutting and running. I'll tell you something else: if I'd known that opening my mouth onstage that night would end up with me sitting beside you on your porch watching a storm with you again, I'd have said it stone sober."

Luann gazes at Colton for several beats. She reaches over and takes Colton's mason jar. "You need a refill." She stands unsteadily and totters.

Colton springs up and catches her, steadying her with one hand on her hip, his other on her hand holding the jar. Luann puts her other hand on his biceps, as though they're dancing. Adrenaline fizzes in his chest.

Their eyes clasp. Colton runs his hand slowly around Luann's hip to her lower back, resting on the curve, pulling her closer. He starts to bend down to her. She closes her eyes and goes still. He's seen this look on her face before, many years ago.

This is happening.

This is happening.

This can't—

Colton straightens up, abruptly breaking the spell. They sputter breathlessly, nervously, simultaneously.

"Sorry, I almost—"

"Yeah, no, I—"

"No, don't—must've been the wine—"

"I should—"

"It's—"

"I should probably get going," Colton says softly.

"Petey got a big meeting in the morning?" Luann smiles sadly.

"Yeah." Colton returns her smile. "He's hoping to touch base with a few clients. Build some synergy. Grow his network. Sleep on his back in a sunny patch on the floor."

"Stay five more minutes. Watch this storm with me."

Colton vacillates.

Luann holds up five fingers and waggles them. She flashes him the confident-bordering-on-cocky half-smile of someone who knows she's too alluring to resist and won't hesitate to use it.

"You've always gotten your way with me," Colton says.

"Not always."

They watch the storm clouds fade into the distance like a film's end credits, the thunder almost inaudible now.

"Smells good out here," Colton murmurs.

"It's Honeysuckle Summer."

He stays for another hour, in the perfume of flowers, measuring out every minute with her like doses of some rare and precious elixir.

CHAPTER 55

"Pass the flour." It's just the two of them opening. Luann rolls out biscuit dough. "And there's something we need to discuss about the other night."

"Okay," Colton says, giving her the container of flour, the interrogative note in her tone making his hands jittery.

"And I hope you'll be completely forthright with me."

"Okay." His apprehension rises.

"Can you shed light on why my girls now call each other Scooter and Possum?"

Colton, exhaling in relief, grins and ducks his head. "Well... Chef... in the spirit of forthrightness: I might've given them nicknames while we were playing football."

Luann sighs loudly, shakes her head, and keeps working.

She tries to hide her smile but fails.

Colton tries to hide how much he loves seeing her smile but fails.

CHAPTER 56

June 2016
Venice, Kentucky

Colton, Luann, Derrick, and Gabrielle sit in the balmy warmth of Colton's backyard, drinking iced sun tea and eating charcoal-grilled churrasco with chimichurri that he prepared. Luann and Gabrielle have hit it off famously and chat away. Tonight is for celebration and sorrow: marking one year of sobriety for Colton; lamenting the twins' imminent departure for the summer. Their father will be coming by the restaurant tomorrow to pick them up for the long journey to Denmark.

The ambrosial bouquet of honeysuckle, clover, gardenia, and linden permeates the yard. The nightdrone of cicadas and frogs waxes and wanes in chorus like the vegetation breathing.

Evening falls and fireflies paint the sultry dark with spectral trails of neon green. Xavier, Imani, Freja, and Esme—who've also taken to each other—give pursuit with shouting and squealing, catching and releasing. Petey hobbles behind them, simultaneously an old man and one of the kids.

Colton's eyes can't escape Luann's gravity. All night, he watches her in the waning light, smiling, not turning away even when she catches him. He remembers the amber of the sun setting through the mahogany of her hair, illuminating flyaways like strands of Tupelo honey.

Maybe love doesn't die when you run from it. Maybe it waits by the door for you to come home.

CHAPTER 57

Colton gets to work earlier than necessary to open. He was up at daybreak anyway, having slept poorly. All night, knowing he'd finally come face-to-face with Luann's ex and the twins' father today, apprehension coiled around him like a boa constrictor. He's ready to call Leon at a moment's notice.

He's alone in the kitchen, and the restaurant is unnervingly quiet but for the muffled patter of animated exchange leaking from behind Luann's closed office door. He chides himself as he creeps close and eavesdrops, catching snippets.

No, you didn't say that...

I distinctly remember...

Fine. Then I forgot...

You forget a lot of things when it's convenient...

...need to open...

...I'm sure you...

Colton continues listening. The dispute grows in pitch until he can hear Luann's voice clearly.

It's never been about that. It's always been about you finding every imaginable—

Keep your voice down.

No one is scheduled to be here for another half hour, plus I own the place;

I'll talk how I want. It's always been about you finding every imaginable reason to belittle me.

No, I simply…

Yes. And they see it.

They…

They're eight, not idiots, Henning.

Colton can hear Luann on the verge of tears, and it's more than he can bear. Rage begins churning in him. He knocks and simultaneously opens the door, not giving anyone a chance to tell him not to enter. "Hey, Chef, sorry to interrupt." Luann looks depleted, flustered, and tearful. Colton turns to Henning Madsen. Henning's hair is shorter than in the photos Colton's seen—spiky, thick, silver, impeccably coiffed. He's wearing glasses with heavy black frames, a slim-cut khaki twill suit with a tailored black T-shirt (probably angora or some other luxurious material), and oxblood Italian dress shoes with no socks.

"Hey, y'all," Colton says, offering his most winning smile despite seething inside. "I thought I'd show—Henning, right? Is it Henning?—around the restaurant before we open up." He takes Henning by the upper arm in a calm but don't-try-me grip, mastered while working briefly as a bouncer after first moving to Nashville.

"Colton," Luann says weakly, clearly lacking the wherewithal to bid him stop.

Henning lodges a protest: "Excuse me, we were—"

But Colton is already leading him out. "Such an honor to meet one of the great Danish architects of the 2000s. So, now we're passing through the kitchen. You can tell because you've got your stoves, your pots and pans. We basically use this area for cooking food that we serve in the dining area, which you've probably already seen. Now here we have the alley." Colton ignores Henning's objections, opens the door to the alley, and shoves Henning outside. "A great place for a little chat." Colton closes the door behind them, releases Henning's arm, and smiles at him, but lets his eyes stay icy. "What's up, man? How you doing?"

Henning regards Colton like he just appeared onscreen during a fiberoptic colonoscopy. "Beg your pardon," he says brusquely and starts toward the door.

Colton moves to block him, his arms folded across his chest. "Naw, brother. Let's hang a sec. Have a little man-to-man. By the way—all those buildings you draw? *Big* fan."

"Stand aside, please." Henning speaks with an almost imperceptible accent.

"You're upsetting her. We're gonna give her a minute."

"Who are you? The busboy?"

"And if I were?"

Henning starts to say something but stops himself. "What did you say your name was?"

"I didn't. I'm Colton Gentry. Pleasure." He doesn't offer his hand.

"Colton..." Amused recognition dawns across Henning's face. "Luann's teenage boyfriend?"

"The very same."

Henning snickers. "Ah. Captain of the football squad," he says with a scornful inflection in his voice.

"Until I got injured. And we call it a team here." *So Luann talked about me to you. We would call that a touchdown.*

"I confess my bafflement with the nomenclature surrounding American football, particularly the name of the sport itself."

"Freja and Esme told me you had that hang-up."

"You've spent time around my daughters then?" Henning's voice is tense.

"Some." *Guess that haymaker landed.*

"So Luann moves back to Mayberry with our daughters to be around the faded American football star and hire him to work at her little diner? Make her own quaint Hallmark movie?"

Henning's turn to land a punch. Colton keeps smiling serenely. "Don't forget faded country star, chief."

Henning smirks. "I didn't know if that was a sore spot."

"I'll treat your question like it's sincere. No, she didn't move back to be around me. She came here to start something amazing, and she's done it. I ended up back in Venice when my life imploded and I was trying to keep from drinking myself to death—"

"She—"

"Don't interrupt. My turn to talk." Colton speaks with a perilously soft tone. "She hired me as a sous chef. She put me to work creating again, after I thought that part of me was dead and buried. She saved my life and my dignity, and as far as I'm concerned, that building behind me represents a greater achievement than every building your ass has ever designed." Colton's smile has faded, and he glares lancets into Henning's eyes.

"Fitting that you two should end up working together. You think you honor her by treating this as some grand achievement. I honor her by not accepting her wasting her life in a backwater town, squandering her promise behind a grill, and taking our daughters along for the ride."

"I think she'd prefer my way."

"I'd remind you that I've known her for far longer and more intimately than you. We have children together."

Colton is grudgingly impressed at how keenly Henning's managed to sniff out, in mere minutes, how that comment would sting. He runs through possible responses. But Luann saves him yet again.

She opens the door to the alley, her eyes tear-swollen. "Wrap up whatever this is. The girls are here." She retreats.

Henning moves to follow. Colton stops him with a hand on his chest. "From now until you and the girls leave, it's rainbows and sunshine and no more about squandering anything. Got it?"

Henning regards him with a cold, impassive stare. "Or what?"

Colton brings his face very near Henning's and speaks with a menacing calm. "Or I make you my next bad decision."

Henning scoffs. "You ought to mind your own business, tough guy. And I doubt that will take you long." He heads inside, brushing past Colton.

Colton waits for a while in the alleyway, trembling with fury as adrenaline recedes from his veins.

After what could have been seconds or minutes for all Colton can tell, Luann opens the door again, nose running, tears streaking her face. "The girls want to say goodbye."

Colton hurries inside to the dining area, where Freja and Esme stand with their bags. Luann's parents are off to the side. Henning paces outside the front windows, phone to ear.

Both girls sob. A heavy lump rises in Colton's throat. He hurries to them and kneels on his good knee.

"Hey, hey," he says softly, dabbing tears from both their cheeks with the clean bandanna he'll use later to mop sweat from his brow. "Y'all gonna make me blubber, and I can't be crying into the food. Makes it too salty."

"We're gonna miss you and Petey," Freja wails.

"What if Petey dies while we're gone?" Esme asks. Her weeping, already at a solid eight, goes right to ten at her invocation of Petey's demise. Freja's too.

Colton takes them both into his arms. "No, no, hey: Petey's gonna be waiting when y'all get back, okay?" *Lord help me if that proves false.*[2] "Now y'all listening good?"

Freja and Esme nod and wipe at their eyes.

"You're gonna be speaking Danish all summer, right?"

They nod.

"Promise you won't forget how to speak English. Because I don't speak Danish. And I know Petey doesn't."

"We won't forget!" The twins shout with the exuberant outrage that

---

2 It won't.

comes over kids on the precious occasion of getting to correct an adult—when a parent calls a mitten a glove; when a parent accidentally calls their child the dog's name.

"Swear?"

"We swear."

"See, I didn't understand that. You gotta speak English."

"That *was* in English!" Esme says.

"I didn't understand that either. Y'all keep speaking Danish."

"We're speaking *English*," Freja says, giggling. "You're lying!"

Colton looks up at Luann, brow wrinkled. "You getting any of this?"

The girls laugh and wipe their eyes.

"All right," Colton says softly and hugs Freja. "Bye, Scooter." He hugs Esme. "Bye, Possum." He hugs them both. "Did y'all pack your footballs so you can practice over the summer?"

The girls beam and nod.

Colton glances out the window at Henning, grins, and says, "We'll throw the footballs and play with Petey when y'all get back. Have us some nice big banana splits, okay?"

They nod and resume weeping.

Colton hugs each one more time, kisses each on top of their head, and stands, suppressing tears with all his force. He steps back for Luann to bid farewell once more. Then the twins leave.

Luann, who had largely kept her composure, crumbles. She goes to Colton and buries her face in his chest. He holds her as sobs rack her body. Feeling her weight, he's acutely aware that he's the only thing preventing her from collapsing on the floor.

Finally, she composes herself enough to go back to her office to answer the phone, dabbing her eyes.

As they watch her leave, Luann's father claps Colton on the shoulder and gives him a somber but firm nod.

After allowing her space to mourn, Colton finds Luann in the alley, crying and gnawing one of his toothpicks.

"I need a real cigarette," she says in a thick voice. "If I give you cash, will you run and get me some American Spirits?"

Colton stands next to her, close. "That's about the only thing I wouldn't do for you right now, Chef."

"You're the sole person on Earth who has my back. Can't you be a better smoking enabler?"

"Sorry."

"It never gets easier," she murmurs. "Sending them off like that."

"Hope he's a better father than he seems."

"He is. You saw him at his worst."

"You think? I almost had to knock his ass out earlier."

"I'm glad you two didn't get into it. He does Brazilian jiujitsu as a hobby." She exhales, shakes her head. "Of course his pastime involves dominating people and causing them pain."

"Cool."

"He's not quite the prick he appears to be."

"Defending him now?"

She sighs. "Myself. You probably think I'm insane for having married him."

"This glass house resident ain't big on throwing stones."

"I read that Maisy parks in handicap spaces at the nail salon."

"Where'd you see that?"

"Sleazy celeb gossip site. Is it true?"

"It, uh...sounds true. What were you doing on that site?"

"Gathering evidence that I'm not the only person on Earth who married a jerk."

"Glad you found it. What were you and Henning discussing when I arrived?" Colton pauses, then quickly adds, "If that's not too personal."

Luann sighs loudly. She looks down and flicks her toothpick like she's knocking ash from it. She speaks with a quaver. "This is the first time he's been to Venice since I started the restaurant. He thinks I'm wasting my life and talent here, but more importantly, he thinks I'm wasting the twins' lives here."

"He is aware that you're from here, right?"

"He misses no opportunity to make me feel small and provincial."

"Jeez, Luann."

"Hey, I tried the adoring boyfriend in high school. I managed to run him off. So I told myself the next time around I'd settle for someone who doted on me less but would be harder to scare away. And I *nailed* the less doting part."

"You never ran off your adoring high school boyfriend," Colton says after she meets his eyes. "He was an immature coward. But guess what he never outgrew."

Luann lifts her eyebrows in query.

"Adoring you," Colton says.

Luann looks at Colton for a while and her gaze softens. "You're such a cheeseball," she says with an unmistakable note of affection.

"Don't assign me a cheeseball recipe."

"You earned a long homework reprieve with the Nashville hot chicken. Ever since it hit the menu, we're doing better than we were doing even pre-Haggerty hit job."

"Speaking of, Chef, I better get to opening. We're running behind thanks to one of the most celebrated Danish architects of the 2000s. But try explaining that to an irate lunch guest." He starts toward the door, Luann at his heels. "Hey," he says. "Take whatever time. I got this."

Luann follows him in. "There's nothing I'd rather do right now than make food with you."

Colton turns and stops her with his hand on her upper right arm. He looks her square in the eyes. "Chef, do not ever believe anyone who tells you that you're wasting your talent here."

CHAPTER 58

July 2016
Venice, Kentucky

Colton dabs his brow with his sleeve. "Hey, Dani, is my bandanna by you? I was working on the field pea chow-chow earlier."

"Don't see it," she calls back.

Colton grouses inwardly and goes to the locker room, where he keeps a stash of extras. He opens his locker, pulls out a blue bandanna, folds it, and puts it in his pocket.

As he's leaving, his eyes fall on a coworker's purse—he's not sure whose—with a copy of *Us Weekly* poking out. He can just make out *Martin* on the folded cover. His pulse quickens. *Leave it. You'll ruin your day or worse. Even just seeing her.*

Perverse curiosity compels him closer. *Maybe it's an article about Chris Martin or Ricky Martin or Martin Sheen or Martin Freeman or…*

He looks around furtively and pulls the magazine out, eyes scanning the cover.

"Maisy Martin Steps Out Showing Baby Bump." A paparazzi photo shows her holding hands with the Hockey Player. Both wear sunglasses. Her lower belly has a pronounced swell.

Something tips over inside Colton, and he feels like he's just gotten his arms pinned at his sides while exploring a cave. His breathing becomes quick and shallow. Red spots swarm the periphery of his vision, and his extremities go cold and prickle.

A crest of searing pain hits like an elbow to the temple. He steadies himself against a locker, stares at the floor, and tries to breathe, nauseated.

He's somehow managed to hold himself together for the past year and keep from shattering. But this is a maul strike directly to his most precarious fault line.

He pulls out his phone and scrolls through his and Maisy's sparse history of text exchanges from the past year. Most strictly business. She wished him a cordial happy birthday. When he got Petey, he sent her a picture. Nearing the end of the twelve steps, he asked her to talk so he could make amends. He's never mentioned his new job—not because he was embarrassed but because he just didn't feel like telling her.

He steamrolls the voice in his head telling him to wait and cool off, and texts, Congrats on getting knocked up. Guess you changed your mind lol.

I didn't mean for you to find out however you did, she immediately texts back.

On the cover of Us Weekly? Thx.

I planned to tell you.

It's fun learning about your life from tabloids. Take care.

His phone vibrates with her response but he can't look. *She said she never wanted kids. Or maybe she just didn't want them with me. A second-rate country musician was never going to be good enough to father her children.*

He doesn't know if he'll survive the next breaker of agony that crashes over him. He needs medicine to dull the edge of this feral, howling hurt. He tucks the magazine back into the purse without great care. The bag's appearing undisturbed is the least of his worries.

He staggers into the kitchen, its sounds a wash of white noise. He feels like he's barely survived a potent bomb blast, his vision blurry, ears ringing, unsteady on his feet. Dani says something and he vaguely nods. He looks to see that Luann is in her office, talking on the phone. He goes to the station where they keep the bourbon they use for glazing.

No one notices him furtively grab it, palms sweating. No one sees as he walks with it held as low as he can without hunching over, obscuring the bottle with his body and the counters. Dani and Finn are too preoccupied with the tasks before them to notice anyway. He slips into the locker room and sits on the bench with the bottle. Its smoothness fits his hand like it was made bespoke.

One year.

You made it one year.

He glances at the magazine poking out of the purse and another violent surge hits him.

Just a mouthful or two. Not even enough to kill the pain entirely; only to turn its edge, just sufficient to manage it along with the adrenaline and distraction of the kitchen. When you get off tonight, you can go for a long run and try to forget the rest of the way.

Another wave washes over him, dragging him deeper.

He unscrews the bottle's cap and lifts it near enough his lips to smell the vanillic, sour-sweetness wafting from the opening. His hand trembles. He can hear the amber liquid lapping the sides of the bottle.

Only what you need to survive. Then you start the path again.

He puts the bottle to his mouth. It's hard and cold on his lips like the barrel of a shotgun. He can taste the alcohol vapor.

"Colton?" Luann calls from outside the locker room door. She knocks and starts to open it. "Hope you're decent in here."

Colton curses and slaps the cap back on, hurriedly screwing it a couple of turns. He shoves the bottle under a locker right as Luann walks in.

"Tonight could you—" She stops, having clearly heard the hollow, glassine ring of the bottle skidding, the liquid inside sloshing as Colton straightens up quickly.

He can't look at her. He rests his forearms on his knees and hangs his head, staring at the ground.

"Colton?" she says softly.

He can't speak or meet her gaze. He clasps his hands together, as though praying, to stop their tremor.

She walks over, kneels, reaches under the locker, and retrieves the bottle. She looks at it like she wishes she could transform it into something else.

Colton presses his fist to his lips and weeps. "I'm sorry, Chef," he chokes out. He starts unbuttoning his chef's jacket. "I didn't drink any, but I was about to, and you should take it out of my final paycheck."

She kneels beside him. "Colton."

"I know I'm done. You need to can me."

"You said you didn't drink any."

"Please just fire me. I told you I wouldn't quit on you again and I'm not, but you have to fire me." His voice quavers as he finishes unbuttoning his chef's jacket and starts to remove it.

Luann stands and puts the bottle on top of a locker and then kneels to him again. "You have a sponsor, right?"

Colton nods.

"Call him now. He'll tell you to get to a meeting pronto. I'll take you."

"Please, I deserve—"

Luann grabs his forearm hard, nails digging in. "Look at me. *Look* at me. Call your sponsor *immediately*. I'll wait outside. Get me the second you're done." She grabs the bottle of bourbon off the top of the locker and leaves, closing the door behind her.

Colton calls Leon. Leon says, "Much love, brother, you got this. Now get your dumb ass to a meeting right now. Quit your job if you have to."

Colton leaves the locker room. Luann waits outside, keys in hand, having doffed her chef's jacket too.

Luann turns and hollers back into the kitchen, "Dani! Honey and Thyme!"

They exit through the alleyway.

"'Honey and Thyme' is what Dani's going to name her restaurant," Luann explains. "It's our code for when I need her to run the restaurant solo."

"I don't know where there's a meeting right now," Colton says. "I can't think of—I don't know. My brain isn't working right."

"I saved a schedule on my phone in case something like this ever happened."

Luann pulls up in front of the Cumberland Presbyterian Church, where a meeting started seven minutes ago.

"You don't have to wait for me," Colton says. "You can just drop me off and I'll figure out how to get back."

"If you'd cut your hand open and I was taking you to the ER, I wouldn't just leave you. How does this work? Can I come in and support you?"

Colton hesitates, uncertain he wants Luann to hear him being as honest as he must be, but also needing her. He chooses needing her. "Yeah, you can come in."

The meeting is truly anonymous. It's not Colton's usual group and he recognizes none of the five other people there.

He bounces his legs and rubs the bronze one-year sobriety chip his mom gave him—a tree on one side, the Serenity Prayer on the other. It comes to his turn. He clears his throat. Luann is sitting outside the circle, within his view. He makes brief eye contact with her, and she gives him a supportive smile. He stands. "My name is Colton, and I'm an alcoholic."

"Hi, Colton," the group says.

He breathes in deep. He holds up his chip. "One year sober. I almost lost this today. Less than an hour ago. I was sitting there with the bottle in my hand. Cap off. I put the bottle in my mouth. Ready to throw away more than a year of hard work. Some close calls but no slips. If my boss—she's here. She's a good friend too. If my boss hadn't walked in on me, I'd have done it. I'd just encountered the trigger of triggers. See, I'd found out my ex is pregnant, in about the most humiliating way possible.

With the dude she cheated on me with. And the thing is she always told me she didn't want kids. Said we'd never have any. Her career was too important. And that was okay because I was focused on my gig too. But my drinking caught up to me after a buddy of mine got killed and I flushed that and everything else down the toilet. Because of the booze. And so my wife left me. I don't know if that one was because of the alcoholism. Probably it was a lot of things. Doesn't matter, really. The drinking sure didn't help.

"And so I got sober and moved back home to Venice and started a new life. I didn't have much, but I had my sobriety and I was proud of that. My boss gave me a job at her restaurant. I got to be pretty decent with a skillet and a spatula. I started seeing my friends' kids and I realized how much I'd given up. For a life that's over. I started wanting—" Colton's throat tightens with emotion and he pauses to regain his composure. "I started wanting for myself what my friends have. Sometimes I dream it's not too late. But I think it probably is. That's why it hit me so hard when I got that news. It reminded me of how much I've lost. And it seemed like I might as well add this chip to the list of things I've pissed away.

"But I didn't. Maybe it was my Higher Power who put my boss between me and the mouth of that bottle today. I don't know. Here I am, still one year sober. One day at a time."

They sit in Luann's car, idling in the parking lot, the AC blowing. Neither says anything for a while. Colton looks at the floor and rubs his coin.

"I read we're supposed to talk through the why of you almost drinking," Luann says. "So Maisy's pregnant, huh?"

"Yeah." Colton gazes out the window and watches a bird groom itself on the power line.

"Tabloids'll have a field day with that."

"That's how I found out."

"Oh Lord."

"I went in the locker room to grab something and saw a copy of *Us Weekly* with it on the cover."

"I'm banning tabloids from the restaurant."

"Don't ruin everyone's fun on my account."

"You feel better after going to group?"

Colton scratches at a spot on the thigh of his pants. "Don't know if *better* is the right word. *Different.* I feel different."

"How so?"

Colton ponders for a moment. "I felt like I was sliding down an icy slope and couldn't stop. Now I just feel angry."

"Angry?"

"At myself. For almost taking a drink. For still *wanting* a drink. For still considering it an option. For missing the way it killed pain and made me feel like I was listening to everything from underwater. Now all those feelings of hopelessness and guilt and shame come rushing back."

"That sounds tough."

"Tired too. Of losing things I love."

A long silence passes between them.

"Do you still love Maisy?" Luann asks quietly, staring at the floorboards.

"I don't know," Colton says with a joyless laugh. "I didn't think so. I guess it's more I loved being able to live with the fiction that it wasn't some great shortcoming on my part that made her not want to start a family with me. Like she wasn't lying when she said it was her career. But nope. It's just me. And I get here and see Derrick and Gabi's beautiful kids. I see Freja and Esme. Then I realize what I've sacrificed. And for what?"

"Your dream."

"Yeah." Colton drops his coin and has to bend and pick it up.

"And you did pretty damn great at it. I heard you on the radio."

"Seventeen-year-old me really wishes thirty-nine-year-old me were making a better showing for you than washed-up alcoholic failure."

"Both seventeen-year-old me and thirty-nine-year-old me want you to know that they like you just fine."

"Yeah?" Colton takes a deep breath. "Thank you for intervening today. Being here for me. Giving me the job that put you in a position to stop me. Which you really should still fire me from, by the way."

"That what you want?"

"Not particularly. But it's what I deserve."

"For the record, your answer didn't matter."

"I figured."

"It's my restaurant. I make the decisions."

"I know."

"I'll be the judge of what you deserve. I've always been better at that than you."

"I know."

"I have never been interested in giving up on you, Colton. Not ever."

"I've never felt like I was good enough to be part of your life. In any way."

"You are, somehow. You've always been."

CHAPTER 59

Colton's phone rings so infrequently at night, it startles him when it starts buzzing and chittering across his coffee table.

He grabs it and answers. "Luann? What's up?"

"Hey."

"Hey, everything good?"

"Yeah, what're you up to?"

"Been a pretty chill Sunday. You just calling to chat or—"

"Yeah, am I allowed?"

"I welcome it."

"You don't have a lady over?"

"I don't have *a* lady over... I have three."

"Oh I better let you get back to that."

"No, no, it's fine. Lemme just—I'll tell them to—" Colton holds his phone away from his head and calls into the empty house. "Hey, Amber, Sasha, and..."

"That joke would have landed better if you had a third woman's name ready and didn't have to scramble."

"Next time. You been having a good day?"

"Got a bunch of housework done. Cooked dinner for my parents. They say hi, by the way."

"Hi, Luann's parents."

"What are you up to right now?"

"Watching a *Chopped* marathon on Food Network, kinda drifting off every now and again."

"I took a late nap, so I'll be up all night. I have a hard time sleeping anyway when my house is so quiet."

"You missing Scooter and Possum?"

"Like you wouldn't believe," she says wistfully.

"Oh, I might."

"How's Petey?"

Colton sighs dramatically. "Meetings all day. On the phone with his broker nonstop."

"This running joke where Petey is an overworked businessdog will always be funny to me."

"So you just sitting at home being lonely?"

"Yeah."

"Wanna come over and watch TV? Be lonely together?"

Luann hesitates. "Now?"

"No, on the eve of the next full moon after the first turnip harvest. Yeah, now. Come over. We'll holler at the screen, shout about how serving up 'deconstructed' dishes is a copout and fools no one."

"I look like garbage. No makeup; hair's a mess."

"You felt hot enough to call me and fish for an invite to come watch TV with me."

Luann gasps. "There was *no* fishing. How dare you."

"You can't see me, but I'm pantomiming casting a fishing line."

"I'm pantomiming catching that fishing line and attaching a note to it. Reel it in and see."

"I'm reading it and it says I'm getting a fifty percent raise?"

"If you hold it up to a flame, that writing disappears and new writing appears that says you're now responsible for developing a Nashville hot catfish entrée to put on the menu."

"I swear, if you keep giving me new assignments every time I make a joke, I'm gonna stop making jokes."

"Colton, *no*. Oh you *mustn't*. However will I go on. How will I *live*. What purpose will I—"

"So, circling back to you fishing for an invite: you look great."

"You can't see me."

"I know, and I stand by my statement. Come over. Let's watch TV and eat popcorn out of a big metal mixing bowl and drink expensive artisan root beers from glass bottles."

"You got popcorn?"

"Microwave."

"Need I tell you I don't touch that?"

"I suppose you needn't."

"I'll pick up some on the way. I have nutritional yeast we can sprinkle on it. You ever done that?"

"No."

"It's good. See you in a few."

"Okay."

Colton flurries around the house, tidying up, washing his sink full of dishes, giving his bathroom a quick spraydown.

Luann arrives wearing makeup.

They stand on Colton's small front porch, yawning under the miniature silver moon of his porchlight. It's 1:12 a.m. and the air is cool with dew.

"I'd win for sure," Colton says.

"I'll tell you what I've whipped up in the kitchen: a certified monster," Luann says.

"I'd bring a taste of that Sweet Colton G Mojo Magic Sauce to the *Chopped* kitchen."

"Mmmm no, I hate it."

"What, the idea of me winning *Chopped*?"

"No. The phrase you just used."

"What phrase?"

"You know."

"I want to hear you say it."

"And I don't want to end up on the sex offender registry, which is where the mere uttering of that phrase would land me."

"You hate the phrase 'Sweet Colton G Mojo Magic Sauce'?"

"It sucks. I forbid you from ever speaking it again."

"Are other people allowed to say it?"

"Not even if they wanted to. It's uniformly forbidden."

"Can I say it at home? Whisper it into my pillow?"

"If I ever find out, you're fired."

"Wait, so you're effectively banning the phrase 'Sweet Colton G Mojo Magic Sauce' from the English lexicon?" Colton raises his index finger in warning. "Don't—"

"*What?* I wasn't gonna say anything."

"You weren't going to express surprise that I know the word *lexicon* and use it correctly?"

"I... was maybe a little unprepared for that."

"I can read you like a lexicon."

"Not to interrupt your musings, but I have a question. And you can say no."

"No."

Luann ignores him. "I was going to bring it up at work Tuesday, but I might as well now. Next weekend, I'm catering a private party out of town. I was going to fly solo, but I just got updated attendance numbers and requests for menu accommodations, and I'll need help. Late notice, but do you want to come? It'll be overnight."

"Is Dani good to hold things down alone?"

"Her boyfriend's coming down to help out, and they're going to run it as a Honey and Thyme popup. But here's the thing. It's a party in

Nashville—Leiper's Fork, technically. Pay is incredible because it's for a lot of socialite bigwigs. Not just entertainment industry, but there'll be plenty of that for sure. So..." Luann's voice fades out.

"So you're wondering if it'll be a triggering environment?"

"Basically."

"Stuff is way less triggering to me when I can prepare myself mentally. I can have my plan for not drinking in place. I'll let my sponsor know; he can be ready."

"They'll have a waitstaff. It's not like you'll be wearing a bowtie and serving canapés to your old manager or something."

"I went to a lot of those things back in the day, and I don't remember ever encountering the chefs. I'll be fine."

"So? That a yes?" Luann seems bashful. Her cheeks are pink.

Colton turns to her with a cocksure grin. "Hang on. This negotiation ain't over. Now that I'm holding some cards: I want to be able to use the phrase 'Sweet Colton G Mojo Magic Sauce.'"

Luann scoffs. "Never mind, I'll make some calls and hire some temp in Nashville. Lord knows there are enough chefs there looking to pick up a little extra work." She starts down the porch steps toward her car.

"No no no no, okay, okay."

Luann turns, snorts, and rolls her eyes. "You backtracked so quickly you almost ruptured the space-time continuum. You are the worst negotiator. If you'd gone a few rounds, you might have ended up being able to say it exactly once. Pick me up at my parents' place on Friday at seven. We'll take your truck, because there's stuff I wanna carry in the bed." She turns and continues down Colton's front walk, giving Colton a *toodle-oo* wave over her shoulder.

Colton follows Luann to make sure she gets into her car. "Text me when you get home safe, okay?" They hug for a few beats longer than they need to.

He walks back to his house, muttering to himself, "I really am a crap negotiator."

Nevertheless, he feels victorious.

CHAPTER 60

August 2016
Venice, Kentucky

COLTON'S BREATH DESERTS HIM AS HE PULLS UP TO LUANN'S PARENTS' HOME at sunset.

The structure, done in a modern farmhouse style, is dazzling. It's the perfect balance of vintage and modern, rustic and elegant, like a rough-hewn nineteenth-century barn meets a Chelsea art gallery. Massive windows and multiple decks set with outdoor furniture overlook the picturesque vistas. A grand stone chimney features prominently on the front, as does what looks to be reclaimed wood.

Colton has seen, been in, and lived in some awe-inspiring homes. He's never seen this home's equal. He rings the doorbell, and Luann's father answers.

"Evening, Eddie," Colton says.

"Colton. Step on in."

"I'm getting a little déjà vu here, except the digs are even nicer."

Eddie chuckles proudly. "Got Lulu to thank for that."

The smell of sage, basil, and fir greets Colton as he takes in the foyer. It's as breathtaking as the exterior. Heavy, worn timber beams with dark-patinaed iron accents crisscross above the flooring crafted from wide, lustrous whiskey-hued oak planks. A chandelier made from hempen rope and interwoven antlers hangs from the ceiling, and bronze industrial light sconces line the walls.

"Lord almighty," Colton murmurs. "Look at this place."

"Lulu's our decorator too."

That woman could have five different careers, all at the highest level.

Eddie continues. "She's finishing up a few things." He leads Colton into the kitchen.

The focal point is a colossal Viking gas range with a commercial-grade ventilation hood. One wall is exposed whitewashed brick. There's an island on which you could land a helicopter, with butcher-block countertops, surrounded by antique drafting stools, and a pot rack suspended above it. White stoneware plates, bowls, and mugs sit on exposed live-edge wood shelves.

Luann glances over her shoulder. "Almost ready."

Colton rests his elbows on the island and leans forward. "Hey, I'm still taking in the grandeur of this place."

"A lot of the wood you see is salvaged from an old tobacco barn, railroad ties, and bourbon barrel staves. We also used trees that were cleared to make room for the house. The stonework you see is local river rock. I designed the kitchen so that I could use it to run a catering business if the restaurant ever went under." Luann finishes loading trays into a plastic bin and slams the lid down tight. "Before we go, I'll show you my favorite part."

Colton follows her up two steep flights of narrow stairs, to a tiny crow's-nest deck off the side of the roof, with two chairs. It overlooks the river.

"This is the other touch I put in for myself. For storm-watching."

They sit in the half-light in reverent silence, watching bats flutter like excited thoughts against the purpling sky.

"This is the only building I've ever designed solo," Luann murmurs after a bit. "I'm proud of it."

"You should be."

Viewing the river from this lofty perch makes Colton ache with nostalgia, jarring in its potency, buffeting him like the gale before a storm. And he's known some formidable aches in his life. Lord knows.

CHAPTER 61

THEY FORGO THE INTERSTATE IN FAVOR OF BACK ROADS, WHICH THEY BOTH prefer, even though (and perhaps because) it lengthens the journey. It's an unseasonably cool, dry night. A hurricane in the Gulf has drawn heat and humidity from the upland South like a paper towel soaking up spilled wine. They drive with the windows down, lapping up the mild, verdurous air that washes over their faces. Fireflies wink in the insect-song blackness lining the road.

They introduce each other to favorite songs from the past twenty years. They chat happily and easily. A mirthful energy prevails between them.

"Nope. Never made it to the real Venice," Colton says. "We had plans. We went to Italy once, but it somehow never made it onto the itinerary."

"You missed out," Luann says. "It's my favorite city on Earth. All these gorgeous old buildings and winding narrow streets. It's a fairy-tale place."

"Are those gondolas real?"

"Yep."

"Man. How about you get us a catering job there next time?"

"Because Italians famously need culinary help from Americans."

Colton shrugs. "Depends on the Americans."

"You know what tonight reminds me of?" Luann asks. "Our first date."

Colton looks at her and smiles. "That was a damn good time. I wish we had some Bucky's."

"Let's not get carried away."

Luann props her feet on the dashboard, the way she did when they were teenagers. She's wearing a thin, button-front indigo cotton sundress, and it rides up to her mid-thigh. The sight sends a sensuous, warm weakness through Colton's lower belly. He steals quick sidelong glances as he drives. He's pretty sure Luann catches him multiple times, but she seems unbothered.

He admires her profile, the line of her nose. The swell of her lips. The fine architecture of her cheekbones. He wonders for the millionth time how it's possible that someone so accomplished is also so impossibly beautiful.

Ahead, there's a break in the trees. Colton slows as a pair of motorcycles turn onto the road from a gravel parking lot ringed with orange sodium lights. Country music wafts from the open door of a small, white cinderblock building, adorned with a neon Budweiser sign in a dusty, barred window, and a hand-lettered placard that reads "Sunny's Stateline Saloon." Harleys and pickups dot the parking lot, and biker types, both men and women, mill around outside—smoking, sipping tallboys, and shooting the shit.

As Colton starts to accelerate again, Luann gasps. "Colton! Turn in!"

He hits the brakes with enough force to make their seat belts catch them and obeys. "What?"

"Listen."

"Is that..."

"'I Will Always Love You.' Dolly's version." Luann looks at Colton. "Park. Get out."

"I don't really wanna go in—"

"Like I would take you into a bar. You're dancing with me in this parking lot."

Colton parks and they get out. The lot is redolent of a rowdy Friday night in the country: dust, spilled beer, exhaust, cloying cotton-candy body mist, and cigarette smoke. Amber-colored june bugs orbit the white light illuminating the bar's sign as though tethered to it, batting their bodies against it with faint chitinous thumps.

Luann and Colton stand close, and he puts his hands on her hips, her arms around his neck, the way high schoolers dance, swaying slowly. Her body seems to welcome his touch. They meet each other's eyes, smile, and draw nearer.

"Remember when we danced to the Whitney cover of this song in the hall at homecoming?" Colton murmurs.

"Yes, Colton, I do."

"That's why you wanted to turn in here."

"Yes, Colton, it is."

Colton nods sheepishly. "I've always been quick."

"Girl, you got you a nice-lookin' boyfriend," one of the windburned and bottle-blond biker ladies calls over to Luann in a whiskey-and-smoke-rasped voice.

Luann laughs. "Don't let him hear you say that. I like him better humble."

The biker lady and her friend cackle and clap. "Get it, honey," the friend calls.

The song ends.

"Gimme five bucks," Luann says.

Colton knows better than to ask. He rummages in his wallet and hands her a five. She goes to the back of the pickup, grabs a foil-covered disposable aluminum serving tray, and heads for the bar.

"What are you doing with those biscuits?" Colton calls after her.

"Little community outreach technique I learned from someone."

"She don't come back for you, baby, we'll keep you comp'ny," one of the leather-clad biker ladies calls over with a wheezy, lascivious chortle.

Colton grins and tips an invisible hat. "Thank you, ma'am. I'm hoping she comes back, though."

Luann does return, the opening strains of Dolly's "I Will Always Love

You" following her. "It's like a two-minute song," she explains. "So I put it on the jukebox five more times and left a tray of free biscuits in there so no one would complain."

"I certainly won't be complaining," Colton says. "Now, I believe we were..."

They join again, and this time Luann stands so close her breasts brush his chest. He can feel the warmth emanating from her skin. She smells like green ivy and blossoms and figs.

The world tapers to a focal point and all other sensory input dissolves away in the margins of evening.

Luann lays her head on Colton's chest and murmurs, "You can't take your eyes off me tonight."

"And I don't particularly care to, either." Colton moves his hand to her lower back, and then gently onto the rise beyond, drawing her hips to his. "Not tonight or any other."

She makes a faint sighing sound, and Colton can feel the heat of her breath and then her lips caressing the hollow of his throat.

Colton puts his hand on the side of her face and raises it. He brushes a lock of hair back from her cheek.

They kiss like it's the most natural and inevitable thing that could be. Spring flowing into summer. Tides. The moon waxing and waning.

She tastes how she used to—like youth, joy, lust, and possibility. Their bodies remember each other. They fit together still.

They kiss long after Luann's jukebox plays run out.

"What are we doing?" Luann says in a low voice, silken with longing. Her skin is hot and florid as though fevered.

"Whatever we want." Desire has turned Colton's voice husky. His lips hover close to her ear. He can barely make out the bikers' cheers and catcalls in the background.

Luann's nails dig into the back of Colton's neck. "I want to do things they can't watch," she whispers breathlessly. "Take me out back. I want it all."

They drive to a dark corner of the parking lot. Luann slumps into her seat, plants her bare feet on the dashboard, arches her hips and pulls off her underwear. After tossing them into the back of the cab, she straddles Colton, grinding against him while unbuckling his belt with sure movements, her determination betraying her hunger.

He kisses her neck and upper chest while he unbuttons the front of her dress, almost ripping it in his fervor. Luann grabs his hands and pulls them onto her breasts. She moans under his touch, which sends Colton's head spinning with reckless craving. There were so many nights over the past months when he had to interrupt his thoughts, wouldn't even let himself consider what it might feel like to have her now. All of her.

Now, he touches her, feels her body's arousal on his fingers, lets himself run his hands over every curve, brushing his lips over each freckle he remembers and some he doesn't.

They melt into each other like wildflower honey in hot butter.

Midway, he pauses, pulls back, gazes at her in the faint light, enraptured. His blood feels like lava coursing through him.

"What's up?" she gasps, holding his face. "You okay?"

"I just needed to admire you for a second."

If you have learned one thing over this past year, it's that heat transforms things.

Let it.

They lie panting, entwined and half-clad, stray scraps of orange sodium light leaking in through the fogged truck windows. They hear the hollers, occasional revving motorcycle, and faint music of the bar as though far distant. The night is cool and arid for August, but still they sweat together, small pools collecting in the hollows of their bodies.

Luann lifts her head from Colton's bare chest. "You smell good," she murmurs.

"Yeah?"

"Like leather and creamy sawdust."

"Before we left, I sanded a cedar plank into a tub of mascarpone and used it as lotion on my skin, which is where the leather comes from."

"Ricotta's more moisturizing."

"You'd know."

"I can hear your heartbeat," Luann says, resting her head back on his chest.

"Our fan club back there can probably hear my heartbeat."

She draws a deep, shuddering breath. "Oh *wow*, I needed that." She raises a fist and whoops lust-drunkenly.

Colton puts his finger to his lips and shushes her. "Easy, tiger. You're gonna get my ass whipped by bikers who think I'm pulling a Biff Tannen back here."

Luann presses her fingertip into Colton's cheek and pushes his face away. "Oh *please*. There's not a soul who would mistake that for a cry of distress. If anything, I'm more afraid of *your* fan club coming back here and demanding their turn."

"Don't even put that thought out there."

"You are *way* better at that than I remember, by the way."

"What?"

"Colton. *That*."

"Yeah, well." Colton rolls his neck a couple times and stretches out his jaw as if yawning. "I'm definitely going to be feeling it more in the morning at age thirty-nine."

"You'd have been feeling it in the morning at age eighteen if you'd known what you were doing."

"Touché."

Luann reaches up a toe and draws a sloppy smiley face in the condensation on the inside of the glass. They laugh.

She covers her eyes with her hand and shakes her head, nestling it into Colton's chest and groaning. "I just slept with my employee."

"In a parked vehicle. In a biker bar parking lot."

"I'm a sleazy boss."

"I sure as *hell* wasn't coerced into this. Besides, we have a bit of pre-employment history, don't we?"

"Good point."

They're silent for a while. Luann claps her hand over her face.

"What now?"

"Just remembered about the hotel. You're not gonna believe I didn't plan this."

"I already don't."

"I forgot to make you a reservation. I only reserved one room."

"Yep. Don't believe you."

"I'll prove it by checking if they have another room."

"Don't get carried away. Save the restaurant some money."

"There's only a queen bed."

"We'll manage."

"This sounds like a romcom contrivance."

"The lady doth protest too much," Colton says.

"We *will* actually need some sleep. Tomorrow's gonna be intense."

"I'll let you sleep. Some."

They lie there. Colton traces a finger along the valley of Luann's lower back.

Luann strokes the hollow of Colton's throat with her knife-callused thumb. "I still love this part of you." She traces her fingers over the tattoos his T-shirt normally covers. "What's this one?" she asks, pointing at a guitar and a purple orchid on his right upper pectoral.

"That commemorates when I played Tootsies for the first time."

"How about this one?" She caresses an old-timey microphone on his right upper arm.

"When I played the Grand Ole Opry."

She runs her fingertip on the one over his heart. "What's this—" She squints. "Does that say 'Linger'?"

"Why, yes it does."

"As in the Cranberries song?"

"Yep."

Luann squints at it. "The *L* looks exactly how I write the *L* in my name."

"Yep."

"Colton."

"Hmm?"

"What's the story of this one?"

Colton swipes his hand down his face. "That was my first. I got blasted and ended up with it after being dumped by another girl who just wasn't you. I was missing you a lot that night. I go and grab that drawing you did of the two of us on the bluff and lug it in the tattoo place and have them look off the *L* in your signature to do the *L* in *Linger*. Of all the decisions I've made while smashed, this is one I regret least."

"Did you get one for Maisy?"

"I did."

Luann looks at Colton expectantly. "Have I... seen it?"

Colton coughs. "You weren't... well positioned to see it."

"It already makes me want to die of secondhand embarrassment."

"Yeah, it's a sexy green lady M&M on my left butt cheek."

"When we get back to the restaurant, I'm making you sit on the meat slicer until it's gone."

"Said the woman who threw a fit over my standing on one of her tables at the Christmas party."

"Yeah, well, that ass is as fine as any Parma ham, so."

They crack up.

"Your Luann tattoo wins, by the way," she murmurs, snuggling up closer to Colton.

Colton pulls her face to his lips and kisses her forehead. "Yeah, it sure does."

"Remember that night you babysat, and we watched the storm? I told you what I missed about Kentucky?"

"Vividly. Because I'd secretly hoped I was on the list."

"You were."

They lie quietly for a long time. Colton doesn't want to talk about whatever this is. He wants to just let it be—wild and beautiful and heedless. Luann implies the same with her silence.

All around them, crickets and frogs raise their drowsy nocturne to the moon-bright sky.

CHAPTER 62

Colton hasn't been back to Nashville in over a year. The last time was when he was rehearsing his band for the Brant Lucas tour. He and Luann stay near downtown (they do sleep—some) and hit the farmers market in the morning, both for breakfast and to stock up for that night's dinner service:

Nashville hot chicken lollipops

Biscuits with pimento cheese

Wood-fired cedar-plank North Carolina rainbow trout

Heirloom tomato and caramelized Vidalia onion tart

Fried Alabama Red okra with ranch ice cream

Smoky roasted Purple Passion asparagus with Broadbent country ham and red eye mayo

Pickled beet salad with crème fraiche, orange-fennel vinaigrette, and pecan granola

Chocolate milk stout pie with peanut butter whooped cream and peanuts

Crème brûlée infused with orange blossom, rosewater, Madagascar vanilla, and sourwood honey

After last evening's gallivant through the garden of earthly delights, they're mostly back to business—albeit with rather more touching and sustained eye contact than is strictly necessary. Colton's chest seizes with exhilaration at whatever's happening between them. But melancholy starts to seep in, being back here.

Luann watches Colton surveying the Nashville skyline with a haunted expression. "Hey. How you doing with all this?"

Colton points. "See that building there?"

"The gaudy one with all the windows and balconies? The tasteless proportions?"

"Yep. Maisy and I lived there."

Luann sniffs. "I'd have made very different choices if I designed it."

"Brutal."

"You didn't answer me. You doing okay?"

Colton gazes off in the direction of the rooftop bar where he and Duane hung out for one of the final times; the Broadway honkytonks where they partied and performed and watched friends play; the skyline they regarded with hopeful, hungry eyes as younger men, filled with spirit and prospect. The city they thought they could make theirs. "Yeah," he lies.

He wonders if it's inevitable, reaching a point in life when all remembrances taste both sweet and bitter. Inevitable or not, he's reached it.

More memories accost Colton as they drive to Leiper's Fork through the verdant, rolling hills and white-fenced meadows of the horse country south of Nashville—the exact route he drove Maisy on their first date at Puckett's Grocery, which they pass along the way. He wants to take Luann there sometime, to start rebuilding memories that have been razed to the ground.

They arrive at the sprawling, Tuscan-style villa hosting the event. Horses graze in an adjoining pasture. Blessedly, its owner (and their hostess) isn't in the music industry—she's CEO of a company in Nashville that buys and operates hospital systems. The prospect of not running into anyone he knows, even by accident, fills Colton with cheer, and he works in high spirits. Being at Luann's side feels especially sweet today.

They prep all through the afternoon. The kitchen is lavishly appointed—clearly designed with entertaining in mind—and they want for nothing. The hostess is gracious and kind. "I'm something of a foodie," she says with retiring humility. "Please let me know of anything you need," she says to Luann. "I've been following your career, and I'm a huge fan, obviously. It's an honor to have you working in my kitchen." She doesn't recognize Colton, even by name.

The waitstaff arrives and begins setting up. Luann confers with them regarding the menu. A few are aspiring musicians and recognize Colton. They shyly ask him for an autograph. But their hushed whispers and bashful glances as they exit the kitchen tell Colton that he's become a sort of country music cautionary tale. He hopes it's the last time he's recognized tonight.

Colton shakes it off, and he and Luann set to work in perfect tandem. Falling into the rhythms of cooking, the smells and sounds of the kitchen, calms him quickly. They're well prepared as the house starts to buzz with guests' arrivals. The mansion is large enough that Colton sees no one—the party is located largely in a ballroom, spilling outside onto a patio. On the few occasions that they need to confer with their hostess, Luann heads out alone.

As they're wrapping up dessert service, Luann calls Colton to the well-stocked pantry. "Colton? I need you for a sec."

He comes. "What's up, Chef?"

"Get the door."

He does.

"This." She puts her arms around his neck and kisses him hungrily, jumping into his arms and wrapping her legs around his waist.

He presses her against the pantry shelves, bottles clinking, and they make out in the hungrily illicit way of teenagers stealing away at a wedding. Luann cups the back of his neck, gently tracing his hairline with her fingers. Using the shelves as leverage, Colton too allows his hands to roam.

Luann eventually slides down and wipes her mouth. "We're not gonna be able to do that at the restaurant."

"Can't stop me from thinking about it, Chef."

"Let your erection subside before you come out. For the waitstaff's sake."

"Could be a while."

"If nothing else, I know how to wait for you."

Colton and Luann stand in the kitchen, facing each other wordlessly, no longer one step ahead of the exhaustion, the last desserts having gone out.

"Probably good I came along to help," Colton says, releasing a long exhale and dabbing his brow with a bandanna.

"For many reasons." Luann gives him a weary but sly grin.

The hostess enters the kitchen, aglow. "Y'all. That was sublime. Unanimous raves. Y'all need to step out here and take a bow. I'm serious."

"That's so kind of you but—" Luann starts to say.

"Come. Let us celebrate you and your art. I insist." The hostess grabs each of their wrists and starts leading them out to the party.

"I... think Luann should go solo. This is her show," Colton says.

The hostess gawks. "You kidding? I saw the work you did. You are accepting your laurels."

Colton's stomach writhes. He shoots a this-is-what-I-wanted-least look at Luann. She answers with a she-signs-our-check-remember look.

They arrive in the ballroom, set with tables. The hostess picks up a glass and clinks on the side with a knife. "Y'all. Y'all, if I could have your attention quickly. Excuse me. Standing beside me is Luann Lawler, owner and executive chef of Field to Flame in Venice, Kentucky, and her sous chef, Colby...is it Colby? Oh, Colton Gentry. Sorry, Colton. It was these two who so lovingly prepared your food this evening."

At the sight of Colton and the mention of his name, there's a stir among the assembled guests, a flurry of whispers.

Is that—

I wondered what had become of—

I would've never expected—

Shame what happened—

When they entered the room, Colton had been staring at the ground in what he hoped appeared to be an attitude of humility but was more designed to evade eye contact with anyone he wished to avoid. Now, though, he lifts his gaze. He doesn't want to seem ashamed of working at Luann's side, because he's not. He scans the room quickly. Now he sees people he knows. Other musicians. Label execs. Agents. Managers. Nashville high society.

The hostess continues. "Chefs, please, take a bow for your sublime performance tonight."

Luann and Colton look at each other, smile, and join hands with their fingers interwoven. Luann raises their hands high and they bow. By the time they rise back up, many of the diners are on their feet, clapping. Someone shouts "Bravo!"

Colton makes eye contact with one of the standing applauders, the head of an artist management group who he knows is sympathetic to the sentiments that got Colton fired from music. He gives Colton a contrite smile that says, *Sorry, man, you know I wish there was something I could have done, but I'm happy for where you've landed.* Which Colton returns with a smile that says, *I get it. And it's all turned out okay.*

Colton clears his throat and says, "Scout's honor; I didn't poison any of the food."

Those in the know chuckle appreciatively, the tension broken. The hostess looks at Colton strangely but joins in the laughter, so as to not be the odd woman out.

Then Colton sees a face, accompanied by a sensation akin to getting T-boned by a dump truck at an intersection. If it was a visage he knew less well, he might've had to do a double take. At a table in the back corner, Maisy Martin stands and applauds. When their eyes meet, Maisy mouths, *What?*

A searing geyser of adrenaline erupts in his chest, followed by the sense that his lungs and heart are being pressed under a sheet of plywood with an elephant atop. But he manages to answer her with a nonchalant shrug and a *surprise!* smile—which evaporates immediately when he sees the Hockey Player sitting at her table beside her. His legs go boneless.

Struggling to maintain his impassivity, he turns his eyes from Maisy to Luann, who was looking in another direction and appears not to have noticed Colton's silent interaction.

Luann waves. "Thanks, y'all."

Colton gently pulls Luann back in the direction of the kitchen, the hostess apparently mollified. Still gripping Luann's hand, he whispers hoarsely out of the side of his mouth, "Maisy's here."

Luann gasps and covers her mouth with her free hand. "Stop."

"Back of the room."

They walk fast.

"You okay?" Luann asks. "You need to call Leon?"

"I . . . think . . . I don't know, actually. Maybe ask me in a half hour."

"I will."

"I mean, I'm shaken up—I haven't seen her in person in over a year—but I think I got it out of my system a couple months back." *I hope.*

"Let's go to high alert just in case."

Colton's pulse throbs in his neck and his face burns. The adrenaline starts to ebb from his system, leaving behind a dull pang.

"Hey?" Luann says gently. "Talk to me. What are you feeling right now?" She rests her hand on his.

"Hurting, for sure. She was with the dude she cheated on me with. So that's not fun."

"Been there. I'm here for you, and if we need to get in the truck and leave right now, we can."

Colton shakes his head like he's recovering from a punch. He exhales hard. "Let's work. I'm okay." He pauses. "It was nice hearing people clap for me again."

"You earned it," Luann murmurs. She kisses him on the cheek.

They go to work packing up leftovers and stowing their equipment. The hostess returns to grab Luann—her adoring masses aren't done with her. And there's potential business to be had. Possible future investors to schmooze.

Before she leaves, she glances at Colton.

I'm good, he mouths and makes a sweeping motion. *Go*.

CHAPTER 63

"Hey, .45."

The familiar voice startles Colton as he loads a bin in the bed of his pickup. He whirls around to see Maisy approaching. All the things he has to say crowd to the front of his mouth, but none want to be the first to jump.

They stand a few feet apart, the silence between them taut as a guitar's high E string.

Maisy nears and rests her hand on the tailgate. "I remember riding in this truck near here the night we met."

"I was going to upgrade to a Bugatti, but they didn't have one in hot pink."

"You rescued me from a party like this."

"The food was much better tonight."

"It sure was."

"You're welcome."

"This is... *so* weird."

Colton leans on his truck and folds his arms. "You're glowing," he says, trying to walk the tightrope of cynical and sincere.

Maisy rubs her baby bump in a way that looks subconscious. "I'm glad I get the chance to tell you in person how sorry I am about how that went down. I meant to give you a heads-up because we—you know, we'd talked about—"

"Maise?" Colton interrupts quietly. "The past is past. It's really fine." *If I say it out loud often and emphatically enough, maybe that will even be true someday.*

"Speaking of keeping secrets, where was this chef side of you when we were together? I always thought cooking was sexy."

"I recall the way you once phrased it was 'I'd let Guy Fieri do me on top of a pile of buffalo wings.' Which, in retrospect, is somewhat less funny now than at the time."

"But it *was* funny at the time."

"You didn't ever, did you? It's a fair question."

Maisy rolls her eyes. "So, is that your job now? Cooking?"

"Yep. Sous chef at Field to Flame."

"And you like it?"

"Very much. I love working under Luann. Who you also saw earlier."

"Luann as in the high school girlfriend you wrote 'Honeysuckle Summer' about?"

"The same. My first love."

"Not denying it anymore, I see. You never said she could cook. You told me she was a good artist."

"That too."

"She's pretty." Maisy's tone betrays the swallowing of envy, and Colton relishes it.

"More so than in high school. Hell of a mom too."

"Wow. She's hot. She can cook. Draw. Runs her own business. Great mom. Perfect woman. Goals," Maisy says, clearly shooting for a tone of ribbing but landing on more jealousy tingeing her voice.

"You don't fail at much. I'm sure you'll rock motherhood too."

"Hopefully."

"I wouldn't have broached the topic repeatedly when we were together if I didn't believe that with all my heart." An awkward but tender silence passes between them.

"So what's going on with you and Luann?"

Colton shrugs. "Oh, you know." *Hopefully you do, because I don't.* "What's ol' Pritchard Martin think about all this?" He draws a circle in the air around Maisy's belly.

"About daddy's lil' girl getting knocked up out of wedlock? Oh, thrilled."

They laugh.

"He's excited to be a grandpa," she says, adding a moment later, "If it's any comfort, you're still his favorite."

"You don't say. He likes me better than a Swedish hockey player? Who'd've guessed. Speaking of, where is the Hockey Player?"

"We drove separately. He has to get up early."

"Aw. Here I'd hoped to meet him."

"He loved dinner."

"He can eat solid food?"

Maisy rolls her eyes. "This again."

"If I'd known he'd be here, I would have whipped up special my garlic-truffle smashed potatoes with smoked marrow butter. No teeth required."

"He *has* teeth. Just lots of them are fake," Maisy pronounces with righteous indignation.

"I want you to take a second and think about the sentence you just uttered out loud."

They both smile in spite of themselves.

"You look good," Maisy says.

Colton meets her eyes in the dim light. "I'm over a year sober. Couple of close calls, but not a drop since rehab. Found a new passion. Moved into a little place with my dog. Got a lot of things going for me, I guess."

"Sounds like," Maisy says, sounding wistful. "I'm glad for you."

"I don't need your pity, Maise."

"Do I sound like I'm pitying you?"

"Lil' bit."

"I'm not. I hoped you would land on your feet."

"All right. Well," Colton says. "This has been fun catching up, but I better finish here."

"Good seeing you, Colt. Don't be a stranger." Maisy stands on her tiptoes and gives him a long hug and a kiss on the cheek. The firm swell of her belly grazes his. He smells her hair, and the floodgates of memory open momentarily.

Watching her walk back inside, he eases himself into the cab of his truck, quaking, and phones Leon.

CHAPTER 64

"I saw Maisy again. While I was loading out," Colton says as he pulls away from the house, Luann curled up against the passenger door. "She ambushed me. We talked a bit."

"How was that?" Luann asks with an expression of distaste.

"It was...strange."

"I debated whether to mention this, but she cornered me too, a little before we left."

"And?"

"Sounded like she's not quite over you."

"Does she *get* to not be over me?"

Luann shrugs. "She strikes me as someone who gets to do whatever she wants."

"Ain't wrong about that," Colton mutters. "So what'd she say?"

"You know. *How long have you and Colton been working together? Did you seek him out or did he seek you out? So do y'all spend a lot of time together?* That sorta thing."

"Huh."

"Yeah. Being confronted by a jealous A-list pop star—not what I expected from this evening."

"What a weird night."

"What a bizarre weekend for you."

Colton looks over at Luann and rests his right hand on her thigh. "More good than bad."

Luann takes his hand, interlacing their fingers, slumps exhausted into her seat, and rests her head on his shoulder.

For a while, they drive in silence, Colton ruminating on the improbable turns of events of the past twenty-four hours.

"Hey, there's something I've been wanting to talk to you about," Luann breaks the quietude, a note of compunction in her voice. "And I was waiting for the right moment, which it feels like this is."

"Don't keep me in suspense."

"So, basically since day one that I took over the Field to Flame location, I've been in talks with the folks next door about taking over and expanding into that space. I'd thought about going the coffee shop route or just expanding the Field to Flame dining area. But I've landed on something different."

"Ah, finally opening that laser tag place you always dreamed of."

"I'm glad running into your ex didn't dull that razor wit. But if you're done, you'll want to hear this."

"I'm listening."

"Another restaurant in the space next door—a lower-priced fast casual and takeout concept, still focusing on high-quality, local ingredients and fresh takes on Southern favorites. And the centerpiece would be your Nashville hot chicken."

After a long pause to digest, Colton says, "So... would I—"

"You'd be running it."

Colton looks over at her. "*Me?*"

"You."

"You think I'm ready?"

"Wouldn't be having this conversation if I didn't. If it helps, we'd still be working side by side. We'd use the Field to Flame kitchen for both places. But you'd be head chef and managing it. Setting the menu, hiring people, scheduling shifts. All that."

"This is... wow. When would you be looking to open?"

"Next summer. Listen, don't answer right now. Think it over this week and tell me next Sunday. Sooner we get started the better."

They pass a few dozen miles in companionable quietude, alternating between stealing looks at one another and gazing into the headlit distance. Luann squints down the road. "Is that..."

"Our new favorite roadside stop, Sunny's Stateline Saloon."

"Turn in."

Colton's hand was already on the blinker.

One last night of unseasonable, hurricane-induced cool; platinum moonlight diffusing from behind a caul of thin clouds and streaming in through the fogged-up truck windows.

They lie woven together as they did the last time, Luann's head resting on Colton's bare chest. Her fingers trace his "Linger" tattoo again and again. "What is it with this parking lot? It's located in some, like, carnal energy sex vortex."

"Dibs on Sex Vortex as my next band name. Could it be that we're just really horny for each other once more?"

"Possibly."

"So this new restaurant thing that you want me to be in charge of, that's not because—"

Luann giggles. "Honey, please. You're good, but you ain't that good. It's all based on your chicken-frying and leadership abilities and not your other... aptitudes."

"Okay," Colton says.

"How disappointed you sound."

"I'm not."

"Liar. You wish you boned your way into being the Hot Chicken King of Venice." Luann tickles Colton and he laughs and squirms.

"How dare you. If I wear the crown, I want to have justly earned it."

"I'm gonna have to be extra mean to you at work now. You know that, right?"

"I mean, Dani got together with her dude at their job, so I don't think she'd judge much."

"Oh, I'm not worried about Dani. I just think it'll be fun."

Colton rolls over, putting Luann on her back, grabs her thighs, and pulls her into position beneath him. He kisses down her neck and clavicle while she sighs and runs her fingers through his thick salt-and-pepper hair. "How about I'll show you what fun is," he whispers in her ear with a rakish smile, nipping gently at her earlobe as he works his way lower, lower. "Again."

CHAPTER 65

It's Tuesday night and Colton's performance at the restaurant that evening has not given him confidence about Luann's proposal, even as he continues to mull over the notion of helming her new concept.

He's driving home when his phone rings. He answers without looking at the screen, half expecting it to be Luann, rescinding her offer. He wouldn't blame her.

"Colton?"

"Maisy?"

"This a good time?"

"Driving home from work. What's up?"

"I was just... thinking about you."

"Oh yeah?" Colton says cautiously. There's something almost flirtatious in Maisy's voice that throws him, nearly as much as the fact of her calling at all. It's a side of her he hasn't seen in a long while.

"It tripped me out seeing you on Saturday. I was *not* expecting it."

"Quite the coincidence."

"The thing is, I'm not sure it was."

"Uh... maybe elaborate?"

"I've been feeling a little... directionless lately, so I had Selena read my tarot." Maisy's spiritual belief system might best be described as a Cheesecake Factory–esque menu of appropriated Eastern and Indian thought, Joshua Tree New Age crystals and sage smoke mysticism, astrology and tarot, all stuffed in the pita of good old-fashioned American Christian prosperity gospel à la Joel Osteen—all were valid insofar as they pointed to the universe's moving in her favor.

"And?"

"She told me my path forward would be found in my past."

Colton pulls up to his house and shuts off his truck but remains seated. "I assume that involves me."

"My reading with Selena was on *Friday*. On *Saturday*, I go to this dinner and who do I randomly encounter? You. Of *course* it's you."

Colton struggles to form words. "Look, I admit—"

"Just hear me out. I've spent the past couple days working up a plan to reboot your music career."

"Hang on, you know—"

"Yes. It won't be easy. But things are going well for me."

"No argument there."

"Which means I can make things happen. Especially since I'm done with country. It's all pop from here on out. So I bring you back with me. I've already talked with Karl Johan and his team about writing a duet for us and working with you on an album. You come on tour with me next summer. We relaunch you with a complete rebrand: the tortured, sexy troubadour, back from exile after speaking truth to power and wrestling his demons of addiction. You know how many people agree with you about guns? You won't need the fans who turned their backs on you. You'll have twice as many new fans. And I'll be right there with you to help make it happen."

"Maisy. No way will anyone buy that sort of—"

"This is a great moment for you to reinvent. Lots of male singer-songwriters hitting big. You got Hozier blowing up a few years ago. James Bay. Ed Sheeran. Passenger. Laydee just released that duet with that Dearly kid from Tennessee and that's catching fire."

Colton reels. In his calculations about the end of his music career, he never accounted for anything like this, the one thing that might actually work to give him back all he lost.

"Colton?" Maisy says.

"Sorry, I'm processing. What about the Hockey Player? He can't possibly be down with all this."

"Well…and that's…okay. He doesn't dictate my professional and artistic decisions."

After a prolonged pause, Colton says, "Maisy. What's happening here?"

"I told you. I was feeling directionless. I sought guidance from the universe. I got it."

"Why do I feel like you're speaking in code?"

Maisy's turn to hesitate. "I feel guilty, okay? That what you want to hear? Seeing you the other night drove it all home. I feel terrible for how I treated you and how I didn't do everything I could to help you salvage your career because I was scared for my own. You're not the only one trying to make amends."

Colton sits in confounded silence.

"Say something," Maisy says.

"Such as?"

"That you'll let me help you. I know you miss making music more than anything. How could you not?"

"And you know this how?"

"I saw it all over your face. Look, you're a great chef. But you're the kind of guy who's good at everything he does. You need to do what you were *born* to do, and that's music. Everyone who's ever met you knows it. Even Luann herself. You said she was the one who got you into music to begin with. And tell me you don't think about it and miss it every day."

Colton starts to tell her exactly that but stops himself. The truth is that he doesn't know if it's that he hasn't missed it or he hasn't allowed himself to miss it because he saw no way back to it. "This is…a lot to consider."

"It probably sounds crazy. It feels crazy. But I have to live with my eyes open to possibility and my truth. I see it here. And I want to do this for you. I want you to be happy and doing what you love."

Colton is unsure how to answer. "I really appreciate it," he says finally, inwardly cursing his inability to summon some clever or insightful response.

"Talk to you soon, Colt."

"Bye, Maise."

After hanging up, Colton lets his phone drop in his lap. It was not out of character for Maisy to make a momentous life decision based on a single tarot reading. And why not? She's the sort for whom things almost always go well. It's fun to be able to attribute that, in retrospect, to some grand, unknowable design as opposed to being rich and beautiful with an uncanny instinct for making art that multitudes enjoy.

He rests his head on his window, shuts his eyes, and rubs them until red fireworks materialize on the backs of his lids. He envisions himself standing again before a capacity crowd wildly applauding a song he wrote. A bolt of exhilaration passes through him—from his fingers, where he can almost feel the metallic buzz of his guitar strings—to his ears, where he can hear his own voice reverberate through an arena.

He pulls himself out of his truck to his door, the whiff of the kitchen trailing him. He can tell already it's going to be a night of tossing and turning, despite his exhaustion.

He knows he'll need to figure out how much of the last year he's spent lying to himself as inoculation against pining for what's irretrievably lost.

There's already a part of him that wants a shot at undoing the humiliations and trauma of his life's and career's implosions. How sweet—no, *just*—it would be for the Hockey Player to have to hear him and Maisy on the radio, for Shad Haggerty to have to eat crow, lovingly prepared Nashville hot style by Colton.

Above all, he wishes he had a better track record for sound decision-making.

There's one good choice he can make right now: he calls Leon.

CHAPTER 66

"HEY," LUANN SAYS GENTLY, WIPING A SMUDGE OF FLOUR FROM COLTON'S brow. "You okay?"

"Yeah, just got a lot on my mind." While working tonight, he envisioned turning on the radio again and hearing one of his songs. He imagined never again working over hot stoves and with sharp knives, his back and knees aching after the hours on his feet. He daydreamed about redemption from all the ways he's been brought low over the past year. He remembered the hours and passion he poured into something that was lost but may now be found.

"Thought I might've been too mean to you tonight."

"Naw, you were fine."

Luann looks at him for a while. She puts a hand on her hip. With her other hand she beckons. "Spill."

Colton sighs. "Maisy called last night."

Luann's face registers passing aversion. "Did she."

"She had a, uh, proposal."

"A proposal." Another expression of distaste.

Colton braces himself. "She wants to engineer a musical comeback for me. She's got a whole collaboration plan."

"I *knew* she had something brewing," Luann murmurs. "I could tell when I talked to her."

"Apparently she felt guilty, like she didn't do enough to help when the world took a big old dump on me."

"I can see why she might feel that way." Several seconds of silence pass. "That must be a tempting offer," Luann says quietly.

"I don't know what it is. I don't know what to think."

"Hence your obvious preoccupation tonight."

"Sorry."

"So. Did Maisy give a timeline for this grand plan of hers?"

"Next summer."

Luann folds her arms and shakes her head. "Naturally. Right when we'd be rolling out the new concept."

"Yeah."

Luann is mum for a long time.

"Say something," Colton says softly.

Luann shakes her head and doesn't look at him. "What?"

"Anything."

"I'm sorta speechless. You considering her offer?"

"I mean...I don't know. I feel like I have to at least *consider* it. After everything."

"Everything," Luann repeats in a murmur and fixates on the ground. She pulls out a toothpick and gnaws on it.

"The last thing I want is to let you down again," Colton says.

She looks at Colton, and he can see the raw pain in her eyes. "I've learned how to lose since the time we were kids."

"I don't want to be the source of more loss for you."

"I know what music means to you, Colton. No one knows it better. Not Maisy. Nobody. I watched it save you once. And if you need it to save you again, I won't stand in your way. I care about you too much. But I need you to promise me something."

"Say it."

"Whatever you decide, make that your decision and don't look back. Choose what won't leave you wondering *what if* on your deathbed. I know this life isn't the one you chose for yourself."

"If I try the music thing and it doesn't work out, maybe I can—"

But Luann's eyes stop him. "Colton? *Choose.*"

"I promise." He almost says *Whatever I choose, we could still be together.* But it feels like a lie. *It would feel like a lie to Luann, too. And she would say so, and I couldn't bear hearing her say that.*

They stand in the alley, facing each other but not making eye contact.

Luann starts inside. "I better get back."

Colton stops her. They look at each other, but neither has anything to say. By unspoken accord, they enter a long and wordless embrace. The sort where you're trying to make someone part of you, absorbing some essence—to carry their scent on your clothing and imprint the warmth and corporeality of their body on your skin's memory. The kind with the weight of history. One with which you welcome someone after a prolonged absence.

Or perhaps with which you bid someone farewell.

CHAPTER 67

It's late Sunday afternoon and Colton sits on his porch with Petey, listening to the trains pass and his wind chimes lazily toll. He watches the breeze sway the boughs of the oaks and maples that ring his small and quiet yard, in front of his small and quiet house, which contains nearly the entirety of his small and quiet life, in this small and quiet town where he grew up. The one he toiled, sweat, and dreamed so hard to escape.

He's spent the morning at his mom's house, trying to trace the source of a water leak, which he tracks down to her rusted-out water heater. It will need replacing—one more thing in her house on the decline. He wonders again if he might yet be able to give his mom that big, new house he always wanted to buy her.

He remembers how he loved music. How it imbued him with meaning and purpose, justified his existence.

He imagines standing once more on a blackened stage overlooking a sea of glowing cell phone lights, the palpable animation of the roaring crowd making the air glitter with electricity.

He tries to conjure what Duane would say if he could sit beside Colton, just once more, in one of those white plastic chairs that collapses if you rock back in it. No cold beers this time. Just the sweet intoxication of friendship and brotherhood, bound by love for one another and music.

He considers calling Derrick or his mom, but he knows he has to make this decision solo, with no other thumbs on the scale.

He gazes down at Petey, who naps and snores in a sunny patch. "What do I love most, boy?" He murmurs. "What's the life I want?" *Which do you love more? Luann and cooking, or Maisy and music?*

He owes both Luann and Maisy an answer. He's been thinking for days. He could think for the rest of his life and the decision would be no easier.

But the time for thinking is done.

CHAPTER 68

Colton knows he should tell her face-to-face—he owes her at least that after all their history—but he can't. Second best would be to call her, but that's also out. He has too much experience with a phone call like this going horribly awry. He wants to say what he has to say better than a (highly emotional, certainly) voice conversation will allow. And after his last interaction with her, he doubts his ability to say what he needs to in the way he needs to if he has to hear her voice. So he composes a text message.

> I want to thank you for offering me this opportunity. I need you to know how deeply grateful I am for this and for everything you've done to help me. That's what makes this so difficult.
>
> I have to decline your generous offer and pursue a different path, one in which I do something I love, at the side of the woman I love. I had a good thing with her once and it ended badly, but now I have a second chance to write a happy ending and that's what I hope to do. Every time I ever told you I loved you, I meant it, and I'm grateful for the times we spent together and the things I learned from you. For the good times

we had. I'll remember all of that fondly. I'm grateful for the occasions that fate led us to each other.

But there's a life I want. I lived it for a while and it got interrupted. Now I have a second chance, and I can't let it slip through my fingers again. I hope you understand.

I want the very best for you. I wish you great happiness in this life and tremendous success in all that you do. Of course, you don't need my wishes. You never have.

Goodbye again,
Colton

He sits with the drafted message, trying to breathe himself calm, and wonders one final time if he's making the correct decision.

After this door closes, it will not reopen.

He hits Send.

CHAPTER 69

COLTON RINGS LUANN'S DOORBELL. SHE ANSWERS, HER FACE TENSE AND SOMBER.

"I had an idea for what we could name the place," Colton says.

Luann visibly releases into herself, smiles, folds her arms, and leans against the doorjamb. "Let's hear it." She makes a *gimme* gesture.

"Flame to Fowl. Huh? Field to Flame; Flame to Fowl. Nice symmetry, right?"

"Very. Wanna hear my pitch?"

"You're the boss."

Luann meets Colton's eyes. "Duane's Hot Chicken. That has a nice symmetry too, don't you think?"

It hits him with the force of an ocean wave on a warm summer day. One that sends you tumbling, but when you rise and breathe again, you feel like you could fall upward into the sky. Colton's voice cracks. "I sure do."

"Thought you might."

"You know me well."

"I should by now."

"I'm scared."

"I'm not. You're gonna do great." Luann starts to say something, balks, then allows herself. "Colton?"

"Yeah."

"Maisy still loves you. You know that, right? This wasn't just your opportunity to return to music; it was your second chance with her."

"I don't know. I mean—"

"No, Colton, she does. I saw it in her eyes. I heard it in her voice. It's coming through in her actions. She's still in love with you, and that's why she wanted to work at your side. You need to believe me on this if you've never believed me on anything else."

Colton draws close to Luann. He strokes his finger down the side of her face, tracing the line of her cheekbone, then resting his hand on her cheek. "I believe you. Now I need you to believe me. I love you, Luann. I choose you. Over music. Over Maisy. Over everything. And I will keep choosing you." He says it softly, and tears well in his eyes for a reason that's not quite either joy or sorrow alone.

Luann pulls Colton's face to hers and they kiss, long and deep—a kiss that speaks the language of lost years and also of years that await.

"How would you feel about inviting me in to celebrate this decision?" Colton asks finally.

"Hey, Colton, wanna come in and celebrate this decision?"

Colton steps inside but doesn't make it far before he's pressing Luann against the entryway wall, jackets on a coat rack serving as padding. Their kissing swells in intensity. Luann pushes the front door shut with a toe and starts tearing off Colton's shirt.

"Careful," he says with a wolfish smile. "That's a vintage Waylon Jennings T-shirt. It was a gift from my girlfriend."

"Shoulda thought of that before looking so hot in it." Luann carefully peels his shirt off. Then she attacks his belt like she's unbuckling someone trapped in a burning car. Her face and upper chest flush. Her scent of figs, crushed ivy, and coconut blooms from the heat of her skin.

Colton's hands move on her body as though drawn to it by some irresistible force. "I want to touch all of you," he says in a rough whisper. He unbuttons her cutoffs and slides them to the ground. She steps out of them. He pulls off her tank top, tosses it behind him, and kisses her neck and breasts as she sighs and dissolves into him.

He hoists her by the back of her thighs, and she wraps her legs around his waist and her arms around his neck. He presses her against the wall again, clutching her ass, pushing her underwear aside, and thrusting slow and deep inside her.

She gasps, her eyes glassy with pleasure, bites the flesh of his shoulder to stifle a cry of ecstasy and murmurs, breathlessly in his ear, "I tried so hard not to fall in love with you again."

Colton closes his eyes in rapture, as though tasting the nectar from an impossibly perfect sun-ripe peach. "I didn't try very hard at all."

CHAPTER 70

COLTON STROLLS UP THE FRONT WALK, CARRYING A BROWN PAPER BAG. LUANN waits with her front door open, leaning against the doorframe. "Hey, cowboy."

Colton doesn't answer but sets down his bag, picks up Luann by the waist, whirls her around, sets her down, and kisses her long and slow.

"I haven't told the girls yet," Luann whispers when they come up for air.

"That's what that was for, in case they're watching from around the corner."

"They're in their room, crashed out after the trip."

"I hope I didn't miss getting to say hi to Mr. Madsen, the most celebrated Danish architect of the 2000s."

"Oh so that kiss was for him too?"

"Hadn't occurred to me."

"He was gone thirty seconds after dropping off the girls."

Colton tuts and snaps his fingers.

"I know," Luann says. "Told him you were coming, and he suddenly had somewhere to be. Shame for both of us. He said to say hi, though."

"Did he?"

"In his own way—through stony, hostile taciturnity."

"I've come to accept that this life is a parade of disappointments. Put not getting to see Scooter and Possum on the list." He holds up the paper bag. "I brought them something."

Luann waves him off. "If they find out you and Petey came by and I didn't wake them up, they'll never forgive me. Hold on." Luann returns after a few minutes with the twins in tow. Their normally fair skin is sun-kissed and aglow from summer afternoons on Danish Riviera beaches. They look taller.

They rub their eyes, yawning and looking grumpy—until they see Colton and Petey. "Petey!" They snap instantly from their torpors, shriek, and run to him.

"See?" Colton says. "Alive and well. Did I not promise?"

They brush him off and skid to Petey on their knees, hugging and kissing him. He sneezes with delight, and his tail whips furiously in a propeller motion, batting Colton on the calf.

After a couple of minutes, Colton says, "I'm feeling a little left out up here."

They stand and hug Colton.

"We missed you," Freja says.

"What? You gotta speak English."

"You already did that joke!" Esme says with ecstatic outrage.

"You're right. I need new material. I haven't had time to develop any on account of your mama bossin' me all the time."

"We listened to your music in Denmark," Freja crows.

Colton gasps. "What?! Are you sure it was me?"

"Yes," Esme says. "Because our dad made us stop."

"Then maybe you'll like this song: Are you ready for some football?" Colton sings, in his best Hank Williams Jr. voice. That it is an exceedingly good impression is tragically lost on the twins. They jump and cheer nevertheless.

"Okay, then you're gonna need..." Colton pulls out the contents of his bag. Two junior-sized Tennessee Titans jerseys. One with "Scooter" on the back. One with "Possum." The girls squeal and pull on the jerseys over their T-shirts, hanging baggy on their small frames. They dash back to their room and return with their footballs.

"Can we have banana splits too?" Esme asks when they return.

"What about some nice broccoli-kale cake with fennel cream cheese frosting instead?"

"No!" they scream.

"I'd have to run to the store," Colton says.

"Actually..." Luann says. "I might've stocked up in anticipation of this request."

Colton grins. "Well now."

"Do *not* get cocky."

Colton turns to the twins. "Football first, or you'll get sick."

The girls tear into the yard. Petey limps behind them.

"Hey," Colton says softly to Luann as they leave earshot. "Can I tell them?"

Luann looks at him for a second, sighs, and beams. "Since I would have made you tell them if you took Maisy's offer, I guess fair is fair. Sure."

Colton trots after the twins. "Hey, Scooter and Possum, remember how your mama and I used to go out in high school?"

"Yes," they say, giggling.

"Scooter, go long and cut right." Colton picks up and palms one of their Nerf footballs and points to a far corner of the yard. "Possum, play D. Anyway, what if I told y'all that I never really stopped loving your mama?"

CHAPTER 71

October 2017
Venice, Kentucky

Luann answers her parents' door and scans Colton up and down. "I assume you're going to reveal why it was so damn important we meet here instead of one of our places. And also why you have your guitar with you."

Colton smiles. "All in time. Where's Scooter and Possum?"

"Asleep upstairs. They really wanted to see you, but they've gotten to bed way too late for the last week. How were the interviews for Riley's replacement?"

"Great. I think I've narrowed it down to a pick."

"Do tell."

"Kid named Travis. Did his time in the KFC and Cracker Barrel trenches. Sweet guy; seems like a hard worker, genuinely interested in food. I think he'll be a good fit. You wanna sit down with him before we offer?"

"I trust your judgment. What about—"

Colton cuts her off with a long kiss. "Hey," he says gently, brushing a piece of hair back from her face. "No more business tonight, Chef."

Luann smiles and blushes. "Sorry. Hard to turn off."

"I know. Let's head to your storm-watching deck."

They climb the stairs and step into the cool, bonfire-scented October night. The moon is refulgent and bathes them in pearlescent light. They sit in the two chairs. Colton bends over, opens the clasps on his guitar case, and pulls out his guitar. He strums it a couple of times and tweaks the tuning.

Luann sits cross-legged in her chair and rests her chin in her palms. Her eyes sparkle in the darkness. "Getting serenaded under moonlight, huh?"

"You probably won't remember this, but back in high school, you told me once you hoped someday I'd sing to you in a building you designed."

"I remember well," Luann murmurs, beaming.

"Then you'll probably recall this song."

Colton plays her "Linger." Luann watches him the whole time, her face suffused with adoration.

When he finishes, she sighs and hugs herself. "Better than the first time you played it for me."

Colton kneels to put his guitar back in its case, rummaging for something in the string compartment. He retrieves it, wrapped in a white T-shirt that's over twenty years old. Luann will know it. Still kneeling, he says, "Now, I have two questions for you. First: how do you think Scooter and Possum would feel about having Petey live out his days as their older brother?"

Luann stares at Colton blankly for a second, as though she didn't hear him—or did but doesn't trust her ears. Then she slowly covers her mouth with both hands and her eyes brim. She nods quickly and says, voice breaking and quavering, "I think they'd love that more than anything."

He sees in her face his heart's whole chronicle—past, present, and future. A story they wrote on each other in the hours of youth and its spring-green color of love. A history inscribed in lightning across the sky in the witness of storms on their westward passage. A gloriously inescapable orbit.

Sometimes the wind that pushes your house off its foundation carries you to a flowering garden.

Colton smiles through his own tears. "Which brings me to my second question."

EPILOGUE

November 1995
Venice, Kentucky

They sat on a blanket at the high bluff overlooking the Cumberland River. They cradled each other for warmth against a blustering north wind as the sun sank below the horizon. Behind leafless branches, civil twilight fell, the hue of purple silk pressed to a window.

They watched the river make its patient exodus to sea, a braid threading through the earth.

The raw wind blurred his eyes as he looked at her, her face a silhouette against the gathering night, her wind-tossed hair and rose cheeks. She made his heart a creature of delirium with her beauty.

"You believe in fate?" she asked without prompt.

"How do you mean?" he asked.

"Like, were we meant to find each other?"

"What made you think of that?"

"I was remembering a dream I had before we met. You were in it."

"I wanna hear."

"Don't get excited. It was pretty tame."

"Still."

She paused, like she was removing the memory from a locked museum case. "I was walking through this field of golden, waist-high grass. The air was warm like summer. I was running my hands along the tops of the grass, letting it tickle my palms. Then I looked up and you were walking beside me and I said, 'I waited for you,' and you go, 'I know.' That's it. The dream ended. I wanted to talk to you more. I woke up feeling really happy and peaceful. I tried to go back to sleep to see if I could restart the dream, but that never works. I saw you at school the next day, and I smiled at you, as though you'd somehow remember *my* dream. Couldn't help it. But you weren't looking, and good thing, because I would have been embarrassed."

"I wish I saw you. I'd have smiled back."

"Promise?"

"I promise."

"So, do you believe in fate?"

"Yes," he said finally. "I do."

She laid her head on his shoulder, and they said nothing more for a while.

He held her until nightbreak and then after. In the quiet dark, he rested his lips in her hair, whispering her name in his mind until it became as shapeless as the starry sky above, as if blessing the name of whatever unseen hand had brought them together.

ACKNOWLEDGMENTS

Throughout my creative life, I've had to make several exciting but terrifying pivots, and this book was certainly one. I couldn't have done it without the support of many incredible and wonderful people.

Thanks to my brilliant agent, Charlie Olsen. This book will be coming out almost exactly ten years after we started working together. Here's to many more. And to Liz Kossnar. I know you get thanked in many authors' books for your sublime editorial hand, but how often does someone thank you for marrying Charlie?

Thanks to my amazing publishing team at Grand Central who made this book exist and what it is, inside and out: Lila Selle, Sarah Congdon, Ivy Cheng, Kamrun Nesa, Janine Perez, Leena Oropez, Lori Paximadis, Anjuli Johnson, Karen Kosztolnyik, Ben Sevier, and last, but most certainly not least, my genius editor, Jacqueline Young. Your insights, intellect, and keen eye made this book the best it could be.

My eternal gratitude to:

My BFF, Kerry Kletter. As if it weren't enough that you show me the possibility of language with every book you write, you show me the possibility of adulthood and life more generally by keeping cans of whipped cream in your refrigerator and excusing yourself periodically to shoot some directly into your mouth.

Brittany Cavallaro and Emily Henry: my bandmates. Except I think/hope we like each other far more than if we were actually bandmates.

David Arnold, for being my bizarro twin (this is more of a compliment to me than to you).

Alex and Amy Saville, for the invaluable guidance and feedback. And for being generally one of the coolest couples I've ever known.

Natalie Lloyd, for making me believe in this story and my ability to write it.

Emily Easton, for ushering me into this beautiful world and showing me what a truly great editor is, so I knew to settle for nothing less on this book.

Rob Bokkon, for being the best Southern foodways / Western Kentucky sounding board a guy could ask for.

Silas House, for disproving the axiom that one should never meet their heroes.

Lamar Giles, for being the first person I text about almost every piece of pop culture.

Shane and Angela Nasby and Andy West, for your invaluable restaurant knowledge.

Lee Adams, for your invaluable country music industry knowledge.

Jenny Howard and Heather Iverson, for maintaining the sort of day job environment that not only leaves my spirit intact to write books but makes me feel like I'm making a positive difference.

Rob Rufus, for being a rock star in every possible sense.

Jessie Ann Foley, for making me believe in this book and just generally being the coolest.

And finally:

My beautiful Sara, my love, my heart. My maker of music and grower of green things. Everything I get right when I write about love, I learned from loving you. Thank you for all your support. I could never write books without it.

My son, Tennessee. Heaven is Marvel movies and McKay's and the greenway and the Asheville Walk with you. I love you. I'm so proud of you.

ABOUT THE AUTHOR

Jeff Zentner is the author of *New York Times* Notable Book *The Serpent King* and *In the Wild Light*, as well as *Goodbye Days* and *Rayne & Delilah's Midnite Matinee*. Among other honors, he has won the ALA's William C. Morris Award, the Amelia Elizabeth Walden Award twice, the Muriel Becker Award, and the International Literacy Association Award, been long-listed twice for the Carnegie Medal, and been a two-time Southern Book Prize finalist. Before becoming a writer, he was a musician who recorded with Iggy Pop, Nick Cave, and Debbie Harry. He lives in Nashville.